EVA VERDE

Lives
Like
Mine

**SIMON &
SCHUSTER**

London · New York · Sydney · Toronto · New Delhi

First published in Great Britain by Simon & Schuster UK Ltd, 2021
This paperback edition published 2022

3 5 7 9 10 8 6 4 2

Simon & Schuster UK Ltd
1st Floor
222 Gray's Inn Road
London WC1X 8HB

Simon & Schuster Australia,
Sydney

Simon & Schuster India,
New Delhi

www.simonandschuster.co.uk
www.simonandschuster.com.au
www.simonandschuster.co.in

A CIP catalogue record for this book is available from the British Library

Paperback ISBN: 978-1-3985-0285-7
eBook ISBN: 978-1-3985-0284-0
Audio ISBN: 978-1-3985-0286-4

Typeset in Palatino by Hewer Text UK Ltd, Edinburgh
Printed in the UK by CPI Group (UK) Ltd, Croydon, CR0 4YY

MIX
Paper from
responsible sources
FSC® C171272

For Glennie – the mother-in-law
of every Monica's dreams x

Contents

1

Love, Honour, Obey
(and Conform)

Way back in the day, on the bus stop outside my childhood church, in great Tippex capitals, were the words: *Virtue is Valium*. After Saturday school or Sunday mass, Mum would tick me off for reading it out as we waited for the bus home. Funny what comes back.

Outside a different church, in my grown-up different life, is how you find me, now. Despite all I've been, this is what I became. Mother, wife. Good. Grateful. So grateful. Perhaps, at last, a daughter she might be proud of.

Perhaps not, though. All wholesome contemplation gets smothered by the fast-approaching pastel linens, complete with grabby hands, like those amusement machines on seafront piers.

Penny; my mother-in-law. Only by law.

'At least you look hot,' Dan says, sharing my emotions

like we've learnt to share everything else. His soothing hand on my hip works. 'After the speeches, we're off – I promise.' Dan's beautiful eyes are disarming, known to have me feeling like there's no earth and he's the centre of everything and all it means. It's unsettling – revealing, too, how feebly teenage I can be. How romance very much still rules.

'You pair. That's proper love.' Penny's kisses give way for the giggles. 'Love and good hair, Monica!' As those grabby hands reach for my neat ballet bun, I laugh along, too, with a mockney cockney twitter that makes for the oddest of feelings. 'I never did take to all that frizz.'

Virtue is Valium.

Outside this different church, in my grown-up different life, those little white words from the bus stop stick.

My sadly thinning hairline meant calling time on the relaxers. I'm now transitioning, in love with the very word of the process I'm slowly adapting to. At thirty-nine, I'm at last embracing my 3c curl pattern, trying to dismantle what went before this transitioning – my conditioning that natural hair was unruly, unsexy, primitive.

Comedic.

My big black hair is a tiny rebellion.

Yet today the rebellion shrinks. Here it's best to fit in, even if that means taming myself insipid, overlooking this early – yet predictable – banter, cloning the woman I am truly from, back at that bus stop. Mother, wife. Good. Grateful. It's a trick that's become like armoury, protecting my little brown self from this family of people still as alien to me as the day I married into them.

Budgie Crane's reception is in the crumbling Old Court Hotel opposite his boxing club. Eight round tables seat eight guests apiece, each with a central floral arrangement, bubble-gum pink and draped in so much bling even Barbie would wince. Budgie stands, the pinkness of the room matching his shiny head, an unlit cigar in one hand, a pint in the other. With his waistcoat undone, there's no disguising his gut, pouched on his belt like a hot-water bottle. 'It's an honour to introduce my third time —'

'Final time, brother dearest!' Penny heckles. Side-eyeing me, she confides behind a cupped hand. 'It won't last.'

' — Third time's a charm, spanking new, trouble and strife.'

Budgie's bride play-slaps his thigh, exploding into nerv-ous hiccupped laughter — Gracie Crane, three decades younger, and three trillion light years better looking. Though she seems fun and rather charming, since the church I've thought of nothing but her lack of guests, how she'd stood in front of those half-filled pews and seemed so very small. There's something, beneath the giggles and over-styling, that makes me want to hold her.

But I'm still chomping to go.

I've not forgotten Dan's promise, nor the one he made to the kids — which was more bribery — about stopping at McDonald's on the way home. Fran on my lap acts as my fortress. Little girls can be so useful. Our twins, Joel and

3

Toby, are glued – admittedly most discreetly – to a phone screen, likely the Year Seven group chat I've recently lost them to. How quick they are to seek distraction.

How bloody lucky.

They're not the only ones. As Budgie talks on, Gracie straightens the tablecloth, then her cutlery. The fizz set out to toast with she's already polished off, her restless hands now playing with an empty flute.

Where's her mum, her family, today?

Where was mine?

But we've not put in the hours for any real familiarity yet – where anything deep might slip. She might be a closed book on purpose. The thought strangely warms me. Struck as I am, there's sudden toasts and cheers and smiles all round; well-wishes, heartfelt, even from me – now we're on the cusp of leaving.

As the tables begin to disperse, making way for the evening dance floor, the DJ strikes up with Sinatra. 'Can we play outside?' Joel asks, and I don't blame him.

Before I can sow the seeds of school tomorrow and early nights, Dan agrees. Quickly. 'Seems all right, doesn't it?' Back in the thick of his family, the great Crane Petersen clan, Dan's happiness levels are on the rise. Our little house seems suddenly moons away as the boys stand, grinning, Toby raining a handful of ready salted into his mouth.

'Hark at this lot.' Budgie's bald as a peanut head appears between the boys, blinking at the kids as if he's peering into a Petri dish. 'Still sure they're yours, Danny-boy?'

'Only the good-looking ones,' Dan claps back, never suffering the stumble, the hitch of insecurity preventing that kind of quick-comeback confidence in me.

Hens lay eggs in different bloody shades every day and no one bats an eye – yet when I do, it becomes the anecdote of every family get-together for the past decade. Our incredible sons are identical, only Joel is black-haired and brown-skinned, looking every bit as mixed ethnicity as me, while Toby's as green-eyed and golden as his father. It's been pointed out in every waiting room, classroom and checkout queue they've both ever been in, but to me and Dan, it's no surprise that they look as they do. They are perfectly us.

Left to myself, away from here, the only time I give skin any real consideration is when I'm worrying about Fran's eczema, or selecting a new foundation – the recent abundance of brown shades at high street prices sparking sheer joy.

When I'm left to myself, away from here.

'When you gonna get some gloves and teach me a thing or two, lads?' Budgie asks the boys in his rufty-tufty-books-are-for-nobs-get-it-down-your-neck-son way. 'Or are you both too soft?'

'Mum don't let us fight,' says Toby, and I feel a pang of treachery. I've no problem with fighting sports as such, am rather enthusiastic in fact, when watching Anthony Joshua.

'You've a dad, ain't ya?' Budgie dashes back and forth as if sparring, shielding his face with his hands. 'Might've been all right himself – if he weren't so pretty.' Sitting beside me, he ruffles Dan's hair, and if this annoys Dan, he doesn't show it. 'All them girls, d'you remember, boy, hanging round for a glimpse of you in action?'

As Fran slips off to join the other kids on the cleared dance floor, Dan's nana shuffles over from the top table. She parks up next to Penny, closing the circle, swallowing me whole, her mean little eyes never leaving mine, and I know, with supernatural conviction, that she's thinking of the church earlier, of me and Joel sat six rows back from the fit-to-bursting family pews. Dear Nana Yvonne, who spent half the ceremony rubbernecking, with a look that said it was apt for us to be separated from the rest, like some godly apartheid in her favour. After all the bitch evils I could muster, I turned to God myself, asked if he'd make it so the alabaster Jesus, strung above her from the ceiling, would come loose and flatten her, there and then.

But the prayers didn't work. Nana Yvonne's very much still here, every bit the mother-of-the-groom today. Eyes and teeth and swathes of old cobweb. My wicked old witch crown of thorns. The worst of the bunch.

Toby pokes a subtle, coded message on my back.

'Go on then,' I say. 'Behave yourselves.' And the boys vanish so quickly it's as if they've vaporized.

'That's it, love,' says Budgie, 'cut them a bit of slack.' With his hand on mine, I get a troubling image of later, of Budgie's raw chipolata fingers all over Gracie's young peachy loveliness. 'You don't want to turn them into mummy's boys, do ya? Not pretty girl's blouses, like old Danny-boy.' Budgie bats his lashes. 'One bird you had, Dan. Proper little sort – d'you remember? Legs up to her armpits, and all that hair.' He chuckles. 'Proper Goldilocks . . . Look at him, sat there like he can't remember. Didn't you dump it for this one?'

'This one?' Dan gives a forced little stretch-smile. 'This one's my wife.'

'And a wife is for life. Reckon a woman made that up.' Budgie's arm loops my neck, his mouth almost grazing my ear. 'I bet you could still taste her on him.' He squeezes me like a kind Father Christmas, the rest of the table oblivious.

Except Dan. Dan's awkward shifting like he's shat his pants says everything.

'Let's get you a drink, Monica; knock that frost off.' Budgie squashes my shoulders, so brittle beneath his hands I fear they'll crumble. 'Help me get a round in, Danny-boy.'

Our well-finessed telepathy falters as Dan follows Budgie to the bar, just as Fran's back at the table, the only one still heaving with dirty crockery and foggy prosecco flutes. 'I'm bursting.'

Taking her hand, I stomp down the corridor to the ladies', my fingers trembling on the lock. The floor's wet, and so's the seat, so I pick Fran up to hover her over it.

'Don't drop me.'

'I'd never drop you.'

'Not even tomorrow, when we're at the top of the castle?'

Shit. The bloody school outing. Today's loomed for so long in my thoughts it's eclipsed everything else. There was me dreaming of an easy, silent day of just me, myself and our dog, Sir Duke. But first trips are first trips. 'Not even at the top of the castle.' I don't skip a beat. 'I've got Percy Pigs for the coach.'

Holding her steady, my feet avoid the clouds of bloated loo roll that cover the floor. *Could I taste her on him?* Odious man. Odious family. Poor Gracie.

And poor bloody me, too. It's never not wounding, how I'm the one that dips in submission to their rudeness, because, among all my many, many faults, it's that strong strain of acquiescent procrastination that remains the most constant. Still. Even here at life's tipping point, halfway through – if I stay well and out of danger. Knocking on forty – and that's never not startling, either.

'Wash your hands. Properly.' I direct Fran to the sinks, jumping from my already shaky skin when I see Joel in the mirror behind me, semi-slumped in Gracie's bosomy comfort. His grazed face stains her dress – his lip split and swollen too; a rising dark purple.

'I said we'd find Mum in here, didn't I, love?' Gracie mothers him, looking at me. 'I don't know what went down, but I'm sure it looks worse than it is.'

Fran begins to cry.

'What on earth's happened?' Panicked, packing handfuls of wet paper towel against his face, I get nothing back. 'Let's find Toby, then, see if he can talk. I'm so sorry about your dress, Gracie.'

'No bother,' she says, as if it really isn't any bother at all. 'Wedding's not a wedding without a punch-up, is it?'

8

'Was it a dog, Joel, or a wolf?' Fran's voice climbs like an air-raid siren as she runs along behind us. Cutting through the hall, Dan's suit catches my sight just beyond the patio doors, where an evening buffet that looks suspiciously like a re-hash of earlier is being arranged on fresh platters.

A furious Dan flings Toby at me with such force I stumble back, just in time for Budgie to steady me.

'Is this you, your silly play-fighting?' I shake him off, alarmed I've bitten, but the words are out before I can think, my heart thudding like I've sped up six flights of stairs.

'No need for all that temper. I pulled 'em apart when that one came squealing.' He pokes a thumb at Joel, though I know Budgie knows his name. 'Just lads being lads. Love.'

'It's nothing, Mum.' But Toby's eyes, edged with rare fury, say different. 'Honest.'

'It's time we were off, anyway,' Dan remembers, before giving Toby a nudge. 'But you can bloody say sorry first.'

Budgie makes a meal of their mumbled apologies, soaking up the tension with relish. 'My boxing club's the place for all that. For you, perhaps.' He nods to scruffy but unhurt Toby, before turning his eyes, hooded and now hostile, on Joel, who shrivels beneath his stare until he can no longer look anywhere but down to his dust-speckled good shoes.

The moment shifts as Dan scoops up Fran, bundling us towards the car.

Penny, leaning against the patio doorframe, begins welling up, Jesus Christ, as we pass. She gives me a tiny smile, but I've not forgotten the hair bants, so pretend not to notice. The car, still hot from earlier, welcomes us back like a warm blanket as Dan starts the engine. Despite the forcefield of emotion in our Ford Focus, the little green numbers on the dash illuminate my heart. 19.23. Regardless of what comes next, we're still off-ski. The agonizing scaffold underwear can be peeled off. Home in time for a big fuck-off gin and the iPlayer.

Outside the hotel, straddling the crumbling wall in her bloodied dress, sits Gracie. She takes a long swig from a prosecco bottle, then, noticing us, waves. We wave back, and as she looks in as we drive past, blows Joel a big kiss.

After remorseful hugs and crappy rushed attempts at apology cards, the kids are finally asleep. Three school bags sit by the front door, sandwiches dressed in tinfoil wait in the fridge, ready for the appropriate lunchboxes first thing. The floor's swept, even the dog bowl is clean – housewifery efforts to keep things right.

Now, in our bedroom, Dan lies next to me in the almost darkness. The whites of his eyes have been blinking furiously at the ceiling for the past fifteen minutes.

'They've said sorry. All night.'

But Dan doesn't thaw. 'We can't take them anywhere.'

Shocking as Joel's face seemed, after cleaning him up, Gracie was quite right, only surface damage. Even his lip, though still a plummy purple, is again its normal size. But both boys are being proper shifty, sitting on something between them; I know the signs. I also know that pushing them won't get us anywhere.

Pulling at the covers, Dan makes a big show of rearranging them before nestling down again. 'Budgie laughed it off, but it definitely upset him.'

'It was an act!' My hands flop either side of me on the fresh duvet cover, a little treat I did on the quick this morning, knowing I'd be grateful later. 'He owns a bloody boxing club, makes his living off rough and tumble. He just likes our kids nervy and licking his boots.'

'You're sick.'

'You're blind.' My face feels spiteful, teeth bared and yappy dog-ish. 'But you're not deaf. What about what he said to me?'

Dan huffs, the micro-signal that he'll now begin rejecting the conversation. 'What can I say? You know what he's like.'

Our whole life together has been a dozen variations of that phrase.

To me, back in the early days, Dan's lot seemed a beautiful example of what family meant and should be. Kinship to emulate. With my family all but forgotten, we'd been strained and cold for so long; I entered the fold a lone ranger. I adopted their patterns readily, their mindset of kids and kin first, abandoning my shitty old job to stay at home when the twins were born. This, I admit, is one of their better values.

It sits light years from their worst.

'I do, I know exactly what he's like. What they're all—'

'Don't. Don't start all that,' Dan says crossly. 'Kids fight – even siblings.' He does the familiar as-an-only-child-Monica-you-can't-possibly-understand face. 'It's just the disrespect . . .'

11

But I'm cross too. Cross for hoping, for believing a day with his family could end any other way than with an argument. I'm cross for putting on clean sheets, for the brief spark of us at the church earlier. Our spark – smothered the minute I'm reminded that my everything is part of them.

Watching one another, the atmosphere relaxes, a necessary reminder that it's here, home, our own young bud fam, that's most important. Dan touches my shoulder, back to soothing, just enough. 'It's done, Mon. Go to sleep.'

This is where you find me. At the tipping point. Where the big thing, too volatile to detonate, surrounds us like static. Invisible, yet obvious to all my senses. I don't expect any sort of magical existence, know very well that this is just my turn, yet I still can't help but wonder how many rounds in the world pass, semi-sedated – for an easy life. Like this.

Virtue is Valium.

Closing my eyes, I perform the ritual of pushing it all down and trying to forget. I obey him. But the honour's eroding. Daily.

2

Trip

As all good school trips start, there's a rush for the waiting coach, and a bagsying of seats before the backpacks and coats are even off. And they must come off. Everyone's sopping. We've had the prerequisite pelt-down, leaving me damp and itchy, while my curls shrink to fine frizz (think Michael Jackson, circa 1982).

'Can we sit upstairs, Mum?' Fran's eyes turn in mischief towards a tiny staircase my arse is bound to get trapped by. It's on my lips to invent a knee playing up, or that upstairs travel makes little girls sick, but her excitement keeps me quiet. Instead, I smile. She grabs a hand and drags me up, racing down the aisle to the front window.

'Can you see our house?' I ask, looking out, though there's nothing beyond us but the trees we're level with.

'Mu-um.' Fran rolls her eyes, big and brown like Galaxy Counters. 'We live half a mile away. Exactly.' Because Fran's watched Penny type postcodes into Rightmove since birth, I've taken to hiding our address book – though Penny's interest revolves more around property values than the distance to school.

With her nose pressed piglet-like against the glass, we watch the tops of heads below us, still dithering. A mum I've known for years without speaking to, wearing a polka-dot raincoat, counts heads and shrugs shoulders as Fran's teacher Miss Banks looks up and points at us. I get a flash-back school sensation, as if I'm in trouble – which was often.

'Are you Mrs Petersen?' A male, vaguely familiar head emerges from the staircase, amused when I say that I am. 'Your group's down here.'

Group? With so many helpers today, I'd sincerely hoped for the best. Me and Fran follow the fun crusher, his shoulders making a swishing sound as they brush the walls of the staircase, leaving behind a faint scent as he descends. Lemons and cigarettes. It's oddly pleasant.

Two small dripping kids are pushed towards me, a red sticker pressed on my jacket. Another is torn off for Fran. 'Girls, this is Franny's mum. She'll look after you today,' Miss Banks tells them. 'Twins,' she adds, emptily. 'Like yours.'

The girls watch me with exaggerated mournfulness as I usher them aboard, piling in across the aisle from Mrs Polka-dot raincoat and the lemons and cigarettes fun crusher. I've acknowledged him before in passing and can never decide whether he looks like a brooding weathered Hollywood actor, or a brooding weathered secondary school teacher. Flashes of striking, flashes of nondescript. Masculine, in a hefty, old-fashioned sort of way. Capable-looking. Mildly appealing.

With a smile like we're the oldest pals in the world, he sticks out a hand. 'Joe.'

Leaning forwards, I shake it. 'Monica.'

'First trip?'

'No; two more. You?'

'First trip. Not first child.'

'I'm Lynda,' efficient Mrs Polka-dots interrupts, sanitizing the hands and wrists of her son sat opposite. He stares ahead in glassy-eyed surrender. 'Done every trip, me and my side-kick.' She leans back to call into the row behind. 'Haven't we, Kathryn?'

'Duxford. Colchester Zoo,' says the invisible Kathryn. I'm familiar with her too. She's the friendlier of the duo, though I've never seen them parted. 'Name anywhere, and we've probably done it – twice.'

The engine rumbles into action, sparking excitement and swallowing the adult prattle. The pavement crowd waves with aching arms, their smiles now frozen, as it takes days for us to reverse out of the school. Then we're off, retracing the journey we took on foot earlier. Down the tree-lined road to the village green, and then our house, which whizzes past with an excited squeal from Fran. It looks strangely quiet from this distance, all higgledy and asleep, the thick lace nets at the old original window frames striking against the brick-work that could do with a sandblast. The Virginia creeper that Dan's still furious I let take over shines red-gold and wonderful in the sun that's fought through and won. Then home's gone, as we're hurtled off the main road, towards the A12.

'Mum, look – Nanny and Grandad's!' Penny and Clive's bungalow moves by in a flash of hydrangea and yellow rendering as we reach the edge of the village, their ancient BMW missing from the drive.

'What a lucky girlie,' says Lynda in the condescending sing-song voice that adults often use when addressing small children. 'Having Nanny close by.'

'Mum doesn't like it.' Fran gets a face that I hope trans-lates as 'stop bloody talking'.

'I had my in-laws round most of Sunday.' With a twinkle in his eye, Joe shakes his head as if he doesn't know what the world's coming to. 'Weekends pleasing other people's parents.'

In-law tensions are, of course, a common perennial in many a strained dynamic, yet I admit that mine – towards Penny, anyway – have matured into lukewarm appreciation over the years. Penny's a brilliant mum and nan; I give her credit. Watching her grandkids thrive – accepting that I've had something to do with that fact – means it's reciprocated, too. But as much as she is glued to me these days, my elephant memory means I can never, ever be her friend.

I say no more, though. As the world unravels through the window, I simply relish my escape.

Now we're city status, locals like to call where we live 'The Village'. I confess that my associations with the word village are either obscure or uncomplimentary – Idiot, for example, often springs to mind, living here – and People – muscular lads in fancy dress, complete with compulsory dance routines. Though they'd certainly make life more interesting; an American Indian and a black bondage policeman would likely spark panic on the village Facebook Community Hub.

Round here, though, the unanimous view of village life is that it's special. How many postcard-perfect villages sit fifteen minutes from a John Lewis and an Everyman Cinema, a hop-skip from urban life? The village is safe; affluent, green and settled – glorious positives.

The negatives need explanation. They don't apply to most here.

Though there are no candlestick makers that I know of, there's an artisan bread shop and a family butcher's; three generations of jovial, ruddy types. On the green, there's a pond full of ducks, free from rusty shopping trolleys, and free from any ne'er-do-wells roaming its periphery, too. The city centre's the place for urban dysfunction; out of sight and safely kept from little village thoughts. On the edge of the green, at the corner opposite the church and our house, stands the Fox pub, clad in Tudor beams. Its internal nooks are perfect spots for the local OGs to suss out the newcomers – suspicious territorial eyes over their pale ales.

Everybody has a decent car. Even us, though I can't drive. It gets used by Dan on weekends to do the things we think as adults we should be doing – turns around the retail park just outside the city centre, sourcing replacements and upgrades on our already acceptable clothing / furniture / fixtures – depending on sales and seasons, stopping at the on-site Costa to stare from the huge windows at others performing the same free-time routine. On these types of days, I keep an internal headcount of every brown face I see. And with each head I count, my heart gladdens. In the city, I almost forget I'm a minority.

A milk vomit whiff hits my nose, breaking my thoughts. It comes from the small brown kid Lynda's looking after, a slight girl with magnificent braids, clutching a paper bag.

'Don't worry,' Joe's saying from his haunches in front of her. 'Shall we swap that for a nice clean one?'

'I'm done,' the girl says, a little out of breath. She takes a tissue from Lynda, who begins panic-searching her cross-body bag. Out comes the hand sanitizer again.

'What's your name?' Joe asks, taking her sicky bits without any silly flinching.

'Immy something,' Lynda answers for her. 'Such a mouthful and I've a terrible memory. I'm calling her Emma instead.'

Immy something? It ruffles me, inside out.

A girl with the same grey eyes as Joe tugs at his coat, coaxing him down into a whisper.

'Mummy's working.' Lynda gives a judgy little nod in Immy-something's direction, as if it's the crime of the year.

Christ, if it weren't for the meticulous balancing act of Tax Credits and Dan's wage, I wouldn't be here myself.

Joe offers the girl a Polo mint. 'D'you think one of these might help, Iyamani?' She takes one with a quiet thank you.

'You've got such pretty hair,' I say, keen to boost her spirits, too. 'I had braids when I was little.' Rows of neat plaits that'd meet sensibly at the nape of my neck, all week long. I'd love freeing it, my candyfloss 'fro bouncing as I'd shake it round to the top twenty on a Sunday evening, that magic time before my dad would switch it for Radio 4 and Mum would pin me down and braid me tight for another spell at school. 'D'you go to the hairdressers, or do you know someone really clever?'

'Auntie Claudette.' Iyamani blooms before our eyes. 'She can do braids like this.' She flicks her fingers through them with a flourish. 'And canerows and box braids—'

'First school trip, though,' Lynda says under her breath, with a shake of her immaculate bob. 'Shame.'

Joe and me catch eyes. I'd like to look at him more, make up my mind properly about whether he's dishy or not, but the coach is slowing. The castle shades us out as we dismount, its grey stone presence reminding me of yesterday, of the church and all that followed. Old places that have seen it all before.

I'm so very glad it's today.

After a brief tour, the Reception class regroups with a storyteller and their bag of puppets in the deep rooms of the castle foundations. These are lovely kids. The stories hold their attention and Iyamani is picked to hold some armour before my group settles around a picnic table at midday. I take the cellophane off straws, assist with opening tiny Tupperware, and pinch most of Fran's Doritos.

With another twenty minutes left of lunch, we opt for a turn around Castle Gardens. The trees aren't yet winter bare, the pathways a carpet of russet. From the pale white sun comes a sliver of warmth. Knitwear weather. My absolute favourite.

The girls just ahead of me chatter non-stop; their time together making them less inhibited. With arm grabbing and hands clapping and the covering of mouths, their unfolding friendship is an honour to witness. But bittersweet; I miss Fran at home. Since she started school, my days are too still, our home hung in waiting till her afternoon return. When she's back – usually fractious, only to drop off in front of the telly – her presence fixes everything.

Those six, silent school hours set me thinking of the silences from my own childhood. Of that little house on Horn Road, quiet and tense with a hole in the middle – filled at last, now that I've stuffed the gaps with Dan and our own inventions. As the old drag of the negative creeps through me, I do what I always do, and shut it down. It's self-preservation; mentally distancing from where those bunny-hole thoughts lead me. It's an art.

Trailing the girls, I notice Joe's group a stone's throw from an ice-cream van. His gang of three sit cross-legged under a big tree, chatting in whispers about their unorthodox treats. Both kids have Fabs, and both wear faces that say this is surely life's pinnacle so far. Joe has a lemon sorbet. As he licks clean the melted dribble of yellow that's almost reached his fingers, his eyes meet mine – leaving me in no doubt. If we were in the first flutterings of humanity, he would simply stomp over, put me over his shoulder and take me some-where to instantly copulate.

I am seriously lamenting, with all the wickedest parts of me, how unfortunate it is that humanity ever evolved. If I'd an ounce of sense, I'd run, but my hand's already waving, the other in my purse, hoping I've enough for four lollies.

'You've led us astray.' It's the best I can come up with. The girls squeal around my legs, clutching their Calippos. 'May we join you?'

'Yes, please,' Joe says. 'Budge up, kiddos.' The girls slip into the gaps as he pats the grass next to him. 'You should've seen Lynda when she spotted the lollies – reckon she's already called the fun police. Sorry, if you're mates.' My face gets him laughing. 'I didn't think so. You don't look very schoolish.'

I don't ask what 'not very schoolish' means. I'd rather just think it's a compliment. 'I wondered whether you were a teacher, looking after Iyamani like that. Poor kid.'

'Imagine, being stuck in that group.' He stops to retrieve someone's lolly from the grass, pushed up with too much force. Looking it over, he plops it back into the wrapper and the broken parts into his mouth. 'I work up at the hospital, in mental health. You get some vomit, but not much. What about you?'

'I'm just at home.' God, I sound feeble, the meek martyr of domesticity. I can't leave it there. 'But now she's at school,' I nod over at Fran, 'I'll go back to work. Or study. I'm not sure yet.'

'What would you study?' Joe asks, not feigning interest, but with proper inquisitiveness.

'I don't know. I've not done any learning since my GCSEs.' Mocks. I only showed up to one real exam. Art. I got a B.

'GCSEs? Crikey, you're a baby—'

'*You're* not, Daddy. You're old.' Molly wears a wicked little grin. 'And very hairy.'

Joe cuffs her around the ears. 'I'm forty-eight and beards are all the rage these days.'

'My dad's smooth,' says Fran, 'like my Ken doll.'

The talk stays light and easy, with a hovering sparkle that floors me with disappointment when all too quickly it's time to reassemble in the castle. The groups split once again, and I wonder if I can drag out our final hour in the shoebox-sized gift shop.

Me and Joe return in the seats we travelled in – handy for us to indulge our in-joke at Lynda's off-the-scale parental peacocking. While she bleeds the eardrums of everyone around her, the kids stay silent until the coach stops. Such noise on take-off, but their placid return journey proves that they are every bit still very much five years old.

'We must swap numbers. Lynda does a book club.' Kathryn beams over the seats as my mind panics, shrivelling in on itself. An invitation. Punishment for being too friendly. 'One a month. We rotate houses. Are you much of a reader?'

I can't deny my books. My sanity. 'I am, yes.'

'We're reading *The Woman in the Well*.' Lynda swats Joe with her brochure. 'You're welcome, too – be our honorary male.' It's delivered rather flirtatiously, with a final lingering glance, as she chases down an escaping Iyamani. Kathryn tails her, waving goodbye.

'I'm game.' Joe's raincoat makes the swishing noise again as it rubs against the window. His corduroys, taut around the thickness of his thighs, jolt in jest along with the rest of him. He's joking. Thank goodness.

'I'm not the most sociable of souls,' I admit.

'But regardless a very decent one.' Joe puts his hand out again, and I let him make mine disappear within it. 'Thank you. For a lovely day.'

Collecting the wrappers Molly's left in her seat, Joe straightens upright. Though there's a clear gap between us, I'm now eye level with his crotch. I pretend not to notice – nor him pretending not to notice that I'm trying not to notice his crotch. The absurdity of this on a damp coach with its lingering scent of breakfast sick is not lost on us either, but we pretend not to notice that, too.

Walking home, me and Fran cut across the green and round the duck pond. 'Did you have a lovely day?' I ask her.

'The best. I made three new friends. No. Four.' She kicks at the leaves on the path. 'Four.' Kick. 'New.' Kick. 'Friends.'

'Four more mates for your party.' I humour Fran's big birthday plans, though she's got till next September. 'Who's on your list now?'

'Nanny,' she begins. Of course. 'Grandad. You. Daddy. Joel and Toto . . .' Her eyes are lively in the bright afternoon. 'Sir Duke!'

'Chubby Labradors can't go trampolining.'

Her laughter, that open, natural joy, stirs a vision of a grown Fran in a far-off future. I picture a happy moon-faced old lady, full of the same fun and mischief. The thought makes me ache with love for her. With hope. Yet it feels like mourning.

We wait at the edge of the road for the traffic to slow. 'Will Nana Yvonne come to my party?'

My self-inflicted sorrow pops. 'If you want her to.' I can't help myself. 'Do you want her to?' But she breaks from my hand to chuck her arms around Joel, who's caught us up. He has impeccable timing; we're just about to pass the Co-op.

'Can we get some strawberry laces?' Yvonne is forgotten as Fran does her best begging, batting her lashes, holding her hands together like some long-suffering woodland creature in a Disney film.

Along with three bags of laces for a lovely round pound, I pick up a bottle of Merlot despite it breaking my plan for a dry night. I feel I've earned it, being a good mother today – a good wife yesterday. A quiet wife, until last night. Those boozy units I'll claim as reward. Like the light-level flirting earlier, the discovery that those forgotten muscles still

24

remember what to do. At the queue to pay, rather than feeling drained by such an unusually sociable day, I'm refreshed – more at peace.

There's a startling, rather remarkable pang of energy in me. Perhaps, after all these weeks of ineptitude that I've excused as adjusting to Fran at school, I am ready to stand tall, and go-get again. Or, at the very least, scrub the fucking bathroom.

3

Guests

Days slip by in routine ease until tonight. We have a social, ringed on the kitchen calendar with a worn-out stump of a pencil. Like every second Thursday of the month, Dan's sister and her husband visit us. On Nancy and Hunter's arrival, there's a stand-ard hour of excited chaos, then the kids will be packed off, so the grown-ups can have a lazy late supper, thanks to Just Eat.

It's not yet six when Sir Duke barks a belated and non-threatening welcome as Dan returns home. Pausing in the doorway, he gapes at the mess our three offspring have abandoned in favour of the telly. The dining table's disap-peared beneath rucksacks and lunchboxes, the early founda-tions of a Lego spaceship and Fran's art, lavished with so much poster paint it will likely never dry.

'You know they'll be here soon?' Dan says, setting a box from Majestic on Fran's wet pictures.

'It's only a takeaway.' And only his sister, but I leave that and offer him tea instead. 'I bought the drinks. I told you yesterday.'

'Weeknight Chenin?' He unloads his Chablis, an epic-looking red and some trendy lagers. Taking the last slither of after-school angel cake, he collapses it into his mouth, moving in the direction of the living room. Shrieks and giggles fill our downstairs as he reappears with a clean, damp-haired daughter under his arm.

'Clear up your mess for Mum.' Dan sets Fran on her feet, taking his tea from me. 'Busy day?' He peers judgily around again, but I turn it by asking about his.

The daily briefing begins with Dan's superiors; pompous creatures I don't know, but who Dan thinks matter, so I pretend to care about. Sir Duke settles at Dan's feet, and as he twiddles the dog's velvet ears, he talks up a Thursday of life in the City of London. The residual wedding aggro ebbs as Dan gossips, eyes gleaming as though he's spent the day rubbing shoulders with the Kardashians. Bookkeeping. Office life. An environment to which I am allergic but thankful for all the same. The world he thrives in gave us a home, security, a non-return to the job I despised.

I'm grateful when the volume of kid chatter overpowers our own. I can just enjoy his face, now he's been muffled almost mute. It's a fantastic face; well-sculpted, clean-shaven, with neat brows the colour of wet sand shielding the grey-green slants of his eyes.

'You're not listening,' he says, but he's not offended. Relaxed and released now from all of work's trappings, Dan melts back into home Dan. My Dan. 'Come here.' He takes my hand, pulling me onto his lap. 'How was your day?'

'Easier.' Embracing our flush of feeling, Dan's hands assume their natural place, on my hips, where they best belong. 'Plus, I've had this to look forward to.'

'This?' Dan's face is nothing but filth as he grinds against me. 'Or the takeaway?'

A round of bickering kicks off upstairs; our speck of perfect knocked back into normality. Rolling eyes, we smile – admittedly, a little bit smugly – in mutual awareness of our good fortune. Our fabulous family.

Dan stretches out of his seat, slaps my arse. Says, 'Laters.'

Through the kid noise, the television blares alongside someone's computer game, our home alive with the vibrant, boisterous sounds of domestic life. I use the energy to press through the duty with my good wife's head on, the epitome of maternal and domestic precision, ready to take on the additional role of host. Knowing Dan will like it, I search for the matching glasses at the back of the cereal cupboard. Avoiding stray Cheerios and Weetabix debris, I find them; hefty great globes, purchased with showing off in mind. Thick with dust. The bathroom's clean already, but I know as Dan gets ready for his shower he'll straighten towels and adjust the toiletries on our shelves. Labels will be teased into jaunty angles, the fancy ones coaxed to the front. Though there's still a good inch of the hand soap left, Dan will replace it with the new one under the sink. It makes me feel sad, rather like when I realize that I've overdone the lipstick.

The irony – which makes all this even more agony – is that Nancy couldn't give two shits about any of it. Though undoubtedly from the same Petersen keeping-up-with-the-Joneses gene pool, she now has so much accumulated wealth that the competition's pointless.

And though she's from them, I like Nancy. Should I have met her independently, we still would've been friends.

Though I'm all chill compared to Dan's obsessive neat-ness, I am not so relaxed that I'm happy to sit about with a shiny face. Heading for a quick gussy-up, I pass the twins' room. Dan stands topless between them, holding an Xbox controller, a hint of a beer gut resting on his work trousers, as they all stare, zombie-transfixed, at the cars looping the screen.

'D'you reckon Hunter will play tonight?' Joel sets up another round.

'He might.' Toby sounds hopeful. 'He's epic on Black Ops . . .'

Nancy's all smiles as she bundles the kids into her arms. From beneath an armpit, Fran gazes up at her adoringly, reaching to stroke the blonde silkiness she didn't inherit. She got brown curls instead, with a mismatched Caramac halo of frizz around her hairline; fabulous, in every way.

A bottle of champagne dangles from Nancy's hand as she hugs me, resting cold down the middle of my back. 'I went for a sparkly drop – thought you'd need it. After Sunday's punch-up.' She shoves her tongue in the side of her cheek, playfully.

'Neither will say why, so there's no treats till they do.' I say this, remembering the strawberry laces slip-up. When I catch Fran's eye, she presses her lips together tightly, stashing the secret, should Joel wind her up later.

'It wasn't our fault,' Joel says for the billionth time.

'So embarrassing.' I take Nancy's mac, steering her into the kitchen. 'Budgie was disgusted.'

'Oh well,' she says, as if she couldn't care less, dumping her bags on the table. 'He didn't try,' Nancy makes groping gestures at my arse, 'all that again, did he? Because that really was disgusting.' Her brows arch, eyes pure devilment. 'Dan still don't know?' Much as I like her, Nancy cannot be trusted. 'Mum's sulking has hit new levels over us not going, but I swear . . .'

I let her dissect them. However appetizing an epic slagging-off fest would be, I'd rather preserve my reputation for never bitching within the folds of their family.

'Mon, you beautiful creature.' Hunter bursts in, his chiselled cheeks outdoor cold as he presses them to mine for air kisses, before helping himself to a packet of Mini Cheddars. 'Your kitchen's awesome.'

I love my kitchen too, and not just for the snacks. It's a colour riot, against the mostly neutral rest of the house. Nothing matches because kids break shit and I'd be foolish to get sentimental. Each year, millions more unfortunate teaspoons go missing, never to be found. With every opened cupboard, a shower of empty sports bottles or tea towels or – lucky for Hunter – crisps rain out. I'm expert at barely organized chaos.

With a rumble of footsteps, Dan jogs down the stairs in an out of character white vest with his hair combed back, looking like he's about to mount a Harley-Davidson. Nancy kisses him hello. 'Let's order quick; I've been having dirty pizza urges all day.'

'We had Tesco frozen.' Joel slumps next to her.

'Poor little sod,' Nancy fusses, stroking his hair. 'Must be just like the workhouse, living here.'

There's much love between Nancy and all my children. The adoration goes both ways, but she never indulges or babies them. They are mates more than anything else. No matter how old Nancy and Hunter get, and they're both forty now, they will eternally remain the coolest aunt and uncle ever. When Penny's around too, she gets all misty-eyed and stuck on how Nancy would make a fantastic mum. When she's reminded that it's never going to happen, Penny's misty eyes turn into the sulks. Nancy prefers last-minute city breaks, after-work fabulousness in cocktail bars in Soho – and her sanity.

There's resentment, too – unspoken of, naturally (Dan would never readily admit to any personal shortcomings, even to his wedded and beloved) – towards Nancy's success and independence. She's leapt from one dazzling opportunity to another, marrying a dazzling, successful man along the way. Dan didn't leave home until he met me. The sweaty, magical nights in my tiny rented studio drifted into weeks, until one day he was at last fully disentangled from Penny and her industrial-strength apron strings.

As militantly as I fight it, I am equipped with the same core motivations as my parents. Though these days we're no more than strangers, similar drivers sit in my veins. I never follow trends or the crowd, for example. Even when a little bit of me would like to, my stubbornness won't let me get my nails done, enjoy chain coffee shops or watch *Friends*.

The Petersen siblings inherited Penny's competitiveness. When Dan secured his City job fresh from his A-levels, Nancy and her First in Digital Enterprise eclipsed him by gliding across the Atlantic to a shinier skyscraper than any to be found on Liverpool Street. Our end-of-terrace at the less appealing end of the village pales to invisibility when compared to Nancy's home, worth (last time Dan checked online) four times more than ours. Their three-storey Georgian on the wooded east of the Central Line heaves with Bose and Boch. But no babies, much to Penny's lamentations, no babies.

'Hunter, d'you wanna play Xbox?' asks Toby, as Dan, performance playing, gets him in a Dad of the Year sort of headlock. I wish he'd have a bloody beer and relax.

'Of course, man,' drawls Hunter. Hunter became Hunter when he moved to America in his teens and took to using his surname instead. He claps his hands, rubbing them together. 'Order me anything, as long as it's thin base.' As he follows the boys out, I hand him one of the trendy lagers. 'I do love your house.'

'So, you've no idea what it was over?' Nancy asks, as Alexa comes to life with some dreadful Ibiza chill-out music that Dan's selected for background.

'Can't believe they know the first rule of Fight Club already.' I'm two big glasses down, far more laissez-faire on the subject than I have been.

'And the second.' Nancy laughs. 'Proper little Kray twins.'

Dan's forehead creases into four horizontals, the ceiling light ageing him into a sudden and startling resemblance to Joe. A flutter erupts in my stomach, gone as quick as it was there. I light some candles, just in case that wicked light bulb's adding years to me as well.

'And they're stubborn as hell.' Dan glances across at me as if I'm to blame for that.

'They argue like hell, too.' I kick at Dan as he catches my foot with his own, keeping it trapped beneath the table. 'But they're not violent.'

'What's this?' Hunter opens a box, making prayer hands before taking a slice.

'The fight,' says Dan. 'They've both clammed up, shady little shits. But no one likes a grass, do they?'

'Sounds like it was justified.' Puzzled by Dan's clearly gobsmacked face, Hunter asks, 'What? They said, just now upstairs.'

'Just like that?' Dan's forehead recrumples, our linked

ankles disentangling. I know he's thinking that their telling Hunter equates to some slight on his own good fatherliness, but I'm just pleased. Pleased that the silence has popped, regardless to whom.

'Well, spit it out, then,' says Nancy, 'don't keep the parents waiting.'

'Some cousin – Callum, is it? Used the N-word. They got triggered. What,' Hunter says, looking at Dan's blank face, 'do I need to say more?'

'It's a disgusting word.' Dan's careful. 'But attacking your own—'

'*Defending your own*. Callum called Joel a N—' His raised brows fill in the rest of the word.

As it all begins to register, I leg it up to the boys' room. 'Why didn't you tell me?' I look from Joel to Toby, sprawled on the bottom bunk, hiding behind an upside-down ALDI catalogue. I push it away, revealing his face, hot from upset.

'Callum deserved it, Mum. It's the worst word. *You* said that.'

'Yes, but that doesn't mean—' I stop. 'Please. Just tell me everything.'

'He wouldn't pass that ball we found – said he didn't have to because Joel was a stupid . . .' Toby nods in the place the word fell. 'He wouldn't take it back – said that . . .' His breath catches, trapped, his chest rising. 'I don't want to say.'

But I think I can guess. Stroking Toby's cheeks, still defensive and burning, I am for a moment stuck, blank of the words I need to soothe them.

'He said I wasn't one of them.' Joel's voice comes quiet from above. 'Said they all just put up with me. I hit him, but he was quicker.'

Clambering out to Joel, I try kissing him over the safety bar, gently avoiding his scabby bits. 'I'm so very, very sorry.' Joel clings to me, sobbing like he's five again, as I brush the tears away.

'I got him, though. Long idiot.' Toby pushes his toes into my knee for effect, using the nickname Dan invented for Callum years ago. 'Next time—'

'I don't want next time. I don't want to see any of them. Ever again.' But even as Joel says it, I know I'm not that bloody lucky. 'And I wouldn't want to be like Callum, anyway. He stinks of onions. And farts.' Joel leans close, pressing his forehead to mine.

From below, Toby's arms wrap around my knees. 'Onion farts. And he still reads baby books. I saw him in the school library. How's he think he's better?'

''Cos he's white,' Joel says. 'And I'm not.'

When the twins arrived early, Joel was ill, needing antibiotics twice daily for three long worrying weeks. Toby – twin two, tiny but robust – slept in the same incubator in the Special Baby Unit because Joel couldn't settle without him. Joel's like me, bookish and left-handed, who'd rather live in the clouds than a tidy bedroom, whereas Toby is Dan: asleep in seconds, brilliant at sports and thrives on a bit of an audience. Both kind boys; funny, unlikely to ever single anyone out for ridicule. I've practised fairness, taught them empathy, too.

But I didn't equip them for this. I didn't think I needed to yet.

They've worked it out now, anyway – this unusual clinginess A-star evidence. In all their similarities, from equal measures down to sharing my womb at the same time, things have shifted. Toby's natural protectiveness has curdled into aggression. It won't be the only time. This new negativity, laced with paranoia, is a sensory burden; a sixth-sense gut instinct for prejudice.

And Joel now will hesitate, overthinking every new interaction. He'll notice little significances, like how when the boys follow me around M&S on a Saturday, Joel's the one trailed by plain-clothed security, too. How, while he waits for a bus, folk will hold their bags closer when they notice him in the queue. It's a self-awareness that will scar a boy plenty self-conscious anyway, as he's judged by his colour before anything else.

It's an honour, an earthly privilege for Joel to be my image, but it hurts, knowing all that'll bring.

'You both standing up to Callum is by far the bravest thing I've ever heard.' I hold them both close, my babies again. 'Seriously. Martin Luther King brave. Black Panther brave. Bloody long idiot.'

I sense Joel's search for a connection, a common story; for me to open, share, say that I get it, have learnt to spot all this shit instinctively, as an animal would. That these behaviours come from knowing you're different, knowing it's best to keep palatable, sounding bright enough, friendly enough.

White enough. Camo, for the easy ride, which turns me inside out.

But I'm unprepared.

'Callum's mind is ugly. Just like him.'

His parents' fault, on both counts.

Rocket lollies and half an hour more telly make it all as if the upset was worth it, but I'm glad it's out of them. Secrets are toxic. Families die because of them.

First checking in on a sparked-out Fran, I head downstairs.

Dan's voice slows my steps. 'He's picked it up and is testing it out; it's not Hitler Youth part two. And Christ, her music's full of it. Nigger this, nigger that.' *He says it.* Even *I* don't say it. Not even when I'm rapping out perfect verses to KRS-One and Kano, cooking with my Spotify blasting. 'He's the bloody long idiot, but any money you like this'll be another wrong that I'll take the blame for. You know, we can't even watch the news together? She holds me personally responsible for every wrong in Westminster.' Beer's given Dan a careless tongue.

As Hunter starts about how mindfulness improves one's personal responsibility, I stalk into the kitchen, heading for the freezer.

'Is that for the boys?' Dan touches my forearm. 'I'll take it up, talk . . . let them know it wasn't their . . .' He trails off as I shove the lollies into his chest.

'I got you something,' Nancy says, changing the subject.

I slump into my seat. 'Is it a lifetime supply of disco biscuits?'

'You're so funny. Clever. It's all wasted.' Nancy splats a handful of brochures on the table.

I swing one closer to read it. 'I can't go to a proper university.'

'I knew you'd do this.' Frustrated, Nancy grabs up her hair, lets it fall like a sleek sheet over her shoulders, making me miss my old and very trusted look. 'Remember in the summer? You asked—'

'Begged,' says Hunter.

'*Begged* me to kick you up the arse when Fran went to school. Well, it's time.' She taps the brochures. 'They're only ideas.'

Any authority school held vanished as soon as I knew that I didn't have to be there – but I'd love to explore what I was good at then, those sweeping little stories I'd write in my diaries, brighter than my own day to days, that I'd repackage for my homework. How I'd paint, just for the joy of it, page after page of outrageous colour. I've now the time, but not the confidence.

Yet I did ask for this. And I did beg, one drunken night spent wailing about missing Fran before she'd even started school.

A satisfied Dan reappears. 'Frozen treats and all's right in the world.'

'Perhaps self-defence is a good idea,' I think aloud. It couldn't hurt.

'That's a good shout,' Dan says approvingly. 'I'll ring Budgie. After all, he—'

'You *are* kidding?' I'm baffled by how normal I sound.

'A bit of discipline, light boxing, learning to defend themselves against . . . all that.'

'Can someone help Dan out, please, because I don't think he gets it.' My voice rises, girlish and wavery. I absolutely mustn't cry.

Nancy's hand closes over mine. 'It's all right.'

'It's not though, is it?' I blot my lashes, cross I'm emotional. 'It's suffocating.'

'I'm suffocating?'

'She doesn't mean you,' Nancy says. 'She means all them.'

Dan tuts. 'You make our family sound like a cult.'

'Maybe it's not till you've got away that you see it. Why d'you think we bought in Epping?'

Dan stays silent; teeth clamped tight.

I don't want Nancy and Hunter to go, but it's not long before they do. And as we whisper goodbyes on the doorstep, Dan withdraws into the sulks.

'That's it, then, is it – end of discussion? Don't turn your back.' I tail him into the kitchen. 'I wish you knew how it felt, having someone convinced you're beneath them, just because you're not white.'

'They're children. Callum's likely got it from the same bloody music you listen to.'

'Why are you excusing him? That boy tried smashing the shit out of your sons. That stinky boy with the same awful face as his mother.'

'That's just childish—'

39

'They look like rejects in a doughnut factory. And he's not a kid – he's fourteen. He knows better. Just like Budgie—'

'And what am I supposed to do?'

'Well, you could start by just bloody acknowledging it.' By the armchair, Nancy's Sainsbury's bag bursts with the gifts she's left for the boys' upcoming birthday. 'Uninvite Callum to the boys' party.'

'But I've already—'

'Well, undo what you've—'

'All right!' he barks, snapping me off. 'I'll sort it.'

But it still won't be. 'And Budgie can stay away, too.' *Budgie.* Stupid bloody nickname, anyway. At least Joel and Toby aren't following in Dan's passive footsteps. Their radar's sharper than his already.

'I can't tell you how sick I am of this. My whole life's a tug of war; who's offending who, who do I defend? They're my family, Monica.'

'And what about mine?'

'Who – us here, or the mystery mum and dad that we can't ever mention?' Hands on hips, Dan's neck is a flush of temper. It's a cheap dig.

Moving to the sink, I fling on the tap, waiting for the hot to come through, and when it does, keep my hand within the scalding gush for as long as I can stand it.

Dan leans on the worktop, exhaling his entire body weight. 'I knew this would end up being my fault.'

Dunking the dishcloth and wringing it first, I throw it at him. It makes a hard slap against his chest. His shoulders set, taut and unforgiving as he works it over the table, every fibre of him willing me to lose momentum, so we can all go back to thinking his family are just a bunch of harmless ill-informed old fools who don't know any better.

Thirteen autumns ago, after three months of dating, Dan arranged a meet-the-parents lunch. We met 'on neutral territory' – his words – after assuring me that, though Clive and Penny were 'lovely', they could be a bit 'old-fashioned'. His vagueness neither told me much nor worried me; I remained excited and eager to charm. Not because I was particularly keen to befriend his parents, but because this was a landmark moment. The potential future in-laws. The potential of it all. Dan was serious.

We looked bloody amazing, sat waiting for them in a fancy-pants restaurant, having freshly returned from Rome, our first romantic city break. I'd been longing, since devouring *Bridget Jones's Diary* on a day off school with period pains, for a mini break. Dan did not disappoint.

For someone to be so dedicated and romantic, I knew his parents would have to be decent people. At twenty-seven, Dan already had the good manners and dependability of someone's dad. And from someone who never thought much about babies and children, it was unquestionable that, since meeting Dan, I absolutely wanted a family. With him. I knew it with conviction, my ovaries somehow spiritually fusing to his balls. Dan hadn't yet articulated any words of love, but I had the feeling we were edging to it. Not everybody meets the parents.

But it was instinct, as Penny's eyes travelled over me for the first time, that sent my stomach to my feet. Instant dislike. In fact, dislike may've been easier – this was instant distaste. Penny came across as matriarchal yet marble, no matter how I tried to engage her – and I did try, with topics I knew she had an interest in – she remained cold, impenetrable. Clive was a little more talkative, polite enough, but they both had a very strange way about them. It left me bewildered; I'd never met them, we lived miles apart, with no occasion where we might've crossed paths; their decision to dislike me was made the second they saw me, but still it hadn't clicked why.

It came after our main courses. I was in the loos redoing my lipstick when Penny flounced in. I tried with the small talk, offering something like how her steak looked delicious, but she cut me off.

'Parker,' she'd said. 'A very English surname; how did you end up with a name like that?'

'My father,' I'd answered, still with lashings of deferential politeness, though the old copper coin had at last started to drop.

'So, your mother's the soot?'

The soot? I'd thought, *What are we, fucking Victorians?*

'My mother's Trinidadian, if that's what you're asking.'

Penny raised her brows at this, as with floppy fingers I packed my make-up away, ready to flee before she spoke again. I remember pulling on what felt like the heaviest door in history, and when it finally opened, Penny placed her manicured hand, those pink frost nails, just above my grip.

'My boy's worth more than some trampy little half-breed, so don't get any funny ideas.' She'd shoved past, overtaking, leaving me stopped, still holding that door.

It's peculiar how they happen, the bursts of in-your-face prejudice. They not only pain me, right down to my chromosomes, but they force an acknowledgement as well, a truth, of the very little value I hold to some. It's been a living waiting game; that fear, the revulsion, of being abused in front of the kids, for them to suffer it.

The fact I didn't know is annihilating.

They're old enough for memories to stick, to fester into anger, or vengeance, or just – how I always felt whenever it happened to my mum, and then to me – vulnerable. I want to challenge, be fierce, but this, this bullshit archaic white food chain always, without fail, makes me want to hide. Makes me ashamed to be me.

I swerved Joel's questions because I didn't know how to explain that.

'It must be such a lovely, secure feeling, being white,' I say, softer now. 'Don't get me wrong, I don't want to change who I am, but I do so envy that feeling.'

'There's no feeling. You just are what you are.' Said unthinkingly. So matter of fact.

'Lucky you.' The classic white male specimen. Comfortable. Confident.

King of the hill. Always.

Penny, pinched by her own vileness, sat with clasped hands, her chest reddish clouds of high colour. My return to the table sent her leaping for her glass, but, finding herself unsteady, changed her mind about picking it up. Dan, mumbling about me taking forever, had tugged at my arm, slotting me effortlessly into his side, rather as though I'd always belonged there. He reached for his beer, then had leant back, comfortable and confident.

And naïve. Bafflingly naïve.

In the whole of my life, I've rarely found myself with a competitive spirit. But looking at Penny from my nook of protection, I held her stare that day until her eyes turned watery and fluttered into a pattern of unsure little blinks.

'I don't want them here, Dan. And neither do your children.'

Dan snatches up Sir Duke's lead. 'I need air.'

I don't answer him. I don't wait up.

And, for the first night in forever, we sleep apart.

4

Friends – Not the TV Show

For almost a week, we've watched each other but haven't spoken. This afternoon, Joe stands across the playground from me, his hands behind his back, leaning into his left side. Dark denim jeans, tan worn-in brogues, and umbrella-less, his navy jumper slowly gathering pearls of precipitation. The cold's made his face drawn; his lines deeper than one might expect for forty-eight years old. There's a definite hint of brooding actor about him.

How very wonderful.

Sod it. I'm next to him before I think too much on it, and he seems so pleased with the situation that I forget to be awkward. 'I wondered if you'd been collared by Lynda yet.'

He shakes his head. 'But I am thinking of wearing camo and hiding in the bushes. You?'

'She's back to pretending she can't see me.'

He laughs. 'Friendly bunch up here, are they, the rest of them?'

'Some. Mostly, I just smile and leg it. Small talk kills me.'

'Hell, bloody yes it does. Oi.' He grins, nudging me. 'Let's never talk small.'

That'll mean no correct Calpol measurement debates; no SATS obsessions, no local riding lessons / keyboard lessons / should I get a tutor shit-chat. It means no competition. And it sounds beautiful.

'All right,' I agree, with a smile surely bigger than his. 'Like what, then?'

'Like they all do it.' Joe points his head towards Fran and Molly's classroom. 'With favourites and worsts, and none of the bland filler. That's how you make proper friends.'

After the lemon sorbet and his groin in my face, I've thought about a whole damn lot of things. Being his friend wasn't one of them, but it's by far the healthiest suggestion.

'Favourite chocolate bar?' he tests.

'A Galaxy Ripple.' I don't even have to think about it. 'You?'

'The Starbar. An oldie but goodie. I'm a Cadbury man, myself.'

Few things are better than a Galaxy Ripple paired with a packet of plain crisps – I'll have to stop at the shops. Going by the outdoor clock, there's another lucky minute or two before the school bell. 'Favourite song, then.'

'Christ, that's a tricky one. I'd struggle with a top five. I'll have to sleep on it and tell you tomorrow.'

'Tomorrow's Saturday.'

'Back to pleasing other people's parents.' His gaze slows as it moves over my mouth. 'Perhaps we should run away together.'

Though this is only harmless fun, I still check the faces of the mums closest to us. The group are cooing over a phone screen; the holder of it wearing the smuggest grin imaginable. Today's school gate is no different from my old school days, those girly cliques and hierarchy I remember well. I'm still neither affluent enough to compete with nor similar enough to connect with. And though I've never been a stranger to existing as the outsider, there's a martyr-esque comfort about it here. Not schoolish. For once in my life, I'm grateful not to fit.

But if I were watching us, I'd know. From the set of his mouth, down to his gripped hands. Want is written all over him. Face to face in broad daylight, neither of us has made any special efforts to impress, yet it's clearer every second spent together that neither one of us is disappointed.

'I've a weekend free of obligation. If I keep everyone well fed, they'll leave me alone.'

'What'll you do then,' he asks, 'alone?'

'Read. Nap, if I'm lucky.'

'What do you read?'

It's the sort of question that makes me nervous, that'll reveal I never went to uni, that I'm thick as shit, despite getting through two books a week. I've a cupboard at home, a second-hand lump of old-fashioned wood that I've come to love, where I keep my most precious books that all my life have moved me. Every paperback on those shelves has at some point been restorative, vitamins for my ups and downs. My most recent addition to the line-up is a Booker Prize nominee. Who's only got one GCSE now?

It's the book I choose to tell him about. 'And what are you reading?'

'Work stuff – *Crisis in the Digital Age*.' He watches me, cockeyed. 'You know, some people go a bit funny when I tell them what I do.'

'Not me.'

He smiles, relieved. From a back pocket, he produces his phone. 'I'd best give you my number. You never know, it might come in handy. Playdates and the likes.' He holds it out for me and, as I tap his digits into mine, the bastard bell rings.

Children. Reality bites as they spill through the doors.

And like that, it's snuffed.

I do it without thinking. Seamlessly exiting the school at the same time as Lynda and Kathryn, I catch Kathryn's far friendlier, softer face. As I hoped, she reminds me about the book club with a bonus prompt to invite Joe, too, should I see him.

This month, it's Kathryn's turn to host. She lives in one of the new-builds opposite the school, the three-storey white-brick terraces that manage to be both imposing yet flimsy at the same time. She gives me orders for seven o'clock, next Thursday evening.

Dan goes a bit slack in the face as he takes an eye off the football to check me out. 'Wow, Mon. Well bloody done.'

I've made no more effort than I usually would to leave the house, it's just that on a regular night I'd be bare-faced and in my comfies by now. I clutch *The Woman in the Well* to calm my trembling. Dan sits beneath the standing lamp, with Fran tucked at his side practising her phonics in one of her floor-length nighties that always makes me think of boarding schools and midnight feasts. On the sofa, Joel and Toby kick at each other from opposite ends, still in uniform and needing a good wash. I'd normally be sat between them, my feet tucked beneath Sir Duke's warm belly, balancing my tea and shouting at them not to jog me.

Dan bats his hands, ushering me away from the telly. 'Sorry, I thought we were going to— Yes!' He stands, reaching for the sky. The phonics cards fly everywhere as the boys leap on the sofa to throw air punches with their father, while Fran screams into the chaos in that earth-shattering pitch she's expert at reaching.

A closed front door brings instant detachment, the silent glow of streetlights a godsend. The night air holds a new wintry crispness that lingers in my throat, making me think about changing seasons and life's repeating patterns – and that blasted internet quote, about living the same year seventy times and calling it a life. Though quotes like this plague me, they're perfect Christmas presents for Penny, adding to the *Live, Laugh, Love, Good Vibes Only* and *Dance*

Like No One's Watching plaques dotted throughout her domain.

My unhurried footsteps feel different to how they do when I'm zigzagging all week in the daytime. The scooping heels, in no rush at all, sound forgotten – yet familiar. They sound like mine. But it's not long before I'm at Kathryn's highly polished white uPVC door. A pair of mud-speckled floral wellies sit neatly on her doorstep, like a replica of Dan's jaunty displays of his best bits.

Impressions. Veneers. We're all at it, one way or another.

This is a bit like bumping into work people on a day off – unsettling, yet somehow intriguing. Other than for pickups, when I've had the kids' friends for tea, no school parent has ever spent more than ten minutes in my house. I admit, I come over a little bit Dan when it happens. The once-white fifty-pence IKEA tea towels get temporarily replaced with pristine, patterned variations. I'll clean the floor, do a bit of a declutter, have a quiche or a cake cooling on the table, sowing the fib that I'm an actual breathing reality of a domestic goddess.

Through the glass, a body shape grows. 'Hello, you. We're just getting comfy.' Kathryn, in an animal print onesie, ushers me inside. She clicks the front door shut as I slip my boots off, stacking them next to the other pairs. On the end, a disorderly pair of maroon adidas Gazelles stands out. Joe's, I'm hoping. 'Wine? Prosecco? Or?' she adds, with a down-turned face as if this would be the choice of the terminally dull, 'tea or coffee?'

'White wine, please.' I pull out the bottle of Chardonnay that I paid over the odds for just now in the Co-op because it came chilled and ready from the fridge. Exploitative bastards, preying on the last-minute procrastinators, coining it in.

Kathryn beams, a hand flat on her furry chest. 'That's so kind, thank you.'

I follow her tail out of the kitchen and into the through-lounge. It's the popular template of modern life: a sofa and telly at one end, and a wood dining set at the other. Chairs dot the periphery, and all but one is full. Claiming it as mine, I move it to the brighter, sofa end of the room, where Joe, in bookish dark-framed glasses, has himself a comfy seat, the burgundy armchair beneath the window. There's a dish of nuts on his armrest, and the world's largest glass of red cradled between his fingers. I do no more than nod in his direction.

'I admit, I found myself skimming,' Lynda announces a little later from her cross-legged spot in the centre of the sofa. She sips her red, licking her lips. 'But that was more because I wanted to know what happened to . . .' The name escapes her. It escapes me too. Though I've read it, it was years ago.

'I got a bit lost. It started so believably,' a small woman with a side ponytail that she can't stop stroking chips in. 'I didn't care what happened in the end.'

'What about you, Monica?' Kathryn kneels beside me on a pile of cushions, a strategically placed tube of Pringles tucked just behind her, out of sight from the rest. 'What did you think?'

'It was a real page-turner. I liked it.' Typically tongue-tied, it's all I manage.

The focus shifts to a mum with a kid in Joel and Toby's year, and her detailed plot critique, but even the shame of my bland contribution can't stop me drifting into blue movie thoughts. Joe's hands, those long elegant fingers around that glass, are nothing short of spellbinding. Though I'm happy to indulge my pervy little thoughts, I know better than to let anyone notice. Instead, my eyes skim his circumference while I make interested faces at whoever happens to be talking, without doing any actual listening.

Allowing my body to relax into the chair, Kathryn yo-yos doing top-ups as the book's discussed for perhaps five minutes more, which includes Joe's apology for not finishing it. I bet he hasn't even started. The sole male at a club full of women he barely knows, for a book he hasn't bothered to read.

And, if I'm reading it right, that's very flattering.

An enormous canvas of Kathryn's kids hangs above a bookcase, bowing beneath crime hardbacks. I wonder if they're Kathryn's books, or her husband's – currently barricaded in his study, somewhere at the top of the house. Squeezed on the end, an oddity from the rest, sits a small paperback, its seventies-style font I recognize with a jolt – Erica Jong's *Fear of Flying*, my mother's favourite.

The book's canary yellow spine makes a gaping pit of my innards. Makes me suddenly so empty that I fight to stop myself claiming it from the shelf, to retrace the words neither my mum, nor me, its covert teen reader, could get enough of.

I'd cottoned on, by thirteen or so, that Mum's treasured fiction was a window, a glimpse within the closed book of a person she'd always been to me. Her pages would part in my hands, my thumbs aligned with the invisible impressions of her own, as they offered up their well-read innards, clear as a diary would. Mum's abundance of Jackie Collinses and Jilly Coopers were fast, sizzling, smack-in-the-face outrageous against my father's Corn Laws and Cold War Truth history books. And they made my curiosity frantic; was this the real person, behind all the rules, behind the bible she used to back them up?

I still wonder.

But if I wonder too long, I'll be Facebook snooping before I even bloody know it. Mums, dads – their AWOL kids. I break the thoughts quick. 'What's the next read?' I ask Kathryn inopportunely – she's just popped a wodge of Pringles.

She smiles politely, a hand shielding her mouth. 'I'm so glad you're thinking of coming again because that's our question for you. Newbies pick the next read. We've found it jazzes things up a bit.'

'Weren't you published?' Lynda leans towards Joe, poking his thigh. 'Your wife mentioned you'd been in *Granta*?'

Wife? *Granta*? I keep glued to the bookshelves, doing supersonic hearing at the same time.

'Years ago,' he says, perhaps with a hint of a smile, but doesn't add anything more.

'How clever,' gushes Kathryn. 'Fancy, a published poet at our little book club.'

'And very modest.' Lynda reaches over, perhaps to pat his leg this time, but I just can't look. 'Forgive me, I can't remember your wife's name.'

Joe hesitates. 'Bella.'

Bella. It sounds boring. And posh.

With coaxing, compliments and tummy tickling, Joe reveals more about his wife, which is met with more gushing, as if he's the first man to ever marry. Bella's the Head of English in a grammar school in Colchester. It explains the mystery of why she's never in the playground for Molly. She sounds terribly together. Purposeful. Not remotely winging it.

Talk works its way back to Lynda, as it has a way of doing, and I return to the game of false interest. Pushing the hair from my shoulders, I tilt my head to an angle that I know becomes me, my hand at the base of my neck, across the tiny gold crucifix necklace. Without moving, I make eyes at Joe, before quickly returning to the face of who's talking. I cross my legs, lifting my thigh a little higher than necessary. Resting it slowly on top of the other, I then let my sultry look linger.

Joe's waiting expression is laden, positively dripping, with predatory want. The nuts go everywhere as he blinks, horrified. 'Shit. Sorry, Kathryn.'

With soft assurances, Kathryn shuffles over to him. On their knees, digging dry-roasted from the rug, they bump heads and get the giggles. Cross-legged Lynda prickles disapprovingly, looking down her nose from her raised height on the sofa. Taking the soiled nuts through to the kitchen, Joe brushes past me, his leg connecting with my fingers, leaving lingering lemons in his midst. This is torture.

It's fantastic.

An hour later, I decline when he offers to walk me home.

'Walk me home anytime you like, handsome, brainy, doctor poet,' Lynda simpers, a hint of a slur to the ends of her words, eyes heavy with big blinks. 'But Roger's already on his way.' She leans across Joe to look out of the window. 'Speak of the devil.'

'What book are you choosing, Monica?' Kathryn squeezes my hands. 'Anything you like.'

Naming a book I've enjoyed feels like I'm giving a piece of myself away. And why, when I've read so many, can I not think of one bloody title, anyway? I scale back, thinking of skinny books, a long afternoon in an armchair kind of read, good books for handbags – and for giving as little commitment as possible to a book club I'll likely never return to.

A good skinny book that'll also impress them. '*Bonjour Tristesse*?' Balls, I hope I said that right, but no one corrects me.

We pull our shoes on, exiting at the same time as Lynda, who climbs in beside a sombre Roger in their brand-new Qashqai, their son in pyjamas and dressing gown strapped behind him, with the same unsmiling, tunnel vision look as he had on the coach. Waving them off, me and Joe find ourselves alone on the pavement.

'Well,' he says, putting his hands in his pockets.

'Well, all right. If you insist.'

He watches me, knows as well as I do.

Minutes later, we approach the edge of the green. Cutting across will make for a shorter trip, and though the village isn't exactly a crime hotspot, I wouldn't do it alone at night. Right now, though – weirdos aren't my concern; it's if anyone were to get the right impression. Though I've never stopped noticing attractive men, Dan's never once had cause to be the jealous sort. I don't want that to change.

'It's a funny place round here, don't you think?' Joe says.

'What d'you mean?' I nudge him on, consenting to take the shortcut together.

'Well, it's all a bit . . . samey. Same little routes, same people. At times it all feels . . .'

'Small.'

'Yes.' He snatches at it. 'Painfully pointless. I'm not any kind of thrill seeker, but Christ.'

Has my spell of angst conjured him? An empathetic twin to put the bullshit to rights with. If any belief remained in me, instead of the hangover guilt-complex from the Catholic education I clung to instead, I'd say he was a gift from God.

'I hope one day I get the chance to experience somewhere different.'

'Another country different?' Hands in my pockets, my fingers close around a half tube of Mentos.

'Everything different. Weather-wise, lifestyle-wise. For my eyes not to wake up to this.' He gestures beyond our tree-lined path, arms stretched to acknowledge the neat box hedges and last puffs of hydrangea, crisp and drooping. The quiet liquid of the pond reflects the small set of alms houses, timeless in the crescent moonlight. 'I don't mean this, this.' Joe holds his hand out. 'This, Christ. This right now is perfect.' I drop a sweet into his palm, pale yellow and Eucharistic, just as the church comes into sight. Its golden clock face reads ten-twenty.

'Did you marry in a church?'

'Na,' he says. 'A hotel. Both times. Not the same hotel, of course.'

'Both times, eh?'

'Oh yeah, I'm a proper Liz Taylor. You?'

'No church for me, either. I was very pregnant. We just went off on holiday.'

Thinking of back then stirs something satisfying. At nearly thirty weeks pregnant, Dan and me had been together for little over a year. After the simplest of ceremonies on an Athens beach before my maternity leave, our wedding party of two stuffed ourselves silly on barbecue then had noisy, liberating sex – Dan, I'm certain, high from duplicitousness. Penny and Clive and all the other muppets had no idea we'd eloped.

'I like that,' he says. 'That's what I mean, veering off the path a bit, going your own way.'

'Path-walking's for pussies.' It's out before I think, sending us both into terrific giggles that skip off into the silence. 'I'm the biggest path-walker in history, really. It's terrible.'

'We all are. It's what makes everything so fucking shit.' He pulls out his fags, along with a lighter, *Essex Boys Barbers* written along the side of it. 'Knowing better. Doing it anyway.' He grins, offering me the box. It's been over twelve years since my last. Joe lights it for me, his eyes leaving the flame to watch me back. 'You,' he says, as the spark burns in his hands, 'really are astonishing.'

'I have a very peculiar face.' The ground rushes around my feet in a dizzying whoosh of a headrush; nicotine is a fabulous beast. I inhale again, holding all those toxic dangers in my chest, surprised by how naturally the act returns to me. Then the flat strip of road appears in the distance, the bend that'll put me at home.

'Only because there's no others around here like it.' He can't take his gaze off me. 'That doesn't mean you're not astonishing. Because you are. Christ, you're a goddess.'

Mutual. Reciprocated. Concrete confirmation.

'It's no surprise you married twice.' The single key's fished from my bag, and I motion with it across the street. Though my house is not yet visible, this seems a sensible, respectable distance to part. 'Thank you, for walking me home.'

Risking it, Joe achieves contact with me, elbow to elbow. 'My night stint's over for a while; back to normal hours.'

'And proper bedtimes? How lovely.' His job at the hospital is certainly intriguing. Assessing those just sectioned, his group therapy sessions promote the arts in mental health. It does explain his openness, that clever thing he does called listening.

'As much as the nights turn my brain upside down, there's no job I'd ever swap it for. Helping helps, you know.' He taps his temple. 'Besides, most of my patients have nothing on me.' It's another of those moments where I can't quite tell if he's joking. 'With all my proper bedtimes, you won't recognize me in a fortnight.' He smiles, wide and impressive even at night. 'But that'll keep me going.'

'What'll keep you going?'

'Your peculiar face.' He winks at me. 'I'll miss you, too.' Pleased with himself, Joe walks away, stopping at the green's edge to look back. Unfolding his arms, he reveals two pairs of swear fingers. As I give him the finger back, the mischief across his delicious face grows. 'Have a cracking half term.' Blowing me a kiss, Joe takes a deep bow and turns on his heels, disappearing into the velvet night.

Leaving wordgasms in my ears; this is crush-fiction gone live. It's Mellors and Heathcliff and bloody stern Rochester. It's Rupert fucking Campbell-Black.

The house rests in glorious silence as I creep upstairs. I take off my make-up, stacking the sludge of cotton wool pads until my eyes wipe clear, dotting Nivea round my eyes, neck, then the corners of my mouth. A mouth beginning to rather cruelly turn downwards in resting face mode. Quietly, I slip in beside Dan, asleep on his tummy; his face turned to the wardrobes. As soon as my eyes close, I'm unpacking the evening, ready to revel in its contents. Joe's summoned, right at the part where he says I'm astonishing.

Next to my chosen partner, imagining another, a similar sadness to earlier returns. Mimicking the pattern of Dan's breathing, which always helps me drop off, I curl into his side. His hand finds mine and he draws it up, tucking it under his chest.

'Everything all right?' I check, in a whisper.

'Fine. How was it?'

'Fine, too. Entertaining.' I kiss his shoulder. 'It's something different, isn't it?'

'You been smoking?' There's a smile in his voice, but I am all toothpaste and tobacco.

'What a thing to ask.'

Dan turns, putting me on my back, his mouth on mine. 'Never a straight bloody answer.' He loosens my pyjamas, just enough for his hand to disappear and descend between my legs. He finds me damp. Willing.

Pulling off my bottoms, he shifts onto my body; our kisses edged with the old rare heat that puts us back in my studio flat. We push against each other, in this missionary moment that's ours – until the new thoughts creep in, a Dracula's mist beneath our bedroom door. Dan's silhouette could easily, easily pass for Joe. The nighttime shadows allow the fantasy to gain velocity: Joe's mouth, Joe's hands, Joe's cock.

It's effortless.

Harmless. It took years of practice to get here, to know one another so well we roll apart mutually satisfied.

Dan offers his pants to wodge between my legs. 'We need a night, don't we? Time together – just us.'

My chest rises, lungs opening like doors to free the demons – and, out of character, because I've never been one for post-coital affection, I ask Dan to hold me. I want to tell him everything; how my head's turned, how I've resorted to something as vain and desperate as the night I've had.

How I already know how this goes.

But Dan holds me tight, quieting my thoughts with: 'I love you.'

5

Birth Days

Dan's voice comes from above me, a mug of tea set on the bedside. Through my glazy morning vision, he derobes from his paisley housecoat and begins to dress. 'It looks good down there.' He's woken to balloons and bunting, our table decorated for the traditional breakfast banquet he's about to collect from McDonald's. 'Right. I'm off.' He buckles his belt, slipping on a t-shirt. 'Do you need anything?'

Other than a new identity, or amnesty from the day ahead, there is nothing. 'I'm all right. Thanks.'

'You sure?' He pushes out his bottom lip, like a baby would, then shakes his head, perhaps thinking better of mentioning the twins' traumatic entry into the world, or the blanket depression that followed.

Twelve years ago today.

Downstairs, two cakes wait for decoration. There's also a party buffet to prep, and more balloons and bunting to hang. The second I get up, I'm vanished for the day. Joel and Toby's birthday officially starts here.

For me, it started weeks ago, settling on a mutually convenient party date. Then the hiding of purchases, my range of emotions swinging from worrying the boys' gifts look a bit mean, to being cross I've been guilt-tripped by consumerism. Among the sweets and smellies there's new trainers – both needed them anyway, so two birds and all that – and tickets to watch West Ham play tomorrow.

Rolling into Dan's side of the bed, I close my eyes, try hibernating from the arm's-length list of obligations I've no one to blame for but myself. The birthdays lead into half term, where each day must be filled by some mutually appealing activity, which these days is near impossible, as the kids' tastes change and the age gap grows ever more noticeable. I'll haemorrhage money to ensure they're happy and occupied with a midweek excursion to the Natural History Museum. We'll do eye tests, dentists and haircuts. But I mustn't jump ahead. There's a day of effort and smiles to come first.

It's always the same, crafting a day for the children brighter than all others, trying to be tolerant, because what could be worse than any upset on the day they were born – regardless of the agony they caused on arrival. But the day they made their entrance, that chaos, peril, the instant responsibility for two live things, was a shock, to the very root of my existence. Trauma I am still not repaired from.

A lead thud comes as Joel descends from the top bunk. 'Happy birthday, TO YOU!' he bellows, making the walls shudder.

'Happy birthday, TO YOU!' comes back Toby.

'Oh no, *I insist*. HAP—'

'MUM!' Fran squeals from her room.

Hibernation was always a pipedream, especially at seven on a birthday morning. I rise, rubbing at my face. Behind the curtains is bright sun, the same as the day they were born. And just the same as then, the kids assume their place, forever ahead of me as I seek them out for birthday hugs and kisses.

'I'm looking for Dan?' A man on my doorstep looks from me to the birthday banners pinned across the window in confusion. He steps back, clasping and unclasping his hands.

Smiling, I shout for Dan over my shoulder. 'I'm Monica.'

'Of course. Sorry, I didn't realize . . .' He shakes his head, the rims of his ears glowing pink.

'Michael!' Dan ushers him inside. 'This is the Michael I was talking about,' he says to the living room. Dan does this all so well.

It's risen a few octaves, but there's no mistaking Penny's prattle from the front room. 'You're off to Spain with my Daniel too, next week? It's what I've always said, haven't I, Clive? London spells opportunity – the pulse is in the city. Tell me, has my daughter-in-law offered you a drink?'

She'll be handing him a menu next. Before the door went, she'd been bragging – with embellished fresh detail – about Dan's promotion, forgetting it was back in January and all over her Facebook already. But I'm feeling generous, flexing that very English trait of tolerance and cutting Penny some slack because – heavenly chorus – there's no Budgie today. Absent, too, are the family of smashed doughnut faces, currently contaminating Center Parcs – saving Dan the trouble of uninviting them. Yes, Yvonne's here, mummified in misery, her presence hanging over the celebrations like a wet fart, but, hey, I can tolerate that, too. It's baby steps, but it's progress.

Who knows? Perhaps next year, Yvonne'll be gone as well.

'Barcelona's gorgeous, isn't it?' Penny chatters. 'We cruised there, a few years back. Two weeks of heaven, wasn't it, Clive?'

'Or fourteen gold-plated nights, depends who you're asking – it bloody crippled me,' he replies, quick and humorous. Mostly, I like Clive.

In an empty kitchen, I'm happy to linger while I wait for the kettle, idly pulling towards me the post that came earlier. Among the junk and a Virgin Media bill, there's an IKEA Christmas catalogue.

We could be lifted straight from the brochure; Dan, the tousled hulk of blondness, with his stubbly morning face. Me, the mixed wifey, with the crazy – after six gazillion years of styling – morning-perfect curls. The couple gaze adoringly at each other as the kids – trendy combinations of their parents in milk-white pyjamas – smack the shit out of each other with pillows at the end of the bed.

On the next page, the same family sits at a makeshift row of mismatched tables in their festive child-friendly loft apartment, now filled with friends and family. In a red party hat, the woman laughs from the centre of the multicultural utopia. Unlike my house, there are no daggers from a snarling little nana in a brown coat in the corner. Nor any buxom, ash blonde matriarchs treading on her toes in full-on hostess with the mostess mode.

On cue, Penny bustles in with a stack of dirty plates. 'I remember all this; organizing in the background.' I'm nudged aside as she dumps them in the sink, moving me without really being touched into the far corner where the big cupboard is that fits both the hoover and the ironing board. There'd be just enough space for me to wedge in, too. 'Did you pick up any brandy? Mum's fancying a tipple.'

'I knew I'd forget.' I slap a hand on my forehead, pulling what I hope is a suitably sorry expression. 'What about a sherry?' There's a dribble of an old cooking one left, full of sediment and past its best. No tipple would suit Yvonne better.

'That'll do. Best make it a small one.' She dunks another plate, her rings and Fairy bubbles sparkling in the water. 'Glad the rain's holding off.'

Lightweight and gentle rotations of conversation is how Penny and I best communicate. We talk cookery, children, ailments and the weather. Occasionally I'll broach gardening, and she may try with the books, but we always stay on the surface, the thin ice of placatory chatter. Like our vicious beginning never was.

'I remember Daniel turning twelve,' she says, twinkly-eyed. 'Bless – you could see the man he'd grow into. Driven, even then.' I think of the daily manhandling to get the boys in the bathroom, or round the table for homework. I struggle to imagine Danny-boy being any different.

While washing and rinsing, Penny talks me in the most intricate of detail through Dan's birth story, and, as an act of tolerance – because this has to be the thirtieth time I've heard it – I try blocking my life out by remembering songs with the word 'hate' in their lyrics.

Once my own babies came, in the ferocious panic that they did – not Penny's bearing-down sensation; Dan slipping free without so much as a whimper, at home, in under an hour – Penny could neither keep away nor do enough to help. She'd show up announcing she was staying for a few nights, which would provoke the most peculiar reaction in me, a kind of grateful claustrophobia. Childbirth annihilated both the health and good spirits I'd always taken for granted; vulnerability was a new notion. Someone could hurt me, hurt my babies, precious defenceless Toby, and incubated Joel. It was a relief to be incubated by Penny's cosseting, too. I was smothered by her exaggerated motherliness, yet keen for it all the same. And Penny, the self-proclaimed natural-born nurturer, shelved her prejudice for pity.

I'd lose listless days in old episodes of *Gardeners' World* and the Good Food Channel, an easy pet for Penny. And her exception, too. Penny fussed, trickle-trickle, rearranging, a feather-touched influence over Dan and me and our fledgling family disorder of things. She turned our world back in time, reviving her own methods, which were the best ways, obviously. The old-fashioned, trust-me-I'm-a-cockney-you-could-leave-your-front-door-unlocked-with-a-pram-outside, good old East End way.

But she did help. In some bizarre way Penny helped – 'She's confused, Daniel. No mum about. I'll look after her. Don't worry, Son.' Her care, gently padded by a block of counselling and some cognitive therapy, revived me a little. Enough at least not to be petrified when left alone with my sons in case something terrible happened. And once restored, back to my 'normal', it became all but impossible to ever outright question her flaws again.

I am firmly in her pocket because I'm still grateful.

'He'd never leave a football alone, same as them pair. Did I tell you about when he broke that window?' Penny rushes on, as if I've begged her to elaborate. 'About their age, too. Now that caused some trouble. Course, all them in the Paki shop thought it had to be racist.'

Though she doesn't pause for breath, I do, catching my own in a tight little swallow, ignoring what I can't believe she thinks is acceptable.

'The owner only rang the police – though he knew who we were, could've just given us a tap, could've been sorted amicably. Tell you the truth, I never really liked shopping there. Always smelled funny – *off*, y'know. But it was convenient.' I'm heart, soul, DNA aware that I should call her out. Yet avoiding Penny's upset somehow, but always, matters more.

My hurt feelings are permanent companions. They've made a burning, lumpen thing in me, an indigestion – and just as uncomfortable. And though I may kid myself, this is not tolerance. It's knowing my place. I am the passive passenger in this family. Stuck, by the shit of my own shortcomings.

Penny's voice becomes noise again. Rounding up her tale, she hands me a plate to dry. 'Must be odd, with madam at school. Strange for you, Mon – an empty nest.'

On a loop, I dry around the same edge of the dish. Penny doesn't notice. She's watching my face, perhaps attempting concern, but it's hard to tell since she discovered Planet Facial Filler. It's given her the look of wearing a high-shine permanent blusher.

'Still, as long as they're happy, we'll be the glue,' she adds. 'Never a day off, us mums, no matter how hard it gets. And it only gets harder as they get bigger, you only need ask . . .'

Fran runs in, heading for Penny to cuddle. 'Can I have a drink, please, Nanny P?' she gasps, as if she's run a marathon.

'Take this through for Yvonne, first.' I hold out the dribble of Fino in a shot glass.

Fran sniffs it, bunching her nose. 'Is it poison?'

Here's wishing. With a don't-be-silly face I usher her off, following behind with Michael's tea. Work-friend Michael. Dropping in off the back of a loose invite when he bumped into Dan this morning. New to the village. Girlfriend an air hostess. A lot of time on his own. 'Just pop in,' offered Dan, in his sociably straightforward way – but Michael might be regretting it, now he only has Yvonne for company. He stands limp and distant by the front window, as Yvonne sits not far away, parked up for a bit of peace. Clocking my approach, Michael reanimates accordingly.

'White, no sugar.' I hand over the mug.

'That's good of you, thanks—'

'You silly, silly girl!' The shot glass rolls from Yvonne's lap to the floor, cracking in perfect halves, a liquid shadow on the cuff of her coat. 'Didn't your mother teach you not to tear-arse around indoors?'

'It's my fault.' I cross the room, offering handfuls of napkins, but the sly old witch won't take them. Mopping her up myself, I find the smell of her far worse than the literal fucking thimbleful of spillage; a floral headache of hyacinths disguising old kipper. She slaps at my hand, snarling like a snappy Jack Russell would.

Drifting in from outside, Dan's voice cuts the tension. It's football chat, bonding gruff noise. He sounds buoyant. And why not? He is only aware of his gleaming home, the darling boys we've managed to keep alive for twelve years, playing on our small lawn, happy in his blinkered little bubble.

'No harm done. See?' I smile, hiding my hurt to stop Fran's. 'Let's pop this in the bin.' We make it to the kitchen, closing the door for a lucky minute alone. Fran's nostrils are pinched and flared, the sign she's likely to cry. Without fuss, I drop a quick kiss on her forehead. 'We know what she's like, don't we?' I raise an eyebrow. 'D'you reckon it's time to do the candles?' It's more than time. 'Try rounding your brothers up, then.'

Just as I give her a little push into the hall, the doorbell rings. She looks back, startled, unwilling to let me go. 'I'll be right behind you. You've full permission to be bossy.' Her old enthusiasm returns a bit as I open the door to Gracie, dressed top to toe in spectacular leisurewear, as glam as she was for her wedding.

My temples throb, fit to bursting, as I search the street for Budgie.

Gracie clocks me doing it. 'I'm on my own.' She holds out two gold gift bags. 'I hope you don't mind—'

'Gracie?' Michael's voice is unfathomably high.

'Bleedin' 'ell!' Gracie launches past me, kissing him as Michael's tongue, jaw, and perhaps his entire lower face, collapse in admiration as he hangs off her every word. School days. Small world. So long ago now, they reminisce, though it can't be more than a decade since they left.

There's a rumble in my jeans pocket. A text. It's Joe, safe beneath a pseudonym.

Kathryn (School): Still trying with that music top five. I like all sorts, but have a soft spot for hip hop – old stuff, because I am 👓

On a Sunday, approaching five, it's a nothing text – a boredom text. Friendly and innocent. A smidge disappointing.

I reply: *I must be old too then*

I stash my phone, spot Yvonne still sat on her own. My decency offers her quiche and a handful of crisps. Eyes fixed on my flooring, she twists her mouth, perhaps to stop an accidental thank you. But there's reprieve. Everybody squashes in the dining room as Dan carries through the first cake. Penny, aglow in the candlelight, stands tight next to him. With her hands clasped, the way she watches the boys emerge from the garden is celestial. Plain love. Its strength is alarming. Undermining.

'Flipping size of 'em now.' Clive whistles from somewhere behind me. 'They'll be downing pints and betting on horses before we bloody know it. Eighteen ain't far off. Twenty-one, weddings – doing all this, with kids of their own.'

So much ahead, each milestone moment a celebration, in a countdown to the last, final event that I'll never ever know. Which means this is it. This is us. Till there's nothing. The thought is one I'm keen to set straight, never wanting to take what we have for granted. I am very aware that this is all very precious. And fleeting.

But so am I.

I'm fleeting.

Joel beams, his cheeks flushed as we sing a tuneless happy birthday to twin one by eight and a half minutes. He blows out his candles, the odds and ends I unearthed, seeing as I forgot to buy any; six blue and four yellow new ones, and two glittery red nubbins. I fly at him to squeeze him tight, pecking his sweaty little head all over.

'I love you, Joel. Make a wish.'

I'm rather choked when he squeezes me back. 'I love you too, Mum.'

'You'll make her cry; never takes much. Smile, Monica,' says Penny as Clive presents himself, buckling beneath his photography gear.

'Shunt in, Pen girl,' he says, in the gruff, gentle tone reserved only for Penny. You'd think him a lamb, but the second she's out of earshot his voice will rise, along with a strong smattering of seventies crudity. But not today. Clive's camera blinds us, preserving the moment, capturing all that's good. And wholesome. Then it's Toby's turn.

After, I light a single candle for Fran to blow out.

'We best make a move,' Penny says, like it's the end of the world. 'I'm not even on that plane, and I'm missing 'em already.' She turns in melancholic desperation towards the kids, fighting their way through the doors and back into the garden. As I'm the only one left, Penny's huge tits mesh into mine and, swathed in her scented embrace, I know I'll smell of Youth Dew for the rest of the day. Perversely, I'm always rather lost when they disappear off to their place in Tenerife, a bit abandoned for the first few weeks. I reckon I've got the beginnings, the symptoms at least, of a peculiar in-law strain of Stockholm Syndrome. 'Come a long way, haven't we, love?' she says, all prosecco and Chardonnay affectionate.

'That doesn't matter now,' I manage, malice-free. Just.

'One of us now, anyway. Look, bless him.' She nods at Dan, helping Yvonne button that horrible itchy brown coat she seems to live in.

Yvonne scowls at me, cleverly, in a way only I can see. Smiling, regardless of the animosity, I shrink myself again for her elderly benefit. Submit. Retreat.

In the kitchen, I cut cake to take away. Checking behind me first, I split Yvonne's piece open and spit very neatly into the jam, before squashing it back together. Briefly, I'm ashamed. But only briefly. Sir Duke nudges my legs, judgy yet still ever hopeful of falling crumbs, as my phone vibrates again.

Kathryn (School): Not old. Just astonishing

I know what I'd wish if these were my candles today. For everything Penny believes, these days, to be true about me. But I'm still the sassy half-caste bit of skirt she thought I was, looking over my shoulder for attention, laden with teenage vanity. And still disappointed, raging within, with nowhere for the furies to go. My biggest wish, my prayer, would be for contentment. For my resentful lonely emptiness to go. And to settle.

With what's already precious. And mine.

6

Half Term

At seven minutes past ten, the London-bound train pulls up to platform 1. The kids wait for the passengers to alight, but they're quick on after that, despite the tuts from a lardy suit who huffs as he boards ahead of them. He turns into first class, watching them from his plush territory each time their volume rises. I'm always sensitive to the adult temperament, other people's offspring annoy the hell out of me too, but the kids can do their worst for all I care about upsetting old gut lord of the train.

The journey's quick. I buy a coffee before the tube comes, dishing out juices from my Mary Poppins bag. Though never knowingly organized and classically unprepared, I pride myself on any small savings on days like today. I've used my discount railcard, and with a packed lunch and the museum being free entry, today should be less of a shock to my poor little purse, which has already taken a good hiding this week.

'Have we got rolls?' Joel stretches a Mr Tickle arm into the bag at my feet. 'What's in them? It's not ham, is it? I hate ham.' He's exaggerating; ham's just not his current favourite.

'Yours is cheese.' I slap his hand. 'Don't bloody squeeze them.'

'I'm boiling.' Fran's opposite me, next to a brown girl with blue bouffant hair, clasping a large portfolio, with the longest nails I've ever seen, covered in glittery sparkles.

'You want some room, little girl?' she asks kindly, as Fran escapes her coat, knocking her by accident.

Fran smiles, surprised. Then her nosiness takes over. She points to the folder, collaged in stickers. There's a small one in the corner that Fran can't see from where she's sat. It says *Trump is a Cunt* in bubble writing. 'What's in there?'

'College stuff. You wanna see?' The girl skims her phone as Fran waits patiently. 'That's me, and that's me. That's not.' She makes her eyes wide and flicks past the picture quick, making Fran laugh. 'See all the hair, and the make-up? That's what I'm learning.'

'And the nails?' Fran's unable to resist stroking one.

'Na. That's just for fun. I do prosthetics and stage make-up.'

'I'm gonna learn that. Mum, I can learn that, can't I?'

'Course you can.' I smile at the girl as they chat, watching Fran note all her particulars: the trainers, the silver rings on her little fingers, the animal-print headscarf holding the blue hair in place.

The boys stay on the half-seats that slump downward by the doors, talking among themselves. They've started doing this, separating from the adult, as if pretending to be on their own. I let them, knowing it won't be long before they're off doing their own thing anyway. But I can't ignore the ache the thought of that brings, either.

'Are you Dominican?' the girl asks me. 'You look just like my auntie. And my cousin.'

'Me? No.' As I press my knees together, she watches me expectantly. 'Here's our stop, kiddos.' The ritual checking for tickets, phone and purse begins. And lunch.

'Say hello to the dinosaurs for me,' says blue hair.

Fran pats her knee, peeking from frayed denim, as though she's been entrusted with something of real importance. 'I promise.'

We exit onto Exhibition Road and into apocalyptic rainfall. The beauty of our surroundings falls unnoticed when I spot the longest line of raincoats I've ever seen. Mums and dads with unsure faces like mine hover near the back, but it's like the seven ages of man as I look down the queue to the ones nearest the front. Unsure turns to fury, to stoic making the best of it, complete with happy smiles and rousing little movements to keep the kids upbeat, to the very front, where everybody looks almost broken.

'Bet the V&A wouldn't have a queue like this,' I mutter aloud.

'Because it's boring,' Joel says, but not really at me.

I feel tired before it's all even started. Snail's pace proves to be an underestimation; it takes forty-six minutes to get in the door. Again, the beauty of the building is lost. It's just high ceiling echoes and fucking cold.

The bag for life looks so sad I bin it.

'What you doing?' Joel's mouth falls open.

'Follow me.' Spotting a sign, I march them as best I can to the café, which is so full of damp evaporating people that real steam mists the atmosphere, so we head instead for the restaurant, the one with warm natural light and pea-green leather chairs that sells pizzas and burgers. And white wine.

Sod the budget. I don't care what it costs.

We join yet another queue as we wait for a table. The boys hold our spot, while I take Fran to the loo. There's lots of put-out faces on the way back, as if we're jumping the line, so I do my best steely look and wade through anyway. I'm just about to use my elbows when the line shifts by itself, like the Red Sea parting, as a man with a toddler on his hip provides enough space for us to rejoin the boys. Just in time; we're three from the front.

After a quick skim of the simplest menu designed for the minimum of fuss, the kids order burgers and I have the same with a large dry white. Every sip of the cool, naughty drop proves restorative, disrobing the cross, damp wicked witch bastard I often become when hungry. Just as I start smiling again, small fingers nudge my shoulder. It's the toddler from the queue, holding Fran's red bobble hat. She's still got that baby softness that only seems noticeable in Fran these days when she's asleep. With a big exaggerated thank you to the little kid, who's adorably keen to please, I take it.

The father of the child sits not far away. Raising a thin pilsner glass filled with beery bubbles, he smiles.

'Thanks.' The hat goes in my bag as the man still looks over, only now rather hungrily down my shirt. I'm not the sort to grow red, nor grow indignant, so opt for sultry disapproval instead, refocusing on the kids.

We chat about the mean-girl Fran partners in PE who made fun of the hole in her tights last week. And about meeting Dan back at Liverpool Street so we can all travel home together. We talk about Joel joining cooking club and Toby thinking it's lame when there's football to play – or is Joel there because Mae from his form goes to cooking club, too, making Joel adorably bashful. And all the time we chat, I exchange discreet glances with the man, rather like me and Joe did at Kathryn's.

Joe. I've blocked all truly saucy thoughts about him since my and Dan's charged coupling the other week, which seems to have made us like each other again.

The kids order brownies as the finale to their meal deal. As I ask for the bill, a woman appears at the man's table, her arms sliding around him from behind. She kisses his neck, and his eyes meet mine.

Shame. On us both.

The woman sits, chats, stores three big bags from Selfridges & Co. beneath the table. Our sole similarity is we're about the same height. She's all gym-bunny thin in boyfriend jeans with a mousy pixie haircut, size eight, top *and* bottom. But types always have legroom, especially once married. It's more about who's willing to play the game. He's not my type, either. Too tall, too skinny, boring brown eyes that are a little too narrow. A foppish salt-and-pepper hairdo.

But it doesn't matter; we're paying and we're out. It's forty pounds well spent as my fun levels magnify. We do the earthquake room three times, skipping the stones and minerals. We gaze through glass boxes into glass eyes of a billion stuffed creatures and birds that makes me itch to buggery just like every time I've ever seen them.

'Why though, Mum?' asks Fran, sadly. Why, indeed.

'Couldn't they paint them or something, instead of all this murdering?' Joel drags a slit-throat finger across his neck, flopping his tongue out for effect.

Ghastly boy. I give him The Look.

The dinosaur queue is ridiculous and, besides, the boys are past this and Fran likes glitter and slime more than Jurassic Park. I let her duck in and give them a wave as she promised the girl on the train.

In the gift shop, I've a moment of impulsive maternal generosity, giving them each a fiver and letting them browse alone – provided they stay together, and Joel holds Fran's hand. I keep a distant eye while mooching among the books, but all this nature and space will only hold me so long.

The kids come back. Fran's waving a scarf. 'I want—' she starts.

'*We* want, actually,' Joel corrects. 'To join our money and get you this.'

Fran beams, holding out a large square of cool ivory cotton, decorated with jungle leaves and miniature leopards in action. 'D'you like it?'

'It's beautiful.' I want to cry. 'You don't have—'

'We just need five pounds more, though . . .' Fran screws up her little nose. Who the hell could say no to a face like that?

'*Look at the quality* . . .' Toby runs a hand across it, like a gameshow hostess.

'I'll have to use my card.' I put my hand out, collecting up their fivers. Another flipping queue to join. But their smiling eyes warm me, loving, grateful for a tipsy mum and the best day. 'Thank you, little people. I'll treasure it forever.'

The cashier scans the tiny label. 'That's fifty pounds.'

Almost dribbling, I snatch it up, squinting in the hope it'll transform the five back into a two. A small numerical error from my girl who muddles her digits. But I don't have the heart to put it back. I slot my Barclaycard in the machine. We'll feed from the backs of the cupboards instead of a big shop next week.

'Could you cut the tag off?' I wrap it round my neck and tie it on the side, as Fran watches, frowning.

'No, Mum. You've got to do it like Jasmine's.'

'Who the hell's Jasmine?'

'The girl on the tube.' She groans, rolling her eyes as if I'm entering early onset. 'It's for your hair.'

'I'll need a mirror, then.'

But before the loos, we make our last stop to the human body section. Joel and Toby have their picture taken against a giant penis, both pointing with mucky grins at the word testes, which we send to Dan. We enter the womb and see the enormous glowing baby, and I think, *never again*.

We're tired. The kids half-heartedly fiddle with the activities, and it's time to wind up anyway. It's past four, and we're meeting Dan at five.

'Toilets then the tube, mates.'

And no one disagrees.

Dan stands outside Upper Crust, frowning at the huge timetable above. The kids charge him, and the frown melts. 'Fancy seeing you lot here. Have you had a good day?' He looks around. 'What've you done with Mum?' Fran points at me, stuck to his hip as he strokes her hair. 'Na, that's not Mum.'

'Cooourrse it is,' she squeaks, still pointing at my head, now wrapped in its new scarf. 'We bought her a present. D'you like it?'

'Very nice,' he says, grinning. 'Very, who's that woman you like? Very Zadie Smith.' I kiss him, can see in his face that he does like it. 'Bagsy I sit next to Mum on the way home.' Slipping my arm through his, he squeezes it against his body. 'Head for platform 11, gang. We've got five minutes.'

We're home and around the table in less than an hour. My feet have had it, so it's pasta – and a pat on the back to me for freezing leftover sauces.

'I dug out your passport earlier,' I tell Dan. 'It's near the fruit bowl, with a handful of euros; about twenty quid, I think.'

'I wish they wouldn't ask me.' Mournful, he lifts his glass to his lips.

'It's fine once you're there, you know it is.' Four five-star nights in the centre of Barcelona isn't half the chore he tries making it. 'Besides, you've still got the weekend.'

'And tonight.' The maudlin melancholy lifts a little, as he tilts his head towards me.

Blimey.

'Dad,' Fran whines. 'You're not listening. Jasmine said that Mum looked like everyone in her family.'

I sigh. We've heard the name a dozen times, Dan fully filled in about the girl from the tube. Once home, Fran went straight for her Barbies. Christie's now Jasmine, the same as Fran's first child, which will, of course, naturally be a girl. Any boys, we're told, will have to stay in her tummy. She'll flat refuse to push them out.

'Was Jasmine from the most beautiful family in the whole world, then?' Dan asks her, the saucy sparkle still playing around his mouth.

'She was soooo pretty. Wasn't she?' Fran turns to the boys.

Joel shrugs. 'If you like Elsa from *Frozen*.'

'Elsa has white hair.' Fran thumps her fist on the table, close to tears and overtired.

I've had enough, too. 'Go on. Go and watch the telly or something. I'll be up in a bit.'

Just us, Dan tops our glasses up. Generously. On a Wednesday with work tomorrow. His lovely eyes are captivating in the flames of the candles. 'You look gorgeous,' he tells me.

So does he.

Sir Duke gets his dinner, plus leftovers, as Dan stacks the dishwasher like he's on fast-forward. I make haste too and relinquish, letting the kids sleep in travel dirt, so long as they brush their teeth.

'Where's your mummy?' Fran snuggles up as I tuck round her duvet. In the fairy-lit softness of her room, curiosity twinkles in her eyes. 'From when you were small. Back in the day.'

'Cheeky.' I push her covers down between the wall and the bed frame, smoothing, focusing on other things. Any things. The plump duvet covered with kittens in top hats. The dusty disorder of her little bookcase, the naked Sylvanian fox family, scattered in her fluffy rug.

'Was she so mean we can't ever talk about her?'

'Where did you hear that?' Sitting on the edge of her bed, I feel my libido recede into memory. 'It's all right, I won't be cross.'

She hesitates. 'Dad said.'

'When?'

'When Nancy and Hunter came. When they got treats and not me.'

'It's rude to eavesdrop, madam.'

'Did you need a policeman?' Her small, sad voice pains.

'She wasn't mean like that, Fran. We just aren't very good friends.' The worry vanishes, replaced by a look that matches how my words sound: unconvincing. 'We don't see things the same way. We clashed – do you understand what I mean by that?'

'Like you and Uncle Budgie.'

Uncle fucking Budgie. I'd like to scribble the uncle away until there's a hole in him. 'A bit.' I smile. 'You're too bloody nosey for five, Frances Petersen.'

'Would she like me?'

My throat shrinks as I pretend to be busy, picking socks and knickers up from the carpet. 'She'd love you. And my dad.' Her night-plug throbs womblike and hypnotizing from the corner as the fairy lights go out. I kiss her forehead. 'But sometimes, things break that can't be fixed.'

'Even families?'

Shit. 'Sometimes. It's rare. But sometimes.' I do bend the truth, but never outright lie.

'Do you know where they are?'

I know where they were. The tiny mid-terrace in South Essex, quieter than the cemetery at the end of the road.

'Do you miss them, Mum?'

When I'm lost. When everything stretches similar as the chances to reconnect fade. I snuggle her. 'How can I, when I have all you lot? What does Dorothy say?'

'There's no place like home.' Smiles and cuddles and warm ever afters.

'Thanks so much for my scarf.'

'You must wear it every day.'

'I'll wear it every bad hair day, how's that?' I get another smile, slower this time, my drooping little flower. 'Go to sleep, now. I love you.'

I banish Fran's questions by finishing off tidying the kitchen. Dan seeks me out almost instantly, dropping his head to kiss my neck. As he gathers up my skirt, at the clink of his belt unbuckling, the determined prod of his cock on the back of my thigh, all the weird parent-shit evaporates. This has always been my very best method to blank it all out. There's no need for the attentions of nondescript narrow-eyed men in museums, either. Nor dishy older chaps who think I'm astonishing . . .

Because when we're like this, me and Dan, when we're left alone, we're good. We're—

His laughter vibrates in small bursts at the nape of my neck. 'Sorry, Nan just popped in my head. It's just, Christ, can you imagine her face if she saw you in that?' He kisses me again, squeezing my hips like he's kneading bread. 'Converted to— Oh, come on, don't go funny. Where's your sense of humour?' He lets go with a huff. 'Bloody hell, don't take it off. I didn't mean—' He sighs, irritated. 'You really are a porcupine at times.'

'Of course. Always me.'

'Perhaps I just shouldn't speak at all. Perhaps that'd be

better. Can't have an opinion if it's not your opinion, can't have a joke—'

'You could – if there weren't any truth in it.'

'I'm not doing this again.' He pulls himself upright, refastening his trousers. 'The same old fucking circles.'

'Yes.' Two teabags flung into our night mugs. His navy blue, mine spinach green. 'The same old circle. The never-bloody-ending circle.'

'Isn't life terrible? Three healthy kids, a husband who cares, provides. You know, a bit, just a sprinkling, of appreciation—'

'Thank you, Dan. For my life.' Waiting for the kettle, I pull the blind and lock the back door. 'I should never forget how blessed I am. Cleaning your pants, the toilet, feeding everyone, keeping you all clothed. Organized. Loved. Holding it all together.'

'Here we go, the billion thankless tasks you do that nobody else notices. It's half the trouble, you, here in your own thoughts all day . . .'

Women thinking. All day.

I'd like to leap, all nimble and accurate and grab his silly ears. Scream into their dark narrow pits. Fragment his drums. But I'm calm. And shouldn't I have learnt by now anyway, how my loud thoughts are only truly loud to me. 'You know what, I'll stop, then. I'll get a job. Fran can go to a kids' club, the boys can have a key, come home and vegetate on screens. Everyone can live on baked beans.'

It's easy to forget. Think it's always been this way. I did have a job once, not a very good one, but a life unconnected to him. But it's not that Dan's purposefully done this to me; it's utterly self-inflicted. Allowances have been made for his apathy, my thankfulness for the life he provides silencing me ever since.

Another pocket. Ever beholden.

'That's what I'll do. I'll apply to Tesco. ALDI are looking, too.' Pour the kettle, stir. Tight and efficient little movements. But I don't raise my voice. There's no point; we've done this a million times. We never outright rage at one another; our snippy stirrings of dissatisfaction instead have become small vicissitudes in our everyday life, where we've slowly become less vital, less bonded. Just less, of everything.

'Fran's too small for all that. And besides, we still haven't decided.' He hesitates. 'Whether there'll be a fourth.'

When Dan's fam finally swallowed me as permanent, we began repeating the pattern of generations before. If the Crane women aren't themselves twins, then they give birth to them. It's been traced back on an Ancestry.com subscription by almost two hundred years. Penny, sharing a womb with Budgie, passed the joy to me and Dan. We didn't get it quite right, though, having muddled the chain with two willies and my godforsaken pigment, but it got overlooked, because above all else, family's what counts. Crane women stay home, keep house, nurturing until they metamorphose into noisy matriarchs that no one dares disagree with. Neither Yvonne nor Penny worked once they'd given birth. And though it's been beautiful being at home, the kids are growing. They don't need me in the way they once did. Perhaps, I've got to grow too.

'You said to forget another baby. What if we had two again, and I went off my trolley?'

'I never said anything like that. I said it wasn't the right time. But now there's the promotion and Fran's at school, it's, it's a possibility.'

'We're almost forty. Can you imagine going right back to the beginning, the night feeds, the tiredness, and them lot as well?' I nod upstairs.

Our world's shifted. Babies now seem an exhausting possibility; for me, anyway. The idea of stairgates and sterilizing and stretching out again. I'm done. It's just that, until now, I haven't voiced it.

The baby phase, ticked off and moved on from. Like a premonition, I sense a new stage dawning for us, an absolute shift. Our familiar ground's precarious.

'Well, what then?' Dan's knuckles are bone white as he clasps his hands together. 'We just carry on as we are?'

'Yes.' I hide the uncertainty in my voice, just as he did. 'We just carry on as we are.'

Dan takes his tea, the stairs creaking beneath his footsteps, as I mooch rather aimlessly downstairs, straightening cushions, blowing on surfaces to put off polishing them for a few days, until I can't resist any longer. Switching on the laptop, I turn snoop. Facebook reigns top for boomer prying, so I start there, hitting enter as the worldwide list of Avril Parkers pops up.

She's always the fourth down, a private profile with one photo. Mum's leaning on a wooden gate to a field, stood slightly on an angle, in a red scoop-neck jumper and denim skirt. Knee-high flat brown boots. A hand on her hip, chin tilted in a way she knows flatters her and that flatters me, too. My father doesn't have a Facebook account, but I already know that if I Google his name, I get a very small piece about a prizegiving evening at Topham Jenkins Secondary, his place of employment for as long as I've known. The article is three years old. *History Teacher celebrates record A-level results – two students bound for Oxbridge!* There's a photo accompanying the paragraph of an article, so distant his face could belong to anyone. But I see his posture, slightly stooped and humble, taller than the man behind him, shorter than the one shaking his hand. I see he's wearing a dark ink blue. His favourite colour.

My eyes drift from the screen to my bookcase, to the top shelf where I keep my battered little New Testament, handed out one school assembly by two bearded men who came in the name of Gideon. Before I know it, it's in my hands, the grubby fake red leather and grubby fake gold print. The tracing-paper pages are framed by a running list of my most fancied, the soap and film stars of the mid-nineties. At bible study, instead of reading, I'd retract into thoughts of them loving me back, as the white noise of my mind and its pixelated snowstorm protected, isolated, locked me in fantasy – like an out-of-body experience, only for less serious shit.

Between the central pages are three photographs, folded into quarters. Folded so carefully, there's only a faint cross on the pictures. The sole three pictures that I have of us three. Me, my mum and my dad.

Fran's words return. My own, too – *'some families can't be fixed'*. But these photos make me question that. Make me doubtful. There was love, once; I just chose to erase us. Forgetting even the good bits.

And what if there's the faintest, most microscopic possibility that on just the other side of the same bloody county, they've simply done the same?

Regardless of our raw distance, I can't help wondering how it would be to have them in my life. Whether things would be better – now that I'm older, older than they were when I left. Because it's dangerous to never admit being wrong. Worse, to never admit love. For as long as I can remember, I thought loving them was a weakness.

But perhaps it only really meant that I have a heart.

7

Blisters

Monday rolls around quickly, with Dan leaving for the airport before the rest of us even think about vacating our comfy little pits. There were shadowy farewells before sunrise, saying all the things we should; be safe, love you, call should you need to, text when you land. Though we are and have been amicable, the rising fog around us prevents any real connection. We are dutiful, yet distant, and they are empty roles.

Restless sleep blights all apart from Fran, still alien to the nerves of a new term, or the apprehension of a work trip you'd rather a broken bone than attend. I've ladled out motherly assurances to all who needed them, doing the billion thankless tasks that nobody ever notices. School shoes found and cleaned, Dan's washbag magically stocked, his two favourite suits back from the cleaners just in time. Homework projects swiftly finished and bagged away, and just when the morning nerves took too much of a grip, the dangled reward; whatever they want for dinner, I'll cook, no questions asked. It's sausages and mash night.

Joel and Toby leave the house a little before me and Fran, their absence from the school run still noticeable. Walking was a good way to stay current, the ten-minute chat every morning, their days tumbling out at record speed during pickup. All I get now is a series of grunts whenever I enquire.

Still. This week ahead, the luxury of choice without compromise, is beautiful. I've a list of tasks and self-improvements, and am planning to volunteer, too – if the village can't staff it, our tiny demountable library will close. The application to help is a month old. This week I'll send it. My time will be well utilized, full of positivity and progress.

Because this glue we're in can't set.

I return with a bounce in my footsteps, the front door shutting me in and the world out – apart, of course, from Sir Duke. We've a six-hour stretch of absolute silence for two pencilled in. Praise be.

He waddles up, happy to have fuss from his second best now his first choice has deserted him. Our moments of affection are rare, but he is never not appreciated. I run my hands over his head, gliding down his silky back and cup his face. His fat black tail goes wild. 'Cup of tea, Sir? A biscuit?' Far too big for any grace, he bounds around my legs as we go to his favourite place in the world, the cupboard next to the fridge, where he knows all his treats are stored. Such raptures from food and affection – Sir Duke is as basic a creature as I am.

But even my basic-ness can't stop this restlessness. It percolates. Escalates. I need a harness, a focus, or I'll become a living tornado of misspent frustration. Study or work. This week, I'll choose.

I sort the growing pile of paper from the comfort of my armchair, the sole item of furniture I ever independently bought, that came from a time before family life. Before Dan. The retro purple flower detail would never be his choice. I found it at a house clearance, in some fleapit flat above an off-licence in Shoreditch, back in the long, long ago, before it became saccharine trendy. I scrubbed for hours, refusing to pay for reupholstering, even feeding and treating the wooden arms and legs. I love this chair. And I'll never be parted from it.

The pile shrinks as I sift out the old *Evening Standard*s that Dan's picked up on his way home from work. A bank statement to be filed. A Dan list of odd jobs: 1. Sort guttering by back window. 2. Jet wash conservatory. 3. Dentist, with a big question mark. Beneath is a wodge of A4 folded down the middle. Crane Boys' Club and Gymnasium. Application forms completed in neat black ink capitals. One for Joel. And one for Toby. Boxing, Thursday nights.

I'm beyond expletives. Unsurprised, too. Sir Duke nudges his way under my arms as all the papers and my nearby coffee upturns onto the floor.

'Shit!' I lift Nancy's book, Oprah's *What I Know for Sure*, from the puddle before it's ruined. The outer cover's fine, still shimmering beige with its ribbon-like green trim, but the innermost pages are sodden. As I spread it on the radiator, a stained Post-it floats loose. 'Like I said, Mon – every woman should read this. Nancy x.' I picture her writing it, leant against her impossibly expensive kitchen worktop, chewing the top of a posh pen. Free from them all, in her escape hatch of Epping Forest.

I could make a list of things I know for sure, a weekly shop for a family of five length of truths. I could even categorize them, into truths about me, and truths universally – some even cross-contaminating. Lately, certainly since the boys' fight, I know for sure that prejudice has subtly invaded every square inch of my life. My antenna's alert in places as ordinary as the doctor's surgery. Only a month ago, my new neighbour introduced me to her puppy, Clint, a gorgeous yellow Lab with paws he kept falling over while he raced around dribbling wee in excitement. She also introduced me to her mother, who looked as if I were the one spraying piss around, instead of simply breathing in her daughter's kitchen. She neither acknowledged me nor said hello. Recent times have made her kind bolder. But I can't prove it. Nor can I prove that when Dan's grandfather died, after I'd sympathetically shaken Yvonne's hand, she wiped hers off on her dress.

Of course, I could just be silly. Oversensitive, as Dan would claim. Paranoid. Too little to think about, stewing on the small stuff. But racism's not dead; it's alive and fucking kicking; in our politics, on our streets – in happy little families, too. For Dan to validate me, take my side – even once – would mean the world; instead, his playing deaf and absence of understanding have bled together, impossible to separate. It's all that keeps our fragile peace.

I know for sure that I'm pointless, too. Needed, yes – and useful – but failing to flourish when everyone else here has. They love me because I'm Mum, because I'm here, and routine. Kids make time move so fast, yet most days are identical to the next. What I don't know is how to pull back, to stop myself from morphing into just another fading flower, a docile shadow of a woman halfway through life, relevant as dust.

And I'm scared that I am the only one who feels it.

Even the potential of our crumbling home has been realized, room by room, but for the plan to extend for a downstairs loo one day. When we've cleared the credit card, DIY-phobic Dan will get three quotes, and when we're at last a family with two lavs, we'll sit in our finished castle, and for a moment it'll feel like we've won.

Then, the kids will fly away, our castle will decay – and so will we, inside it. The same as our village neighbours, with their tight-knit death-grip on a home patch emptied of atmosphere, of spirit, where it feels like everyone's neatly waiting, a held breath, till the end. And if that's that, what's the point of all this? The castle, the family, the smiles, the pretending. Pretending to be satisfied, grown up, normal.

Keeping Dan happy, the kids secure, and the fights and the tensions and the awkwardness at bay.

Always someone else first. And always the guilt, that perpetual cloud, of me neither ever being enough nor knowing how to truly be. From the way I hold and conduct myself, to the new questions about my parents that I'm gluing myself tight to avoid.

I'd cry, but when my trap is examined, I'm ashamed. Everywhere, daily, are real tragedies – like just now on the radio – people drowning in icy bottomless seas trying to reach the place I take for granted; my troubles aren't worthy of comparison. Because who doesn't have in-laws they could sometimes throttle, a persisting disenchantment as the middle years take hold? First-world headfuckery.

As I prep a lunch hopefully more fulfilling than my dark little thoughts, I opt for being slowly anesthetized by the Christmas adverts in between segments of daytime telly, even though we've only just had Halloween. My viewing's interrupted when the house telephone shrills from its forgotten corner. Wiping my lunch fingers on a tea towel, I turn down the sound before answering.

'Dan didn't ring.' It's Yvonne. 'He always rings on a Sunday.'

'He left for Barcelona this morning, it must've slipped his mind.' Dan forgetting's unheard of. Since his grandad died, Dan's faithfully called or visited Yvonne every Sunday. When the kids are pests, I've been known to dangle the threat that they'll have to visit, too. It's always worked as spectacular bribery.

'Just checking he's all right.' Yvonne clears her throat. 'Thought those kids might've been up to no good again—'

Though she's old and this is the most she's ever said to me, I interrupt. 'Those kids?'

'Pains in the arse. I'm not getting any younger, won't see many more celebrations like my Budgie's – not that you lot would care.'

In the light layer of grease on the cooker splashback, I catch my reflection; the frown, the deep pair of 11s between my brows, my lips set in abject distaste. I look just like my mother. Not the glamorous Facebook profile, but the real her. The indoors, head of the household version.

'Always making trouble.' Yvonne begins to cough, loud enough to make crackles on the line. '. . . the jungle . . . more order in a zoo.' There may be distortion, but come on . . .

'Why don't you just say it?' Trembling now, I am slow. Clear. Possessed. 'I bloody dare you.'

The phone rings off; is jammed back onto its platform.

Sir Duke, striking gold from my sudden lack of appetite, wolfs my sandwich while I tear back into the housework with unprecedented fury, and a vision of Dan's return unfolds in my mind. He'll come back tired yet pleasant, so long as all talk remains small. He won't want to hear about his shit-stirring nan. And he'd shut me down anyway, should I broach Yvonne, with the clichéd soundbites he's been brainwashed by: 'respect your elders / they've lived through a lot / they don't mean any harm'. There's no hazy middle ground for Dan; contrast is absent. Blindly obeying the elders, because every elder deserves respect – well, that worked out a treat with those good old boys Sav and Rolf, now, didn't it?

There have always been words in my head, fantastic ones that really could challenge, but they've never once emerged right. They're either unheard and reabsorbed, adding to the acid ball in my gut that'll probably kill me, or come out dipped in so much venom that I'm aggressive. Stereotypical. I become what the Cranes already think of me and my kind.

Dan and me. Our one-sided existence has become as predictable as dying, making me question just what I've created, what I've allowed, within my own four walls – what's now affecting the children. I'm stuck, my soul shrink-wrapped, forever the quietly furious woman, who struggles applying for an adult learning course, let alone challenging her own family over their truly suspect leanings. I've swallowed back, ignored even, the undercurrent, because I've been allowed in the circle. The tolerated exception.

I may be half-black, but I'm all right. Usually.

Other than my children – and perhaps the armchair – I'm not particularly proud of anything I've ever done, have always existed without much purpose. Beyond my nest, beyond Dan, the cut-throat hustle of the real world roars on, awake and ambitious, while I'm just softer, everywhere. And left behind.

No real friends, no parents, no career, no fucking soul. All that effort, for the family life I tried so hard to believe in.

I did choose this, made my bed, but I don't have to die in it. A girl can change her mind.

Dan's boxing forms shred satisfyingly into paper rain, and into the compost bin.

Right now, it's all I've got.

There are two karate clubs within a five-mile radius. Clubs spoil weekends so I select the one in town on Tuesdays. It starts at 4.45pm, which'll give us plenty of time to get there, and plenty of shops for me and Fran while we wait. Completing an online enquiry form, I note that we can drop in before committing to a class.

And if Dan wasn't so underhand, I'd tell him we're doing it.

'The outfits are awesome. Can I get one?' Joel springs about beside me, enthused from his first lesson.

'It's called a gi.' I put a pound in a shallow Tesco trolley, unlocking it from the chain of others. It's blanket darkness, with a wet sparkle of pavements. A quick turn for essentials before catching the bus home.

'A gi, then. Do we have to carry bags?' Joel moans, and I give him the look. 'Can we choose some sweets – Haribos on offer.' He blinks his eyes quickly, like he's half-boy half-machine. 'Big bag. £1.99. Promise. To share.' Out come some robotic dance moves.

'One more moan, and they go back.'

Chuffed, he lets me get on as the trolley mounts. I pick up lunchbox fillings. Green beans or broccoli? I put the broccoli down – I have frozen, I'm sure, at home.

'I hate beans.' Toby slides over with some Oreos, also on offer, and a begging face. 'Dad hates beans as well.'

The beans go in the trolley.

After he'd landed, it took an entire day for Dan to call. In the same space of time, he'd been tagged on Insta by his boss in two swanky eateries. Party-time Dan makes a background appearance in one picture, and is more prominent in the second, laughing at something off-camera – 166 likes. I'm not envious; his boss is grotesque – inside and out. It's more the freedom that's appealing.

'If you want to eat Oreos you have to eat beans.'

'Excellent negotiating, Mrs P,' Joe says, from nowhere to right here, prodding my arm with his French stick. He's wearing those fantastic glasses and a navy roll-neck, cradling the baguette and a bottle of Pinot Noir. 'I'm late tonight. Fending for myself.'

'We've been karate-ing. Dan's away. Work.' I point in the trolley at the chicken nuggets. 'I'm slacking off, a slummy mummy this evening.'

'Hardly.' The word hangs as we look at each other for a little too long.

I never leave the house bare-faced. Not necessarily in full make-up, but enough to stand fortified, should I need to tackle ancient enemies, bigots, exes (though they could mostly be filed under enemies, too), flirting, or (if God were particularly cruel) my parents. These are one-in-a-million scenarios, but I know, absolutely, that the day I step out without my eyebrows will be the day said scenarios strike. Right now, my motto serves me well.

'This is Joe. From Fran's school,' I announce, all motherly smiles, keen to bleach things clean. 'Toby, and Joel.'

'Fantastic name,' Joe says. The boys return his smile with that distracted politeness children do, when they know they must. And though I'd love to talk, it all feels rather exposing.

'How're your normal hours?' I ask him.

'Too normal.'

'You're mad.'

Joe smiles again, bigger this time, his face breaking into the lines that only work on men. 'Probably.'

Bored, the kids drift to the newspapers. Toby puts his hand out to cover the '*Es*' on the display for the *Essex Chronicles*. Both he and Joel crease into giggles as Joe peers in my trolley.

'Haricots and Haribos, what a woman of complexity you are.' Moving along the aisle together, Joe helps himself to a bag of salad. 'I'd usually skip the garnish,' he shakes it at me, 'and save a quid. But I'm trying to impress you.'

'You're never a fussy eater?'

Joe looks disgusted. 'How dare you.'

'It would put me right off.'

'That, then,' he says, after a long moment, 'would suggest you're on.'

Christ. Our attraction brings a happiness I was unaware still existed, so pleasurable it hinges on excruciating. He'll be back in my thoughts with a vengeance now – without question at the top of my fancy list should I ever start another in my battered little bible. Who says we grow up, anyway?

'So, it's dry bread and wine for tea? With a baby portion of salad.'

'Don't be silly. I've bacon at home.' He picks up a share bag of crisps from the end of the aisle. 'D'you want a lift? I'm happy to wait.'

A strange man on my own is one thing. But a strange car – with my kids?

'If you're sure. I'm pretty much done.'

The kids are happy to be saved the bus back, and secretly so am I. I don't mind public transport, but I do hate waiting for it to turn up. Joe's parked on the ground floor, and the kids lead the way on the instruction that he's in the far corner. With a double beep, an enormous grey Range Rover comes to life. It's not the car I imagine him driving.

The kids climb in while we load up – strangers, playing husband and wife. Returning my trolley, he collects the coin, pressing it into my hand. I expect wild excitement from the contact, but it just feels moreish.

'Thank you.'

'Nah,' he says, starting the engine with a little sideways glance. 'It's a pleasure.' Radio fills the quiet as warmth puffs from the heaters. Wriggling my toes, I knock the leather satchel in the footwell. It's packed with paper, a stuffed disorder.

'How d'you find anything?' My feet hit against something in the depths, like empty bottles. 'You're even messier than me.'

'You're never messy.'

'She is,' pipes up Toby, sat with Joel on one side and Fran in Molly's car seat on the other. 'Especially when she cooks.'

'But is your mum a good cook?' Joe catches Toby in the mirror.

'When it's our favourites. I like roasts, Joel's favourite's paella. Fran's is nuggets, but even *I* can cook them.'

'Mum does the best cakes,' says Fran. 'Sometimes I help.'

'Help make more mess.' Toby ducks, avoiding a slap, while Joel keeps silent.

'My mum did glorious fry-ups. "Another sausage, Joseph, another egg?" Being ten was heaven.'

'We're twelve,' Joel says, in a flat, final sort of way that might be awkward if we weren't almost home.

Turning into our road, we stop a few houses back. Swinging the front door open, the kids kick off their shoes, legging it up to their rooms. I shout after them that dinner will be as quick as I can cook it.

Joe waits with my other bags, doesn't step in.

'When are you back on nights?'

'A week Thursday.' He wiggles his brows, jangling his keys.

'I'd ask you in—'

'Nah,' he says as his eyes take in everything, the crumbly path, the house in need of a haircut because of the creeper. 'Signed up for any courses yet?'

'I'm still considering. Still keen, though.'

'While you're considering, I don't suppose you fancy lunch?' He's the picture of innocence, yet I sense, absolutely, he's nothing of the sort. 'What harm ever came from a sandwich?'

'Thanks for the lift,' Joel says, thudding down the stairs.

Dangling an arm around me, he surveys Joe, his assertive straight shoulders reminding me of Dan.

It's the grown man with the similar name who lowers his eyes first.

'I best feed this lot.' I shift focus, my good mother routine easing the little pricks of guilt.

These little pricks are reminders. All is not quite lost for me.

After polite platonic goodbyes, Joel stays till Joe's gone, but by the time I've locked the door and pulled the curtain he's back in his room. It's not until later that Joel becomes more himself. As I'm rounding them up for bed and almost winning, the boys bring out their favourite staller of all time – questions.

'Were you messy as a kid?' Toby watches me remove my make-up, at my extraordinarily untidy dressing table.

'I'm not falling for it. It's twenty past nine.'

'What time did you go to bed as a kid?'

'At twenty past nine.'

'Jeez. You're so hollow, Mum.'

'What does that mean?'

Thinking, Toby clicks his fingers. 'Like you've got no memories.'

'I've got memories.' Cheeky shit. He makes me sound horrible. Empty.

'He means no backstory.' Joel folds his arms, mirroring his brother entire – their likeness never not amazing. 'Like as a person you only start with us.'

'With Dad,' Toby corrects.

'Rubbish,' I say. But it's not.

Other than the obvious things, such as good manners, my personal influence on the children is lightweight. They clean their teeth well because they know the story of Dan's Ribena obsession that led to three extractions at seven years old. They know Nancy was head of Year Six because of her kindliness to the new starters – another classic Penny drags out in support of the Nancy-starting-a-family appeal. They plug every gap, every open question with their stories, their bygone bullshit. And their perspective, that vision of how the world works, and where they belong. They've always had just enough money, comfort and white mobility to exploit all those things. The bungalow bought outright when Penny and Clive moved from East Ham in the nineties. The love of brand names and personalized number plates and their pièce de resistance, Villa Clivenny, Los Cristianos, Tenerife.

Joel rubs his hands together, as if he's warming up. 'Tell us about when you were twelve, then.'

'Well.' Shifting in my chair, I resist changing the subject. 'Well, I looked like you. Watched too much telly, like you – pushed my mum's buttons at bedtime, probably, just like you.'

'And she, your mum, looked like you – like us?' Joel asks.

'Well, yes. She's . . . we're Trinidadian.'

'I wish I was Trinidadian,' says Toby.

'You are. You all are.'

'But me and Fran don't look it. That's not fair.'

'It is.' Joel squeezes my hand. 'You match everywhere. So, I get Mum.'

His words are a gravity on my heart.

'You'd get Mum's mum, too,' Toby says after a bit, thoughtful and serious. 'But she's a witch, so—'

'My mum's not a witch.' Bloody Dan. 'We just don't get on.' It sounds even weaker than when I said it to Fran. But there never was an epic fallout, no drama to detail – more, a parent–offspring impasse. Troubles never settled, and so the distance grew.

I thought when I had children I'd tell them everything about my life, the isolated, prickly childhood, all the things in the gap between then and them, and I'd never be lonely again. Dan says, often, how lost he'd be without Penny and Clive. How they mean everything. My parents, on the other hand, erased so effectively from my day to day, have become instead a fiction to me, an unnecessary prologue to skip past, the fragments of our old story tucked in a bible, on a shelf left mostly forgotten. The kids – Dan too – used to my closed reticence, never asked much about my family history at all. Until recently, anyway.

My family history. Not theirs, or ours, but always mine – my mother's daughter all right. Packed tight and resentful beneath my careful layers of protection, there's a gnawing in my heart as I fray between the versions of myself.

There's the me truly, when alone or in the rare ease of close company. Or I'm the fraudster. Like here, as I play blasé, unbothered by the boys' words. I switch for anyone, without really thinking about it, the pretending dulling the ancient and now rather delicate layer of my true self. But I never thought I'd ever end up behaving the same with *my own kids.* Then again, I never foresaw any benefit of having someone beyond me to balance the family pattern, either. Joining familial dots is a comfort when you're made from a vastness of holes. I know that, far better than most.

I've drifted. The boys gone. Saying goodnight, I go down-stairs, making a mental note to delete my internet searches when I'm done. The laptop comes to life and I find myself looking at Fran's last viewed page, the Rightmove website. Nosey habits.

I type it in rather absently, my behaviour not exactly new – but getting a result is. Our old house fills the screen. Horn Road. The narrow terrace, the black front door, the brass letterbox at the foot of it. For Sale, £229,995.

My clammy hand clicks for more pictures. Finds none.

Private, closed books – even on Rightmove.

My phone starts to ring. Expecting Dan, I'm thrown that it's *Kathryn (school)* flashing up at me. Joe's convenient alias, because I learnt the tricks young, have always been a fast learner.

'I wasn't sure you'd answer.' His voice makes the Rightmove panic ebb, just a little.

'How was the sarnie?'

'Heavenly.'

I think of Dan, his ketchup-smothered bacon – Heinz only.

'Look, you can tell me to do one – and that's fine.' Joe hesitates as I hesitate, staring again at Horn Road. 'But I like you. Far more than I should.' He sighs. 'What that means I don't know, with both of us being married for Christ's sakes, and I didn't mean to disturb—'

A moth collides with the desk lamp. I bat it away. 'You're a lovely distraction.'

'Remember school, bunking off? Finding a bit of park to vanish in, with your tunes and fags and notebooks – something pinched from the back of the drinks cabinet.' He must sense I get it, for he adds, 'We should do that.'

'Notebooks?' I leap on the word, diluting the proposition. 'For your poems, even then?'

'Not as prolifically as now. But I didn't know you then.' Though he's colouring me in, using far brighter colours, for a more impressive sketch than I truly am, I know, absolutely, that he's sincere. All lives should be full of flattery like this. Fat with delicious diversion.

'For a psychiatrist, you really do talk a lot of shit.' His laughter feels good in my ears, erasing the worries I struggle to stifle without Dan's alleviating presence. Alone, with no one to fake it for. 'I'll meet you for lunch.' I swipe the moth again, must catch a wing, for its dust.

'Are we bunking off?'

Closing the screen, Horn Road vanishes. 'Why not?'

8

Reparations

'All the shit's lifting.' There's an aura around me, I'm sure of it. 'And everything's special.'

'The beauty of the green in a nutshell.' Reaching across the grass, Joe gives my arm a lazy prod. 'Though you are, undoubtedly, very special.'

And lucky. We've been on this riverbank all morning and have only seen one other person. According to Joe, it's remarkably unchanged since his own school days. He's got the bunking off starter kit perfected, right down to the marijuana and Curly Wurlys, though he's shown his middle-classness by bringing blackberries and pistachios as well.

Two weeping willows dip their branches in the water, curtaining us from view. We lie beneath one on grass tufts, long as chives, and dried patches of mud, me on my raincoat for comfort. It's one of those last-ditch sunny days that set me at odds because my scarves and hats are already back in circulation. Apart from the trees nothing is particularly picturesque, but it's certainly private, which is, after all, what's most important.

'We'll feel terrible later, after this.' I down my last inch of beer. 'Tomorrow, too.'

'I'm off tomorrow. Football.' Balling up his wrapper, Joe reaches for his tobacco tin. 'Come – if you like.'

My tummy turns in a rising flump of a sensation, like when a fast car takes a humped bridge. I couldn't go, even if I liked football. Childcare for three must be prearranged weeks in advance.

Unless you're Dan. Pitch and putting, early rounds, still schmoozing around Barcelona with the letch boss.

Checking the time, I throw my arms up, flopping backwards as the sky moves far too fast behind the amber glass of my shades. Spinning out's what I'd call it, back in the day.

We've got ages.

And ages still isn't long enough.

'Can anyone else pick up Fran?' Joe asks, clearly thinking the same.

'Penny's in Tenerife. So sad.'

'What about your mum?'

'Ha.' Taking his joint, I light the end. God, the smoke feels good. 'A terrifically long story. I'd bore you shitless.'

'You'd never.' Off come his sunglasses, showing me he means it. 'Go on.'

'My parents' version or mine?'

'Whatever the truth is.'

I can picture him at work, all stern concern, epic-looking in a white button-up coat, though he's already told me he hasn't got one. Whatever the truth is. He did ask.

'Well, they're both such cold stuck records, it's easier pretending I don't need them.' Don't miss them. 'When Dan's with his lot, they treat him like he's Jesus.'

A scattering of magpies peck at the crumbled earth not far away. I count seven. For a secret, never to be told. But what the fuck do magpies know?

'I had an affair when I was sixteen. My parents blamed me.'

Aloud, it's not as earth-shattering.

Joe pulls a face. 'Playground triangles.'

'There's your trouble. He was forty. And very married.'

'What does very married mean?'

'It means like us. Outwardly happy. No need for more. We never got past it. I left home and the gap just stretched.' Stretched into years. 'My mum – you've never met anyone so proper. She'd come to parents' evening in her church clothes. Nothing was ever good enough.' Mum, fully conjured now before me, is almost too vivid to stomach. 'And my dad, a dictionary on legs, always late for something. The most under-the-thumb man ever – till I met Dan's dad – but that's another story.' Stories. Lives chocked with the moments that define us. 'Being an only child with them was shit.'

Subject aside, though – without doubt, this is the best I've felt in months, my world altogether more endurable through the fog of a big zoot.

'Parents are cunts.' It comes out so boldly that it sets us off in the laughter that makes tears and stitches and puts me at twelve again. 'Well, Dad was – Mother's all right. She keeps her distance, mostly. We rented a villa in Porto once; Mum, me, Molls. Bella and her parents. It was proper fucking hell.'

I try slotting my lot into his setting. The Parkers and the Petersens – together at last. Polar worlds and backgrounds. Clashing opposites. Being grown up should mean being free of the parent-shit, yet even in middle bloody age, we're still carrying the weight. Joe, on his Portuguese jollies. And me. Wearing the remnants, like a nappy full of it.

'My mum was a doctor's receptionist,' I tell him, like the words have just been waiting. 'I remember once, she'd just got in, was talking to my dad. *Top of the Pops* was on.' Every Thursday, after stuffing myself with tinned peach slices for afters, I'd tune in, bursting into the running-man and the snake, like I was there in the studio, getting zoomed in on by those cameras on wheels, thanks to my killer Salt-N-Pepa dance moves.

'I could hear them, doing the hushed voices; trying to shield me.' Avoiding Joe's face, my throat grows a little bit tight. 'She said the weirdest, saddest thing.'

I see her now, through the glaze of the serving hatch, Dad's hands on her shoulders, trapping her in a hug that lasted for ever. Dad hugs were rare, saved for necessity; scraped knees or bad dreams. Or for his wife, fucking jangling in her skin from the chants of 'nigger bitch' on the bus back from work.

'Four grown men,' I say, once I've told him the story,

though there are countless others like it. 'And a bus full of bystanders. She said that all she'd like was a day without a comment or an insult.' The joint won't catch. Joe takes it from my hands, lighting it for me. 'Melancholy.' I sniff a little. 'Christ, for a second I almost missed her.'

'Where's she from, your mum?' he asks gently.

'Trinidad. Came here in her teens. Whenever I asked about then, she'd come over all "meeting-your-father-was-when-my-life-started" bullshit.' As a kid I'd have this vision of her, on a dusty landing strip, the wind flapping wildly at her dress and hat, as she modestly clung to both, avoiding exposure. There's a suitcase, old-fashioned and jarring, that she leaves there in the dust to board the shiny white plane. She takes a seat, closes her eyes.

Then England. Trinidad private, done with. Me denied the code to a culture I'm expected to know, yet have never, ever been shown.

And no amount of sentimental snooping should mean I ever forget this.

'Odd woman. Such an odd, beautiful woman.'

'I don't doubt. Look at you.'

'Married, though, Joe. Kids, older than me. I went to a bloody Catholic school.'

'Exactly,' he says simply, offering a blackberry. 'You were a kid.'

'Dan doesn't know.' I plop one in my mouth, my taste buds swooning. 'Thinks I'm all sweet and decent. I never wanted to shatter the illusion.'

'But it's those things that make us, us. It's all bollocks, otherwise.'

'Twelve years married isn't bollocks.'

'Divorce spikes spectacularly around the twelve-year mark.'

'That's convenient.' I bat my lashes. 'How long have you been married?' I avoid using Bella's name.

'Seven years. The classic itch.' His laughter startles the magpies and, taking flight, they distance themselves, leaving Joe and me completely alone. 'Your mum. D'you talk to Dan about that?'

'Never. You don't have to look at me like that. I know.' My black mother is a sticking point for all of us, in very different ways. 'What about you, anyway? No one gets to forty-eight without a few secrets.'

'I'm too ordinary for a cupboard full of skeletons.' But Joe's wearing an expression I haven't seen before that morphs our hazy morning back into focus. 'I had a problem. Years back – with alcohol. For most of my twenties. Fucked my first marriage, and the relationship with my son, Henry. He's too old to need me for anything beyond paying his uni fees these days.'

I don't say anything. Instead, I do as he does, and listen.

'I never wanted to be a GP, never wanted to be like my father. Drinking made all that bearable – till I got chucked out. I've just learnt how to manage it over the years. It's like being on a constant diet.' He parallels me, leaning on his palm propped by an elbow, all angles. 'Bella knows nothing about it.'

'And *I* live a lie. Bloody hypocrite.'

'But this isn't.' With care, Joe sets the joint on the grass above our heads, his expression again full of shadows, though not anything to fear. His is a velvet darkness, luring and deep. Unapologetically carnal. I see it all. What he wants. What he'll do.

And there's always been the absolute certainty that he'll be very, very good at it.

'Since that stinking old coach, you're all I think about.' Joe's words are hot, damp, fucking millimetres from my skin, his hands digging into the pits of my hips, as his mouth finds and learns mine. 'The most delicious thing I've ever seen.' Our fingers thread together, crushing onto his crotch.

There's no resistance. I'm languid beneath his touch; conflicting emotions dead. Outdoor humping is surely illegal; public indecency, I think. Adulterous outdoor humping in clouds of marijuana more so. Three bad things, then – in one day.

He slowly licks his fingers, urging aside my knickers to slide his thumb along the length of me, as the gaps between his shirt buttons gape and contract as he breathes harder and faster. We're coated, slathered in absolute wrong, yet this is everything I hoped for. My adult life, now like my adolescence, scratched out by the base appetite that burns harder within me than anything else. I've just become expert at my Stepford part all these years; the truth of me harnessed somewhere, black and buried.

Until now.

But this is my moment. My unwholesome resurrection.

He begins unbuttoning my blouse and it's a peculiar sensation, being partially dressed in front of another man, in front of Joe; two stone overweight and beginning to grey.

Who's not a patch on Dan, but's as lonely and disillusioned as I am.

Joe breathes into my neck, creating gorgeous goosepimples of excitement, soaking me, as my shaking hands work his belt. He catches my lips – and all I can think is how my mouth is being invaded so deliciously in perfect sync with my cunt, as Joe's fingers fluently slip-slide, then are held, so instinctively, by my warm tightness; the very core of me. With the tip of my nipple between his teeth, he grazes my slit with his cock, studying me beneath him, as if keen to know, to remember, every flicker from the joy of this.

And I, I could roar from relief, from the blessed relief of him at last having me, those knowing grey eyes seared to mine, with everything magnified to magnificence. I come without thinking, without having to focus on making it happen.

It's wrong. It's fucking blissful.

But there's a nagging sludge, too, that I know will never shift.

Surrendering beneath the weight of him, Joe takes unrestrained advantage. He has the look of the decadent; greedy, selfish, pleasure-driven. Without doubt, my duplicate. His body slows, tenses, his unhurried tongue trailing my jaw and onto my lips.

'I'd live in you,' he whispers, clamped to my body.

What a glorious, glorious thing. 'I'd let you.'

Joe waits in his usual spot. 'Do you feel wrong?' he asks, straight to the point, proper greetings unnecessary in our new phase. He hands me a note with a look that says it's not for now. Like me, he's showered, changed and is back in the playground an acceptable six minutes early.

And, to the rest of the world, we're the same people we always were.

There's a saying, some blasted inspirational thought that does the rounds on the net, about how if you were to see your soul instead of your physical appearance, would you still be beautiful then?

'Yes and no.'

'You would answer like that,' he says, and this cheers me somewhat; he's getting to know me. 'Honestly, how do you feel?'

My body's rather in shock. Legs as if they aren't my own – jellified and Bambi-ish. But there isn't the terrible regret I thought there would be, whenever I imagined the reality of sex with him.

Instead, there's bizarre calm. An acceptance, perhaps. The feeling that the tiny seed, the essence of me truly, has been nurtured into bud.

'Awake.'

'Yeah,' he says, getting it. 'That'll do.'

*   *   *

Memory. And Truth. By sixteen, tired of the plaits I considered childish, I felt it was time for hair like my mum's. She'd long abandoned her 'fro for Caucasian fluidity, and I begged to join her on the quarterly visits to her salon in Stratford. Mum would go alone, claiming I'd be bored, and to be fair, getting her hair done did seem to take all day. But I'd always look forward to the confidence of her return, the softness of her hair, the way it would move around her face; both of us fully indoctrinated by western beauty standards.

Between appointments, she'd make do with the minuscule selection of black hair products in the town centre pharmacy, the only place that remembered black people had hair, too. Once, after school, behind her back, I traipsed around all the local hairdressers with my birthday money, only to be turned away with varying versions of, I wouldn't know where to start / I can't touch that / You need an expert – as if afro were a tropical disease. If I hadn't been sure that white lady salons weren't for me before then, that sad little afternoon proved it.

Mum's next visit became a joint appointment. Her tiny salon was no bigger than our front room, run by three unsmiling large-breasted women in their sixties, where my hair was relaxed for the first time. And it did take all day. The shop heaved with clients, while I was left for indeterminable lengths of time with old magazines, and the occasional passing hand on my shoulder to prove I hadn't been forgotten.

After my first hit of the creamy crack, I was hooked. I left the hairdressers with a James Brown bounce, all styled and sheeny. My hair was straight, just like everybody else's, like the girls in *Just Seventeen* with their Kate Moss-inspired middle partings. I could (ish) emulate. It sparked a tiny confidence, a little more belonging. I felt, at last, pretty.

Visible.

Mum sensed the shift. Warned, 'There's no room in your clever head for boys yet.'

But she was too late.

I was a dishwasher, hired by his wife to work weekends, on the promise to my parents that it wouldn't interfere with school. At first, Jason (J-Man to his friends) didn't talk to me – but he didn't have to. His expressions were enough. His mouth would twitch as he'd lick his lips in such a way it left my knees useless. I was already learning a young woman's power, blooming like a bloody daylily at car beeps and wolf whistles, but at school, the brown and black girls – four of us, none in the same year – were invisible. We weren't fanciable, certainly never beautiful; 'different' was a backhanded compliment. And we'd likely be on Zimmer-frames before anyone tried snogging us – perhaps never, if we waited for a decent classmate. But no one decent would ever have taught me all that J-Man did. Shaping me.

From the oddity, into the fetishized.

I looked forward to my job, to washing up, to the eye contact between me and this huge Barbadian lump of man darker than my mum, eye contact that grew longer, stronger, how he'd bring things to the sink, and, for a thrilling, throbbing second, press his crotch into my back. His chef's whites made a stark and delicious contrast to his lovely skin and my mind couldn't process anything beyond how we might look, skin on skin, bare flesh connected. Awed by the finesse of his chef skills and the dictatorial way he ran his kitchen, he'd bark at everyone but me – an absolute alpha. I'd been boy-mad forever, imagining desire when it worked both ways – when it became reciprocal. Finally, my prayers were answered.

Only, J-Man wasn't a boy.

One late night, after an evening of cooking action, J-Man stayed back, helping with my last few dishes. Just us, I was shy as he coaxed and flattered, him unfalteringly attentive to the very little I said. He insisted on taking me home, and as he helped me into my coat I'd felt a magnificent danger.

His car stereo, the headfuck of Magic Tree, Paco Rabanne and Pledge played like disco lights in my senses, turning me plasticine before he'd even touched me. J-Man knew he'd cracked my code already, knew exactly how to gain entry. All he needed was privacy. And permission. He'd driven, utterly distracted, his twig-like fingers moving across the roundness of my mouth, then down to the breast closest to him, then down again, to settle on my fanny, outside of my clothes, as the A13 became small roads, narrow lanes, then a countryside seclusion of flat black British wilderness.

'Are you the "V" word?' he'd asked, softly, kindly; me, embarrassed that I was. We kissed all over late-night KISS, my first kiss, as the heater spilled round our feet, lubricating our limbs, until he was limber enough to manipulate my seat into recline. I was willing. It wasn't special. It didn't hurt. And I was glad that it was done.

I was gladder still to find that the more we did it, the better it got. Better even than Mum's books described – and back at home, she was full-on suspicious. She'd hover around doorways, making me repeat where I'd been, muttering about the Devil and changelings. But she'd been the best teacher for keeping secrets; I'd learnt, exactly, how to be a closed book. I kept myself the same, quiet and friendless – but out of sight, I owned my new role. Monica June Parker – Temptress Extraordinaire. The kind of woman who collected all the gazes. Men were suddenly so very easy, and I had the hottest one, risking his moon and stars.

I played the part inside out; an Oscar-winning performance. Because anything was better than returning to the old life, to the awkward silent geek I'd been before, who no one ever tried to know. So grateful, I swallowed everything he said. Of course, his colossal nob couldn't be constricted by a rubber; of course, there was no bareback danger, he'd only been with wifey, for years and years – they didn't even hug any more. I went to the doctor for the pill, so J-Man could hump without consequence.

'Look how he's taken that little brown girl from Horn Road under his wing; she looks like she could belong to them lot.' Locals would smile and wave at J-Man in his sleek BMW when he picked me up from school like some kind uncle, while all the time his hand would be alternating between the gearstick and my fanny.

My one-track focus meant that everything I valued beyond him crumbled away. Neglected things often do. I didn't care, though. I preferred the illicit helpings of sexual gratification, even if that meant J-Man slowly shutting me away so I could be only his. Because those moments. God, those moments. The thrill of appealing to someone I shouldn't, the aching resistance. I was born for it.

Until Dan. When I changed again; reset to pure, while I hid the rest. More layers. More protection. Another gash split in my psyche.

AD and BC; those prominent dividers of time. Shrink to person size, and we each contain our own. That moment when something enormous occurs, spurring a whole new life phase – like the transforming time of my affair and leaving home. But, at thirty-nine, it's not hard absolving myself, for the most part, from my relationship with J-Man. I was sixteen; a child, really. And he wasn't.

This time around, though.

This time, I'm the grown-up; know from experience the devastation of deceit, still chose to push the button. But I was always going to push it. From Kathryn's book club, I knew. So did Joe.

And that's the sort of woman I really am.

9

Return of the Mon

'He-lloo.' Mum's telephone voice fills the thick carpet stillness of the front room, the same as it always did. *He-lloo*; rolling across the biscuit-coloured shag-pile and chocolate three-piece suite, over the After Eight mahogany wall unit, filled with knick-knacks and Dad's non-fiction.

Her voice paints a picture from memory, puts her neat on the edge of the armchair, *her armchair*; knees together, prim and spine upright, as if to impress the invisible caller. Only, back then, should the caller be me, the *He-lloo* would be followed by *Monica!* All quick and stern and altogether different-sounding, as though she'd come over all *Exorcist* and conjured another soul from her voice box. She has always been two people.

'It's me.' I want to acknowledge her, but the only word I can think of that should fall out with such ease is 'Mum'.

But it's stuck. My heart won't let me say it.

'Moni. Is everything—'

'Everything's fine.' I hold the phone away from my ear, from the distant breath of her sigh. 'You?'

'We're both fine.' Curt now, with a skim of chill.

'Look, I'm nearby. Could I pop in – if, if you're not busy, that is?'

'Your father's not here, so if you're hoping—'

'I'm not hoping for anything. Mum.' Mum – coughed up; flobbed at the end of a sentence. 'I just wanted to see you.'

'Well,' she says, quiet. Tentative. 'Well, that'd be nice.'

The phone goes silent. Joe, cruising down the old high street, reaches across to give my knee a squeeze – a calm, warmth of support by my side.

The exposure, though.

But, had I not over-revealed – which has left me feeling more vulnerable than the al fresco shagging – I wouldn't be here now. Joe's a pleaser, I can tell – but it comes with a certain pushiness. If I thought it manipulative, I'd be wary, but it's more like guidance.

Like steering me here – delivering me. To her.

Panic flares in my gut. I close my eyes, avoiding Robinson's Grill, J-Man's restaurant, though I'm unsure it's even still going. Joe turns off, towards the concrete Lego brick of a school building and the smart houses opposite, their distinction hidden behind iron gates and lengthy drives.

And then the estate; row upon row of pebble-dashed magnolia, indistinguishable. But for a box hedge or a dropped kerb, nothing's changed here. And if nothing's changed ... but it's too late. Joe finds Horn Road easily. Spotting the For Sale sign, he stops a few doors back. I try remembering my last proper connection here, which must be the picture I sent of a newborn Fran, her perfect pea face poking from swaddling blankets the colour of buttermilk.

Five years ago.

I've a terrible feeling – know, in my bones, nothing here will be good for me. 'This is madness. A silly panic because they're moving. She even said everything's fine, just now.'

'Because you called her. The hardest part you've cracked already.' Joe pats my knee again, still so kind. Because it is kind; to ferry me about on his day off – on the minimum of information, too. 'But, if you'd rather go home—'

'No.' I pull down the shade to look in the mirror, checking up my nose. 'It's not just them moving.'

'Take your time. If I'm not here, I'll be stretching my legs.' Nodding to the cemetery, he starts the engine. 'Remember, it's just your mum.' Joe falters, hesitation in the action, before he leans into the passenger side and kisses my mouth, off-centre, somehow exactly as it should be.

It takes mere seconds of contact for the energy to change, the blues lifting from the edges of my mind into something better – extinguished, when I climb from the car onto the kerb, a giantess shrunk for the child world. Always a grey place, even in the hottest of summers.

My head and my heart, unified by some one-off earthly miracle, urge me to get the hell away, from that house and the people inside it. I broke from the guilt they cloaked me in by choosing not to see them. I swapped their judgement for my freedom. I made that choice. The right one.

And yet.

I notice her face, that creaseless oval at the kitchen window, before I'm even across the street, and by the time I unlatch the gate she's at the door. Her nyloned drumstick legs slipped silkily into sheepskin slippers, her hands clasped together as though she's frightened to separate them. Because what then – hugs or handshakes? We share polite almost smiles instead as she welcomes me inside.

Time's stood still in Horn Road on first impressions, until I enter a space I don't recognize. The kitchen and dining room, once separated by a serving hatch, is now open-plan and refitted. Cabinets of soft sage complement the wooden worktop, which looks (compared to mine at home, anyway) brand new. Everywhere's neat, to polished, crumb-less perfection. Ivory metro tiles gleam by the window, the road beyond now empty of cars. She has an island; a Kenwood mixer and a stack of cookbooks on a fashionable slant that reminds me of home, of Dan. The comfortable family space, whose capacity never peaks two, makes me desperately sad.

Sicky little hooks tug at the back of my throat. Like sorrow, or loss. The remedy for both in touching distance, but always, always impossible.

Her silent footsteps come to a halt as she sets down cups and saucers. She's kept the same table; a thickly varnished square, tiled in terracotta. 'Sit. D'you want something to eat?' She glides to the fridge as I slide into a chair.

'How's Dad?' I sound grainy, strange, must say the words Mum and Dad a hundred times a day, yet they sound like I've just learnt them.

'Too busy for his own good.' She offers a side plate assortment of biscuits, a black-speckled vanilla sponge. Always a teapot and a homemade cake at the ready, should she ever need to prove her Britishness; she's even wearing a twinset and pearls. Cutting off a piece with a black-handled knife, she pushes it towards me.

'Thank you.' Traitorous against myself, I take small deceivingly dense bites that lodge in my chest as I look around. From the décor to the plates to the feel of the place, there's nothing that stirs a homely memory, no hint that I ever existed.

But it always was an anonymous home.

'How's your family?' *Your family*. 'Must be growing up, now?'

'The boys just started secondary. Tall as me, too. And Fran, she just started school – but thinks she knows it all already.'

'Well, we all know a child like that.' There's a rare fondness in her tone. 'And what you doing to fill your time, you back working?'

'I'm studying,' I lie, pleased to surprise her. 'English literature. And . . .' Why did I say 'and'? 'Art – modern.' I try again. 'The history of modern art.'

She sniffs. 'Better late.'

'I volunteer too.' It's not another lie, exactly. 'Two mornings in the library. Keeping busy.'

'Well,' she says, like we're the type of mother–daughter who chat daily on the phone and live in each other's pockets. Like she knows me. 'You never were good in your own company.'

I could snip back, but the effort it would take to find something slicing tires me.

'Sugar?'

'No, thank you.'

'Sweet enough.' She sits to my left as the TV in the front room spurts canned laughter. 'What do you want?'

'I don't know.'

Mum sighs. Apart from the hum of gameshow voices, we sip our teas in silence, observing, but not observing, one another. Her hair's in the same sleek bun, only now flecked with mixed greys, like an out-of-tune television. Rather than ageing, it's becoming. A tender bubble of nostalgia swells inside me as she sits frozen in her perfect posture, still a generous size fourteen; plump hips and tidy waist. Unfussy, shining nails. A hint of blush, still the same sunset sweep of orange, a fleshy coral on her lips. A light whizz with the wand through her lashes to define and separate, but that's it. There's nothing flash or overstated about her.

She's still the most perfect woman I've ever seen. In all my life.

'Why're you moving?'

'Economic uncertainty.' She rolls her eyes, using one of Joe's 'what's the world coming to, downward spiral' faces. 'If we're offered what we're asking, we'll take it. Alan can retire whenever he likes. And there's nothing keeping us here.'

I'd like to ask where they'll go, but don't feel I've the right to.

It's months before she speaks again. 'Your dad will be sorry he missed you.'

'Another time.' I look through her streak-free window to the freedom beyond.

'Another decade, then.' She tuts. 'Stubborn.'

'Touché, Mum.' There's a glimmer, a momentary connection, that's gone before I know it's even real, returning us to stone. 'But there's been nothing stopping you, either. I've had babies, *am your baby*, yet it's me—'

'All that, yes. All that and we've never been necessary.'

'You've never been curious? Wondered what they're—'

'You know he's still here?' She turns her lips into a small pouty 'o', her eyes wide and innocent. 'Come, you can do better than a face like that, girl. Y'know exactly who I talking about. *Him*. Jason Robinson.'

I don't know how she does it, how it works, how I'm a grown woman – so mature that I recently found three white pubes – but in front of her I'm a kid again.

'He has another restaurant – three thriving businesses now. Another new blonde wife; another kid. Happy ever after.' She stops, giving a little. 'Being fair, he looks more like a grandad. But regardless, he ain't doing badly.'

I still picture desolation. Me the grenade, launched through the letterbox of J-Man's family home. His grown children, unable to love or form bonds because their dad let them down. Because their dad abandoned them for a teenager in a tiny dress.

But then yesterday. Speaking it, Joe's unfazed response to the sin I've worn like a fucking ball and chain, and none of this feels the same. My crime doesn't command the same power as it did before, when I only had their shame with which to measure it. The only thing it does do is make me certain this is futile.

My chest aches. I'd like to blame her cake for that, but the truth is that I was hopeful. Now all I am is reset, back to child status; muted by the power of her tongue. The only thing that's moved on here is her perfect kitchen.

It still hurts, though.

Then I'm upstairs to the bathroom, sat all furious on the side of the tub before even realizing I'm repeating the dormant behaviour of long ago. Nudging the bath panel, I find the wobble gone. She's modernized; wicker baskets store her lotions and potions, an assortment of Palmer's and Simple, and still with the old Dark & Lovely. The neighbouring basket is a makeshift medicine cabinet, and I'm intrusive enough to read the labels. Mrs Avril Parker, 56 Horn Road, Ranitidine, Omeprazole, names and names I'll never remember. She could open a small chemist.

I hate how I want her to want me – hate still caring what she thinks.

But I can't resist, hovering in their bedroom doorway for a little nosey. Mum still sleeps on the left, her bedside ordered; a small dish for jewellery; a cream-coloured study lamp that bends over her pillow like a crooked elbow, for reading. There's only one book. Her fixture, the Roman Catholic missal bible. I whizz unthinkingly through the pages till one catches, revealing an edge of paper. Hesitating, I check behind me for a sign of her presence. It's clear.

My trembling hands discover the photo of day-old Fran. The other paper is a printout, of me not long after giving birth, hung from a hospital drip, wearing one of Penny's bed-shirts that she rushed in for me, when I bled through my fancy new Mamas & Papas nightie three seconds after putting it on. I'm weary, pale and bloated. The cruellest of pictures, saved only by my two new sons, Joel in a buttercup Babygro and Toby in mint green. Penny chose this picture for her Facebook announcement. Becoming Nan. The day she fell in love so deeply, it even swallowed me.

But we've had a secret spectator. Watching our lives through the prism of Penny's timeline. What that might mean brings weak knees, tears, makes my breath jagged and irregular – but now's a bit shitty for any deep emotional reflection. Hurriedly, I push the pictures back, until another page separates, near the back. A small photo of a tiny baby, with jet black hair and a tube in one nostril, like Joel had at birth, too. I read: *Baby Ashley*.

Suddenly nervous, I put everything back and slip out, past Mum's dressing table loaded with products, which, when applied in the right marvellous medicine order, create her smell. It wafts through the bedroom, steeped in her belongings, her bedsheets, her true space. I want to bottle and treasure it. Have it salve the parent-sized hole in me, gaping and uncertain. Always hungry.

Best ignored.

Back on the landing, I look across to the closed door of my old room.

I choose to go downstairs.

'I did all right.' In the kitchen, I hover by the window. 'Twelve years. My happy ever after. Doesn't that count for anything?' Outside, Joe's back. The car window lowers. Fag ash tapped into the road, he glances across at the house, as if sensing me. 'If you're still wondering what this is really about, what I'm here for . . . it's only because I want the kids to know you.' It's out – in top distracting time, too. Good truth masking bad truth. Hiding in plain sight, like all the bad motherfuckers. 'Because they are missing out, Mum.'

'You want more?' she asks, quietly.

'Do you?' I bite my lip while she leans against the wall, a hand over her mouth. 'We could try, don't you think? Help them understand who they come from.' I swallow. Unable to read her face, what her hesitation means, I glance back outside. 'And I know Dan—'

'That him?' Mum peers over my shoulder, eyes on Joe just as mine are. Ten-ish years between me and him, ten again for him to reach her. Still comely and cougar-ish at fifty-nine. I wonder what he'd think of her. What she'd make of him.

'Yes.' Smoothly delivered, without hesitation.

'Even if I didn't know what your own darn husband looked like, I'd still know he weren't it.' Mum's knock-back laughter sends me into her trap. 'I could feel it when you came in. You're deceit, Monica. And you wear it like it's custom made.'

I barge past her, fleeing up the tiny hall, and slam the door with such a bang it echoes out in every direction.

Joe asks no questions. He starts the car and drives away, leaving me to my thoughts, to my shame. To J-Man, his imprint, clear as it ever was.

I'm deceit.

Like I didn't fucking know that already.

It takes till we're nearing the village for me to speak. 'That was horrible.'

'That was brave.' I flinch as Joe tries wiping my tears. 'Oh, love, there's no crime in showing your feelings.'

'My mum's more likely to lick my tears than be kind because of them. She hates me.'

'She doesn't hate you.'

But Joe doesn't know her.

My tears gather momentum, the emotion and stress of the past few days chasing me down at last. 'I knew it'd be like that. Now look at me – all weak in front of you.'

'Not weak – human. Try writing it down.' Joe stops behind the park, near the quiet bit of footpath that leads back to the village. 'Think of it as a facial. Cleansing.' He smiles. 'Just get it out.'

'You're therapizing me.' I think of the mood diary I kept, those sessions of cognitive therapy at the hospital twelve years back. Joe might even have been there when I was.

'We're not exactly in a position where I can look after you properly. This is all I've got.' The fervency about him begins to wilt, like a slow puncture on a bouncy castle, a hiss as he empties his lungs. 'It hurts that you can't see. How good, *how special*, you are.'

'You're only saying that 'cos you fancy me.'

Joe smiles at this, biased of course by my immense tits and arse. I could cook kittens for breakfast and he'd likely overlook it. I wipe my eyes again, a touch more collected.

'I do,' he says, 'but it's still true. And I'm here – if you want me.'

If. I want him so badly, I'd like to roll him up, pop him in my gob and consume him. I don't tell him this, but going by the way he's watching me too, he'd understand. Kissing my fingers, I press them to his cheek and keep my distance. Any contact will tip the smoulder into outrageous flames, our seclusion becoming a dogging frenzy before we know it.

'What we've done, Joe. It's massive.'

'Massive. Yes.' He looks me straight in the eyes. 'I'm not sorry.'

'Neither am I.' But the enormity of events still reverberates my body; an aftershock of guilt – and clarity. Clarity that makes me want to puke my guts over Joe's fine uphol-stery. All the badness behind Dan's gilded back. Because he does seem so very, very golden now; his crimes feather-weight against my dense wrongdoings. 'But I do need to let it sink in.'

Joe needn't worry; it won't take long. Ironic, how deceit's the most honest part of me.

And the most burdensome.

10

Earnest Domesticities

I'm sorting the house out, top to bottom, getting ahead of all the mum stuff so I can be dedicated to Dan and the kids all weekend. I forget I can be like this. Energetic. Purposeful. Our bathroom's one bright clinical sparkle. The medicine cupboard cleaned out, restocked with every wintry requirement.

I've even disinfected the wheelie bin. The Virginia creeper is shedding now; the leaves, curled pink and weightless, blow into the hallway every time the front door's opened. Net curtains washed, the downstairs windows inside out.

As Friday passes through treacle.

I make mental notes – too exposing to write down. One: to shut the door on my mum – Dan mustn't pick up on any weirdness. But her Facebook prying is beyond my control. And haven't I been doing the same to her all these years?

Our pictures in her bible, the mysterious Baby Ashley – and that head-bomb contradiction of us, so distant, we share the same bloody hiding places. I could dwell, cling to that, a speck of humanity to warm myself on, but I know better. The only way to repair from her rejection is to shut her out completely.

Besides, my heart can't take any more.

I mustn't crack, either. Which leads to point number two: no gaps are allowed in this fuckery.

On the mantelpiece is a picture Toby drew of the five of us, years ago, our crayoned faces like apocalyptic suns. We're holding hands, identical apart from our heights, descending across the tiny A6 canvas. The sadness shifts as fear stirs in the shadows of my conscience.

Mental note number three: don't be scared.

But, I am. Of Dan's return. Of him seeing the same as my mother did. I've a strong, banging in the throat sort of heart-beat while I study Toby's drawing; the five of us, holding hands, same as always. But Joe and the parent-shit need be no different from the myriad of other me-shit that Dan's clueless about. All I need do is pack it away, cast another veil over the truth of me.

The boxing forms are now tiny wet squares, fraternizing with old teabags and veg peelings in the compost. I don't know when Dan will notice them missing, or when he'll tell me we're at his bloody parents' again for Christmas. I don't know when he'll learn about the karate, either – or if the lift home from Tesco in the car of his dreams will slip too. It's a greasy dance on a knife edge, moves I'll have to master.

Mental note number four: be normal. Pleased to see him.

The cupboards restocked; two Peronis chill in the fridge. Lamb, studded with garlic and tufts of rosemary, cooks slowly for later. Dauphinois potatoes, laced with a hefty biting cheddar, plips away on the shelf above. Rioja breathes on the worktop, next to the good glasses. The kids showered, their homework completed. Legs shaved, decent knickers on. Perfume. Lipstick.

The only thing pending is walking Sir Duke. But Dan will want to do that.

Everything's how he'd want it.

His Spotify plays in the background as I wait for the key in the door, the swollen wood given a shove. A happy—

But Dan's baffled, boyish arms flop uselessly at his sides. Only my hands reach for him, otherwise I'm frozen to the spot. Not my brain, though; the nerves set it clicking, searching through the archives like a Rolodex, trying to pinpoint how the hell he's caught me out.

'They said it was quick. That she wouldn't've—' Dan's eyes give, tears spilling down his cheeks.

He is limp in my arms. Delicate.

'Daddy!' Fran races down the stairs, jumping from the last with a plop.

'C'mere, love. Don't be worried.' Dan scoops her up in her cow-print onesie, his staggered, halting breaths stirring her curls. 'I've something very sad to tell you.'

Joel shuffles down too, followed by Toby. He leans against the bannister, giving Dan a wave. 'You all right, Dad?'

'Your Nana Yvonne.' Dan gulps, tears streaming. 'She's died, Son.' He crumbles, sobbing into my neck.

God. All these fucking, fucking feelings.

Toby's wide-eyed. 'Sorry, Dad.'

'Yeah. Sorry, Dad.' Joel scratches his nose as I give them proud, approving looks.

'It's so good to see you all.' He holds me so tight, I feel his heart.

Yvonne's dead.

Later, Dan picks at his luxury dinner between calls to family, on the same phone that, only this Monday, I fought with her on.

Yvonne's laughing somewhere. She'll know I'm going to hell.

Penny's eyes are hot slits of emotion, as red as her sunburnt nose. Clive, nursing one of Dan's Peronis, pats her leg rhythmically, shaking his head, doing all but saying 'It's just not fair, is it?'

Two hours in their company, and I've had not a single wicked thought. I'm channelling my Sunday school nuns; their selfless, unquestioning devotion to God – but just the selfless part.

Penny strokes my face. 'You look terrible, girl. I know, it's a shock, but eighty and all your faculties is a blessing.'

'Tough old bird,' chuckles Clive. 'Two cancers. A World War.' He puts an arm around Penny, glancing at his watch. 'But we've kept you up far too long, young Monica.'

'There's the sofa-bed in the boys' room. Why don't you rest a bit, get over your travelling?'

'I do feel much better being here.' Penny, as I knew she would, leaps on the invite. 'I don't much want to go home.'

'Stay if it helps, but I best be off back,' says Clive, which I know translates as making sure the bungalow's secure and as he left it, while he smokes a few Bensons without a lecture.

'Look after 'em, lad.' Clive slaps a hand on Dan's shoulder, the gesture stuffed with comfort, as Dan nods, his mouth determined. Dependable. Sincere.

I get out the spare bedding, still trembly – knocked for six, old Yvonne might've said.

'You're worrying me.' Penny reaches out, bloody stroking me again. 'You haven't looked like this since – you're not pregnant, are you?' Her hope fades fast; knows she's wrong. I may be in mental torment, my mind bloody shedding like a cheap fur coat, but I'm not stupid. 'Go on, get some rest, darlin'. He's going to need you.'

I cream my hands, watching Dan on his tummy, back where he belongs on the left side of our bed. Slipping in, I press myself to the warmth of his back, the safety of his smell. And falling in with his breathing, I break.

'Shh.' He pats my leg, sleepily. 'It's all right.'

'It's not.'

'No. It's not.' He wraps my snot and wet emotion in his arms, in his love. 'But I've got you – hey, I mean it.' He pulls my hands from my face, with a look so tender I want to purge my own beating heart. 'You're the best wife, Mon. The best wife.'

He wouldn't say that, wouldn't look at me that way, if he really knew me.

All these falsehoods.

Warped truths.

Waking into a hangover of sleeping pills, it's further cruelty to hear Budgie's voice downstairs. The two pills at 2am made for a fitful night of mostly tears – and the terrible gut intuition that Yvonne's dead and I'm the cause. Despairing in the darkness, I fought every taunting demon, trying to rationalize the impossibility of all my shit mysteriously aligning to slay Yvonne down. Because I can't escape how every wrong this week rests solely on my shoulders – and behind Dan's back. Me, the lapsed Catholic, knows far too well that sinners get punished – Lord, often without any sinning involved at all. Thou shalt not . . . I must've done the lot by now, and if it *was* the phone fight that set Yvonne on her way to Paradise City . . .

. . . I reckon she might've found those pearly gates closed. Even with my fatberg guilt, nothing could change my thinking that Yvonne was anything other than rotten.

But I still feel terrible about it.

I'm unfamiliar with death. For the family it is ritualistic, a chance to gravitate back as one. Unity. Their collective grief is mind-blowing.

'Remember when you got picked on; what were ya – six, seven?' Budgie reminisces, loud from downstairs. 'Proper good girl Pen was, y'know? Well, Mum, blimey – when she found out . . . She went marching up his house, ho-ho, didn't she?'

'She did,' Penny says in a flat-lined voice. 'She did.'

'Got that little bugger, gave him a right good bollocking. Never bloody did it again.'

It's 8.05am. Joel pokes round my bedroom door, his curls abstract and misshapen. 'Do I have to go down?'

I slip into my dressing gown. 'If you want breakfast.'

'I'll starve, then.' His moody little screw-face disappears.

Sir Duke rushes to greet me as I stick my head in the living room, keeping him close. 'Morning, everyone. Tea?'

With a weak smile and a sniffle, Penny says, 'What a godsend you are.'

I wasn't always a godsend. Penny's got form for altering the contrast of her online photos of me – or posting them in sepia. My choc-a-block house grates; the nun-inspired self-lessness clearly left behind in yesterday.

Despite my double layers of brush cotton and arctic fleece, Budgie licks his lips, asking, 'Sleep well, did ya? Where's them boys, bloody layabouts.'

'It's Saturday.'

'Ha – Me 'n' Ray would've been up an' out with the old man by now, wouldn't we, Pen?'

Ray – Big Ray Crane – his reputation inflated, I suspect, by his absence – is the revered third sibling, who, on a business trip to Florida in 1986, never returned. No one knows much human detail about his life there, but everyone's curiosity is routinely sated by pictures of the beach houses he renovates. An earworm, from Penny's classic collection, is 'I've a brother across the pond. *In Real Estate*,' delivered with as much pleasure as if she were on the Keys dabbling in the property game herself. I've never met Big Ray, but now that it's likely, I've everything crossed that the distance might've opened his outlook – rather like it did for Nancy. I can only hope.

Penny pats Budgie's leg, small, placating little pats. 'It's 2019, darlin'.'

'Kids are wet flannels nowadays,' he sniffs. 'Doughballs. Useless.' He narrows his eyes, king of the castle in my living room, manspreading on my flower-power rescued Ercol. 'Two sugars, love.'

Dan's in the kitchen, stirring five mugs. With a gentle smile, he nudges mine towards me.

'I thought I'd take the kids out. Give you all some space.' Hugging him, the sicky strange gurgle in my gut returns. I'm starving, but not hungry. I don't think I'll ever be hungry again. And, shame on me, seriously – that despite all this angst, the thought it may mean I drop a dress size really does cheer me. 'Just a burst of air, to run off their energy.' And give us some respite, too.

At a little after eleven, me and the kids return with baguettes, only to find Dan gone to fetch Nancy from the station. His cousins bookend Penny, squeezing a hand each.

Gracie's here as well, sat at Budgie's shoeless little feet, snug in their Donnay socks. 'Need a hand?' she asks, prising herself from the floor, but Budgie puts a hand on her shoulder.

'Monica knows her way around her own kitchen.' He gives me a flashy one-second smile, but I don't flicker, just collect the dirty mugs, and exit.

This is my penance.

'Let me do something.' Leaning on the kitchen door, Gracie whispers, 'I'm begging you.' She's wearing a grey jumper dress, draped in such a way that it exposes a smooth round shoulder, like a boiled egg. Her tights have cat faces on the toes. Fran will want a pair when she spots them.

'Do everyone tea with milk. They can sugar themselves.'

Gracie claps her hands together, a bounce in her step as she heads for the kettle. 'I never know how to act at things like this,' she reveals immediately, turning the tap to pour straight into the spout. Water dribbles over its roundness, like tears. 'I know it's sad and everything. But—' She leans closer, conspiratorially. 'She was so old.' It comes out as, *soooo ooooooold*. 'Eighty. Can you imagine? *And* in her sleep. I'd call that perfect, though God help me living till then—'

'But I thought— What d'you mean, "in her sleep"?'

She beams, delighted to impart fresh gossip. 'You're well out the loop, mate – we were only just saying how the care home rang Dan in the end.'

So, Yvonne wasn't convulsing on her carpet squares, desperately ringing for help because I'd wound her up so spectacularly – the sole repeating image I've had since Dan's shock announcement.

'It was Dan who had to tell Penny. The home left her a message, but she couldn't bear to listen to it. Said she,'

Gracie's eyes grow wide, 'knew what it'd say. Freaky, eh?'

Christ. This'll no doubt trigger another round of mediums. I've been with Penny before, when I had no excuse quick enough. Whenever someone came through for me, the psychic used words such as 'tribal', 'earthy' and 'cultural-connections'. Watching *Gardeners' World*'s as earthy as I could ever stretch the dots, but I do believe in something higher, something after. I like to think God would be all right, if the church and the relics and the rules all vanished, and we were all just open-heart honest. Or sorry.

At my most open-heart honest, I'm not sorry Yvonne's dead. I'm glad she didn't suffer, but I'm gladder still that it had sod all to do with me.

And though I do try searching, I can't find it in me to be sorry for the sex, for this thing with Joe. Guilt I locate, without any effort at all. Shame, too, is easily found, highlighted by Dan's sorrow that I don't deserve to repair.

Without picking up her feet, Gracie shuffle-slides over to the fridge to view the photos stuck to it. 'Your kids are so cute.'

Head down, buttering the baguettes, I smile. 'I know.'

'And your other half.'

My smile grows. 'I know.'

'I'm always saying what a good-looking family you are. I asked where you're from, but Budgie – being Budgie . . .' She rolls her eyes, leaving it there.

'My mum's Trinidadian. Originally.' *Originally*. I loathe how distantly, how emptily I say it, like I'm talking about three-hundred-year-old ancestors and not the person I grew inside.

Gracie scans the fridge. 'I can't see her up here.'

'Na.' I act lightweight, engrossed in my task. 'We fell out.'

'Snap-sies.' Ignoring the small dish for used teabags in front of her, she makes a neat stack on the corner of the drainer. 'Mum thought Budgie was after her. We'd always been rocky, but that really broke it. Proper. You should've seen her face when she heard he had a bloody hot tub. Out of all my family, I've one cousin still speaking to me.'

'I'm sorry.'

'If they turn so easy, they're not worth knowing.' Though she couldn't look any downer, her mouth stays smiling. 'I got that off Pinterest.' She loads the tray I offer, and we carry our goods through to the front.

'Proper pickaninny-looking.' Budgie's got my New Testament splayed across his knee. 'No wonder they all flock here. Taste of bloody civilization.'

'Keep your voice down,' Penny hisses, its tickie-off ring hiding her amusement. Almost. 'I've never seen—' Reaching for my pictures, she spots me.

Budgie raises his denim-coloured eyes – sorry, but not sorry. 'Coming up with some comforting words.' He taps the red cover with his uncooked sausage fingers.

Heart banging, I snatch the pictures back, just as Budgie pulls out his old trick of playing defenceless, shrinking from me like an abused puppy – which is ridiculous, especially when he's got to be the second most intimidating man I've ever met.

The first was my own grandfather; the Giant.

It never takes much to fall into remembering Dad's family – so very similar to the family I now find myself part of.

Life's shitty repeating patterns.

Budgie and the Giant; noisy, empty cans – identical types of men. I've an identical memory, too, of a moment just like this one, the big man in the thick of family, who hang from his every sentence. Back then, the very same way as now, when I sit with my babies in the corner, I'd find a little spot to vanish in. I remember sitting tucked by my dad's feet, messing about with one of those portable record players – the kind recently reincarnated that has everyone thinking they're the first to appreciate vinyl. It came in a pale blue box, and I'd lost myself in the act of pretending to play the records. Then, in all the Giant's talk, I heard Mum's name.

I see the Giant, in his slacks and smog-coloured slippers, sporting a similar sneering look to Budgie's now, as he licked along the edge of his Rizla. I hear him again, too, those words, stitched deep in the early fabric of my four-year-old head. That mouth, snarling at my dad – '*your dirty black cunt of a wife*'.

At three foot small, I watched, as the Giant's audience laughed with him, playing along with the monster. That strained amusement, same as Budgie's wedding.

Dad, so Jesus on the cross defeated-looking, set me crying, as more words came, dipped in hate, aimed at her, Mum at home, with a 'headache'. I remember my fear when the Giant scooped me up, looking just like my dad, but only the shell, only his surface. *'I wasn't talking about you, Monica. Never you, love.'* His pity and tickles lifted me free of those words about my mum. Words I came to hear with frequency whenever I eavesdropped, words that filtered through regardless. Words I didn't understand, yet was glad, so very glad, weren't meant for me.

What came next was. Though aimed at Dad, full of fault, for breaking their norm, the fresh words were undoubtedly about me. *'It's a cruelty, poor mite. Better she'd not been born.'*

Dad tried, but the hurt had made his voice small, like he was vacuum-trapped, while the Giant pressed me to take home that lovely pale blue box, with the brass handle and hinges.

So, I did.

For years, I thought it was me that made the strain on the car journey back. My fault, too, for the look between my parents when Mum spotted that bastard record player, growing heavier and nastier and more burdensome the longer I carried it. Mum, swerving family get-togethers whenever she could. Dad, struggling to challenge the ignorance of his own flesh and blood.

Life's repeating patterns.

But I know better now.

Clinging to the residue of that shit-stirring memory, my heart's frantic.

'Give that back.' I point at the bible, do the clear, strong voice again, like I used on the phone to Yvonne. 'Find your own comforting words.'

Eyeballing me, Budgie reverts to his other stock expression. On two occasions where we've been alone, he's put his hands on me, with the same deadpan arrogance he's wearing now – as if I'm only meat. As if that's all I'm for. Though he's not touching me now, he may as well be.

And it's just fucking typical that Dan's vanished – never knowingly the witness.

'That's your two sugars.' Gracie breaks the moment, handing the biggest mug to Budgie, who barely nods a thank you.

I wish he was dead. That it was him in a mortuary drawer instead of Yvonne, so he'd never stick his fingers in my life again. Or touch that poor daft girl, so desperate to please him.

'Common thing, y'know, Monica.' Budgie's oozing everything I long to kick the shit out of. 'Storing personals in bibles. First thing we learnt on police training.'

There's a steadying sensation as Nancy pokes her head over my shoulder, carrying the freshness of outside and the glorious whiff of the chip shop. 'Weren't you a Special Cuntstable, Budgie?'

Eyes back to narrow, his lips pucker into a cat's bottom. 'It's Uncle Budgie to you.'

But Nancy's so dismissive, it's like he's made of air. Cradling the chips, she grinds a reassuring elbow into my side. Whispers, 'Old wanker.'

The bible gets a new hiding place, as everyone, including the kids, scoffs the delights from Nancy's crumpled chip-paper. My baguettes begin to harden, rather like my generosity of spirit. Revived slightly by emergency cling film and refrigeration, they'll do for lunches tomorrow.

If tomorrow ever bloody comes.

Sunday. 7.45pm. The third night of grief. With a Monday to prepare for, only the oldies remain. Gracie, too. Gracie and The Crones – it sounds like a really out-there prog-rock band. From the speaker pours piano and harmonizing, as out comes the brandy I'd finally replaced, Dan topping everyone up.

'Connie bloody Francis. What a voice.' Swaying to the music, Budgie raises his little shot glass to our ceiling rose with a wistful glisten in his eye. 'God bless you, Mum.'

I can't be hospitable for a single second longer.

Gracie, upstairs on the sofa-bed with the kids arranged around her, shifts to make room, and the scent of Penny's bedding wafts around me, her constant Youth Dew presence – Penny will never die. They're all glued to *Strictly*, munching their way down a box of mint Matchmakers like beavers.

'Where's Nana Yvonne?' starts up Fran.

'Cold and stiff in the hospital morgue,' huffs Toby.

'What's a morgue?'

'Where dead people go, before they're buried.' Toby leans closer to her. 'Or burned.'

Fran squeals as I give him a warning look. They're tired, though, out of sorts – more like me than I realize. This takeover is wearing thin for all of us.

I seek refuge for a bit in my bedroom and check my phone, hidden in the pile of uniform I'm yet to iron, despite the perfect order of Friday. The battery's dead. Connecting, it comes to life with a blank screen. No missed calls, no notifications.

'It's a relief, really.' Dan perches on the edge of our bed to put his socks on. Grey today, with a wacky splash of neon green at the heel and toes. 'All planned. All paid for. We just alert the directors when Big Ray gets the go-ahead to fly. He's had all sorts of health trouble himself.' Sinking into my comfort marks his first falter this morning. It's hard to let him go. 'Maybe it's time we did a will.'

'Stay home, Dan. They'll understand.'

'They'll think it's a Barcelona hangover – I can't have that.' His good posture returns, shoulders back, broad and go-getting. 'I'd like to invite Mum and Dad for—'

'I'll do a cottage pie.'

'It's just . . . the kids are a distraction—'

'I know. It's fine.'

Eyes soft, he smiles. 'Love you.'

And the guilt stirs again.

I abhor lateness, but to avoid Joe, Fran gets to school at 9.15. With apologies, I quickly inform Miss Banks of our weekend tragedy, requesting to collect Fran early, too.

Back home, I vacuum crumbs and vanish the mug stains from surfaces, removing all traces. But the weekend still feels a violation. It makes home not feel like mine. And I keep replaying Budgie, mocking me and my absent parents.

Absent. Until someone dies. Or goes all amateur detective when a house goes up for sale. Until our distance shrinks so small that they're looming again.

But I must tidy, before the next grief invasion. Make my home mine again. Take back control. It takes three hours to put things right. Only in the polished order of things do I return the bible to its rightful spot.

Though I know it's only temporary.

A night in her own bed has helped infinitely; the crumpled desolation's smoothed back into the rounded, buxom Penny we all know – only a little quieter, with moments of great distance in her eyes, as she passes beneath the kid chatter about schoolmates and unjust teachers.

I clear up while Dan puts Fran to bed. It's when we're on the last dregs of coffees, moments before they'll slip into their coats and depart, that Penny mentions the photographs.

Straight away, Dan's on it, full of questions.

'Budgie found some pictures,' I explain, loose and easy – as if none of it matters. 'In that little bible up there.'

'Of your family?'

'I didn't know they were there.' Smoothly; margarine over his doubt. 'D'you want to see?'

154

'Oh, Mon, if you don't mind.' Penny's grabby hands are out before I've even lifted my arse from the sofa. Grief, clearly, can only hold the eternally nosey down for so long.

In an agony of slow motion, her eyes move over the first image. It's as if a surgeon's made an incision down my chest. There's a rivet of blood, like a pulled zip, as she gobbles the picture up. Wedging in a sterile implement, the surgeon jacks up my breast plate as Penny peers deeper into the gap.

She gasps, covering the image like she's won at a game of cards. 'Couldn't you be Joel.' She's holding the Polaroid. A Christmas Day new camera test shot. Me, cross-legged near our artificial tree, baubles on the tinsel branches, cradling a Tiny Tears. I'm beaming, delighted to be a child mother, the yellow-haired doll in one hand, her matching yellow potty in the other. The contrast of the picture is so high that if I hadn't all that hair, I'd pass as white. An enormous afro, any curl eradicated because I've overbrushed. I look white. I've had the same thought every time I've ever looked at this picture.

'Look at those eyes! Brown as gravy boats.' It's not the most flattering of parallels, but there's no malice in it. She passes the picture to Dan, which he takes with great reverence.

'We should blow this up, put it somewhere, the kids . . .' Dan's handed another. In this one, only the strong colours remain, the rest bleached and faded. A little black girl in a red cotton dress. Red bows round her hair worn in bunches, like Minnie Mouse ears. She's stood among rocks and sand and great tufts of foliage as a distant sea churns and froths in the background. A skinny, serious girl in a red dress. The same gravy boat eyes as mine.

The surgeon, rooting around, discovers a nerve. Gives it a push.

'What a find,' Dan whispers. He takes the final one. Me, Mum and Dad on holiday. We're sat on a sea wall, me between them. Mum in a tangerine jumpsuit and matching court shoes, her limbs oiled and sheeny. Dad, white tennis shorts, a lemon shirt, unbuttoned halfway. I'm about ten, with large gappy front teeth, and those braids. Dan turns it over. Looping writing slants to the right – *Malta, 1990*. 'Crikey, the kids are going to love these.'

'Yes.' Dismissive, evasive, closed. Their eyes linger over the pictures as they pass them back and forth with little gasps.

'I can see Dan in him.' Penny points to my dad. I wonder what that means.

Did I seek out a man like my father on purpose? Have I issues – not Oedipal, exactly – maybe Oedipal for girls. And Dad was a good man, the sort you'd want to replicate. A decent man, just like Dan. Entirely undeserving of a daughter like me. Of a woman like my mother—

I'm saved, by a cool hallway and a text message. Joe.

Kathryn (School): Next week? 😎

I close my eyes, press my forehead against the smooth gloss of the bannister. As I breathe through my nose, Joe and me return in flashes, on the tumbled earth of that riverbank, lost in absolute urgency.

There is nothing, nothing, nothing I want more than to get out of this house. To do it again.

'Only Nancy.' I take my place back on the sofa, smoothing my skirt that's pleated and therefore never smooth. The material quivers beneath my touch, and I sit on my hands quick, just as Dan's clamps down on my thigh.

'This is a sign, Mon, don't you think – to get in touch.'

The air disappears as my claustrophobia returns. How the fuck to tell him I've already bloody done it? I can't breathe, can already see Dan's mind working, plotting some purposeful Cilla Black hero mission to reunite us.

'Think about it. That's all I'm asking.' He squeezes me again. 'It'd be nice, wouldn't it, if something good came from all this?' He looks to his mother, who's gazing at him like the second coming.

But not all families are like theirs. Dan and his would never understand.

Talk of tomorrow begins, kind rounds of thanks for dinner. Coats on and arms linked, Penny blows us dramatic kisses goodbye like they're skipping town for ever.

Driving away, with my history on their fingertips – which I can't ignore any longer.

11

YOLO

I kick off my boots, shedding my winter layers across the navy carpet of a Southwark Travel Den; seconds from Borough Market, a stroll from Tate Modern. Miles and miles from our lives in the village.

The room is chilly with inoccupation. It needs heating up and bringing to life, for the windows to steam and the heat to rise. Just like me.

'Anyone'd think you only wanted my body,' Joe says, removing his jumper anyway, the one he wears quite regularly, now I'm growing accustomed to the contents of his wardrobe. It's a revelation – getting to know someone in tiny snatches of moments; what might be discussed by freshly dedicated lovers over an intense weekend, we've been drip-fed over weeks at a time. It's kept us hungry.

It's kept us desperate.

'What's happened?' he tries, but I shake my head. Joe's got to silence it all, snuff it gone; I don't want to think of anything but this.

My climax leaves me sharp, alive – an unexpected laughter escaping from me. It sounds fabulous. Clinging to my shaking body, Joe begins to laugh also.

His weight stops my lungs from opening fully, to have enough air to roar properly, and sandwiched in this gap, breathless between his gut and the mattress, I finally get myself back.

'Better?' he asks eventually, once subdued enough to speak. He twitches his buried cock, prompting an answer, and the reminder of him so connected is rather rousing. 'Let's have a kip – then you can tell me all about it.' Peeling himself off me, he rolls onto his back and, like every man I've ever known, enters instant slumber. I close my eyes, too.

Because it is all about the YOLO, these days. You do, only live once.

And this, Joe, here. This is my medicine.

I'm not a natural over-sharer, therefore it's again rather alarming to catch myself revealing my woes to Joe – and I don't know whether it's because of his job or our phantasmagorical connection that I'm able to.

'There's something like old Oedipus – Electra.' Joe's thumb draws small circles on my wrist, soothing more than it perhaps should. 'I wouldn't worry. Everyone's got a dash of some complex or another.'

'Unless you're normal.'

'Normal is only what people choose to show you. On my life, nobody is. How're the funeral plans?'

'All-consuming. I'm being kind, but they've taken over – like woodworm, like the Gestapo. *"Proper pickaninny-looking."* I mean, how fucking dare he?'

'You're right, of course you are,' Joe says, 'but it can't be that you've just suddenly discovered they're bigots, surely?'

'Of course not. But I've always just sucked it up. Because I'm paranoid, apparently, thin-skinned – which I can be. And all right, perhaps Penny's easier and, yes, the kids are her world, but, since that fight—'

'What fight?'

It comes out in a rush, matter of fact at first; the Budgie shit and Gracie's bloodied dress. But then I begin skirting around implicating Dan's reaction. And even to be thinking of a word like that implies Dan's in the wrong. He's wrong.

'It's a wonder he can stand it.' Joe nibbles the rims of my ears; an affection I adore, supplied by a stranger with an instinct. He groans suddenly, extending a leg to wiggle his ankle. 'Cramp. Shit, it's agony.' He stands, performing strange little stretches. As he adjusts, his thigh muscles contract. They are magnificent. Solid. Distracting.

But I must ask. 'What d'you mean, *it's a wonder he can stand it?*'

'He should've stamped it out from the start,' Joe says, after a lengthy silence. 'Instead of addressing their flaws, he's projected the problem back on you. It's deeply unkind.'

'He's not that bad.' I say this, because it's natural defence to protect my husband, but Joe's right. Dan's always silenced me, if it meant protecting them. The originals. The important ones.

'It sounds like you pander to a man-child, who offers you zero stimulation or support, so how's he ever going to hit you where it matters? You're far too evolved.'

I prickle. 'Is that your professional diagnosis?'

'Professional, personal – it makes no odds. He's an Essex boy. The offspring of nouveau riche white flighters. The worst kind.'

'And what are you?'

'I'm Joe. Don't box me in.' He kisses my head, spooning me into his warm body. 'Don't spend your life bending, Monica.'

'There's nothing wrong with a bit of bending, for an easy life.'

'There is if it crushes your soul. I don't want you to have a crushed soul.' Joe smooches his way down my body, his clean citrus bite filling my senses. 'I wanted to take you out, not put you in a room – I'd have liked to get you a bit drunk. Watch you eat.' He plants fat wet kisses on my crimplene stomach. 'Perhaps go dancing, to something throbbing and slow, until it all gets too much.'

'And we end up back in a room.'

'There's food from heaven in spitting distance. Let's fill up.' He gazes down at me, this beautiful man, saying all the right beautiful things. 'We can always come back.'

Borough Market on a wintry lunchtime doesn't feel it in Joe's company. Dan's always hated it here, the touristy disorder agony on his senses. With a bottle of rosé, we take our paella and plastic flutes and find ourselves an ice-block doorstep that doesn't smell terribly pissy. Joe leaves me the plumpest mussel, and I let him have the last king prawn. Joe doesn't eat, but hoovers, devouring with slick shiny fingers that keep my stomach locked in longing.

Holding hands along the South Bank, we see our reflection in a shop window. 'Take a good look.' Joe pulls me closer, as if hypnotized by the glass version of us. 'You'd better get used to it.'

As much as I'm tempted, already more than I'd like to admit, I can't just shed a husband because someone new sparks my soul. It's like Joe's read my thoughts, for there's a sudden strangeness about him, which he smiles to hide.

'What's the matter?'

'Affairs, cheating, it all sounds so . . . it doesn't fit what this is.' Joe's breath plumes into the sky. 'I don't even know if you think this is as special as—'

'I think this is very, very special.' I take his hands, pulling him close. 'You can call us what you like. I'll be anything you want.'

'Didn't we talk about this,' he says, with the most luxuriant authority, 'about no more bending for others?'

'Ah, but the difference is I want to bend for you.' His eyes are like those mood rings I'd wear in the nineties, with the rubbish gemstone that'd change to the light or the temperature rather than to actual feelings.

But Joe's eyes. God, Joe's eyes are the real thing.

'I want to do things to you that words haven't been invented for.' As his voice rumbles from his body into mine, I can't help thinking that I'm the luckiest bitch in the universe. I reckon I could cope with anything if I've got this – my freakout in the intermission; magic, at the middle of my life – that no amount of time apart, or reasoning, makes the slightest bit weaker.

We duck into Tate Modern, with its chimney of handsome brick, and are soon giggling over random slashes in canvas, and scribbles we're sure we could've done, could even replace for these ones, and no one would be any the wiser.

'It's always the way.' Joe deflates just from saying it. 'The minute someone of note says something's brilliant,' he waggles his hands in the centre of the stark white box of a room, 'then everyone – *even if it's shit* – will say its brilliant too. Sheep mentality. Humans are bastards for it.' It seems to have upset him, as if all the world's problems are toxic to his delicate free spirit. 'Pretending's bred a world of frustrated people, blaming their faults on everything but themselves.'

'Shall we just say bollocks, then? Vanish off somewhere, untouched by civilization.'

'Wouldn't that be something, me and you.' Joe kisses me, unselfconsciously, as if we're already there.

We could live in a ramshackle cottage, miles from everyone, where clocks and phones have developed the same

dangerous reputation as heroin – and it would be so beauti-
fully quiet. At night, we'd eat from the garden by candlelight
and listen to French radio, before retiring with cognacs the
size of goldfish bowls to fuck each other sideways.

Passing the gift shop, in the vast echo of disorienting
concrete, I remember the kids' beautiful present, my scarf,
not so long ago. It makes a flash of sorrow in my chest. A
disconnect, too; of the wrong way around telescope kind.
My family becoming small.

Unreachable.

'Another drink?' Joe suggests, saving me, pointing
upwards to the café in the clouds on level nine.

We kiss in the lift, hold hands while we order, and sit
glued tight at the strip of table overlooking the Thames. In
the violet sky of late afternoon, conquering my vertigo for
the sheer view of it, London is captivating. All that history
beyond the glass skyline, and all the people, too – their
stories; the big, bright superstars that've glittered here,
still twinkling in their deaths – and the little lives, those
lives like mine – the insignificant, blink and miss it's. With
all my heart, I hope that every breath ever taken here, of
those gone, and now, and the little glimmers coming,
know happiness. Happiness like mine and Joe's, in this
moment in the sky, looking out on the place I've always
loved most.

I had happy days as a kid here, too. Big loops around
Hyde Park. Stumbling on landmarks. The urban anonymity
was freeing, for all three of us. The memory stokes a little

warmth; a little hope. It makes me think of trying again. Of Dan in supporting role.

Dan. I'm shocked how very quickly I regressed into the duplicitous. The adulteress. It's like that old adage, of remembering how to ride a bicycle – which I can't – but the principle's the same; the contraption between my legs may change, but the skill is all my own.

My eyes move from Joe's thick platinum wedding band to the delicate slip of a ring I never take off, letting my fingers fall with delicious ease between the gaps of his. I wonder what he's thinking, what he hopes will come of us.

Nothing good. I could tell him that right now. Weak at the knees is an expression for the lightweights; this power between us floors me. Thrilling, as it's terrifying.

But not off-putting.

Our window speckles with rain as life teems on beyond, lights zipping across a distant pretty Southwark Bridge, the same colours as my dress. An unintentional match.

Like us.

12

Forwards

'Now.' Kathryn squishes her chin into her neck, with a look as if I really should take notice. 'Returned books are checked. Like this.' She flicks through *Wolf Hall*, creating a concertina blur of pages. 'You'd be amazed what falls out.'

I wouldn't. Not these days.

She breaks into laughter, her glorious bosoms quivering like perfect panna cottas. 'I couldn't believe it when I saw your application. I thought we must be destined.'

'Destined?' I follow her to the small YA section, a triangular structure four feet wide. She splits her pile of paperbacks, and we begin our searching.

'To be friends. We're rarely busy; it's mostly tea and convo. And biscuits.' She nods across to the central desk of peeling pale wood laminate, the packet of Hobnobs poking from her crossbody bag on top of it.

'So, who else volunteers?' All I can imagine is Lynda, taking over with her passive-aggressive energy, sterilizing the library shelves, Febrezing old people, snotty toddlers and the poor.

'Sooz and Fiona help. Gary too, when he can – and Lynda, till it clashed with her Wednesday yoga lunch. No one wanted to keep swapping.' Kathryn gives the shelf a quick dust before returning the books. 'Surname order, Monica. Top left and onwards, like an alphabetical snake. I'll pop the kettle on.' She stands, opening a door with an inside no bigger than a closet. There's a short bit of worktop with an old-fashioned silver tea kettle and a mug tree. 'I suggest you bring a mug; people can get very territorial. Use Lynda's for now.'

Shaking out the returned items, from a book drops a well-folded piece of A4, covered in rows of alternate coloured ink. In red biro reads: *R u going 2 talk 2 him?* Then the reply, in loopy blue: *No point, he's going with Tiff now. Slag.* Teen-girl notes I remember well. Perhaps Tiff's a modern-day me.

'Told ya.' Kathryn reads over my shoulder. 'Kindest thing is to chuck it. I once found a picture of Teresa in a Margaret Atwood. Naked, she was – in a deck chair. I'll never forget it.'

I can't help laughing with her. 'Who's Teresa?'

'You know; does mornings in the Co-op. With the wispy hair,' she confirms. 'Legs like a supermodel. Bald as a badger.' Kathryn works to steady the mug she hands over, lost to the giggles. 'So,' she says, going for the biscuits, 'sick of your house, too? I dreaded Thomas starting – madness, when I've got here, the WI, Rainbows.'

'Exactly that. Sick of cleaning cupboards that are already clean.' My fibs fall out so convincingly smooth these days. 'Sick of my own company.'

'Now, my sister barricades herself indoors instead; studying Child Psychology. If anyone needs a degree like that it's her. And, I know, Monica, that they're my nephews, but they're nightmares. Insomniacs, if you can imagine, all three of them.' Kathryn dunks a biscuit, turning the chocolate shiny and wet. A perfect half disappears in one mouthful, as she rolls her eyes in delicious delirium. 'She took an access course, through the Open University. They send the books, and every so often she sends them an essay. She's loving it, says her brain's having an affair with knowledge.'

I nod – do understand. My affair's flesh-based, I know, but I'm loving it all the same. I'm infinitely more organized, slimmer, happier in general. In the bath or when Dan's asleep beside me, I'm brave enough to text, deleting Joe's replies instantly. Our bite-sized communications come in texts and memes, from songs to delicious plates of food, to 280-character furiousness on the state of the world. With politics banned at home, it's another means to bond.

The sole evidence of us is the note Joe gave me after the first passion. On instinct, I touch the side of my armpit, pressing at my bra for the scrunch of it. Though I daren't put it down anywhere, I doubt many could read his truly atrocious handwriting anyway:

You are happiness.

Kathryn chats away, dragging an old rag across the crime fiction, as a woman opens the door, her hands clasping a stack of leaflets. She strides over, raising one for us to read.

Keep our Village GREEN. Hands off our open spaces!

'Building on the green?' Kathryn's aghast. 'Surely not.'

'Our outskirts, Kathy.' The leaflet lady is wax-jacket posh, just like the woman who chastised the boys recently for uprooting the tree in our front garden – until Dan showed his face. Because there's always a busybody, ready to interfere, some sneering, pinched misery, intent on making the small feel smaller. 'We'll be joined to the city centre before we know it, inheriting their problems.' She sniffs. 'The common cold is catching.'

The clichéd old bat's a bit late for protests, anyway. A new development is already approved for the edge of the village, bridging the gap between us and the city centre. A new school's proposed, a new train station – things that would be wonderfully useful. But it's progress. And cloaked by the nation's current penchant for nostalgia, progression incites tomato-faced furies – of epic proportions.

Before my own face betrays me, I return to the books, unwilling to kill my vibe. Things are pretty good right now; we're riding the wave of Dan's life's-too-short trip, making home altogether more sufferable. Sadly, Dan's renewed appreciation of us extends also to the extended, and if that wasn't enough, out further still, to the chilly periphery of the estranged – who he's still bloody desperate to contact.

Dan doesn't know about the friend request from Mum. Her slightly dated Facebook profile picture is a fresh ticking timebomb on his *people you may know* feed of semi-familiar faces. I'm still nurturing this secret, keeping her mine until I'm more comfortable with our connection, but even the mum stuff doesn't scare me much; Joe's monster cock and cracking good company make all that sufferable too – even if that does mean another olive-branch try with my parents. Because there's no escaping it; the kids needing the full picture of who they are and how they fit together. How they match. And so do my parents.

But I don't need to rush things. I'm in a nice warm spot, volunteering, doing shit, living my—

'. . . Infrastructure can't cope at the best of times, not to mention the rough sleepers – two on the allotment, only last week – *Albanians*,' she adds, as if this should make a difference. 'Living it up in someone's shed—'

'Is that a car alarm?' Kathryn cocks her ear towards the shut window and silent street beyond, but it gets the right reaction. Perhaps the allotment Albanians have ventured into carjacking. The second the woman disappears, Kathryn slam-dunks the leaflets into the bin. 'Living it up – on a bit of rock-hard winter veg?' Her reaction makes my own ground frost shift in a rush of sudden fondness for her. 'And I thank my lucky stars for my new-build, too.'

Our shared views are salving. Kathryn putting Westminster to rights makes me think of my dad, who I know without knowing will be as politically flummoxed as me right now.

Families. A kaleidoscope of matches. Deeper than skin.

By the time my first shift's over, I know how long Kathryn's worn a coil (three years – it'd be nice to test it out more), how long it took Lynda's hubby to recover from his vasectomy (five months, or was he holding out on purpose?) and that Miss Banks, Fran's teacher, is up the duff (look at her from the side, there's no disguising it). I also have an Open University access course application to fill out.

'I'm only saying, because I worry,' Dan tells me later, in the same simplified way he'd use with the kids. 'You're terrible under pressure. Isn't the library enough?'

'It's only home study. Part-time and a student loan, which I'll never earn enough to repay anyway.' I catch myself selling it up, when it's not even down to him. It's not as if I was consulted when he tried shoe-horning the kids into Budgie's boxing lair. Or when he said yes, yes, yes boss to another business trip in the spring. 'They mightn't accept me, anyway.'

But they'd better.

He forks up his peas, pushing and squeezing them into his mash. 'What did you choose in the end?'

'The Arts: Past and Present. History, philosophy – literature, too. A taster of it all, I suppose, to see what tickles your fancy. Going onwards.'

'Onwards?'

'Working towards the degree. Finished by the time Fran hits secondary.'

'At home?'

'Nothing's going to change.' I keep the 'I promise' in my mouth, must do a good enough job, for he nods, quite amiably.

'And your mum and dad.' Dan sips his red. 'At Christmas, Mon – of all times. I'm sure they'd be thrilled—'

'You don't know that.'

'How could they not be?' He nods upstairs to their three snoring grandchildren. 'When they meet them.' His pureness of answer is exactly how I'd reassure one of the children, with a simple logic, not to be looked beneath. I'm too suspicious for all that, need to inspect the taint always, but Dan smiles, a naïve excitement about him that makes me soften. 'I saw how you looked at those photos. Parents don't just stop loving. Would you?'

'Never. Never ever.'

Squeezing my hand, Dan chats his big reunion plans like it was all his idea, and, like most spouses who try, we compromise. In exchange for a Christmas Day of just us five, I'll invite my parents in the twilight gap between Christmas and the New Year.

13

Meet the Fuckers

'And the kids; putting real faces to those pictures, at last ...'
Hands on the wheel, Dan takes alternate glances between me
and the road, prepping me like this since we left the house.

Soon, we'll reach the neutral territory of – Dan's idea –
Mersea Island, where he'll meet my parents for the first time.
Mersea's all flatness and old folk – rosy cheeks and primary
colour gilets. Wellies, small pets and offspring lost to the
quicksand. And always the certainty that I'll be the sole
brown face on the seafront.

Only not today. Today there will be more of us.

'And look at us now.' Dan smiles so wide it must hurt.
'How fond Mum—'

'She still didn't have to come today.'

I sense the boys picking up our vibes like radars from the
backseat. Dan gives me a pleading look not to start, that

Penny and Clive invited themselves, that he didn't have the heart to correct them – correct her, mummy dearest.

It should've been just us. Affair guilt stopped me fighting for it.

The imminence of face-to-face Parkers and Petersens comes to me on high-tide waves of biliousness.

'And I still wish you'd said.' Dan expertly flips the shit back on me. 'That you'd seen yours.'

I've managed to tweak the Mum visit into something infinitely more palatable. It was behind Dan's back, naughty me, but *after* he suggested it. Grief, work and a busy Christmas have muddled time and place; Dan's order of events now hazy. To my benefit.

And should Mum mention Joe and his gas guzzler, it's my word against her imagination. Yet I'm hopeful – more for the kids, of course – that there'll be no conflict today.

We drive past a chippy, a closed butcher, a phone box sans phone. The sky darkens to proper grey, and Dan starts the wipers in anticipation.

'What if they don't show?' Joel asks.

Dan swipes aimlessly in the back for Joel's legs. 'For God's sakes.'

'But if they don't, though?'

'They texted this morning.' I swallow, picking at the hang-nails I dug free myself. Texts, now. Another technological tentacle lessening our distance.

Toby's head appears between the seats. 'Are you excited, Mum?'

I'm certainly curious. To visually fit us together, see if I've got it right, that the boys do indeed have my dad's weird, almost absent earlobes, and other insignificances that'd never concern the close-knitted —

Dan pokes me.

'I am. Of course I am.' I give big believable smiles and happy eyes, all for Dan. 'It's just nerves. Give Fran a nudge; we're almost there.'

Fran wakes up in the same bewildered angry fog as she entered the world – only now cross with the boys, too. Catching her slappy hands in the mirror, Dan ticks her off. 'None of that in front of your new Nan and Grandad, madam.'

Nan and Grandad.

Everything tightens as, steeling myself, I inhale. Unapologetic. Be unapologetic. I say the word in my head again. My life, my choices. Nothing to do with Avril and Alan Parker. Breathe out . . .

First to arrive, we hover in the bar in our best, the kids sipping from black straws stuck in glass bottles of Coke. Through the double doors, watching my parents approach, I'm officially jelly; if it weren't for Dan's arm around me, I'd be wibble-wobbling all over the flagstone floor. And I can't stop the yearn in me, either, that comes from the sight of my father's keen, open face which makes me long to run and sling myself around his middle. Next to him, my mother takes dainty little steps holding his arm. She's come colourful; beneath a cream coat she wears a parrot-green dress that clings so very cleverly to all her best bits. Bits I'm proud to inherit, even if it does mean I exist outside of recommended weight guidelines.

My father sweeps his hand through his hair left to right, before reaching for the door, as Dan grabs the handle to help. 'I'm Daniel. It's very nice to meet you.' Their hands fly out, ready to shake; Dan's open politeness matching my dad's like a good hand of Snap. Good, gentle men.

'Alan.' Dad's smile leaves Dan. For me. 'Monica.'

My three croaky syllables bring my heart and guts to emotional boiling point. But I don't show it. As his eyes travel my face in wonder, mine head for the floor. 'Hello, Dad.'

'Moni,' Mum says, with an arch of a brow and a smidgeon of knowing, before the look gives as she studies the kids, hanging behind me, one at a time. The only hint of emotion I can find is the sudden tension in her neck, as if all at once it's terrifically difficult to swallow. 'Hello, children.' It's the softest voice I've ever heard her use.

Three sets of eyes take in the new pair of olds.

I dig my nails into my palms for distraction. There are murmurings of replies, but nothing stand-out. And though I'm very aware that this moment doesn't belong to me, I can't help wondering what their minds and eyes are processing, two sets identical to the small dark woman in front of them. Her hair's in its usual ballerina bun, complete with her clever less-is-so-much-bloody-more perfect make-up. Mum's coat, unbuttoned, reveals that vivid green dress beneath.

Minuscule pearls decorate her minuscule ears, as she clutches her bag with a vice grip.

Dan slides behind the kids, gathering them in front of him. 'This is our eldest, Joel.' He places his hand flat on Joel's head, before moving on to pat Toby's. 'Middle child by eight and a half minutes, Tobias. And Frances.'

'Hello,' the children chorus, awestruck.

My mum coughs into a tissue, her eyes luminous, dare I suggest, wet. Blimey, she can't be moved to tears.

'Sorry we're late, folks.' Clive opens the door, delivering him and Penny in another chilly gust. He does the greetings as Penny bustles round with breathy hellos and air kisses, fluttering mostly in the direction of my dad, her amiability miles away from my early treatment.

'Excuse me.' A confident, long boy resembling a Quentin Blake illustration appears with a handful of menus. 'Your table's ready.'

Tailing him, we file out, Fran stopping in front of my mother.

'You're really Mum's mummy?' Fran asks her.

'I . . . I am.'

Fran's arms outstretch for a cuddle. As her little fingers hook behind that cream coat, Mum's shoulders start to shake.

'Bless you, little Frances.' Choked, Mum strokes Fran's frizzy wisps across her temple, chucking her under the chin.

'I'm Fran, or sometimes Franny at school.' Fran's big eyes roll the circumference of her sockets, making my mother smile. 'D'you want to sit next to me?'

'I . . .' It's as if Mum's been struck by a thunderbolt, splitting through her middle, exposing a previously undiscovered centre of mush. Rather than hiding it, her warmth doesn't fade. 'I'd like that. Very much.'

One roast special and half a bottle of Chablis later, and I still can't stop my eyes zigzagging between my parents and the kids, side by side, scrutinizing every microscopic similarity. They don't know I'm doing it, of course. I'd moon at the restaurant before I'd ever give them that.

But I know – can sense them – doing it, too. Matching us up with the last thing holding us together: our motherfucking D N of A.

'Three grandchildren,' Penny says to my parents, sat across the table. 'Your Mon's a brilliant mum, you should be very proud.' She squeezes my hand before performing her security check, patting her perfect hair, then hovering a hand over her throat for a pretend cough. 'I practically lived with them at the start.'

'We're abroad a lot these days, though,' Clive says, as Penny stiffens. She'd be frowning, if the fillers would let her. 'Ever been to Tenerife?'

Even when they're in Spain, Penny's on permanent Skype. And where've my parents been? A one-change train journey, which with good connections could put us at each other's doors in under an hour. The air con, vicious and unnecessary, pours from a ceiling vent behind me. I rub my hands together, warming them, noting their pale brownness, now a sallow winter yellow, then think of Fran's little hands, hugging her nan for the very first time.

They're here. Right in front of me. In a pub on the Essex coast. Making small talk. Breathing my air. Breathing and talking and living and learning my life. Because they don't know me at all.

But I sense how much they'd like to. It's overwhelming – with the same lost and found sensation as when I saw those pictures in her bible. And I can't deny, there's a speck of it in me, too – like the flicker of a heartbeat on a twelve-week scan.

Hope.

I loathe myself for still possessing any at all. I find I'm conflicted a lot these days; assuring myself in one moment that I've found balance because of my outlet with Joe, to then being appalled by my infidelity; that I could even think it, let alone act on it. But then, I'd be lying too if I said it hasn't been tempting to ring Joe over Christmas, to wallow in his clever take on all this. Have him fuss, lick my wounds, let our physical gratification emolliate it into nothing.

'I brought some photos you might like to see,' Penny says to my parents, breaking my thoughts.

Mum sits opposite, next to Fran, the pair of them bookended by Dan and my father. 'If that's okay with you.' She checks with me, careful on the floor of landmine eggshells. Fran crayons in her paper placemat, scribbling slowly over the small dot-to-dot as my mother watches, her hand draped across the back of Fran's chair, the other sipping the same glass of red she ordered when our mains came out. Her restraint is saintly.

I'm a good drinker, only ever becoming louder, or increasingly childish, but I wonder if those rules apply today. There's a delicacy about me, a new vulnerability that's more unsettling than the usual self-criticism. It's like I can't fully trust myself.

With a yes from me, Penny gives an excited whimper and sets about rummaging in the enormous leopard-print shopper at her feet. My father moves smoothly to the side, making space for Penny, who plops between my parents and flicks open an album.

'Look at you, Joel-y. Gorgeous blue eyes then.' Penny rubs a jewelled digit back and forth across the picture, wistfully. 'Both their father, at birth.' She gestures for her glass, still in her abandoned spot.

'That's certainly changed, it seems – they're your image, Monica,' Dad says, with a gentle smile that warms then sets me at odds again.

'Dominant genes. Must be.' Penny reaches to tousle Joel's hair. He ducks her hand, swerving again to stop her from grabbing his nose. Catching himself, Joel looks shyly towards my parents. All the kids are operating in an odd, muted respect. Strange, because we are strangers.

'But you, Toby. You're your father, clear as day.' Penny flicks to another page, her activity of matching genetics always more competitive than necessary. 'And hair like yours and Mon's,' she says to my mum, prematurely relieved she's remembered to add in, 'which though lovely,' before telling the truth, 'would be so hard for the kids to cope with.'

'Oh, I don't know, what about those lovely little plaits your mother would sit and do? They'd last almost the whole week, wouldn't they, Monica?' says my father, and I'm touched he remembers the Sunday ritual, when he was usually drowning in marking. 'I reckon you were the only child at St James's that never had nits.'

'You've never had nits?' Dan's astonished. 'Me and Nancy had them, more than once.'

'Well, nits do gravitate towards clean hair – so I'm told.' Penny raises her brows, forgetting she's meant to have evolved from wank like this.

I can't resist checking for Mum and Dad's reaction, but they aren't looking at me. They're instead doing the very thing I've spent years perfecting – pretending not to notice, letting it glide over them as if it's nothing, though I'd put a nifty on it that it'll be discussed, in a tired, unsurprised, slightly superior way, over cups of tea tonight before bed.

And I thought I was good at pretending. My parents are masters at it.

'Was Mon a mischief as a little girl?' Clive chips in. He gives me a small shadow of a wink and I swallow, tight and grateful.

'A funny little thing. She'd live in a pigsty – always, always, with her nose in a book.' Dad's bushy fair brows compress his forehead into folds. 'Even when she was on the toilet.'

An easiness comes, as the kids crease up laughing.

'What was it,' my father asks, so keen to engage, a warmth about him I've neglected to remember, 'the one you'd read over and over—'

'*Little Women*,' Mum says. 'It was *Little Women*.'

I wonder if she remembers when I wanted so desperately to be Amy March that I smothered my face and the backs of my hands in Sudocrem then talc. How she'd flown at me with a flannel, forever stained by the remnant whiteness; a grease film within its fibres. How I endured the scolding – which was always best – '*What's so wrong with your pretty brown face, Moni, that you want to pretend to be a white girl?*' – as her own laments to be lighter looped my head. How our lives became her accusing me of all the things I knew she was guilty of, too. And me, showing always the respect, that absolute respect not to challenge her.

Proper Trinidadian deference, apparently. But, then, I wouldn't really know.

And where were the books with the black or brown or rainbow-striped heroines, anyway? I'd loved Katy Carr too, and most of the girls at Mallory Towers and St Clare's, though I knew, through both reading and my parents' aversion to Ms Blyton, that should I ever have rocked up to either boarding school, I'd never have quite fitted in.

'What a lovely house.' Mum points to the loose photograph of Penny and Clive, stood outside their front gate in Tenerife, Penny clutching a name plaque with a sweaty gleeful face.

'That's Villa Clivenny,' Penny says proudly. 'Our second home.'

Remembering the swings and climbing frame when we parked up, I choose air. 'Who fancies a run around outside?'

The further the kids get from the table, the more buoyant they become, and by the time they've hit the adventure playground, they're the familiar creatures I recognize once again. Slumping against the pub's exterior, I let loose the world's longest sigh, my breath pluming, dragon-like. It's freezing, but that won't make me rush back. The kids are lost in their world, I don't see why I shouldn't lose myself in mine.

'A penny for 'em, Monica girl – though they must be priceless.' Clive chuckles, the door closing behind him as he approaches.

'I don't know what I'm thinking.' I can't make sense of myself, work out what's taking precedence; me being happy they're here, or me glued fast to the resentment that's powered me to get by, to get on, all my adult life.

Lighting up, Clive nods understandingly, the wind sending his second-hand smoke in my face.

Toby charges towards us, pink-cheeked and vital. 'Can we run to the back, Mum – just to that fence?'

There's only one outcome for the race, and he knows it. The field stretches appealingly before us, the white picket finish line striking in the fading light. It's not far, but it's distance enough for me to pinch Clive's fag without them seeing. There's suddenly nothing I want more.

'Only if when you get there, you wait for Fran and do a fresh race back.'

Toby bounds over to the others with shouts of – *She said yeah! Get ready!* And as soon as they cluster together and begin to run, I swipe the fag from Clive's fingers.

'I think you've earned that.' His laughter morphs rapidly into a coughing fit.

I like Clive. It's always been clear that he's a fair man, just too bloody rigid to be comfortable with change. Years back, he shared the story of what made him leave east London, the only place he and Penny had ever lived. Clive made two things clear; one, he wasn't frightened – just fed up, and two, he was sick of being outnumbered, he was the new minority, and couldn't stand witnessing his patch of England deteriorate. Though I'd appreciated his honesty, I knew he'd have said more, so much more, had I not been in earshot. Unlike his wife, Clive's never directly insulted me. He's been forever just enough tactful.

'I want to punch them both. Really hard. Then hold them, and never, ever let go.'

'Y'know, it's not usually me that does the telling round here, but I give you this, girl – none of us walk through life perfect. Forgiveness will feel better than all that hurt, I can tell you.'

Toby's reached the fence – first, as predicted. Joel is close by and Fran's barely halfway across. I take a final speedy pull and pass it back, before kissing Clive's cheek.

'All right, love. It's all right,' he says, awkward and gruff as he holds me to him, all pub dinners and Guinness scented.

Had I a dad like this, a comfort from the clam shell mum who'd never open, pretending our life of missing parts was normal, things might've been different. But if letting the weight of the past go – freeing myself, of thoughts like this – comes from building bridges, then I'll try. I'll try my best.

Clive pulls a navy glove from his pocket, wiping with great gentleness beneath my eyes. 'Let 'em in. What's the worst that can happen?' Grateful now that he stepped outside, I watch Clive stub his fag, before heading back indoors.

I beckon for the kids, gulping wine to replace the smoke smell. They stagger back, collapsing against the wall to catch their breath, and the dangle of dessert gets everyone seated again in a passable air of good manners.

A flushed and emotional Penny sits with her arms folded, listening to my father.

'But the aggravation.' Dad's shaking his head. '2016 spawned a hostile nation. It's unsettling.' Christ; in ten minutes away from the table?

At least they're not discussing me.

'You're like him.' Penny gestures towards Dan. 'Taking it personal. But no one's bothered about Mon. Or you, Avril.' She smiles at us both as if it's her that makes the rules, her who bestows that big green tick of approval, like the fondness she at last found for me. 'It's them that's here illegally. We don't know who's who. It *is* unsettling – *for us.*' Her flustered face makes me long to flee back outside. 'When we're out, we're out. Besides, we've lived through worse.'

Saving our ears from further savagery, Clive, reading with fixed concentration from the chalkboard list of desserts, reaches out, patting Penny's hand – and her – into silence.

Joel groans, filling the gap.

'Must be all you kids hear these days,' Dad says with a sympathetic grin.

'School, a bit – but we don't talk about it at home. It's too contentious.' Swinging his legs, Joel does a wide Cheshire Cat grin, pleased with the fancy word he's thrown in.

'*Contentious.*' Toby mimics, in a prim and proper voice. '*Soooo contentious.*'

'Shut up. Bet you can't even spell it.'

'Beat you running just now, though, didn't I?'

'Can I wash my hands?' Fran holds her felt-tip stained fingers in my mum's face. Her hard expression melts in an instant, as with a happy little nod she takes Fran's hand.

Ignoring Dan's telepathic plea to stay seated, I follow them.

Mum stands behind Fran at the row of sinks, massaging her hands gently under the tap. 'You're so well behaved,' she compliments, making Fran squirm in delight. Then, beneath the noisy blast of the hand-dryer, Mum approaches me. 'How dare you bring all that back to my doorstep?' she hisses, deadly-looking, away from Fran's eyeshot. 'All that time with your father's kin and you learn nothing? And there was I, hoping for once you'd been honest. Lies. Always. Worms in my head.'

'But I have missed you. Missed you both, so much.' Inches between us. Between closeness. I take her hand.

'Missed?' She shakes me off, and again I'm struck numb. 'You just got sick of being the only one on your team.'

'There's some truth in that. But not in a horrible way . . . Joel's been struggling.'

'Life's one big struggle – not that the Peggys of the world have any real clue.'

'You hate me so much, you can't see past that – even for them?' Crying in front of her. Me weak and her unmoved, as forever it's been. In her marble face, I meet her marble stare. 'Well. I hate you, too.'

The hand-dryer clicks off. Fran dries the leftover damp on her dress, but before she's finished, I've grabbed her and gone.

The enthusiasm over mediocre desserts is excruciating, yet it salves the stop-start small talk as I return to the table. No one notices my upset. The kids smash their brownies and ice-cream, keen to get back outside. Volunteering to keep an eye and checking for his smokes, Clive helps Fran on with her coat, careful not to catch the collar with her chocolate ice-cream moustache.

'This here reminds me of your old workplace,' Mum says to me, smooth as a fresh polished ice-rink. Ignoring my dad's pained rigor mortis expression, she does what she's best at. I only wish I was surprised. 'Such a hard worker. And quite the favourite.'

'Avril—' Dad stops before he's even started, with a floor-grazing look of utter disappointment that gives me the old sinking feeling. It's the look I fear the most, that comes to me in premonition when I'm verging on sleep – but on Dan's face, instead of my father's. Omens, like rosary beads, preying on my conscience.

'Am I wrong, Monica?' But I don't answer. And I won't look at her.

'Stop.' It comes louder from my dad, making Mum's shoulders rise as mine do when I'm put in my place, setting in brittle ice-pick stiffness. He clears his throat, running a finger around the inside of his already gappy collar.

'I waited tables when I was a girl!' Penny says, as if this most basic coincidence makes us twins as well. 'A barmaid, too – till I fell with Nancy.'

'I wasn't old enough to work the bar—'

'Or old enough for the boss, but that didn't stop you running off with him.' Mum slices through her cheesecake with the edge of her fork. Stabbing it up off her plate, my gut freezes solid.

'Not that it matters any more.' My father jumps on the end of her words. Reaching across the table, his gentle fingers hesitate before he sets them, tests them, over mine. 'Monica. I am . . .' He stops, swallows. 'Thank you, for having us here today.'

Everything blurs as his touch grows a little stronger. Snatching myself away, protecting my hand within the grasp of the other, someone's wine topples, glugging over the tablecloth like a slashed artery.

Penny dives for her shopper before the red rainfall reaches it, knocking it out of the way like a Premier League goalie.

'Can we have a cloth here, somebody, please?' She stands to inspect herself, relief all over her face from her good sense to wear black.

Quentin Blake boy drags over a wheelie-bucket as the roomful of gilets and windswept hair pretend not to notice my tears and snot and crude open-heart surgery from the hands of my own fucking mother.

Tempered slightly by the post-op care, administered by my out-of-character, personality-transplant, compassionate father. My head's spinning; could likely vomit if I put my mind to it. I'd aim right for Avril's dress.

Dan rises to his feet, holding me close against him. Clinging back, I sob my lungs up, yielding in a way I'm not used to, that scares me shitless because I need him. Too much.

'I've asked for the bill.' Penny marches back from the bar, swerving my parents in favour of fussing me. 'It's been a big old day, Mon, hasn't it?' she mothers, kindly.

Fran, back from outside, bursts into floods of her own, just from the sight of me.

'Mass hysteria. Like Salem,' my father quips, catching my eye as I peek out of Dan's arms. 'Please, won't you get your-selves home. I'd like to settle up—'

'Oh no,' Dan says, before Dad's even finished his sentence. 'This is our treat.'

Treat? I'd slip from his arms to join the spilled red if I could. Dan peels me off, and Fran takes his place, removing most of my blush and base as she tidies up my damp face with a napkin.

'All better,' she says, with a little pat on my head. I hold Fran tight, her rabbit-like heartbeat racing against my body.

Through the glass of the doors, the boys do made-up karate moves on one another, oblivious to the drama inside.

And my mother.

Now with her coat on, she eyes me and Fran with curious regret.

And envy.

It's late. Knowing I should be asleep brings the panicky restlessness that only makes dropping off harder. I've tried lying on my stomach, rotated countless times. I could get up, have a wee, but if I leave the covers, I'll fuck the ambient temperature and set myself back even further.

'Do you want to talk?' Dan whispers, touching my elbow beneath the duvet. 'Don't say what about.'

'What's there to say?'

'That bloke. The man with the restaurant.' He edges closer. Lifting his hand free, he places it warm on my shoulder. The kindness leaves me breathless. 'He didn't hurt you, did he?'

'It wasn't like that.' And it wasn't, then.

I did once see J-Man. I'd been pregnant with the twins, and despite my hugeness, I'd hidden from him – and quickly. The thought of his eyes on my tummy, on my babies, pure and safe inside, disturbed something I'd not recognized as disturbing before.

Something like misuse. How different I'd been, before J-Man turned me adult. Like the flicking of a switch. And no return.

But we are what we are.

I take two tissues from the box on my bedside. 'He took advantage, but I wasn't coerced.'

'Course you were. Sixteen; bloody hell, I didn't even have proper pubes.' He snuggles into my back, securing me in his embrace. 'I wish I hadn't pushed this reunion stuff—'

'I didn't have to.' The meal earlier seems unreal now, like when I first saw Mum, an awful but quickly forgotten bruise; distant till you poke it.

And fucking wince.

'I'm sorry.'

'What on earth for?'

'I'm sorry you learnt that way.'

Dan kisses my cheek, his empathy for all I've ever dreaded him knowing making me sadder still. 'I hope you know, hope you've always known, that you're my heart, Mon. I'll look after you. Forever.' He hugs me until the trembling stops, and I'm emptied and can't cry any more. After sleeping pills and back in bed, I'm held again through my broken shallow sleep, until blanket oblivion.

14

Getaway

Our summer clothing's unearthed and packed in the large shared suitcase; jumpers and waterproofs worn to save room. Looking after me forever has translated into Dan having the unusually spontaneous – but very much appreciated – idea to buy five last-minute EasyJet returns to Tenerife. By the time I wake from my crashout, he's booked us all on the 14.23 Stansted–Tenerife and swiped the keys to Villa Clivenny.

Penny's simple beige villa comes as a soothing change. I unpack, while the kids reacquaint themselves with the few belongings they keep here, mostly a few old toys and a bit of Lego. Their leftover clothes look miniature.

Once we're straight, and I've cleared the fridge of the gremlin milk and other spoils, forgotten in Penny's panic return home, we head out to the small restaurant at the foot of the hill that does proper paella and good, cheap red in pitchers. I'd normally glam up, but am too limp to even attempt it, would rather be invisible. Would rather be alone, but that's not going to happen now.

Dan's disbelieving face glows from behind the lantern, at the centre of our patio table. 'You're the dead spit. Dead spit.' Our travel tension is now floppy exhaustion – relief, too, for the distance we've created. 'She even does that face. That prim look – what's it called?' Clicking his fingers, he tries to think of *resting bitch face*. I won't remind him.

With gusto, the kids work their way through our shared pan of seafood and rabbit (they think it's chicken) paella, but just being here is all the nourishment I need tonight. Dan's still watching me, trying out his new thing of not pushing, reminding me more of my dad by the second. While they make beach plans for tomorrow – pancakes first, of course – I tune their chatter out. Enjoying the stillness of my body, the soft chill of evening on my face; my senses are at last kind to me. But yesterday's never far from my thoughts.

With Mum, I expect frostbite – though I never imagined she'd be quite so ruthless. The surprise was my dad. His effort – and obvious hope. It's typical that here I am, on an impulse holiday, surrounded by the people who matter most, feeling guilty for my dad's hurt. Because Mum was right when she spoke about his family. Of Dad in the middle, the blighted spot that Dan shares too – stuck between wife and wankers. Wankers that are family. Flesh and blood. Thicker than water. And don't you forget it.

Every family get-together, Dad would shrink into the background, Mum never far behind him. She'd wear the drabbest of garms from her usually colourful wardrobe; her hair ironed so straight it looked drawn on. Their tension was so enormous that I'd swear it was visible; a white heat of zigzags emitting from them both, repelling the world to keep a distance. For their own protection.

Mum was always out of the circle, but she'd tack herself onto the gossiping women usually in the kitchen, despite their hostility. It was a way in from the cold, while Dad got swallowed by the people who despised her the most.

Mum was black – but it couldn't be just that. Anything that simplistic would've made them simple racists. Black Avril was *difficult black Avril*. Her shy quietness proved it. The college qualifications didn't help either, because they meant that she thought too much of herself, had forgotten her place, on her knees, before them.

Dad's family liked to remind her. They'd do it behind veiled comments about the other black people they pulled apart, once done trashing the Pakistanis. The shrinking gaps in the kitchen gossip corners reminded Mum, too; with their backs turned, there were no easy ends to stick onto.

Dad was the first in his family to go to uni, the first to have a job that didn't involve wearing overalls. Despite his books and lefty claptrap, his new job as Head of History was reason for family revelry. At a party that overshadowed then killed off Avril's celebratory plans, the praise of him curdled into talk about his pushy wife, who called the shots from behind the scenes. Little untruths, wearing holes through their marriage where their hearts were kept.

Like a replicating chain of paper dolls, me and my husband wear thin in the exact same places.

And have I done it on purpose – recreating their life as my punishment? My own cross to bear, for my adolescent mistake.

Joe would be able to tell me.

'I can hear your brain whirring.' Eyes kind, Dan taps the bowl in front of me that he's filled with a Fran-sized portion. 'Eat. Rest. Tomorrow's tomorrow.' I'm weak and weepy as Dan lifts my hand, pressing it to his lips.

Matching paper dolls. My brain aches over our similarities, our repeating patterns. Behaviours following cycles, genetics – like addictions can, in families. The shittiest game of pass the parcel, forever handing our fuckeries on to the next gen.

But I'm refusing to pass it any further. The burden stops with me. Avril won't spoil my life for another moment.

'Don't cry, Mum.' Joel's hand rests on mine, as Dan keeps the other one.

'Yeah, Mum, we all love you,' says Fran, entirely desensitised and unfazed now by my tears. If I were on some Saturday night entertainment show, I'd get through solely on the back of this, my rollercoaster reunion story that I'd spill on stage, all the judges welling up along with me, milking it just enough to guarantee myself another weak and desperate performance next episode.

'We'd love you more if there's churros for afters,' Toby chips in, making me smile, making me feel safe and blessed.

And utterly loved.

By lunchtime the next day, we're on the beach. Me and Dan lie side by side, our towels smoothed to his exacting stand-ards, small tins of beer in the cooler by our heads, shaded beneath the parasol. The boys are set up just in front, closer to the sea, using the new set of spades. Watching them from this distance, I've a refreshed perspective of their ever-blossoming characters, in a way that's only ever possible when away from home. Fran, less bothered by the sandcastle and drawn towards the sea, is being sent for water, lingering at its edge for a paddle. The water's a bit too chilly for much else. I've always needed eyes up my backside with her.

Toby, with an attention span even flimsier than Fran's, drifts too, now playing football with three boys of a similar age, all with shaggy black hair – brothers, I think, as they're periodically shouted at by the same gruff woman. The boys wear shorts; two in red and one in a yellow pair. Toby, in yellow shorts too, turns the game into teams. He gestures animatedly to the kids, who nod back with thumbs-ups, as Toby uses the smidgeon of Spanish he's collected from the beach over all the years of coming here, like Fran's seashells.

And Joel; Joel's working on the detail of the sandcastle like some neurotic architect. A boy, slightly younger, keeps trying to assist, but Joel's pretending he hasn't noticed, hoping the kid will shove off elsewhere.

'Unsociable little shit,' Dan says, watching him as well. 'Can't think where he gets it from.'

'My mum's like that, too.' There she is, popping up again. Any mention of her to Dan is still leaving me rather naked. 'Anything to avoid conversation. She wouldn't ask for help in shops; she wouldn't even answer the front door.'

'Same as you.'

'Yes.' I turn, pushing my sunglasses onto my forehead. 'If you don't stand out, you're less likely to get any hassle.' I sit back, checking for Fran, now with Joel again, faking interest in his progress.

Dan unzips the bag and takes two cans out. He stares into the sea, flipping the pull, taking a sip. 'I understand why you did the karate.'

'You know?'

'Course. I always know when something's off. It was the right thing. I'm sorry, Mon.'

Dan's sorry torments. His family have always been my punishment, yet here's the first real acknowledgement of any of their nonsense. What to blame my affair on now? Everybody needs an excuse.

'I still think Joel's mostly an unsociable shit, though.' Kissing him, sand rushes into the dent my hand makes. 'I take full responsibility.'

'Your eyes,' Dan says, 'they're lighter.'

'It's the sun.'

'Happier.' He strokes my face. 'Like you're here again – back with me.'

'I never go anywhere.' I hope with everything my new light eyes hide the truth.

'Y'know what I mean. There've been things, moments lately, that haven't been great.'

Things. Moments. What'd happen if we said the real stuff – things meaning our relationship; moments that could avalanche. Could defeat us.

'I love you, love this, what we've made – our little shit-heads.' He smiles, reaching for his sunglasses. Pushing them up his nose, Dan turns his face to the sky, all George Michael, Club Tropicana, and sips his beer. 'We're lucky.'

We are. God, we are.

Back at the villa, while the kids loll on inflatable pizza slices, with Dan, half-asleep, keeping half an eye, I slip off for a nap.

Sleep comes so much better in the summer months; I'm improved all round by the heat, and in Tenerife it's no different. Penny's cool sheets drift me into light dreams; the kind where there's just enough consciousness for slight autonomy over their direction. I dream we're home; it's morning. Everything's normal – exactly as it's always been. And when I take Fran to school, Joe's gone. It's as if I imagined him, made all of us up and nobody knows who he is. It creates a weightlessness in my body, a brief absolution.

But there's still enough consciousness for life's hard facts.

For my black-hole guilt. Because slowly, it's now mostly guilt.

Keen for more time in my head, I pop to the shops. Prawns are on offer, so I add them to my basket, as well as some plump tomatoes, so deeply red and ready to burst that I take great care handling them. Pasta and Penny's ample spice rack will make a decent dinner. Fromage frais for her highness. Eleven euros. *Gracias*. Smiles at the checkout-girl, her skin and eyes matching mine, lips the same deep red as my tomatoes. I wonder what it's like to live here permanently. Penny's said forever that I look like 'one of the natives', how I 'fit right in here', in a way that perhaps at home I do not.

Back up the hill, road dust chalks my flip-flopped feet. Warm in my cardigan and the late afternoon, I can't help but give thanks for the birdsong, for this out-of-season peace. The tonic from these few gentle days is one I'll be sad to give up.

People I know who've tried living abroad never return. I could work on the checkout with tomato lips girl; Dan fulfilling his fantasy to at last chuck it in and become a gardener. There's an international school a bus ride away. Enough Spanish between us to get by. Packing away the house that my babies came home from the hospital to. Our nest, swapped for sunshine distance. If the school's too pricey, I could home-teach. The possibility's delicious, heady and freeing.

Away from Mum, her truth serum spite and Mr Hyde tendencies, I'd even put up with Penny here – anything's possible when the weather's nice. Budgie hates planes and never travels past Dorset, so that'd be another bonus. And Joe. Our smutty, secret loveliness.

Who could stay just that.

A secret.

'Was she wearing a dress, Dad – did she look pretty?' Fran's voice drifts through from the back of the villa, into the hallway.

'She wasn't wearing a dress. She had shorts on.'

'But you dress up for carnivals,' Fran says, disappointed.

'She wore a green shirt, tied around her tummy. And black shorts.'

'That sounds boring.'

'Well, she didn't look boring. She looked.' Dan stops. 'She looked amazing.'

'And then you asked her to marry you?' Fran squeaks.

'Don't be ridiculous,' Joel chips in, his voice more of a distance from theirs, likely the pool – he never gets out. 'No one gets married straight away. They had to get to know each other.'

'Did she have glass slippers,' Fran asks, 'or ruby ones, like I got for Christmas?'

'No fancy shoes. The biggest whitest trainers I've ever seen.'

She's prompted him for this. Dan's regressed to Notting Hill Carnival – though it was the Tuesday, the morning after, when I met my future husband.

Good, from the start.

After an alcohol-confident farewell to some mates, I'd climbed aboard the train for Liverpool Street, packed to bursting with suits in every shade of depression. Wedged in the gap by the doors, my self-assurance shrivelled instantly;

I was far too brightly conspicuous for all those joyless faces. An irritation. They'd barely started their days – I hadn't yet been to bed, having ended up at a party in Ilford. Dan stood opposite, by his own set of doors, and as the train crept along, pausing at every stop, letting more and more people on, we'd been pushed closer and closer together.

And every time our eyes met, we both went a little bit silly.

'Then she wrote her phone number, right here with her eyeliner, so I wouldn't forget,' Dan tells Fran, and I know he's pointing to his forearm.

He leaves out the part before that, when he barked at some old fat-cat letch who kept grinding his paunchy crotch on my derriere. Dan, golden and glorious, shirt sleeves rolled up, tie shoved into the breast pocket, defending the honour of the stop-out girl in tiny hot pants. But I wasn't interested in golden men then. Had it not been for the half-hour stood in his beautiful company, I'd have dismissed him as not my type – yet we couldn't stop watching one another. When he rang, I accepted his date, but, sober and ordinary, I worried that I'd got it wrong.

We'd sat quietly at first, just polite little questions, so very nervous, unsure of what to expect, with no false lashes or hot pants supporting me. But it was gentle; for the first time in my life, sweet. I adored that he didn't rush me into bed, or up a nightclub wall. Dan was proper. And decent.

Without him ever knowing it, he made me proper and decent, too.

'What's the ending?' asks Fran, as I find them hunched together in the kitchen over some crafting activity. Dan beams at me from the breakfast bar, the almost forty-year-old version of that handsome, respectful twenty-something on the train. His hands stick out, star-like, a square of Sellotape on every finger, as the weight of the shopping bag burns across my palm.

And I want to cry.

'It goes without saying.' Lolling on the lounger opposite mine, Dan laughs into the evening sky. 'I'm far more spontaneous than you.'

'You bloody hate surprises.'

'Not as much as you, though.' Dan stretches up into sitting. 'You look proper tasty, lying there.' Leaning across, he nuzzles my neck, all salt and sun cream. 'D'you reckon that sunbed could take me as well?'

'That's very presumptuous.' But I like what he's doing, all the same. Sleepy, happy, my mouth's tart from the tang of our second bottle tonight. Lightweight at being light years from life's current bullshit.

Dan opens my towel, exposing my skin, cool and damp beneath it, grinning to himself. There's a significant swell in his swim shorts as he presses his toes into the arch of my foot, opening my legs. With his eyes on the view, he drinks his wine unhurriedly.

Then he says, 'Don't move.'

He disappears into the house, leaving me with the insect noises, because we haven't yet cleared up from dinner, and apprehension of what's to come. My legs shut with a slam. I can't be a natural adulterer, all this head-switching between bed partners is tricky.

I remember Dan's earlier retelling of how we met. How good we've been. How lucky that we fell together, in such happy, happy love.

I cannot articulate how much Dan means to me.

It comes like turbulence, the realization of what I've done. What I've ruined. The jeopardy, to life as we know it.

How did I ever, ever notice Joe?

'All out for the count, lovely wifey.' Dan dims the pool lights, leaving us in the pitiful glow of Penny's solar lanterns. He pulls off his shorts, using them to cushion his knees from the crazy paving. 'You're so beautiful.' The flattery lubricates my hesitancy, easing the transition back to my husband, father, good father of my children. Gentle. So very loving.

I never could abide squeamish men; prim, oral duty is about as scintillating as cold toast. In all our years together, Dan's never once flinched from the sight of period blood, lochia blood or cottage cheese mastitis. And there's something deeply connecting as he looks on me, my husband, who's seen my body at its best, worst – at its most awe-defying, who witnessed three babies' birth and exit, as hot for me now as the day we first did it.

Our loving, somehow, despite everything else, feels renewed. I lie back, mellowed by his attention – unguarded – wishing with everything that we could've started like this. Dan sees me – knows it all now. Yet, here we are. Still loving.

More.

Through the open patio doors, a streak of yellow sunshine connects the kids, already water-fighting on the patio, to Dan, frying eggs and the last bits of baguette in olive oil, just inside.

'That was very marvellous of you, husband – letting me sleep.'

Dan smiles, ridiculously pleased with himself. 'After last night, I'd let you sleep all day.' The pan spits, his spatula piercing a yolk. 'Bollocks.'

'I'll have that one.' I'll make all the small sacrifices in the world.

A Joe-sized sacrifice as well.

I set the table as Dan dishes up and shouts for the kids. Their bums squeak on the chairs as, dripping wet, they sit to tuck in, Dan demolishing his breakfast too – complete with the dry yolk egg.

This is the man I married. The man I could lose.

Our crew. The sunlit kitchen. Holiday chatter. Light moods. Love.

Me, underestimating.

The fragility of my stability.

15

Back

I'm earlier than usual for pickup, trying, because we're already out of sync. Starting the new term late has gone down as unauthorized absence. It was explained as rather a family crisis, and I must've done a good enough job of pleading my case so as not to be fined, but I can't dwell because the bureaucratic bullshit's infuriating and I'm already plump on emotion. And churros. There's no room for any more feelings.

I've used the time to catch up with housework; home wasn't as I'd dreamed, instead still cloaked in the hangover of Christmas. Our festive greed overflows from the recycling box, its lid askew, our boozy shame on display, as it waits out front for collection. The rest, that general dusty accumulation of shit that makes me declare minimalism every January, goes in the bin, the fledgling order boosting my wellbeing.

Or it could be being here that's doing that.

The playground slowly fills. This early, most are mums like Kathryn, the stay-at-home wonder women, PTA aficionados (classic helicopters); but for every Kathryn there's a Bella, a phantom, rarely seen dynamo mother, delegating from her city skyscraper to the breakfast clubs, childminders, or, if she's super lucky, the grandparents.

There's also another set, the yummy types, a perfect example just in front of me, scrolling her phone, though I don't know how she can read anything through her stage make-up lashes. It looks as if her day's been spent having every telltale sign of stress and weathering buffed away, perhaps by the same machine that polishes up the Tin Man when he gets to the Emerald City. *The Wizard of Oz* is still on a bloody loop, Fran's now word perfect, her Christmas ruby slippers scuffed silly from all that 'no place like home' knocking.

The yummy is quickly forgotten. As Joe moves along the pavement on the other side of the fence, the very centre of me elevates. Three weeks since we were last alone; his body slamming on mine, those delicious mouth-slathering kisses on my throat. And the long slow ones between my legs.

His eyes are on mine before he's even through the gate. That purposeful strut, the agonizing self-control to keep a modest distance. But I mustn't, mustn't think this way any more.

'All right?' I ask him.

'I am now.'

Kathryn, in her usual, glued-to-the-classroom-door position, waves at me. She's with Lynda, who, wearing sunglasses despite the arctic temperature, pretends she can't see me. She still manages a wave at Joe, though, a flittering of perky fingers in his direction alone. 'She fancies the shit—'

'What's happened?' he interrupts me. Bloody psychiatrists. Joe sniffs out my troubles like a fox would dumped leftovers. He's sharp as ever, but there's a haggard strangeness about him, too, as though he's back on nights, but it's at least a week before he switches shifts again. 'You're supposed to chunk out over Christmas, especially when you tack a holiday to the end of it.'

'It's not for now.'

He doesn't push further. 'What about a little jaunt out, then? Perhaps Penny—'

'How lovely. I'm sure you'll all have loads of fun ...' I smile into the sky, ignoring Joe's momentary confusion, as Lynda approaches with Kathryn in tow. She leans into where I'm standing, shading me out.

'I'll have to dash back in a sec,' says Kathryn, choosing me for convo instead of Joe. 'There'll be tears if Tom can't see me.'

'Thanks for covering me at the library.' Squeezing Kathryn's arm, I search my bag for her present, handing her a small paper packet. Inside is Tenerife lava; dark beads like miniature craters, strung as a bracelet.

'Oh, Monica, thank you.' She looks so pleased I could cry; eleven euros well spent. It's warming to be a good person for once. This is the right way to live. Kindness. Friendship. Friendship with Joe, perhaps – so long as the sex stops. And it really must.

'I was only just saying to Roger what fun we had with darling Bella.' For no other earthly good reason besides being the world's most abysmal flirt, Lynda bursts into rounds of tittering laughter. They must've all gone out – socializing over Christmas, perhaps. 'Stand with us,' Lynda offers, more to Joe, as she slips her arm through his and parades him to the front.

It's not unusual for mums and dads to find friendship, yet I'd be mortified to be under any suspicion here with Joe. So, how's Lynda so brazen? Joe's introduced to her wider circle, while she keeps his arm tight – not clinging, more claiming, her little white mac belted so tightly she looks like a knot in a tissue. 'We ordered your book as soon as we got home. Cle-ver-man.' As she taps his chest on the syllables with her manicured talons, Joe stiffens in politeness overload.

In all my Joe-related in-private browsing sessions, I've never unearthed anything significant, rather like when I Google my own name. And I've never found mention of a book. There is always, however, plenty to be found on Bella. She's pictured in restaurants, at parties in houses like castles, striking poses at tennis and golf, dressed in all the kit. And she certainly knows how to work the camera, too, judging by the clever angles of her mega-filtered photographs. Against Joe's scruffiness, fags and precious vinyl, it's hard wondering how they exist together. Opposites. But, then, I know first-hand how exceptionally well they can attract.

It's not hard picturing Lynda and Bella as friends. 'You must come to us; I'll do you my tarte tatin.' Lynda's full-on purring now – she may as well just mount him and be done with it.

The bell rings. As Lynda's entourage turn in search of their offspring, Joe catches my eye, with quite possibly the most stimulating half-grin of all time.

Our lust is instant.

'Tomorrow,' Joe says, his attention shifting when he spots Molly, scooping her up and slinging her over his shoulder. Her giggles fade as they weave their way out of the playground.

In all those online pictures of Bella, there's one of Joe, stood alone, that captures him exactly right. It's of him caught on the hop, turning as if to acknowledge someone calling his name. That strong, almost annoyed-looking profile, staring direct at the camera. Unsmiling. Fucking gut-wrenchingly sexy.

Unravelled. By five minutes in his presence.

Strip the excuses, the reasons and justifications. Remove everything that got me here, tangled in a man like that.

Not Dan's blinkers, nor my fragile shell. More that Joe is fabulous.

I fancy him. Simple as.

I blink, shake myself, find Fran pulling at my jacket, banging on about a whole school trip to Colchester Zoo, and I very reluctantly tune back in.

For now.

Joe draws the coat from my shoulders, and the moment his lips touch my sun-kissed collarbones, all loyal resolve falls through the floor. My best intentions are only ever intentions – I should know that by now. But just because I'm home, just because I'm easy, doesn't mean I've forgotten Dan and me enjoying each other's company either, enjoying one another; mind, body and soul connected at last. It's just that we're back.

We landed at Stansted into hailstones, minus 1 degrees; Penny and Clive and a fish supper as soon as we got in the door. Dan, lost to work emails from the off, and an it-can't-wait funeral-related phone call from Budgie. Holiday happiness now memory.

And I'm a greedy girl, it mustn't be forgotten – an ordinary, greedy girl.

Only now, just one with a conscience.

Beyond Nancy, I've not really got any close friends, certainly no confidante to have talked me away from all this. But even if I did, I doubt it'd change anything. Because I want Joe in a way that, even if I had friends, bondage loyal till the end companions, I'd still not talk. I'd keep the joy of him all to myself, like my stash of dark chocolate Magnums that no one knows about. Joe's the only thing that's just for me.

But today, something's different. We're cuddling, kissing, but they're not our usual urgent, wanton embraces. These have depth.

'I've missed you.' Joe strokes my face, my hair. 'I'm alarmed by how much.'

I'd dismissed that lifting feeling from yesterday, dismissed us, as simply a base attraction; but this moment's proving we're far more evolved creatures than that. I cry, big gulping tears that even my vanity can't stop. Handing me a great wodge of loo roll, Joe places his hands on my shoulders in calming reassurance.

'We're so selfish, Joe. I can't fucking stand myself. What we've done. What we're doing.'

'Do you want to stop?'

'With everything I've got.' I dab fast at the tears. 'But it's the very last thing I want, too.' Dan and the kids fade as my wickedness triumphs, like clouds swallowing the moon. Omens. If you're a paranoid overthinker, they're everywhere.

'Same as me. The very same as me.' He cups my face, his embrace more insistent, as a hotness ignites between my legs, spreading fast through the rest of me; my own private bushfire. There's no reserve, no self-consciousness as he strips; Joe's as presumptuous as I am hungry for his devotions. He prods his plum head, pink like my mouth, and velvet and domed, against my stomach, but I don't attempt to touch him. I'll follow his lead – Christ, Joe could lead me anywhere. My thighs move together, their tops slick with arousal. No warm-ups will be necessary for either of us, distance a gargantuan aphrodisiac. His hands stroke my body, his lips encouraging a recline onto the bed, and with gentle pecks, we find ourselves horizontal.

Our lovemaking is intense, meaningful. It would be beautiful if it weren't so fucking shameful. Home. Dan. My babies. Their goodness is forgotten as the world fragments into the clearest joy I know.

Then he's gone, abruptly vacated, cradling his head between his hands, perched all anguished on the bed's edge, like he's in a hard-hitting TV drama.

Bloody falling into bed again – which I knew I'd do, before I even got here – when I swapped my ancient sleep bra that I wear most days for a laced and sculpted megastructure. I've failed, like Weightwatchers always did whenever I tried; my hidden Magnums and Joe's fat tool hold similar temptation.

Rejection, though. I'm kicking myself – fucking gutted and ashamed, actually – that it's Joe who's done the distancing. But machismo typical that he'd dip his nob first.

'I hate the holidays,' he says. 'Christmas, winter bloody sun. It's all punishment.'

It's still so early, all day on our terms.

Yet I went back on mine. I gave in. For him. 'I can't magic the seasons to suit you, Joe.'

'And I get all that. Honestly, I do. But I need more than just opportunistic humping.' Joe rubs the back of his neck, watching me. 'I love you. You know that, don't you?'

Of course, I know it. What I don't know is if love makes this better.

'I wish we didn't have to cram weeks of sex into one morning. I wish you were my wife.'

It seems bizarre, impossible even, to imagine a life with anybody other than Dan, yet people do it all the time. Starting again. A fresh set of walls; a new partner in a new bed. And sometimes, *sometimes* it's even better, because you've learnt, thoroughly, what you'll never put up with ever again.

Or perhaps you're left wishing you stayed snug with number one, because they were the first choice, the clean choice, the wedding day, the children, the loving muddle of shared years. Everything comfortable. Everything right.

What do you get with a number two? The association's unappealing.

And yet.

'Are you happy?' The question comes so direct, so personal, it's as if he's stuck a finger in my chest.

But I just don't have the energy. I'm sick of spilling my guts. Sifting quickly through my most trusted habits, I select deflection; Joe may be a brainbox shrink, but all men love a platform. Besides, I am still very curious about them – Joe and Bella McEvoy – what they talk about, how they met. She knows everything about him; from how he brushes his teeth, to his steak preference. All the tricks she employs to get her own way, those commonplace things, the everyday. The curtained off from me. They made a child, said marriage vows, meant them. Apart from the drinking, Bella knows all there is to know about Joe.

'I can't be, can I, if I'm here,' I answer him at last. 'But what about you – are you happy?'

With a shrug, he says, 'Happy enough.'

It sounds rather childish.

I don't push. Instead I dish out food. I've made packed lunches. Salt beef sandwiches and plain crisps are demolished in twisted sheets as January sleet smacks against the windows. But it's not too long before I try again. 'What is your life like, Joe?'

'Look for your bloody self.' He unlocks his phone, chucking it into my lap. 'I'm going for a smoke.'

His anonymous factory settings background glows up at me. Why not a photo – a schmaltzy quote, even? The screen dims, fading to black.

As Joe's key swipes the lock.

'That was quick.'

'Got to the lift, came back. What a terrible idea.' He snatches it back, his thumb racing over the screen. 'Did you look at anything?'

'Of course not.' But I would've, if I didn't already know what Bella looks like.

Flopping beside me with a huff, Joe sips the cold dregs from his teacup, a swift move I catch the tail of that I did myself at the meet the fuckers' luncheon to hide the fag breath. Boozing, in thirty bloody seconds out of sight. But he does look a little frayed, a little wild around the edges. Same as yesterday in the playground.

'I'm comfortable,' Joe says, 'but it's empty. Don't think I don't know how shitty that sounds – Bella's certainly not to blame. It's just, most of the time, life's . . . undistinctive.' He blows out, slowly. 'Like the poetry. Just a dream, put to bed, like everything else. Choosing normal, waiting for the inevitable end, my bones worthless. A grave full of missed opportunity and disappointment. Unidentifiable from the rest. And I can't fucking stand it.'

'Living the life we're conditioned to. Lamenting the life we're scared to live.' There's inordinate comfort in finding your fucked-up parallel.

'If I didn't love you already, I'd love you for that.'

'It explains your outlets,' I try, as he bristles. 'Your need for creativity.'

'You meant the drink.'

I did. Yet it's his own paranoia that confirms my suspicions. For the first time, I sense that the drink isn't just some distant problem, respected in his middle years by firm moderation. But red flags are easily missed when infatuated.

'And us as well.' Two stifled people, therapizing in a standard double room, rebelling against our own apathy.

'Meeting you, it's been like . . .' He squeezes his eyes shut, and when he opens them, they're back to life again. 'Like Dorothy – all bloody monochrome and samey – then a whirl-wind. And colour.' Joe takes my hand. 'You're my happiness.'

Bella's Kansas.

I'm fucking Oz.

Kissing his bristly face, I delight in the sensation of its roughness, the authority of his touch – so very, very different from Dan. 'I hope you always feel like this about me.'

'I hope I don't. You'll never leave him.' Joe runs his thumbs along my collarbones, to the base of my throat. 'It'll be the reason I go mad. Descending into an oblivion of drugs and wild poetry.' A prophecy, as he presses, then releases, like miniature resuscitation. 'My dreams will be full of you.'

Too late. It breaks my own dream about him, which falls out far stranger than it was. Of us, in a big bed, with a seashell-shaped headboard. In the thick of a sinister forest.

'A video nasty kind of sinister?' Joe wears the same humouring expression that Dan would, when I'm chatting what he likes to call girly shit.

'The whole time we're together, my legs in this trap, and you'd think it'd hurt, all bloodied and caught up, but everything just feels really good – why're you laughing?'

'While we're fucking?' The way he says it makes me bashful. 'That's the most Catholic dream I've ever heard.' I could pick the blandest of subjects, and he'd somehow manage to unearth some traumatic root perversion for my choosing it. Joe pulls me close again, sliding his fingers down the ditch of my back to the top of my arse. 'I think we're an excellent match.'

'I haven't got your book, though. Not like Lynda.'

'One page in an anthology – a bloody decade ago. I wouldn't get excited.'

I am, though. I'm aroused to a point where it's almost disorienting, it's that vibrant – and affirming. Joe. My prime rib of hotness—

with his words

and his love.

Our journey home follows much the same as it always does. At Stratford, a little after four, platform 10 is empty, a train having only just left. In the drizzle, Joe urges me towards the shelter, and alone we're able to sit close, be modestly tactile – as if we're allowed.

Being with him always makes for the best side effects, like I've woken from the best sleep ever. It's a buck's fizz morning in a silent house sort of feeling. A vitamin C, rejuvenating, clock-rewinding, twerking, perking, regenerating kind of feeling. All fucking over me.

'D'you think people suspect?' I say, for a little self-sabotage. A little penance for feeling too good.

'We're very careful.'

'We're together a lot, though.'

'Well, friends are.'

'I don't fully trust platonic friendship. You're either one-sidedly yearning for his babies, or the thought of snogging him makes you heave, but he hangs around ever hopeful, pretending friendship's enough.'

'That's very callous.'

'But I'm right. You couldn't be my friend. Not once you'd dreamed up all those things you wanted to do to me.' I stop, let his glorious eyes eat me alive. 'That words hadn't been invented for.'

Gripping me tight, Joe's hard, domineering kisses have my toes squirming deep in my boots. As a freight train speeds through, blowing hair and brollies and papers to buggery, Joe presses his leg against mine. Chocolate jumbo-corded thighs – jumbo cords now officially erotic – to my burgundy 70 deniers. I press back.

'Sometimes, the idea of being under suspicion is, I don't know,' he says, 'quite appetizing.'

'What on earth good would that do?'

'Perhaps Dan might leave you, and Bella might leave me.'

'And we can live happily ever after?'

Joe yanks me closer. 'What's so wrong with that?'

I see his vision of the future, the idyll, where he somehow emancipates me and my offspring from our ignorant and stifling existence and we elope, becoming one big liberal blended family, with free-thinking children who cycle everywhere and can recognize a picture of President Putin as well as Paddington Bear; and us, *Guardian*-reading, allotment-owning, weekend pothead bookworms, drifting around our sun-drenched home, purchased because of its good light and oodles of character, in loose clothing for easy sexual access, with a giant gin in one hand and a poetry pamphlet in the other – though I draw the line at Croc footwear and veganism.

I've imagined it, too.

A giggling couple skitter up the steps, ducking into our shelter. She shakes her little dark bob, and as she leans up to kiss him, her lovely face comes into my view.

It's only fucking Gracie. With her arms around *some other bloke*. He's smartly suited, wearing a coat like Dan's best work one, only in black. An office bod – a man with hair!

If I weren't struck frozen in terror, I'd be slapping her on the back in congratulations. Acting quick, I drop Joe's hand and, spotting a damp *Metro* by my feet, hide my face in it.

Peeking over the top, I spy on office bod. Brown hair, smart, something oddly familiar . . . Michael – Dan's Barcelona work buddy. Joe, getting it, does his best to play at strangers, but our falseness makes my paranoia skyrocket. Even if she hadn't seen us glued to one another twenty seconds ago, the odd sitting in repelling directions looks guilty as fuck, too.

A train slows, stops, opens its doors, as Gracie pulls Michael aboard by his coat cuff. Me and Joe stay seated – know to sit tight for the next one. The doors close, the hiss of movement begins, as Gracie looks out.

And we catch eyes.

Home around the table, deep in the thick of family normality, my stomach keeps on churning. A sick-making, adrenaline, organs plummeting to my knees, kind of churn.

Stupid. Careless. The rules all but blown to pieces. Top of the list – no public affection – broken before we barely even started, by the riverbed humping. And all that snogging along the South Bank – flouted further by the lashings of outercourse in the lifts of Tate Modern.

Phone calls and texts, another classic to be snagged on, was also on the list. My early ease with deleting everything means shit when an itemized phone bill drops through the letterbox. Destroyed immediately, but only because I got to the post first.

I'm an idiot.

Dan says, 'It's handy you could cover, but don't let that library start taking the mickey.'

I'm better than this. Or maybe I was just cleverer spinning the shit at sixteen. But, I'd do well to remember that I got caught then as well. How, after almost a year, those escalating rumours and snatches of gossip blew my mucky little romance into big news.

Glaring that it was J-Man, the family guy in his forties, wielding the power in our relationship. Everyone disagreed. Even my own parents blamed me, the nubile female. I looked the type to have that kind of power, to grant a grown man both amnesia and a hard-on – being only sixteen.

It's a familiar template. First come the laments over the poor innocent children, caught in the sordid crossfire. Next, the pity for the poor perfect cuckolds; saint status in seconds. Then, from the scandalous duo, emerges the true culprit.

I bet my soul on a plate it'll be the woman.

When the dots, however ill-fashioned and gappy, join enough, it'll be the same this time, too. And though I understood the likelihood of Joe and I curdling darkly, as fantastic passions often do, I never expected it quite so quickly.

I'm tired. Aching tired. Joe's remnant handprints wearing as heavy as the mask now for Dan.

'So, can she go?' He rolls his eyes at my blank expression. 'Life on Planet Mum must be fascinating, mustn't it, kids?'

I should've just played along. Dan does a knowing face, and they all look knowingly back, bonded in their little in-club that from time to time they like to exclude me from. It mostly happens when I've been out, like their past hour of

FIFA, Fran on Dan's shoulders playing hairdressers with the inch he's got, before my return from the man I've sold them out for. My values. Our life. Again.

I wish I knew if Gracie saw us.

'Molly's fancy dress birthday!' Fran's gripping her fork so tightly, she's trembling. 'It's the Wizard of Oz.'

This is what happens. Cause and fucking effect. Whenever I see Joe, fresh calamity follows. 'I think we're busy that day.'

Dan shuts his eyes, rather superiorly if I'm honest, and shakes his head. One tiny hour and he thinks he's got all the mum-shit down pat. 'She hasn't said what day.'

'Well, we'll see then,' I say, quick to claim my role back. 'Besides, we don't really know Molly.'

'But Mu-um,' Fran starts, while I pray the ground gives and swallows me. 'You talk to her dad – like every day.' She has my full attention now, but it's safer to pretend that she doesn't.

'Yeah. Fatso from Tesco,' Joel says, watching me as Toby laughs.

'Oh, *that* Molly.' I sound bloody ridiculous. 'Did you see, the caravans are back?' But Joel keeps burning holes in me. Adjusting my face into the most expressionless I can muster, I meet his eyes.

'Despite the bloody bollards and the trees.' Dan's bitten. Thank God. I sit back while he grumbles, arranging myself into normal posturing, when I've all but forgotten what normal is. 'It's all over the village community hub. Everyone's gone doolally.'

I noticed them on the way home. Nine caravans on the green, like supersize paracetamol capsules in the dark. I wonder if it'll be like the last time they came. In one month, not a single bloody crime had been committed, yet going by the reactions in the local news comments section, you'd think Travellers had been burgling in wicked pairs night on night, striking fear into the hearts of sleeping village children.

Bollocks though – to the village children and their sleep. I'm never going to sleep again. Because who's to say I'll be the one Gracie confronts? She could message Dan. Tell him what she saw, me more affectionate with another man than she's ever seen me be with him. And even if it's not Gracie that blows it, a million other things could. Molly's upcoming party, or the phone bill – perhaps that's sent electronically, too, straight to Dan's email, as well as our front door? My paperless trail of sin. What if I talk in my fucking sleep?

Despite that risk, I can't wait for bed. There's two hours to go; surely nothing else terrible can happen in two bloody hours.

'Oh yeah,' says Dan, all smiles again. 'Sorry, love – I forgot to mention. Your mum rang.'

16

Bridges

BBC News takes to the high streets of Essex, asking the question: *What does Brexit Day mean to you?* A breakfast special; passers-by offering snapshots of local opinion. Recognizing our town hall, I take a little more interest, choking on my Cheerios when Penny appears on the screen.

'I'm glad we're out,' she says. No shit. She gives a firm nod to the camera as I holler at the kids to be quiet. 'It's time for a bit of self-care.'

Trust Penny to get the platform, to push the impression that she speaks for everybody. All this upset over the most pointless quest of all time. Even those who weren't politically inclined before 2016 have been forced to become experts, chained as we are to the demon of getting it done. It's a class A, first-world fuckery – like England's pressed Rewind, but Craig David's nowhere in sight. And it's a good job Dan's already left. In less than a week, our return is regressive – Dan slipping into his old skin of home-shit equals my world and work-shit equals his. No mention at all of the problems we ran from. That we're back to.

But at least my paranoia's fading. Nothing's been said, no mention of Gracie. I'm certain Dan's none the wiser.

On telly, the reporter offers another question. With the sun in her face, Penny does the same odd blinking routine that Budgie often does when thinking.

'We're an overcrowded nation,' she says authoritatively. 'And I'm not saying other people don't matter, but when everything's crumbling – healthcare, schools, communities – we need to put ourselves first. Save our own souls.' She wasn't bloody saying that to Yvonne's Syrian carers. Generous, patient and nothing less than saintly – considering who they looked after.

'Cheezus, is that Nan?' Slurping milk from his bowl, Joel yells for Toby and Fran.

This must be a recording. Penny's with Dan and Budgie, talking final arrangements, as the funeral directors can't delay any longer. Yvonne's been on ice for over a month, at Penny's insistence that she mustn't be cremated without the presence of Big Ray – who at last has the go-ahead to fly. Penny's been preparing for his imminent arrival ever since, ensuring all his needs are met. The trouble with his legs and heart means his needs include two plane seats. The funeral's a week on Thursday; fresh obligation already dooming my thoughts.

On screen, the reporter thanks Penny, but she interrupts, saying, 'Haven't we suffered enough at the hands of them all – pretending to be refugees, when they're terrorists?'

She's a soundbite goldmine.

It doesn't take much for it all to flood back; Penny's pre-referendum likes, shares and retweets of clubbed-to-death sealions and Turkish invasions. On she'd bang, about fishermen's rights, when I'd watched her hold her breath at the fish counter in Tesco – always opting for a battered sausage in the chippy, too. The fallouts me and Dan had over her posts, as they turned ever more ridiculous – and dangerous. One, stuck fast to my memory, was about the greatest men in history, one being Enoch Powell and another Nigel Farage. Another I remember well was a picture of a little white girl, blue eyes like Wedgwood dinner plates, staring beseechingly out from a sea of black burqas, with the tagline – *Why didn't you stop them, Daddy?* I've been tempted to buy one ever since, a burqa that is, and jump out on her wearing it when she visits.

'And I'm far from prejudiced,' Penny continues. 'I've a half – *brown* – daughter-in law, and a friend who's black.'

I watch the TV through my fingers.

'Why's she saying that?' If Joel didn't look so miffed, I'd be glad he'd at last caught a glimpse of truth.

'What's Nan on about?' Toby, beside himself, snatches up the remote to record the programme.

'Brex-shit.' Joel points crossly at the telly. I put my arm around him and he stiffens, but I keep it there anyway. 'I thought it was over now.'

So did I.

Fran maypoles round our legs, shouting, 'Nanny-P-is-on-TV,' while Penny's moment in the spotlight culminates in a power to the people air punch.

Lord, take me now.

'I'm not liking this.' Mum's mouth makes an n-shape as she looks me up and down. 'Box dresses suit nobody.'

I put my bag under the table. 'It's comfortable.' I should get a season ticket to Stratford, for all the journeys I'm making lately; the Travel Den visits, coffee at Westfield with Avril now, too. But my mental promise needs keeping. Contact, no matter how difficult, is better than no contact at all.

It's for the kids.

'It's shapeless.' She sips her tea, the cup almost empty. Clever Mother, being early; she's had time to relax, time to plot how to get me on the back foot – though, and let's not forget, it was her who rang me.

'Well, I'm not exactly trying to impress anyone.'

'No? Not even your,' she chucks out a flouncy arm, 'chauffeur in that big flash—'

I sod off to buy a cappuccino. The barista pulls levers and knobs as I study Mum from the counter, watching the comings and goings of everybody else. Her eyes follow the buggy of a screaming baby, stopping at the legs of a security man in the doorway of GAP. He looks like Tom Selleck. She's at such an angle that I can't see her expression – but I catch his. The security man smiles, wider as he taps his lips with his thumb, an obvious twinkle about him.

A registering of interest. She's finessing the shit out of the very same game she taught me.

I was seven, perhaps eight. Knowing. Always listening, imagining a conspiracy against me, even then. We had guests over this one night, music – with the couple across the road. We dressed the table with napkins and the good plates, purchased ramekins from Woolworths, just for the occasion. To keep me occupied, I'd been made an honorary waitress. Once the records were louder and the food had gone, Dad sent me off for a beer, and in the dark of the kitchen, the only light coming from the fridge, I saw my mum; her back leant against a cupboard, hands tucked under her backside – the man – the neighbour – parallel to her. Hipbones almost touching. She wore a red dress and a red smile; her painted lips a snake charm effect. I didn't understand desire then, but I felt her power. The ability to bewitch.

In my whole life, that moment was the happiest I'd ever seen her.

'Who is he, Mr Chauffeur?' She's on me as soon as I'm back; Tom Selleck security forgotten. But I'm prepared.

'A friend with a car, because, like you, I still haven't learnt to bloody drive. Dan was at work—'

'Dan.' Mum smiles, looking for once like she means it. 'A good egg in a tainted basket.'

'Like Dad.'

'Yes.' She sips, looking down into her cup.

'How is he?' I've not forgotten how much he tried.

'Still cross.' She adjusts in her seat, clearing her throat. 'He's right. I didn't need to say what I said. But Peggy.' She makes a *pfft* noise as my eyes stay on her movements; I'm mesmerized, despite myself, still ravenous for every expression.

'Penny can be . . .' Cloying / grating / racist. 'Hard work. Sometimes.' I talk slowly, running through my words before I say them. Dan calls me the porcupine – I've never known anyone as easily triggered as Mum. 'I should've warned you. They remind me of Dad's family, too.'

'What's left of them. He's dead now. Your Giant,' she says, zero fucks given – and rightly so. 'We didn't know until William got ill. You're an uncle down, too.'

I don't even remember William. Costa grows busier, the counter now eight people deep, the volume slowly rising. Every spurt of jet liquid that screams through the machine goes right through my head.

'That wasn't all that made me . . . spiteful.' She wears the same odd envy as when she watched me and Fran in the pub. 'You're so tactile with your little ones. It shamed me.'

'You weren't that bad.'

I'm letting her off. From all the bitter little shards of memory that've always taunted me, like that bastard record player I wished I'd clubbed to death but loved Five Star too much – the sole reason I'm proud to come from Essex.

But I am letting her off.

Lately, when I'm thinking of those memories, once I've shaken off the sediment they left behind, I've begun changing perspective.

Mum and Dad, lepers because of their love, which raged despite the shitstorm from Dad's family, and the people he'd known all his life. Mum and Dad, who stuck it out.

The seventies. Power cuts. Perverts. Pot Noodles.

Prejudice.

Pretty fucking brave to have bothered with each other at all.

'I knew it inside, I wouldn't have you long.' Mum's mouth clamps tight, her eyes full of the same old sadness, like they're hoping for so much, but then they see only me and it's never, ever enough. 'Your babies can't be on my conscience as well.'

'But you said, on the phone. You want to try.'

'Of course I want to try. Why else are we here?' she snaps huffily. 'Girls always leave.'

'So, if I were a boy you'd've been Captain Cuddles?'

'Don't be impertinent.' She tuts, doing the *pfft* again. 'You were always a wilful creature. Stubborn.' There's a tiny, tiny smile. 'I see nothing's changed.'

'I think you should look in the mirror.'

She beams now, not trying to hide it, like the sun's come out. 'We were both so very glad to meet the children. We'd very much like to see them again.'

She's a pain. A mammoth pain in my arse, thorn in my side, fly in my brain. Always has been.

But it's enough.

Enough to commence our thaw. 'Me too.'

17

Parents

Of the two available dates for open evening – an informal talk, before proudly poring over our darling's first efforts at school – I booked tonight, assuming Joe would choose the other, thus avoiding any potential fuckery. There have been enough risks lately. Yet, here he is. I spot him, well before he does me, next to a slither of a person I can't fully see, yet know, with scorching certainty that claws at every living fibre of my being, is Bella. They talk quietly, his body tilted, eclipsing hers, responding to each other as only people who've spent forever in each other's company can.

But however snuggly their twosome is, Joe still struggles to hide the gratification when his gaze falls upon me, dipping into the far-away back row. Glad now that I made the effort, Joe's eyes change again when straight-from-work Dan fills the seat beside me. They fix on Dan's hand, slightly draped on my knee as an undoubtedly pregnant Miss Banks starts talking.

Shit. Bella in the flesh is agonizing, but I sit very still, channelling my discomfort into focusing on the perfect parents and playing Simon Says. And, wounding as their togetherness is, Bella and Joe's positioning in the front-row parent pack is rather telling. Joe cranes back again, looking straight at me, but the strange hurt they've provoked makes me pretend I haven't noticed.

Before it's obvious to Dan, I point out the enormous collage wall mural, the big bubble letters 'I'm happy because . . .', the kids as the centres of all different flowers. Fran, one of the smallest in her class, is a sunflower. Chuckling softly, Dan gives the proudest of dad smiles.

I feel suddenly docile. Empty, beyond reason. Whoever's cooing over upstroke attempts at handwriting, thanking Miss Banks for Fran's gentle transition to school life, nodding dedicatedly whenever Dan speaks, avoiding all, all, all others, is not me.

I slip away for a desperate minute alone.

In the quiet confines of lost property, my breathing evens out a bit. God. For shame. Fucking lashings of shame, entwined now, ironic yet typically, with my side-chick mistress blizzard hatred for Bella; tempered – and only slightly, mind – by Joe's hungry, shameless longing. Teary, I hunt for Fran's actual missing cardigan, as a shadowy striplight buzzes ominously, before giving up for good, making every item unidentifiable, black as outside. Black as my thoughts, which should be light as balloons after all Miss Banks's praise.

None of this is about Fran.

At once, I'm attuned to Joe's proximity. 'It's all right. They're in the hall.' He settles into my back, his hands as cold as his minty mouth; Listerine overpowering. It zips between us, an osmosis, for this is despicable behaviour, and I am barely protesting. 'I wish they'd run off together.' My internal warning screeches red as his fingers disappear under my skirt, cupping me towards him. He doesn't attempt to delve inside my knickers, just slowly applies more pressure, knowing he's got me, throbbing for him, right there in the palm of his hand. 'You clearly have a type.'

'You don't.' However good this feels, it's evoking no goodness at all. Every second with him is a near miss, another white hair. I disentangle, can't stop shaking. 'We'll bloody ruin everything.'

'We're ruined already.' He steps back. Moving to speak again, he vanishes instead.

'Did you find it?' Back in the hall, Dan's next to the 'I'm happy because . . .' collage. Panic searching my arms, all Fran's chalk drawings float to the floor, one landing at Joe's nearby feet. He passes it to me, pinching my fingers beneath the paper.

That throb in my knickers is now an unease in the throat, a pulsating pit of negatives in my gut.

'Thanks.' Dan hesitates, perhaps thinking on whether to stick his hand out or not. He decides that he should. 'Daniel,' says Dan, all smiles – and, thank fuck for something – no suspicion.

It's Joe's turn to waver. Avoiding eye contact, he grips Dan's hand, trying and failing to crush it. 'Have a lovely evening, won't you both.'

Setting off towards home, Dan bounds up the street; his giant gait having me skittering along behind him like some ridiculous little wife. All talk is lost to the biting breeze – which pleases me; I don't want to hear or talk about anything. I glance back towards the school. With no wife in sight, Joe stands alone, his eyes blackly hooked into Dan's retreating figure.

I'm awake, but not ready to announce it. Making my move-ments purposefully lazy, I turn to face the clock. It's almost eight; the house still silent.

Dan's fingers moonwalk across my back as I snuggle into the duvet, keeping my breathing deep and rhythmi-cal. He shuffles nearer, dragging me close, and as my nightdress rides up, he gives my bum a lazy squeeze. Clamping my thighs together, I rest his hand on my stom-ach instead.

'You don't have to worry about lunch,' Dan says, picking up on my shit, his skills for which are troubling these days. 'If things get weird again, I'm here – full support.'

'Thank you, Dan.' I am thankful. Relieved he's still mine, that nothing came from Gracie, or from Joe's grinding semi in the semi-dark. I am so relieved that it was me who invited Penny and Clive to lunch today, along with my own parents.

Because I quite liked the coffee with Avril. It's what made me offer this. And if I can rub along and bite my tongue for Dan's family, I can do it for my mum and dad. But I've made a promise to myself that I won't be an emotional flannel this time. I plan to sit back, dare I say, try enjoying myself, once the oven slavery's over.

'Lovely, wasn't it, hearing all that about Fran?'

'And we didn't have to bribe the teacher.' Dan's the spit of his gossipy sister. 'Your mate's wife – it was a classic. She gave Miss Banks a scented candle. Gifts, on parents' evening.' He shakes his head, disbelievingly. 'Don't get too thick, you'll be drinking Pimm's and playing lawn tennis before you know it,' he says, in an incredibly high-heeled tone, pleased he's managed to crack my face. 'Game, set and match.'

Bella is, undoubtedly, tennis whites perfect, but I've never thought of Joe as posh before. Educated. Affluent. But not posh. It's bothering how Dan's formed that opinion, but thanks to my snooping, and Lynda, and what I've gathered from Joe himself, he's likely right.

Still. It's soothing, how Dan's lumped them together.

'And him. I didn't get him at all.' Though Dan has me spooned and protected, I'm cold, and shudder because of it. 'When you were off being antisocial, he asked what makes me smile – you know, because of that class picture—'

Below us, cupboard doors start banging. Voices rise, mingling into a fresh battle over the breakfast table, as my heart beats a nervous frenzy. There's one Fruit Corner yoghurt and three who want it.

'I said family,' Dan says, 'though God knows why.'

When Penny arrives using her own key – which she rarely does these days – I know exactly why. She's like Sir Duke when he pisses up lamp posts and tree trunks, marking his territory. *I'm a fixture here*, her pheromones shout, *I've been the one involved all these years*.

'Lovely dress, Penny,' I tell her, meaning it. A kaftan in the softest blue, paired with a peacock print scarf.

'Little memento,' Penny simpers. 'To mark my five minutes on breakfast telly.' She begins handing out gifts from Superdry, still ignoring the plastic bag charges. 'Little pressies, beautiful children. I've missed you!'

She saw them three days ago.

She clucks and fusses, Clive dipping his head in politeness around the room, as Dan leaps up with the offer of drinks, telling everyone to make themselves at home. Making a show of removing her heels, Penny retrieves the slippers she keeps in the basket under the stairs. I wish Joe were here as an invisible observer. Perverse, maybe; but he'd have tons to say on Penny's current condition.

'Can I help you in the kitchen, Moni?' Mum asks.

'You'll be lucky – we're always banned when she's creating,' Penny tells her, parting cushions and flopping her arse between them.

'Yes, please, Mum.'

As she rises to her feet, Dad squeezes the tips of her fingers.

And I let myself, for a split nourishing second, bask in the honeyed warmth of his approval.

'What shall I do?' Mum asks, now we're removed from the noise of the kids. The radio plays quietly to no one, two pans reaching a rolling boil as she looks around, charmed. I've cleaned for days, manically. Though the kitchen no longer reflects my personality, its hygiene rating now shits all over Avril's judgy bastard standards.

'Keep me company.' I gather the chopped carrots, ready to plop them in the water.

With a hand on my arm, she peers into the saucepan. 'You cut them too thickly.'

'My house. My rules.'

Amused, she wrinkles her nose.

'So, have a tiny glass of wine.' I raise an eyebrow, encouragingly. 'Dan's gone all out and bought a couple of these.' I point to the Château Neuf, already open to improve my gravy, and my nerves.

'A very small one, then.'

Touched how she doesn't stamp the mischief out of me, I set a glass in front of her, alongside a small bowl of peanuts. 'You can line your stomach with those.' Without thinking, I kiss her cheek, which lifts beneath my lips into a smile.

I don't care. This is always how it should've been. And I'm going with it.

*   *   *

It's hard hearing above the chatter. I left the radio on in case of awkward silences, but we've done okay. Penny's immersed herself in the children's conversation, and I'm not sure if she's still making the dominant point as she did on arrival, or if she's just being the Penny that I learnt to rub along with.

I pinch a rejected parsnip off the side of Toby's plate. He's loading it with mint sauce, which he'll soon stir into the leftover gravy and devour, and today I'll pretend not to notice.

'What's it like in Trinidad, Newnanny Avril?' Joel's question brings the parsnip straight back up my throat.

'Well now, let me think,' Mum says, kindly, though she's taut, uncomfortably upright. 'It's a very vibrant place, Joel – d'you know what I mean by that? Colourful, and very friendly.'

Joel's all enthusiasm. 'Can we find it on Google?'

'Is that all right?' I ask her.

'Why wouldn't it be?' she smiles.

Speeding out for his tablet makes Mum and Dad chuckle, and me relax a little, optimistic that perhaps, dare I dream, this could be it, the kids charming Mum into revealing her life before me. Before England. Until Penny starts noisily stacking plates.

'Leave that,' I tell her, 'I'll do it later.' Penny's five minutes in the spotlight suffers brownouts as she does as she's told, her lips set in a peculiar pout.

Fancy being slighted by the mother of someone you never even liked in the first place.

If New Nan's revelations weren't so all-encompassing, I'd mull on that line of thought further. *New Nan*. 'Nanny' and 'Grandad' felt too soon, so the New Nan hybrid was born. Everybody, particularly the boys, feel rather more comfortable saying it.

'What should I type in?' Joel's back, eyes shining in the screen light.

She coughs. 'Manzanilla, Trinidad.'

After a few moments Joel turns the screen towards us.

'Yes, that's right.' Mum claps her hands together. 'See those trees, never eat the apples – they're poisonous!' She beams at the children, their captivated faces seeming to encourage her. 'Where I lived was very small. I left at seventeen . . . Lord, over forty years ago,' she adds, as if to herself.

Joel flicks through image after Google image of white beaches.

'Proper Swiss Family Robinson stuff,' Clive whistles, admiringly.

Dad claps his hands in agreement. 'That's how I've always imagined it. I read that the sea's quite rough around Manzanilla.'

'You never been?' Clive asks.

'Long haul plays havoc with her equilibrium,' Dad bullshits, with a tender squeeze of Mum's shoulder.

'Ho!' Clive says. 'I'd suffer that, for a drop of paradise.'

Because it really does look like paradise.

Twiddling the stem of her glass, with a pronounced *ahem*, Penny reclaims centre stage. 'Don't get me wrong or nothing

– it's lovely, clearly – but I'm just wondering; why come here, then?'

Cringing, Dan shakes his head at her.

'It's okay, Daniel,' Mum says, but already Penny's fucked it. Mum's again a closed shop, reset to the expression I wear so well myself – our resting bitch face, removed and untouchable. But then she surprises me again. 'It's a fair question. The answer's simple. Propaganda.'

'Propaganda?' Penny gives a little sniff.

'Fake news. I got sold a dream of what here would be like, which turned, oh so quickly.' She brushes imaginary crumbs off my tablecloth, her nostrils pinched like Fran's get. It's the only sign of feeling as she looks unflinchingly at Penny. 'A most unwelcoming place.'

'Did you want to go home?' asks Toby, who knows, because I've started to make sure they all know, about hostile environments and the Windrush scandal, our world of lies and fake news and fat controllers they've no choice but to inherit.

'I didn't plan on staying, but I didn't plan meeting him.' She rolls her eyes as Dad coyly lifts his glass to his lips, smiling so much he's unable to sip. They needed this – the kids always needed this. And I'm sorry that I never told them, showed them more of myself. Of us beyond the others.

But what it's done to me, pickled by the Petersens, stomaching Yvonne, Budgie and now Penny – coming full circle with her freshly resurrected superiority – is an atrocity. All because theirs was the family normal I dreamed of. Because Dan was good, and everything I imagined normal meant.

I make another little promise to myself – that even if all this reunion shit goes tits, Dan's family will never subjugate me or the children ever again.

'But to answer your question, Toby,' Mum says. 'I never wanted to return.' Her eyes seek the reassurance of my dad. 'Trinidad was never home to me.'

'Home's luck of the draw,' Penny says, scraping the bottom of her back catalogue of clichés. 'All that freedom of movement's over, anyway. No more flocking here, draining our resources.'

Past caring, I bite. 'What about Villa Clivenny – you're a part-time immigrant yourself.'

'We're expats,' Penny replies smugly, 'supporting their economy.'

I'm baffled. What does she think happens here?

'Trinidad was a British colony,' I say, tiredly, 'it's not even in Europe.'

'I know that.' She shoots her eyes up and down me, like she's at school, practising her best evils. 'You know what I mean.'

'No. No, I don't, actually.'

Dan lays his hand over mine. 'Monica.'

I stare at it, the wispy knuckles, the hand on which his wedding band sits, symbolizing our togetherness – our supposed unity. But this is most certainly control; his hand lets Penny claim the last word, protecting her delicate misinformed little feelings; a weapon used to silence and suppress. Me. Wifey.

What happened to the 'side by side, full support' in bed this morning?

'Monica, what?' I pull away, before Dan's tricks start to work and I'm done for. 'Monica, don't be rude to my mother when she's sat there being just underhand enough to get away with it?'

'No, Monica,' he hisses back, 'don't be rude because it's her mother's bloody funeral next week.' On cue, Penny's eyes brim, giving Dan precisely what he needs, that daft watery look of the mock offended.

'Just keeping the peace, love.' But Clive's laissez-faire routine's fraying, too.

Penny sniffs again. 'I'm all right. Really, boys.'

Oh my days. I've read about this. White tears. I'm reading so much on white privilege lately, it's like my ears have popped. As Clive passes Penny a tissue, as if she's some big brave girl after the dentist, my whole body turns, like a pressure cooker, on full whack, ready to really—

'We're learning about the British Empire in History,' Joel says, unguarded and sure, rising over the friction.

'Big topic,' remarks my father, leaning forward in encouragement. 'What are your thoughts?'

Dad's question puts me back on a simmer. He'd often ask stuff like that when we'd be together like this, over dinner. He'd throw out a name, like Gorbachev or Reagan, expecting me to produce some fact or statement. I'd always be able to.

I'm not, never have been, stupid. Yet I'm at my most livid, having been so willingly blind.

Observing Joel, it's clear that the pressure hasn't fazed him. Tapping his knee beneath the table, he thinks of a response, excited, almost, to be picked from the homogeneous kid bundle and treated as an adult.

'Well, say if some people just showed up in the village.' He clicks his fingers, like he's struck with a brilliant idea. 'Like those caravans – on the green, right now. Imagine if they tried telling us how to talk and live and who to pray to. Well, it's not fair, is it?'

'It's hardly the same,' says Dan. 'They're pikeys, for starters.'

'They're Travellers. And anyway, who said?'

'Who said what?' Dan asks, in a knock-knock voice, humouring him.

'Well, that's what I was thinking; who said being from England was the best way to be in the whole entire world, anyway?'

Dan's old stretch-smile surfaces as my fury empties. Snarky comebacks are unnecessary; Joel's the ointment, salving all my rage.

And Dan better not pull him up on it.

'You're a very smart lad.' Dad's hands clasp together on the table in front of him.

Ruffling Joel's hair, I just can't resist it. 'Must come from our side of the family.'

If looks could do any significant damage, I'd be cinders by now. Penny's eyes are abnormally wide; red-rimmed golf balls, moist with fury. She stares over Dan's shoulder into the garden behind him.

It's delicious, feeling proud and smug for once.

'Let's have some dessert,' I suggest, relinquishing a tad, because I can afford to – and that's rather tasty, too. Placing the dome in the centre of the table, I extravagantly lift off the lid. Mum's baked a sponge, with sweet buttery icing – she's even coated it in shaved coconut. It's my favourite. The significance of that has not gone unnoticed. 'You first, Penny.' My knife glides through the frost lushness, and, accepting her plate, I give Penny the most cloying of smiles I can muster.

Clive tries claiming a slice, as Penny clasps his wrist. When his face shows a crack of protest, she shuts him down with a raised palm. 'Remember your cholesterol,' she says, to the man who's just eaten half his body weight in cauliflower cheese and Yorkshire pudding.

I offer the cake to Dan instead. He drags the plate towards him, his face set stone and impenetrable.

Cleansing and bathing in our house is never luxurious. Regardless of the temperature outside, our little bathroom is always fridge cold. There's a shuffle of activity as I stand brushing my teeth, trying to get to bed before Dan returns from walking Sir Duke. It's Fran, half-asleep and needing the toilet.

'Can you tuck me back in?' she asks, all small and whiney, gathering up her nightie to sit on the loo.

I set my brush back in the cup, my mood lifting a little at our five toothbrushes, bright and haphazard but always together. I made this, us. I made something special. Nothing can change that.

'Can I have the light on?' Fran pleads once we're in her room. There is absolutely nothing to be frightened of in a bedroom like this; her walls covered in school certificates and pictures of her favourite programmes and films, her special moments. Four walls filled with love and goodness. Which is all I want for them, forever.

Which is why it was right, speaking out earlier – despite Dan's silent treatment ever since. And I'm bored by the predictability of how this always goes.

'Budge up and we'll have a cuddle.'

The diva in her disappears as she hops under the covers, shoving the row of Beanie Babies to the end of her bed. All smiles, the whites of her eyes brilliant in the dark, she beckons me in. I am, as usual, surprised at just how comfortable her little bed is. She throws her tiny arms around my neck as I snuggle her into me.

'You're a good mum,' she whispers, so matter of fact, and I squeeze her tighter.

'I'm glad you think so.'

'I've been thinking,' Dan says from the kitchen table, without looking up from his phone. I'd usually come back with a 'that's a first' or 'careful' but I just can't summon the bullshit. 'Let's give the family stuff a rest. It's too bloody much.'

'More than fine with me.' Finishing my drying up, I rock my head from side to side.

'That's what happens when you sleep in with the kids. Very childish, dragging it into the next day.'

'I didn't mean to stay in with Fran.' I give him that, let his shoulders melt a little. 'But does it never occur to you to take my side?'

'I can't tell you how sick I am of this. Who's offending who, who do I defend? She's my mum, Monica.'

'And what about mine?'

'The one you've always hated – that we've never been allowed to talk about; now it's okay for you, we all fall in?'

'It was you who wanted to get in touch, Dan. You.'

'It was easier before!' he yells, making me jump. We face each other; me twisting a tea towel, him hands-on-hips aggressive.

'You've never disappointed me more.' I sling the best thing I have. If there's one thing Dan hates more than anything else, it's his golden crown slipping.

'Find somebody else, then.'

'That's a very childish solution.' I keep my eyes wide. God, I'm good.

'You've been playing a very childish game from the start. I've been the tugging rope between you and Mum for years. I was flattered once, but between you both, fucking hell, I've never felt more drained.'

'I drain you?'

'Acting all sensitive. Your weird games. One month you're my best mate, the next you're doing everything to avoid me. I have to pre-empt every conversation opener. It's always about you, if you're all right. But what about me – when does anyone ever ask about me?'

'You?' I blast right back at him. 'I do everything for you. Tiptoeing round, making your life easy as possible for your artificial world away from us. You don't lift a finger here!'

'Here we go again, the thankless invisible tasks that only you do,' he spits condescendingly. 'Must be so hard. Being you.'

I gesture toward the ceiling at the stirrings upstairs.

'You started it!' he shouts.

The tea towel in my hands has become a twisted sausage. Turning it back, it doubles over, trapping my wrists. I pull tighter as my flesh puckers and stretches, like a Chinese burn.

'You can't have it all your own way!' Done, he leaves the room, leaving me in my tea towel handcuffs, and to the certainty that, should there ever be an actual side to choose, he wouldn't be on mine.

'Well . . . neither can you!' I don't even get to five before he's back in the room. 'Yvonne wouldn't want me there, anyway.' Dead or not, Yvonne's still a poison. I know there's the old 'don't speak ill of the dead', but there are exceptions. Hitler. Fred West . . . I take a deep breath. 'I'll do as you said. Give the family stuff a rest.'

'It's a funeral, Monica.'

247

'I'm not going. And neither are our kids. Talked at like they're part of a Mengele experiment.' I shake my head. 'No more.'

'But I need you there.' Such a sad little face now the bluster's evaporated. I almost feel sorry for him. 'Mum's broken.'

'You've got your dad. Nancy—'

'Nancy's not going—' Dan catches himself. I raise my brows, embarking on the invisible task of crushing our cardboard for recycling. If real family can escape Yvonne's belated send-off, then so can bloody well I.

I'll be the good wife here. But Dan can't have everything any longer.

18

Goodnight and Thank You

If there's one thing worse than a Petersen wedding, it's a Petersen funeral. Yvonne Constance Patricia Crane. 1932–2019. Beloved, to all who knew her

– my big brown arse.

'Nan – Nana Yvonne – if you're one of my kids.' Hands flat on the lectern, Dan holds his sad words in place. Words he's sweated and crossed out and scribbled over. 'Was a force. A rarity these days. She had what her friends often described as "Blitz Spirit".'

I ought to check the name on the door to see if I'm at the right funeral.

But I know that I am. Even from the grave she's managed to craft a day of abject misery, from the draconian rule to wear top-to-toe black, right down to the four gloomy horses with plumes on their heads – and Yvonne, out of cold storage and boxed up behind red velvet curtains, in the kind of carriage I half expect Jack the Ripper to leap from.

Penny, in front of me, makes a low wailing noise, as Dan clears his throat, speaking louder. 'When her sister Angela died unexpectedly, Nan took on her son, Ray, raising him as if he were her own.'

Big Ray – the nickname an underestimation, now I've seen him with my own eyes – blows his nose into, of all things, a black hankie. Inspecting the contents, he then wipes away his tears, without so much as folding it in half. He sits next to a silent Budgie; head down, eyes on the floor. It'd be nice if he stayed like that all day. Gracie, next to him, is last on the pew. She hasn't acknowledged me, but to be fair – and hopeful – she hasn't turned around yet.

Dan continues. 'And when Mum was ill with the cancer, it was Nan who stepped up. Nan who kept her going. Kept us all going. I was ten when I understood what her friends meant, when they said she had the "Blitz Spirit". She got Mum better.'

Penny crumbles into Clive.

After, while Connie Francis blasts from the speakers, a very sad Big Ray stands looking rather lost by the hymn sheets. It's not nice seeing anyone upset, yet I am a little baffled. This bowling ball of a man in nylon polyester is nothing like the hot-shot property tycoon I've been fed over the years. The Petersen propaganda machine, working at its best. Still, he seems sweet enough.

'I'm Monica, Dan's wife,' I tell him. 'Sorry for your loss.'

Big Ray takes my kindness as an invitation to hug. It lasts a little too long. 'Coming for a drink?' Out comes that terrifying hanky and crusty residue, to drag back and forth beneath his nose.

My empty stomach reaches. 'Briefly. Got to get back for the kids.'

Not strictly true. Joel and Toby have a key and will be fine after school for an hour or so, and Fran – on Joe's insistence to help somehow – is on a playdate with Molly. I'm still shell-shocked that I agreed to it, but anything was better than Fran coming here. I spared them by sacrificing myself – a proper modern-day Jesus.

'Well,' Big Ray says, 'be sure we raise a glass first.'

Yvonne's fellow Greenview residents, togged out in their most maudlin of outfits, line the Groundhog Day reception room of the Old Court Hotel. Dan and Penny work their way down the row, kissing powdery cheeks, all Mr and Mrs Charm, as the olds twinkle up at Dan like he's found their glass slippers. Lucky Yvonne, having such a dear grandson – who always rang on a Sunday.

Good. And kind.

To a fault.

A pair of chairs entice me, near the blessed exit, and I bagsy one before it's added to the ever-expanding circle forming in the centre of the room. The first, second and third generations, second marriages and loose-linked offshoots – the returning brother from another mother. Before my very eyes, they gravitate into their intimidating solidarity, the conversation regurgitation; always the same puffed-up tales of glory days nostalgia.

But I'm beyond done with the noise they make, already drained by what's coming, because once we get past the well-wishes for the grief-stricken, I'd bet my house on it that the talk will homogenize back into: I'm English / I was born here / it's mine first.

'Will you help Big Ray?' Penny calls across to me, smack in the thick of her gang, making room for the chair I drag over for him.

Easing himself comfortable, Big Ray wets his lips and burns holes through my blouse. 'Got a nice spot for you, too,' he says, rubbing the fronts of his slacks. 'Ever been to America, brown eyes?'

'Cheeky.' Penny winces, insincerely, letting me know I'm not forgiven. 'You can't behave like that. She's a modern woman, Ray – off to university. Apparently.' She smiles smugly, pleased to catch me out with the information I didn't know she knew.

I've the feeling there's more going on than I realize. My paranoia's terrible. Every action from everybody has a double meaning, a double edge. I feel exhausted. Sloping off to my chair in the corner, I check my phone. 14.10. Another hour – two at the most. It's all I promised.

'You're like Mrs Invisible.' Gracie plonks an enormous glass of dark pink rosé in front of me. 'That's to say thank you.' I wonder if she can see the worry, the agonizing question mark she's left hanging over me – a bloody guilt guillotine. 'For all the Matchmakers you let me eat round yours,' she says, without a flicker.

'You're welcome any time.'

'That's kind.' She clinks glasses. 'But you don't mean it.'

I catch her sleeve quick before she disappears, noticing clouds of old bruising, faint silvery scratches around her wrist. She watches my reaction through her lashes, their dense black lushness flicking towards Budgie, gobbing off at the bar, hands in his pockets and legs akimbo.

Before her sudden snivelling attracts any attention, I take her arm and lead her out. On a table, next to a recently vacated chair, is an almost full pack of fags. Plucking a couple out, I pinch the lighter.

On the crumbling wall outside, now sit two.

'You been seeing him long?' I don't say Michael. I want her to tell me.

'Since we were eleven. Off and on. Till he went to some uni, Brunel, or something, and thought he was better than everyone else.' She takes a big lug of fag. 'Then I saw him at yours, and—' She smiles, all-knowing. 'Don't ever go into acting, mate.'

'I wasn't certain.'

'All filled out with those gorgeous teeth, and me filled out, thanks to Harley Street.' She pushes her chest out. 'I don't know who I've been kidding, thinking I could be his wife.' Gracie sniffs. 'Budgie don't know the meaning of it.'

'At least you learnt quick.' I sip the wine. It's cough syrup sweet, a migraine in a glass. 'What are you going to do?'

'Wait to be sure. I know it's putting you in a spot, but please don't say anything.'

I shake my head, her secret more than safe. 'He doesn't hurt you, does he?'

'Bless. You're so lucky with sweet old Dan, you've forgotten how the world works.' She finishes her wine in two gulps, and it doesn't kill her. 'There aren't any nice men, not really.'

'Not Michael?'

'For now. Who knows?' She squeezes my arm. 'You look like you've seen a ghost. It's not Yvonne, is it?' She looks behind her, mischievous, reminding me of Fran. So very, very young. 'We fight, me and Budgie, but he don't hit me. And I always give as good as I get.'

'You are welcome at ours. Anytime.' I make my eyes big, making sure that she gets it, kissing her face before we go back inside.

'Churchill!' Big Ray bursts, as I brace myself, jealous now of Gracie vanishing to the loos. 'Greatest politician of all time. I hope your university will teach you plenty about him.'

'Country wouldn't be as it is now if we still had him in charge,' says Penny, snug and protected by the circle of parallel thought, though he never bloody ruled in her lifetime.

They'd never know it, the lava within, as I smile, ever tolerant, because it's still too soon to get my coat. My chair's gone, and without the failsafe trickery of disappearing into my offspring, I'm forced to sit with Ray, Penny and Budgie. Dan's still making his rounds.

'He'd be about a hundred and forty-odd by now – I don't think he'd be that much use.' I give them the old well-practised laugh, then study my lap. Churchill. I never was keen. Mind you, with his prejudices he'd have fitted in perfectly well here today.

But I'll keep things light. I'm in the clear with Gracie, I can afford to.

'Well, at least we've got someone like him again, to set this blimmin' country right.' I don't need to see Penny's face to know exactly the look on it, and though she's mostly attractive, I can't help thinking what an ignorant sow of a woman she's capable of becoming.

'How's that all panning out, for someone like that mum of yours, then, Monica?' Budgie asks me, doing his thoughtful face, but I know where this is going. 'Was she, wha'd'they call it, Windrush?'

'No. She came much later than that.'

'So, she's safe, then?'

'Safe from what?' I play dumb. Looking to Penny, she smiles wryly into her packet of cheese and onion, enjoying herself.

'Our hostile environment.' He shudders, doing a ghost noise. 'Ain't it apply to stay, these days, or go back where you come from?' Budgie winks at Big Ray, who explodes into a laughing fit, clutching handfuls of gut, and when at last he can breathe again he rubs at it, like a proud expectant mother.

'She has British Citizenship.' I say it to shut them up, but I'm unsure if it's true. Years ago, she always had a black passport.

'Back on the scene, ain't she? And quite the looker, apparently.' Budgie makes a point of checking out my tits – Ray still doing the same. 'More your age, 'n' all, big brother.' It's that face, his confidence to say all he likes, and I'll never respond. 'Spicy.' They begin to chuckle, those three smug, smirking siblings in this shitty little hall, where no one with any self-respect would ever be seen dead.

From across the table, I lean right into Budgie's bald cone headspace. 'My mum would rather chew her own tits off before she'd ever let you.' I leg it quick, snatching my first ever victory for having the last word.

'What a temper.' Big Ray whistles behind me. 'Danny-boy needs sorting that out. Pronto!' Leaving him offering his services, I run-walk the room's periphery, managing to get out and into the strip of hall that leads back to those manky toilets. I've the same stuck feeling in my chest as when I was here at the wedding. Still hurting; hurt that I let myself be hurt by these ridiculous people who, not so long ago, I'd hoped were an endangered species. But now I know different. These days, I know that I've never been paranoid.

How daft, thinking Big Ray might've been any different.

Collecting myself, I try remembering what Joe once said about not letting my thoughts drown my actions. Joe. What I'd give to be teleported, to him and Fran and Molly – I stop, know I'm losing myself. Find a positive action and do it.

Right then. I go straight to the bar and order a Courvoisier.

Dan's still mingling across the room, quiet with me since the Crem, and I can't think, think, think what I've done, but it hardly matters – everything I do pisses him off. Penny, thriving on the marital tension, sends me hostile vibes as she chats to Big Ray.

The Courvoisier tastes good.

'Taking liberties, ain't it?' Budgie's centimetres behind me.

'Don't worry, I'll pay.'

'Fucking right,' he whispers, his elbow pushing me into the hardness of the bar – discomfort, rather than pain. But I don't know what to do. Budgie grips my chin, turning my face towards Gracie, his eyes woozy and pink and mean. 'Tell me, what'd I want some fat black bitch for, when I've got her—'

I elbow him in his flabby off-guard belly, hard. 'Have you, though?' From fuck knows where, I start to laugh.

He gapes over at her, mouth wide, blinking rapidly. Perhaps they do all pull that face when they're thinking. 'What d'you mean by that?' He takes quick, shallow snorts, less threatening by the second.

'That's all it takes?' I ask as he reaches the shade of cooked prawn. I wouldn't be surprised if steam started pouring from his ears. It's fucking poetic, beautiful, seeing him like this. 'Intimidation's wrong, by the way. Old bullies like you never win—' He bends my arm, and me, into the bar again, shoving himself against my backside. This time it does hurt, and I yelp, loud enough for attention. The hushed room becomes one giant cocked ear; Budgie's angry snorts, hot on my neck, breaking the silence.

Clive severs Budgie's grip. His gentle hand on my back shatters the spell as, all at once, I'm terrified. 'All right, love?' Bewildered, Clive looks from me, to Budgie, then to me again.

'My mother.' Budgie oozes drama; oiled and wanky and over the top. 'Gone, not an hour ago. And now, this . . . *bitch*,' he points at me with such condemnation even Clive flinches, 'is telling me my Gracie's gonna leave me.'

'Monica!' Dan barks, furious from across the room – and I just can't believe it.

Well, I can. It tells me everything I ever suspected.

My bag. My coat. Shoulders back. No tears.

'Ignorant, thick bunch of twats. I hate you all. Not you, Gracie.' I make a point of acknowledging her, hope to God I've not dropped her in it, but also hope with bloody everything that I've made my point. 'Mostly you – brainless bigots.' The fucking Crane brigade. But they don't seem quite so all-powerful now, in fact they look rather unravelled. Emptied of their bolshiness, they're simply mottled, sagging embarrassments; nothing to be scared by.

Nothing to be quietened for. Ever again.

I burst through the main doors and up the lane, shoving my arms into my coat sleeves as I start the two-mile stretch back to the village.

The fallout from this. What's coming. So much to be anxious over. Best to get home first. Just bloody get home, see the boys, and pick up Fran. Actions. Tears set frosty on my face, my feet sore already, the frown of skin above my heel rubbing its way into a raw bubble of blister.

Scrolling my phone for cab numbers, I try keeping my speed as a white monster of a vehicle slows beside me.

'State of you!' Nancy pulls on the handbrake. 'I'm scared fucking shitless to ask.'

I take comfort guzzling my bodyweight in tea, in my own kitchen. Home sweet home. Toby and Joel are gaming with some kids in Vietnam and stuffed full of Pringles, their violent virtual afternoon tame by comparison to mine.

A face wipe, hooded like a little Klansman over Nancy's finger, sorts my mascara, while I take her, blow by blow – impersonations too – from the Blitz bloody spirit eulogy to Budgie lashing out.

To Clive stepping in when Dan didn't.

It hurts more than anything else. That he's still there.

How's he still there?

'They're dinosaurs. A gaggle of gammons, I know. But why Dan's never—' She stops, embarrassed, I think, to say it. 'Look, I know he's a mummy's boy, and when she was ill—'

'I know. He talked about it at the service. I know he worries about her a lot.'

'But she's fine. Mum got better.' She balls up the wipe and puts it on the table. 'Does he think the sky'd cave in if he called them out—' I hug her, tight as I can, my sad, wet face all over her cashmere. 'I've thought many times that I wouldn't blame you if you had enough, Mon. And to think I was coming for a drink because I felt guilty.' Nancy holds me back as I bite my tongue, stopping any impulse revelations. She's still one of them, lest I ever forget, ever dare expect more. Push to shove, no matter their in-fighting, they're glue.

But she means well. At least her eyes are open. 'Please fix your face,' she says. 'D'you want me to pick up Fran?'

'No, thank you. I'll fix my face, like you say, and go and get her.' But no miracle can make mascara take to wet lashes, just like nothing but sleep will fix my puffy eyes and nose. I can make myself less red, though – a paler powder can fix that. It solves the cheek streaks, too.

Looking like a porcelain blowfish, still head to foot in black, only now in comfortable shoes, I set off for Joe's. Dan's still not back. Neither has he called. The silence acts as another means to divide, the gap between us feeling rather cavernous now.

And scary.

Joe's house sits half a mile in the other direction from school. Double-fronted, double-garaged, double-front doors. A spiffy lipstick-red motor sits on a plum slate drive, perfect privet skimming the bare downstairs windows. When you live off the main strip, who needs nets?

I press the doorbell and wait, warming a touch from the thought of Joe's comfort. Through frosted glass his silhouette appears, looking more and more womanly as he approaches the door. What the fucking fuckery is this?

'You must be Franny's mummy. I don't think we've met properly. I'm Bella,' Bella says, with a wide smile and crinkly blue eyes. 'The girls have been having a lovely— I hope you don't mind me saying, but you look terribly upset.' She steps out into the wet, onto the damp slate in her fluffy little beige slippers, and takes my arm. 'Come in, won't you? Let me make you a drink.'

Breaking another of my own rules, I cross the boundary into Joe's home. His married life. Into stark white open-plan loveliness, furnished by Heal's and John Lewis. I follow Bella to the kitchen, where she whips two mugs from nowhere and fusses around her Gaggia.

'Please sit,' Bella says, without looking up, as I hoist myself onto a stool at their central island, which rises from the Zen space like an iceberg. Beyond the windows that run along the back of the house, wall to wall and floor to ceiling, the garden rambles off in all directions, like a school field. There's a swimming pool. Not a hot tub, but a pool. A size for adequate lengths to be swum in.

Bella hands me a little clay mug full of frothy loveliness. 'A funeral, wasn't it?' she asks gently. 'Someone close?'

I sip, not caring if it burns. 'A wicked old witch.'

She smiles, soft despite the angles. Her honey-blonde hair is in a loose twist, tied on the side, the silken sort of hair that bands slip from with ease. She is silky. Beige cigarette trousers, a white shirt with the collar up, just at the back. Affluent

261

elegance seeps from every Clarins-hydrated pore. I reckon, somewhere in the close vicinity, is a cricket jumper, ready to be draped from her bird-like shoulders.

Joe is married to this tiny silken woman.

'They've been watching *The Wizard of Oz*.'

'It's on a loop in our house, too. Ruby slippers for Christmas, the lot.'

'Joseph found the soundtrack on iTunes,' she says, her eyes fluttering heavenwards. 'It makes a change from his Ed Sheeran morning, noon and night.'

You'd think, in all the time we've spent together, amidst all that rambling, tangential chatter, that insatiable keenness to know the ins and outs of each other's souls, Joe's appreciation of Ed might've cropped up. Because this is musical galaxies from Joe's car park whitey before a Big Daddy Kane gig, his love and encyclopaedic knowledge of East Coast hip hop – music we've connected over.

It's a small thing, but when the world, my world, seems so unsteady, so unpredictable, even the most minuscule of detail – and disappointment – feels like a tipping point. Right now, I need Joe. And I need him rock solid.

He should be here.

She blows into her mug. 'He did apologize, by the way, for messing you about. He's terribly forgetful – had this booked for weeks.' She busies herself as she talks, scraping away the girls' leftovers. I've never thought of Joe, Joseph, as forgetful, either. 'The girls are in the playroom,' Bella says, as if I should follow her.

Back in the hall, a door on the left leads into another bright white space, a wall entirely of cubby-holes, housing toys and books and kid-shit of all descriptions. All Molly's finest pieces of art have been lovingly framed in a mismatched collage, along with family photographs. Molly and Fran sit hunched over a Sylvanian treehouse, as Dorothy and the flying monkeys battle it out on a small flatscreen in the corner.

'Mummy!' The delight on Fran's face quickly turns. 'Do we have to go now?'

'I'm glad you've had a lovely time.' I kiss her head, giving her a little nudge onto her feet to get going, but she's lead resistance. It's the very worst thing about playdates, when the kids don't want to go, then can't find their shoes, then hide, while the adult prattle desiccates till you're manhandling with fake smiles, shoving them out of the door.

But in all the times I've ever had to suffer it, this is catastrophically worse.

'They have. I'm so glad to have met Franny at last. Her name crops up a lot round the dining table.'

'We're very fond of Molly as well.' I feel the words coming, my ingrained manners ejecting them. 'Perhaps in a week or two, she'd like to come to us for tea.'

The girls grab each other's hands, thrilled, making me feel even more of a cunt. 'But we really should make a move. Daddy and the boys need their dinner.'

'Five more minutes, please?' they say together, all big eyes. These beautiful innocent kids.

We're going to destroy them.

'Five minutes won't hurt, will it? Besides, Joseph will be back any moment. He'll be sorry he missed you.'

Course he will. 'Any other time and I'd say yes, but it's been a very long day.'

'Of course. Let me round up Franny's bits.'

As the girls join Bella in the hunt for Fran's 'lost' shoe, my eyes stay stuck to their pictures. Photos of them, in places that look like Provence or Tuscany, Joe in a fedora and cream shorts, manspreading and pompous-looking in an outdoor restaurant. Joe, Bella and Molly on a ferry, with the New York skyline behind them. Bella and Molly, matching outfits at a church celebration, someone's wedding perhaps. Holding hands, overjoyed to look the same. Bella; a good mum – not a distant mum, just a working one.

Bella. Friendly, chatty, not remotely snobby.

'I do love your hair,' she says. 'It's super funky.'

I pull Fran along the road towards home, making her half run. She'd usually be cross with me for doing it, but she's still in the clouds, still banging on at a hundred bloody miles an hour about Molly's house.

'Molly's mum said when it's nice and hot, I can go swimming round there.'

I hope the weather stays like this then; a swamping grey sky and minus temperatures, the perfect conditions to send Yvonne off in, but she's left her remnants; she'd have loved the fallout today. The sky rumbles, threatening rain, as I urge Fran to step it up.

With a crosspatch face, she shakes me off. 'I wish I had a playroom.'

'You've got your own bedroom.'

'It's not the same. And Molly goes horse riding. She might get one for her birthday.'

I'd heard puppy from Joe. But pony talk is posh talk, and we never do talk money. It's the sole thing that sits oddly between us. Not race for once, like my and Dan's permanent issue, but all Joe has that seems too easily achieved. He started with an advantage, Daddy's connections, his future in medicine a certainty, rather than a vocation.

'Well, perhaps you can ride that too, when you pop round for your swim.'

'If you get a job, can we move to a house like Molly's? You could be a dinner lady!' She beams, smiling like she's cracked it.

'Well, you be a dinner lady when you grow up – see how far that'll get you.'

Fran shakes from my grip, and I grab her back, holding her close as we cross the road back towards our terraced slum, my eyes zooming in on everything wrong with it, the cracked brickwork, the wonky gate, all the things that usually charm me because they mean I'm above all this shit.

Fuck Joe. And fuck his house.

'I'm working with Jasmine, remember.' Fran folds her arms, watching me crossly while I search my pockets for the key. 'In prosthetics,' she adds, every bit the school know-it-all, still struck with the girl from the tube. But at least Jasmine's a better role model, knowing what she wants, working for her own dreams. No readymade easy ride, like Molly will have. Which isn't Molly's fault, I know, it's just that, white and wealthy, she's streets ahead already – with no awareness of being so. She might stay that way her whole life.

But she gets the luxury to choose.

'Hurry!' Fran squeals, as for a few cracking seconds the clouds become brilliant white. Droplets of rain fall so fat and freezing, they hurt as they pelt us.

'I'm trying!' On my knees, I go around my handbag again, groping through tampons and hair pins and receipts for mostly the Co-op and Home Bargains and Tesco, my holy triangle of family living.

Then there's no need for a key. The light from the hall falls upon us, as Dan opens the front door.

A speedy chilli is whipped up quick, then eaten by all except Fran, blaming her spice aversion on a still-full tummy from Molly's. Dan's quiet, blaming a long day and tiredness for his silence, which suits me fine. I perform my duties with an autopilot efficiency, even managing to make tomorrow's sandwiches, jam ones, because we're out of anything fresh and exciting, and today should've been food shop day. The house is set straight, an overtired Fran plopped in the bath, fighting me all the way, read to, then placated into bed.

And if anyone were to dare tell me it's easy, I'd smack them in the mouth.

At a little after nine, there's just the familiar tap of Dan on his laptop and the kitchen clock. Peace.

But not for my temper.

Dan watches me pour a drink. 'Not for me, love – I'm fine.' He closes the laptop, clearly ready to converse. 'Thanks for asking.'

Risking whiplash, I flip my head back dramatically, making claw hands at the ceiling. It's better than violence, because, trust me, I've never been closer to lashing out. If I looked at my reflection and found myself at the centre of a ball of furious flames, I wouldn't be surprised. But, in the mirror behind Dan, there's no fire and fury, just a puffy, sad woman instead. Every bit knocking on forty, with the same look women around my age start to get; those dull, defeated eyes, despite the trying and the smiles. It's a look that comes when the best is likely behind us, when the best's been sacrificed to ungrateful kids and partners. Women, hollowed from putting everyone else first, in a world we co-created. And if it's all our own bloody doing, how dare we ever, ever complain?

Age does bring some wisdom. I know that if I had my time again, I would not have been as pliable, as easily led, as manipulated by men, in a world geared from day dot to put them first.

And right now, regardless of consequence, I am more than, more than, done.

'You're fine?' I ask, as Dan winces, doing his keep your voice down sign language, making me want to shout all the bloody louder. 'When your uncle grabbed and shoved me. Called me a black bitch.'

Dan won't meet my eye, his high ground shifting considerably.

'Me. Your wife.' I put my hands on my chest, still draped in the head-to-foot misery of black clothing. 'He groped me last Christmas, too. Ask Nancy.'

Closing his eyes, Dan swallows. 'Today was about Nan.'

'He had one hand on the back of my leg, and the other on my arse. Do you know what he said?' The question comes out high-pitched, out of character it's so girlish. 'He said, "I'd give it a try." '

Dan crosses and uncrosses his legs but offers not a single bloody word.

'*It*.' I lean into his face, baiting a reaction. 'So, what was he? Drunk? Only joking? Just being Budgie?' Dan's back to his shifting, but like a sniper with a target, I've got him pinned in place. 'Why've I had to learn not to bite? Why did you give him that power?' My body's one hot throbbing blood vessel. 'Penny, lapping up the black mother jokes, while you're swanning around hoovering up the compliments; how marvellous you are – how marvellous Yvonne was.' I knock back my drink, the fumes complementing, aiding my wrath. 'When really, she was a racist old bastard.'

'Don't you fucking dare!' Dan leaps from his chair and, clasping my throat, frog-marches me from the kitchen into the living room, raising his fist. He aims, before letting his hand splay open, spending the power of it. Lowering his arm, remembering the other's still on my neck, he lets go as if I've scorched him.

Like a puppy caught pissing behind the sofa, Dan can't meet my eye. He's gutted, it's obvious – but only for letting himself down. Bewildered, clasping his head, he walks away from me into the evening shadows of our conservatory, while back in the mirror, my sad, defeated look becomes stone, unflinching resentment.

It's a far more flattering reflection.

19

Revelations

'You're a liar.' The door to our Travel Den barely clicks shut and I'm already on Joe's case. He tries kissing me, stopping my words, but I keep having flashbacks of their happiness, along with an unfathomable urge to shred it all to buggery. Jealousy. Its power is horrifying. Especially when home's nothing but rubble and I'm desperate for an outlet. 'I saw your happy life – all over the walls.'

'I never said I wasn't happy. I said it wasn't enough.'

It's another thing I'm fuming over – my stupidity. Letting Joe in, only for him to exploit and pick me apart like everybody else. 'How easy I've been for you – d'you like Mars Bars? Public Enemy, Toni Morrison – wowzers, me too!' Every little thing. 'Your in-laws are bastards? Hey, guess what—'

'Stop,' he barks, rather menacingly. 'I never lied.'

'You never told me you liked Ed Sheeran—'

'He's done a few catchy ones. It's hardly the crime of the century.'

'You said Bella was cold. Un-mumsy.'

'I never once said that, either.' But he knows that he led me to think it. 'You're just feeling as I did when I had to shake hands with *perfect Dan.*' He says Dan's name as if it's made from week-old vomit. 'Ken Doll. Cunt.'

'Names, now – because Dan got by without Daddy and his coat-tails of nepotism?' I say it, not to defend Dan, but more because I can't quite quell this rage, my pounding palms and temples; a headache of furiousness that's become permanent. I'm hair triggered, hot on defence, always. 'Because he's not pretending to be some down-to-earth, down-with-the-kids—'

'What about you? The misunderstood damsel – ripe for plucking.' He leans forward into my face. '*Wanting* to be plucked. And you're not so helpless, either. In fact, you've got to be the most Machiavellian woman I've ever met.'

'Ah, the big words at last, *Mr Psychiatric Consultant.* Going into your house was like a *Scooby Doo* episode. I pulled off your fakery and suddenly this big pompous Tory git called Joseph appears—'

'Wash your mouth out; I'm absolutely not. But I absolutely love you. You're everything to me. If you said you'd be mine—'

'You'd leave that lovely house, that lovely, skinny blonde wife. And Molly. Would you?'

'In a heartbeat.' On his knees in front of me, Joe takes my hands in a begging sort of proposal. 'That time; bumping into you and the kids in Tesco. I've imagined walking into your house, into that life, ever since. A home with you.' His eyes, so earnest and sincere, move to my neck, then down to my shirt and bra lace, where they stay. I almost believe him.

'She was nothing like you said. Nothing.' I take a deep breath. 'I wanted to hate her.'

'It's jealousy. And what's jealousy but—'

Distraction. Distraction from everything bigger.

'Love, Mon. Look, I never said Bella was a monster. And neither am I miserable enough to warrant the drama of divorce.' Getting up, he flicks on the kettle, assembling our teacups on the tiny tray. 'Not unless there was an us at the end of it.'

'We're too different.'

'Says the woman who married a racist. Fuck me.'

'Just because he's *from* that doesn't make him like them.' Already, I'm conscious of the holes in my words as I recall Dan's wild defence of his family, my almost smack in the gob for calling them out. His lack of acknowledgement for their abject shittiness hurts more than the physical ever could – and I don't know how we come back from that.

Our fractures now are breaks. Irreparable, perhaps.

'Apples and leopards and all that. Scratch the handsome surface,' he stings, wounding me further when he pulls a new half-bottle of Bell's from his coat, not even bothering to hide it, knocking it back just like Sir Duke would when given something out of the ordinary and delicious – ingesting without tasting – before even fucking lunchtime.

'Better handsome, though. Bella's so equine-looking, she really should watch out on your summers down in France, they might package her up for the supermarkets.' But it's never attractive, running down the other woman. The proper woman. The one, when it all turns to shit, and only woman.

Joe's laughing at me, roaring in fact. If he were a cartoon, tears would be springing from his eyes. 'Little girl, you are terribly jealous.'

'Of course. Because I'm younger, better—'

'Because she's got me and I'm all you want. Even though you can't say it.' Clever Joe, managing to silence the spite in two neat sentences.

Oh God, the crying's back, the nervous shakes that I just can't settle. 'I needed you. It's been . . . you've no idea.' I'm a wreck, channelling the kind of person anyone with any sense would run screaming from, but I'm beyond caring, for once unbothered as to what I look like, how Joe sees me. And I don't know how to claw back any moral platform.

'I'm jealous too, trust me, it's absolute torture to think of your history, your bond – the bond I'll never be able to break – when all I want is to shatter it to fuckery.' He grabs my arms, holding me still against him. 'But I don't hate Dan, I'm grateful. Because every time you're here, with me like this, you become a little less his—' He waits, capturing me in the anticipation, his mouth on my mouth, fusing us closer. 'And a little more mine.'

What if he does think that I'm somehow beneath him, just a spicy bit of fanny, all hot and grateful in comparison to his iceberg wife in her iceberg kitchen? Because, if Joe had sex with Bella the way he has sex with me, he'd fucking break her.

'Please, please let's not fight. Let's not waste this,' he mumbles into the back of my neck, knowing what it'll do, and he uses the moment to begin to undress me, to get his own way. I hate myself, in absolute, as Joe unhurriedly slides his cock inside me, but the slick sensation of his movements soon blots out the self-loathing. He pushes harder, faster, gathering great fistfuls of my hair, and shoves me into the pillow, smothering my groans.

He thinks he's dominating, winning with the most prowess, but really, the bigger the point he needs to prove, well, I'm laughing really. Perhaps Joe isn't as clever a psychologist as he thinks.

I'll fall beneath him, for now.

To make up for the drought.

After, in the bathroom, I'm able to close a door on him. As the taps gush with the heat and steam that will purify me, I climb in, disappearing away from the dysfunction of myself – and Joe, too, with his frankly quite unsettling fixation with owning me.

274

Jealousy's a bastard emotion. It's overpowered and won, spoiling even the tiniest trickles of goodness. It's making us ugly.

I tip the shower gel into my palms, rubbing it into my face. The tiny foam bubbles begin to comfort, before the soap stings my eyes, taking the last remainders of smeared mascara from my face.

Clean, my body wrapped in one towel, and my hair in another, I take a quick peek round the door. There's an absence about Joe as I watch him, unmoved from the bed, only now absorbed in the television. Empty, perhaps. Robotic. Light years from my oil-slick guilt.

'I was going to get lunch, but—' He gestures to the telly, to Jamelia, in all her sleek, on fleek fabulousness, chatting with a very plain and orange guest I presume is off a reality show. Propped by a mountain of pillows, Joe grins soppily at the telly, as if our fight and the fraught jealous sex never happened.

– Was life as hard as it looked, out there on the island? asks Jamelia.

'Island!' Joe laughs, big and uninhibited, rattling the bed and the bottle on the bedside. 'It's a fucking set. Rainy night, ah, how lucky that roof-sized piece of tarpaulin washed up on the beach. Right next to the mismatched flip-flops and fishing net.' He gulps down his teacup. 'I used to fish as a kid. Me and Dad – there was a pub on the common.' He laughs again, but this time there's no fun in it. 'He'd hardly ever get to the water.'

It's rare for Joe to offer up anything truly personal. His revelation throws me. 'Did he do that often?'

'He wasn't like a TV pisshead – hiding bottles under the sink and wearing sunglasses indoors – he was brazen. He'd sign for a parcel with one hand and have a Hine in the other – at ten in the morning. My mother wasn't much better.'

I sit next to him, rest my head against his, my eyes passing from his reddish face to the scotch bottle. 'You're pissed.'

'How very dare you. I had a little mouthful. Christ.'

– And do you think you'll be seeing each other again, now it's back to reality? asks Jamelia, all bright teeth and mischief. The audience begin whooping and clapping. Their enthusiasm is alarming.

'What made you think of that – the fishing story?'

'I don't know.' He looks away, burrowing downwards into the duvet. 'Earlier. It was mucky. I'm sorry.' He licks his lips like an act of replenishment, his eyes unfocused, their rims a heavy red. Undoubtedly plastered.

I pick up the now very lightweight bottle. 'You can't be anything other than fucking steaming.' He grasps for it, but I'm sharper, holding it out of his reach.

'Don't,' he says, a bit too ferociously. 'Don't make me—'

'Don't make you what?' I meet his glare. 'You drank five inches of scotch in twenty-odd minutes.'

'I'm as open to you as I've ever been.'

What a load of shit.

Looking at him ruffling the covers around his neck, like an overindulged Tudor boy, my thoughts crowd in on themselves, avalanching. Joe, in this nothing's-ever-my-fault type of sulk, his lips now two hard-done-by slugs, is the most thwacking turnoff.

I scoop my bag from the floor, feely-bag searching for my purse, the familiar, soft leather finding its way into my hand. 'D'you want a sandwich if I pop out? Please don't ask for anything hot – it makes the room stink.' I fling my damp towel at him. 'Why don't you get in the bath, too?'

'All right, wife.'

'I thought that's what you wanted?' I stand, slipping into my shoes, drag my foundation brush across my t-zone.

'Something with bacon, then. Avocado's fine, but only if it's on brown.' He sounds like the flimsy twenty-somethings that he's always going on about. Millions of them, he often moans, all with the same problem – 'the digital age'. 'Just switch the fucking shit off,' he says, as though he has all the answers, which he clearly doesn't.

There's no way I'm coming back.

Later, starting dinner, I spot Joe through the window, stumbling up the front path. Terrified by what's coming next, I mumble an excuse to push the bins out, opening the door just as Joe's balled and lifted his knuckle to knock. Manhandling him round to the side of the house, I pull the door shut behind me. Heart hammering, I scan back to check along the street. No sign of Dan.

Yet.

'Like Prince Charming, I return your lost property.' With a deeply unsteady bow, Joe drops my forgotten earrings into my hand, full-on handsome, full-on imbalanced, as he props himself normal on my brickwork. 'I've been a dick. A pushy, petty little dick. Sorry, about earlier.'

'You can't be here.' I press my hands to my forehead, cold and clammy under my fingertips. This must be a hallucination, because things like this don't happen to me. They're reserved for television, tense dramas, not my world. I don't want this angst, this awful sense of foreboding when I look at the timebomb that is Joe. At a quarter past six on a flipping weeknight. And he knows, he fucking knows, that Dan will be home soon.

'I love you so much, I'd sleep on your doorstep.' He kicks the edge of it, at the little red lip protruding around the house, for effect. 'You look different here,' he says, studying me cockeyed, the drama either paused or forgotten. 'I don't like it.'

'Look, tomorrow – we'll talk ... properly. I promise.' I'd love to know what happened to that considerate man who took me to my mum's that day, who's kept me awestruck, despite all my weak efforts to end us. 'But you've got to go – now. You'll worry the kids if they see you.' It's the only trump I can think of that might restore any integrity.

'First though – and Mon – I know it's a big ask. A massive ask.' His hope blooms in front of me. 'But I booked. Just now from the train. Like we talked about.'

I look back into the house before answering. 'Booked?'

'The Landmark.'

'What – when?'

'My birthday.' He says it as if I should remember, but all that comes back to me is that he's cusp born. Of course he is. 'February twenty-first.'

'We're *in* February.'

'It's a surprise.'

'But we can't do surprises, can we?' I sound like Dan when he talks down to me as if I'm five. Only, Joe deserves it.

'Say you're on a spa or something, with your mum,' he suggests, with a carefree shrug of the shoulders, happy in his parallel pissed-up universe.

'Oh, of course. Because we're such great bezzies, exactly the mother–daughter to do spa breaks together.'

'It's one day. A twenty-four-hour, out-of-the-ordinary, you-and-me experience. Let me make up for earlier.'

Dragging the bin out of the front garden, the wheel catches on the crack in the concrete where it always does. With reluctance, Joe follows me, taking baby steps of concentration along the path. I check again for signs of Dan, relaxing a bit because I can't see him.

'No more drink.' I grab his hand. 'Promise me, straight home. Yes?'

'You promise me, then. Imagine: twenty-four hours. Tell me you don't want it?'

But I say nothing. Nodding, Joe flings the gate shut behind him. The metal bounces off the handle and swings open again, getting caught in the laurel.

'This,' Joe says, as I close the gate properly. He gestures to the house, turning back condemningly. 'This Garden of Eden jails you.'

I walk back to the house with my nerves multiplying – how reckless, for a pissed-as-a-sack grand gesture. But if twenty-four hours away would reset Joe a little, restoring the early version back to me, I'd do it in a heartbeat. Because I could do with his care right now – I've just got to care for him first.

Leaning against the closed front door, I put my earrings back in.

'What did he want?' Joel asks, as I leap from my skin.

'You startled me,' I say, to stall, wary.

'I see you, Mum.' Breathing through his nose, Joel's chest pounds through his t-shirt.

'What do you see?' But I'm foolish to question Joel's suspicion. The manic end music of *Teen Titans Go!* booms out of the living room, and I pray there's another episode, so the other pair sit tight.

'You both. Watching each other like you're starving hungry.' Joel widens his eyes as though I'm stupid, for a second the image of my mother. 'I watch *EastEnders*, Mum. I know what that means.'

Christ. Do I, *dare* I, deny? If I don't, we implode. And I'm not ready.

I'm also rather furious to be put on the spot. 'I am, yes, very fond of Joe. It's nice to have a friend.'

'A boyfriend.'

I elongate myself, enough to stand a fraction taller than him, to signify the swing-shift of authority back in my favour. *'Friend*. It's lovely to talk about books for ten minutes a day. Conversation isn't illegal, Joel.' I'm being a cunt, hate myself for it, but it's classic preservation mode.

Joel clucks his tongue, his eyes set on mine and refusing to budge. 'What about Dad, then?'

'What about Dad?'

'What's happening?' he asks. 'Everything's horrible. You and Dad whispering – or shouting.' I can't bear the tremble in his voice, can't think of any other time in Joel's life where his hurt's been my doing.

He looks older, his sweet softness replaced with this new, narrower face. Worry. My fault. How I've not noticed is shameful. 'Look, love, mums and dads—'

'Do me a favour,' he says, like he's the adult, knowing the bullshit when he smells it.

'All right. It's hard right now.' I sigh. 'Me and Dad aren't seeing eye to eye – but it'll pass. It's been stressful, what with the funeral – New Nan and Grandad. Nanny P hasn't been helping matters.'

Joel's shoulders give a little from the kindred raw point I'm nurturing in the best way I can. It needs a transparency, though – I can't use it as some personal attack on Penny. I don't want to be the one prejudicing my kids.

'Nanny P on TV.' He pokes his tongue out.

My tactics are clearly proving effective.

'Don't get me started.' There's warmth, a smile, one that's genuine from our in-joke, and I catch it, cupping his face in affection. 'Go on now, go and watch the telly. You've nothing to worry about.' I ruffle his curls, turning them frizzy. 'Except your nan getting knotted in her Union Jack bunting and doing herself a mischief.'

Irresistible.

20

No More Drama

Me and Dan remaining furious is starting to feel rather liberating. I'd be foolish, of course I would, to ignore Joe's wobble on the booze front – especially now, with my rightly suspicious son – but at least Joe never plays emotional games, can look both ways and say sorry. At home, I live exactly what I dreaded, within the shadows of Dan's moods and one-word responses. Yet I'm finding, now that I'm utterly disengaged, that the game only works if we're both playing. I cook Dan's meals and wash his pants and, provided there's well-stocked toilet roll and the kids aren't killing each other, we don't really need to speak at all.

And I don't have to pretend.

Since the funeral, we exist without a glance or a connection, climbing into bed without a goodnight, becoming ghosts. Dan is hardly present; just a faint hologram of handsomeness remains, nothing more than an empty puppet of Penny's. He comes home later now, usually just as I'm dishing up dinner. Because of the kids' rapid chatter and habit of talking over one another, I'd hoped Dan's silences passed mostly unnoticed. But at least I know now. I can reassure Joel, and the others should they need it, that it's life. A rough patch.

Nothing to worry about.

But now we're with Nancy and Hunter in the middle of Soho for a meal out, I wish he'd bloody speak. It's Valentine's Day.

And hilarious that, despite having two men in love with me, neither remembered.

Nancy and Hunter have been carrying the conversation for what's surely an hour now, but a crafty glance into my evening clutch shows we've only been here forty minutes. Our mains are yet to arrive. Hunter's talked us through an acquisition he made this morning, and in the same airflow about their upcoming Cuban holiday and the new crate of Languedoc red from the vineyard they own shares in. Nodding politely, oohing in the right places, I want to claw my own face off.

'You're both so bloody quiet,' Nancy says eventually, while Dan dissects the fishcakes he's ordered, because I don't like – and therefore won't pinch – them. 'Is this Funeralgate – still?' I keep silent, feigning distraction by smiling at the gorgeous dimpled bundle in a highchair at the next table, while she studies me.

'Moms, hey.' We each invisibly wince at Hunter Americanizing on purpose. 'No matter how old we get, we'll always be the kids.'

Dan meets Nancy's eyes, though I can't read behind either of their expressions. Their relationship is peculiar – though of course, I've no real expertise in the mechanics of adult sibling relationships. With only a year between them, or as Penny, failing to see the offence in it, likes to croon out, My Irish Twins – to anyone unlucky enough to enquire about the gap – you'd think they'd be close, more unified in their outlook. If it weren't for me and the kids between them, I wonder whether they'd see much of each other at all.

Our mains, a selection of dishes designed to divvy, are placed before us, though the sharing ethos remains rather absent from our table. 'Look, how often do we do this, the four of us? Tell me what's new, what's exciting.' Nancy tries, but Dan remains concrete boredom.

'I got my acceptance,' I say, offering the first thing in my head. 'Once I've finished this taster course, it's all in place to start the degree in October.'

Cheers erupt from Nancy and Hunter. 'At bloody last,' she says, clinking my glass.

'You didn't say,' Dan says.

'I didn't think you'd be interested.'

He sniffs and shrugs, not looking up from his plate.

'Well, I'm interested,' Nancy says. 'And I want all the goss about your mum—'

Dan huffs into the ceiling. I bite before I can stop myself. 'You know what, Dan, you look ridiculous – a full-grown sulking baby. I've had enough of men like you, bossing and behaving—'

'Men like me.' Dan swoops around, cutting me off. 'Who else do you know, then?'

Remembering how to breathe is all at once rather challenging. How bloody thoughtless. Dan eyes me, straight and direct, and I mustn't, mustn't look away first.

'Crikey.' Nancy whistles. 'I'm more embarrassed by the chemistry than the bickering.' She gives a big romantic sigh, turning to tickle Hunter under his chin. 'I hope we still look at each other like that when we've been married as long as you. You're our inspiration; you can't let us down by fighting.'

'You know,' Hunter interjects, in a camaraderie-type drawl, 'when it gets like that, the best thing to do is just kiss her. It knocks the upset out of the drama; puts it to better use.' Excusing himself, he sashays off to the toilets, turning the heads of a table full of expensive highlights as he flounces past.

It might be the most thought-provoking thing Hunter will ever say.

Our tipsy return to a rare empty house should result in a shedding of eveningwear, our garments strewn like Hansel and Gretel's path of breadcrumbs to the bedroom, where, instead of a candy-land cottage of confectionery, we'd feast on each other. But any urge for Dan to mount me has well and truly left the building. I'd rather please myself, be selfish in the act, than have his wet sulky babyishness anywhere near my ladybits.

But Dan is troubled; there are lilac bags beneath his eyes, a permanent cross expression – smiling like something he's never heard of, despite our full tummies and warm comfortable home. He's still bloody frowning now, more Joe-like by the second, but even that doesn't stir me. It's not his looks that are turning me off, anyway. It's all about what's inside, these days, for me. And Dan feels hollow. He takes forever in the shower while I hurry into bed, ready to perform the grand old act of pretending to already be asleep, preferring my headful of silence, my sacrosanct solitude. When he climbs beneath the covers, I know he sees through it, but sense his relief as well.

Lying in the dark, awake with our mouths shut, we're together, but never further apart. Fearful of the change any real talk might stir, we feel futile.

'Mum was really grateful.' Dan's voice makes me jump. 'Having the kids tonight.'

I don't answer him, know that keeping Penny from the kids was a shitty trick to pull. One I thought I was above, but who else would look after them, so I could see Nancy and Hunter and feel momentarily normal again? I'm not ready for my parents to babysit, and neither are the kids. Any residual fight has fermented into acceptance, anyway. I don't want to battle against Dan and his family, I just don't want them. And if I could pluck them out like a rotten tooth, I'd do it – without anaesthetic. I'm tired.

Sat with Nancy and Hunter earlier, the stretched conversation punctured by my and Dan's sniping, I'd the feeling, a wondering, whether it might've been the last social for the four of us. My disconnect from Dan is so obvious, so visible, that I don't know how we ever fitted in the first place, let alone for as long as we have. Our physical attraction was always the glue, but now, without even that to fall back on, there's nothing left to bond us together.

'You might not like it, Mon, but they were so pleased to see her.'

Nothing left to bond us – apart from the kids.

Still play-sleeping, I keep silent, while he bristles – tolerant Dan mode fading.

I'm wondering how divorce happens, what I'd cite as the reason, if I'd bother – thinking of Joe's 'not-unhappy-enough-to-warrant-the-drama-of-divorce' old guff. Incriminating Joe. Dan throwing adultery around in court sounds far superior to the My In-laws Are Bastards reasons for separation. Would I stay in this house? Could I, considering it was Dan's wages and a nest-egg kickstart from Penny and Clive that secured it? Domestic and motherly duties aren't weighed on a monetary scale; those (ha) man-hours are fluid transactions, invisible, till it all goes tits anyway. All those billions of thankless tasks that nobody else notices.

I could be with Joe. Upset the world by having him on a purely selfish skin-to-skin daily basis. Just the thought of him, and I've that empty vessel yearning in my insides, which I'm not sure has much to do with love, but does enough to tell me that we're not done, Joe and I. Imagination stirs erotic flashbacks of myself, spread and pinned by his tongue, on a sumptuous bed, somewhere a cross between my very Catholic dream and somewhere like the Landmark. The Landmark.

'Things can't stay like this.' Dan pops the fantasy. 'All this bloody tension. Kids pick shit up – Joel, especially. And you might not like me much right now—'

'What do you mean Joel especially?'

Dan sighs. 'Avoidance. Becoming a proper teenager, I suppose – but he's been so quiet.'

He has. Lurking in corners, watching me as my mother would, guilty until proven innocent – which means never, in my case.

'It's not fair on him.' Dan's right. It's not fair. Joel's doubt in me weighs heavy on my shoulders. 'He's like you. Dead cold lately. Like you just switched yourself off.'

'I told you, I'm tired.'

'Too tired to try for our kids?' Dan snarl-whispers, forgetting that he doesn't need to be quiet.

'No. Too tired full stop.' The tears come before I know it. Dan never likes to see me cry.

'I'm not surprised. I've watched you, all week with those bloody books. Essays, here with this lot, and the library, too – I don't know what you keep trying to prove.'

But they're the parts of my life that are the most energizing. Kathryn's constant chat, more up to date than Twitter.

Reading with a question to answer in mind – and getting it, learning, finding shit out. What's really tiring me is him. But I won't tell Dan again.

Yet I don't correct him. Despite whatever I ate tonight that was salty and kicking off an epic headache, my brain works fast. 'My mum did mention a break, funnily enough. She wants to do something for her birthday.' I seize the chance to spin my shit, till Dan's nodding and agreeing about a mother–daughter spa day likely being just the ticket. And how we'll both keep an eye on Joel – together – as we shift into becoming just a little bit more human.

21

The Impossible Dream

The pressure and expectation surrounding Joe's birthday is all I can think about. Our illicit night away – though likely physically rewarding – has me now in constant panic. But I'm going. A spa is out of character, yes, but not particularly suspect. It's the sort of thing mums and daughters do, that kind fathers, trying to set things right, offer as treats. Clive's done the same for Penny and Nancy, gifting vouchers for Ragdale Hall, which – when there's been no excuse lightning enough – I've been forced to tag along to myself. Dan's not to know that in place of my mother at the Landmark Hotel, Marylebone, it'll be Joe. My plan was, at the very last moment, to invent a phone call where my mum tells me she's poorly, and I go 'alone'.

Though it's dealt with by a simple text, the lie feels over-whelming and enormous. And I know I won't be right until

I'm home, round the family dinner table tomorrow night, when we're all back together. Eating in friction, or not.

I pack the exciting things beneath the lining of my case; spectacularly scaffolded underwear, black with white polka dots, and a Jessica Rabbit-type dress I've never worn, unsuitable for most occasions, but perfect for spending a night at the bloody Landmark, where it's true I've always wanted to stay, having wasted many a moment on their social media, drooling over their beautiful atrium. It's the sort of decadence I've always dreamed of; impossible as real life.

And I gave in, went for a silk press that I know won't last beyond ten seconds in a steam room, but seeing as I've no intention of using the facilities, I felt my old sleek glamour deserved a bit of a comeback.

I take my essay to show Joe, too. He'll be pleased, I think, for me at last pulling my finger out where this degree's concerned. Especially if I add in that Dan's not fully on board. I'm like a child of divorce, playing one parent off against the other.

And having my cake.

I dismiss that thought, and quickly. There's nothing quite like a pang of reality to put a stop to any smug gratification. I must never become complacent.

Leaving the house, existing in a permanent pleasure-angst moment, I look immaculate – a sore thumb on the school run, but bollocks. All the essentials are taken care of, too. Clean ears and nails, a trimmed yet respectable hedgerow. Preened, not porno.

I'm ready.

On the train platform, I find myself next to a lady with enormous launderette shoppers, one stuffed so plump the zip has split. It's down to me to assist with those lead-weight bags. Helping her on, I drop, hot from exertion, into a forward-facing seat near the window. The lady smiles grate- fully as she passes, shunting her bags along the walkway with her foot as the train begins to move. Gaining speed, the buildings beyond become a sweeping streak of grey that fragments like Morse code, before blurring into the country green that transcends.

Goodbye town that I adopted, the Petersen refuge from all that's foreign and filthy. Goodbye home, familiarity, offspring, responsibility, husband, disappointment, xeno- phobia, claustrophobia.

Hello Joe, the catalyst for my thoroughly British seedy secret escape.

The catalyst.

But not the reason.

The flawless girl on the front desk studies her screen, then smiles. 'Welcome to the Landmark. Dr McEvoy has already checked in. He's waiting in the Twotwentytwo. May I take your luggage?'

'The Twotwentytwo?'

'The bar.' As she gestures with her dainty, dinky little hands, I miss most of the directions. Just because Joe's in the bar, it doesn't mean he's pissed. With a nod, I set off in what

I hope is the way to the Twotwentytwo, and she doesn't contradict.

This is a beautiful building. By far the most opulent place I've ever stayed – and for a second, I falter, rather lost, in awe of the glorious character of it all. I almost wish I still had my weekender with me, strapped across my body like a wary old bag woman, fortressed by possessions and security. A man holds the door as I enter what reminds me of that grand foyer in *Titanic*, where a baby-faced Leo waits for Kate beneath the clock. The walls are a heavy wood panelling, the colour of glazed caramel, and from brilliantly detailed ceiling roses hang the most spectacular chandeliers, twinkling down a serene dappled light.

And amidst all the glorious detail that I want to absorb and remember is Joe, reclining in a baroque gentleman's club armchair – in full-on DiCaprio glory. Two fabulous-looking gin and tonics sit in front of him – the sort you'd immediately Instagram, if you were the type.

'All right?' he asks, grinning so much it must physically hurt, as he stands to welcome me. He looks delicious and smells even better.

'Hello. Yes.' Because, funnily enough, I am now. 'Happy birthday for tomorrow.'

Joe kisses me on both cheeks, cupping my face. 'This means everything.' Releasing me, he sits back down, picking up his drink. Slipping into the seat opposite and stirring my gin a little, I find the ice is still new. He can't have been here long.

'Is everything to your satisfaction, Dr McEvoy?' a waiter asks, pausing at our table – friendly, yet unobtrusive.

'Very much so, thank you.'

'And Mrs McEvoy, how are you finding the Landmark?'

'It's beautiful, thank you.' I glance disapprovingly at a very happy Joe. I haven't asked about his excuse to the real spouse. I'd rather not think of Bella at all.

With a polite nod, the waiter sets down a small dish of olives, vanishing as smoothly as he appeared.

'Monica McEvoy,' Joe says, dropping two in his mouth. 'I love a bit of alliteration. It suits you.'

'Wife number three?' I raise a brow, with another cautionary look, but he's still grinning at me.

'Third time lucky.' He lifts his glass, knocks it softly against mine. 'Cheers.'

It's only a small squabble, and one that's extinguished more by the joint we share in the hotel grounds than a truce. There's no point in arguing, we're here now, and the marijuana and two large gins have allowed me to relinquish most of my irritation. Joe told me he'd booked the cheapest twin, under the – ha, most believable – mother–daughter guise.

The cheapest twin has now transformed Cinderella-like into the Marylebone suite.

I don't know why it's made me cross, exactly – it just seems showy, too much of a risk, but we're past that now, because how do I answer '*Can't you just fucking indulge me for once, Monica?*' Why indeed? Why fight because he's upgraded to a sunken bath, fruit, champagne and complimentary White Company?

Home's in order too. Dan's got a takeaway for later and is on his way back; Fran collected from school by Penny. And, after spilling my last-minute lie, Dan even wished my mother well – strangulating me with guilt.

'Good God, you look perfect,' Joe says admiringly, sprawled across a delicate chaise, as I materialize in our own flipping lounge in my red cocktail frock. 'We should eat downstairs.' He reaches across for the telephone. 'Shall I try and book us a table?'

'I think I'd rather stay here. It's all a bit too splendid to waste.'

'But your dress?'

'It's for you.'

He smiles, gratified. And typical. Yes, he's my champion, but there's no doubting, despite all that liberal egalitarianism, that Joe would rather have me devoted; a comely sunny home-bird of a wife with a wardrobe full of crimson, feeding and fucking him.

Not a million miles off Dan's preferences, either.

'No,' he says suddenly. 'I'm booking. We'll sit down there in the thick of it all, heads high. Legitimate. Yes?'

I'd regret not fully embracing our fantasy parallel universe, so I may as well go with the happy addled flow of things. Pretend to be the wife, pretend that this, our dream of us, is real.

It may never happen again.

We play the game to perfection. There's contentment, a mellow happiness at our table beneath a palm tree, with the twilight London sky spread above us. When Joe offers me a forkful of duck, I happily sample – the most ordinary utensil brimming with his DNA, for my, legitimate, consumption. Other diners have little interest in the intimacy between us, threaded magnificently through every interaction – and that's the best part of it. Our union is so natural, so effortless, nobody would ever think to question its rightfulness.

And it feels so very right.

As we take a slow walk back to our room, I remember our start, last October. All the times we've been together since, how easy and fun and freeing it's been, until always the time comes to separate, and we fall back into our old selves.

But not tonight.

There are no messages, no panics. Just us.

'Best birthday ever, and not even my birthday for forty minutes.' Amused, he watches as I try swiping the door with the key. He takes it from me, slipping it through the lock with ease.

'How? You've drunk twice as much as me.'

'Practice,' he replies, as the door swings open. 'Decades of practice.' He lifts me, perhaps a couple of feet from the floor, and I curl my limbs around him, convinced that he'll discover me too heavy, but all the same bloody thrilled he's so enamoured. Romance and passion, it's overflowing here in bucketloads.

As I'm set on the bed and he takes off his suit, the knot of guilt finally leaves me. I've never known anything as beautiful and rapturous as this, here tonight. The way I feel when I'm with him.

'Tell me something, Joe, that no one else knows.'

He pulls a face, taking his time to think. 'I piss, wash and brush my teeth in the shower every morning.' Dragging off his tie, Joe grins, happy I'm laughing, happy he's made me happy. 'Some days I add masturbation to the multitask – or tears. It's the most revolting, rebellious thing I do all day. And I need it.'

Blatant honesty. It's what I've been missing.

I could tell him I love him. Because I do. I really think I do.

'What's the matter?' he asks, crawling up the bed towards me. 'You look sad. You're not allowed to look sad.'

Play the game. Don't say anything to alter the joy.

'Hello, hey Joe, you wanna give it a go?' If I wasn't half-drunk, I'd be awash with self-consciousness to have used the back-pocket line I've kept as a guilty pleasure for just the right moment. But it gets the reaction that's needed, because we laugh, and become instantly lighter. 'Happy Birthday.'

Orgasm gifts initial knockout drops, but by around three I'm fully awake. Shutting myself in the bathroom with my phone, I use the time alone to set myself back in order, re-reading Dan's message from earlier – glad to cement its ordinariness. There's nothing remotely off, other than me, at odds now with this flashback version of myself. I can't remember the last time

I slept in full make-up, and avoid the mirror running along the entire left of the marble room. Showering, glad to wash away the decadence and the straight hair, I climb back in beside Joe, unable to resist a grope of his limp clammy treasures. No action. No movement. On his back he lies, head resting in his hands, his bottom lip glistening with sleeper's drool. I'm not used to a snorer. I think of Dan, asleep on his tummy, breathing through his nose – self-taught.

Dan.

I wonder if Fran's managed to sneak a night on my side of the bed. It's an image that hurts to conjure. Better to sleep, if I could, and if it weren't for the snores that I'm sure are sending shockwaves down the hall, I'd think Joe was dead.

'We need to talk.' Joe's beside me, nudging a teacup into my hands.

It takes all the motor skills I have to take the cup and set it next to me. I check my phone. 'It's bloody ten past five.'

'I'm just going to come out and say it, and then no more secrets. Like you say, they're toxic.' He edges closer, a sour sweetness emanating from his skin, already hangover waxy. 'I've been taking some time off. Stress-related leave. It's why I wasn't there after the funeral. I had a meeting.'

I put my arms around him. 'Why didn't you tell me?'

'I didn't want to be compared to your city slicker husband.'

'I wouldn't have been like that.'

'It's hardly an alluring selling point, though, is it? Me hiding at my mum's because I can't work. Look, the long and

the short is, if you leave him, be with me, then I'd be all right.
I know I would.' He leans down the side of the bed, pulling
up a dusky blue document wallet. Slipping the bundle of
papers out, he hands them to me.

I sift through pages and brochures. Estate agent details,
houses. Houses bigger than mine. Rentals.

'What is this?'

'A home.' Joe taps on the folder. 'For us. And all the kids,
of course.' He looks at me crossly. 'Not for right now, but
I've got to plan. Got to make plans. You see.' He takes back
the papers, sifting to find whatever he's looking for. 'See, I
did some workings out. If I were to work privately, we could
afford this.'

'But you've always said you'd hate that.'

'Needs must. Marriage guidance, perhaps.' I can't help
laughing. 'For fuck's sake,' he snaps, irritated.

'The irony. It's brilliant. I'm sorry.'

Joe shoves a brochure under my nose, of a classic Victorian
semi, high spec and half a mile from the city station.

'Why're you putting all this pressure on yourself, when I
could work, too?'

'But you mustn't change at all. It wouldn't be right. Just
you. As you are. As you are with him.' Annoyed, he snatches
it back. 'I know you're not ready. I'm not stupid.'

'*You're* not ready, more like. Binge-drinking like some
broken bohemian teenager. You're not Holden bloody
Caulfield, Joe. You've two kids, a wife – and a mortgage
already.'

Reaching for his tea, Joe misses his mouth, his chest hair an instant sponge. With the towel from my shower, I dab him dry, find him gazing at me in wonderment.

'If only I'd known as a teenager, all those moons ago, that I'd get a girl like you.'

'You put me on too high a pedestal.'

'A stratospheric pedestal wouldn't be high enough,' he says, the greyness of his eyes almost transparent in the lamplight. 'What d'you think it would've been like, if we could have met way back when – us from the very start?' Going for his tea again, he trembles, ever so slightly.

And if I wasn't looking for the signs, I wouldn't notice.

'I don't know. We'll never know.' But I have wondered it. That I'd not let some old perv show me the ropes. That I'd never disappointed my parents – and instead met a boy whose dad was a bloody doctor of all things, with a mother who welcomed me instantly. In-laws – I'd swap prejudiced for pissed up, any day of the week.

And Joe. His poems and attentiveness. The babies we'd have had. The day to day, side by side. I've spent a million moments dreaming beautiful, agonizing, fantasies of it. But we can wish all we like; we're nothing stronger than a dream.

It's not our life.

'It can't ever be.' I tell him this, hoping, also, that by saying it aloud I too will accept it. 'And it's gutting.'

'I think you love me, exactly as I love you.' He slumps into the pillows, opening his arms for me.

'We're not kids, though.' I snuggle close, hating myself for being the grown-up, the one to spoil the hope. 'But I swear, in my whole life, nothing has, and nothing ever will, match this.'

'I'll love you ferociously till I die, Mon.'

If he carries on like this, that'll be sooner rather than later. His earnestness is tainted by the shakes. I'm under no illusion that if I did shack up with Joe, our happy ever after would always be in battle with his thirst. He couldn't stay sober for his own babies, so despite all this feeling, all the loveliness that'd come from being together properly, I can't risk mine.

But neither can I hurt him.

Not today.

2 2

Up, Up and Away

It's always heartening to discover, when returned to the nest, that you're missed – and something else, unaccustomed to most mothers' ears – appreciated, too. The house looks nothing like how I'd do things, yet regardless, things have been done well enough. Twenty-four hours away feel more like a fortnight's holiday. I'm viewing the house with distant and critical eyes; it's looking a little shabby and unloved – mirroring our marriage. But Dan's happy enough to see me, tells me I look rested, and can he spa off now to get over his day in my shoes. I thank him for holding the fort, and he says, well, they're my kids too.

And though we smile, we're static.

Neither of us knows how to push down the barrier. And though it would usually be me to initiate, coaxing for more, I can't any longer.

Our weekend trickles away in polite distance, until Sunday lunchtime. Thanks to a bit of rare February sun, Dan has the idea of finding a beer garden with an outdoor play area. We drive further out than usual, into Suffolk with the windows down, as the car slashes its way through Constable country.

'It's a lovely idea.' I motion to the kids in the back as they belt out all the words to one of Dan's songs. Clocking them in the mirror, he smiles. The happy normalcy of being together encourages more, when Dan joins in himself, making everyone laugh. As the song trails away, he looks across, then beyond me, his eyes lingering in thought.

'What?' I ask.

'Nothing. Doesn't matter.' Focusing on the road, he indicates, turning into the car park of a pub so huge it must surely be a hotel as well. There's a pond, a couple of picnic benches – Adnams on pump.

'There's a climbing frame!' shouts Fran, as Dan makes the decision to park, pulling into a space near the entrance.

'I can smell chips,' says Toby.

And it ticks all the boxes.

I'm so stuffed, I've removed my belt, having scoffed one roast beef dinner, Fran's leftover chicken goujons and several onion rings – lukewarm, but still crunchy. Tensions have mellowed considerably since leaving the house, my appetite returned in abundance. But these days there's no need for gluttonous food guilt; I'm in pre-Dan jeans, and feel rather clever whenever I wear them.

'I hope this sunshine carries on.' I give my sunglasses a polish on my cardigan. 'Makes me dream of holidays again.'

I flipping get him to smile. 'Any suggestions?'

'I wouldn't be fussy. Anywhere but Trinidad or Tenerife.' It's too flippant. Too soon. But he doesn't seem slighted.

'What about Norwich?'

'It's not exactly known as a holiday hotspot. I went once on a school trip, to the cathedral.'

'I was there last Tuesday,' he says, in such a way that I give him my absolute attention.

'You didn't say.'

'We've not exactly been on the best of terms.'

'Were you there for work?'

'Sort of. A client – more a friend now actually – relocated last year, found it a lot easier than he thought, what with the direct trains back to the Old Smoke. He's expanding.'

'Sorry, who's this?'

'Maxwell. Abrams. You did meet him, a couple of years back, at that Brazilian steakhouse, d'you remember – with the drunk speaker?'

I do remember. It was a horrible phase the company went through, encouraging partners at client entertainment; *Mad Men*, without the finesse. Fortunately, it died off quickly.

I don't, however, remember Maxwell.

'Well, anyway.' Dan harnesses the tangent. 'He's offered me a job.'

'In Norwich?' I watch his face, unable to quite believe what I think he's about to say.

'Twenty-one years I've been doing it, pulling myself on and off those bastard trains. I'm a battery hen. And I'm knackered,' he says, seriously. 'And then there's Mum. The shit with Budgie and Gracie.'

'What shit?' There's so much on my plate, Gracie only enters my thoughts at night. Both in and on my conscience.

'Gracie did a moonlight flit, apparently – that's all I know.' He shrugs his shoulders, blowing out, with a look I can't interpret. 'All over, in six little months. It makes you think.'

Doesn't it? But I'd rather not.

'So, moving.' Dan watches me.

Blimey. For a while, I imagine it would be like a holiday, with all the joys anonymity brings. Fresh starts, like clean sheets, can't be anything but positive. Shackles of history, reputation, erased forever, in favour of the blank canvas of the carefree.

Dan talks in galloping enthusiasm about the good schools and cheaper houses; a new direction career-wise. Not so much of a corporate carbon copy, he'd be joining a company of just three others. He even touches on creating a breathing space between us and Penny, which makes me wonder if he's spoken to Nancy.

Which would be massive. To talk to her properly, seek advice. He knows we're crumbling.

Norwich.

My mind begins its usual list-making – the problems we'd lose by moving. I picture us in a hot-air balloon, travelling on an easterly wind.

And when we start to sink, I know just who to dump first.

Out goes Penny, her culottes flapping wildly as she plummets. She might dip in and out of the country to the point where we're free for three months of every year, but it's still not enough. I want her claws and her despicable ignorance away from my children for good. With Penny goes the kind old jellyfish Clive. And Budgie. On the day of the funeral, I swore he'd not get another thought or feeling from me. Erased for evermore, out from the balloon he falls – perhaps just as we're passing over some perilous stony terrain . . .

My parents won't be fazed by any distance, considering how far apart we previously existed. Being in touch is better than not, but we've still a long way to go. Over they go, too.

The balloon rises high.

Then plateaus. Joe. Who's been ringing so much that my phone's on permanent silent, chocked with messages that begin lovely, then sour, now the birthday bubble's popped. My heart, racing through the positives of escape, stumbles. Even now I know better, even though all we have is tipping, any distance from Joe would be shattering.

Norwich. A rather radical solution, to escape the externals that are bit by bit dismantling us. Like moving to Spain – only flatter and windier.

It's still distance.

'All right.' I give his hand a squeeze, which he seems to like. 'Norwich it is.'

'We'll keep it between us, till it's more concrete – I'm so glad you're keen.'

It's Dan's excitement, that rare emotion he saves for strict necessity, that's the most overriding positive of all.

23

Penny Dreadful

'I thought you'd dropped me, now you've got your mum back.' Penny stands, straddling her flowers in the front garden of her bungalow. She's wearing navy Crocs and cropped trousers; her linen shirt speckled with soil from the bed she's weeding. Her face is flushed, pretty, even, from the wholesome exertions in the morning sun.

I'd hoped she wouldn't be here, that I could just leave her autumn bulbs and leg it, but I'm being ushered in, the kettle's being switched on. I put the bag on the table, next to her *Daily Mail*.

'I can't stay,' I tell her, thinking of Joe, who I've also managed to avoid this morning – and every day this week. As much as I long to see him, there's really very little point. He's a walking liability; swallowed by all he's consuming. And it's horrible to admit.

'No thought for us.' Penny's mugs come out of the cupboard. 'Disappearing off to Norwich,' she mutters, flinging teabags into them. 'What's in bloody Norwich? Weather's the same as here.'

Un-bloody-believable. What was it Dan said, about keeping it quiet? 'It's a wonderful opportunity, Penny.'

'Opportunity nonsense – Daniel Petersen has his finger on the pulse in the City. If you pulled yours out instead of spouting all this mature student twaddle, you might be able to scrape a deposit for somewhere hot.'

'There's more to bloody life than egg and chips and *Only Fools and Horses* re-runs in the Canaries, Penny.'

'How dare you, Monica – after all we've done, how bloody dare you?' She slams her fists on the worktop, her voice wavering.

'What do you mean, all you've done?'

'We welcomed you in, we looked after you.'

'Welcomed?' I laugh. 'You've a very short memory.'

'What choice did I have but to welcome you in? I raised a good boy – he took his responsibilities.'

Ah.

'You did it on purpose,' she gabs on, now that the lid's off. 'He was always going to support you. And now look, you've got him to abandon us properly. Upping sticks like this. You never think of anyone but your bloody self. Dragging the kids away from their friends, their school?' Her hypocrisy is mind-blowing. They moved to Essex when Dan started secondary. Nancy hated the change so much she'd rush back to London every chance she got. 'I knew. I knew it. From day one, you were no good.'

'Because I was brown.'

'Because I had a feeling, a terrible feeling. Mothers know.' *Mothers know.* What on earth did she do on the planet before she was impregnated? 'He'd have picked you, y'know, when push came to shove.' She tries frowning, the overplucked brows fighting to pucker in on themselves. 'When he told us you were pregnant.'

'I was never anything but polite, Penny.'

'You bloody weren't – I could tell you were judging us, right from the off!' This is ridiculous. In my whole time knowing them – except lately – I've always been respectful. 'Such a haughty girl – not happy until every man in the room had noticed you. I saw through it. And Daniel,' she clucks, 'my boy – holding you up like some sort of princess.'

'Don't turn it all on me. I've put up with you for years because I love him. I've always loved him.'

'You've just had your big reunion with your stuck-up parents. I'd have thought you'd be in each other's pockets, trying to make up for lost time. Yet you're moving. Makes us wonder what you're running away from.' Penny's eyes swim as she tries to stop her hands shaking, clasping them together across her tummy. Her rings – so much gold and sparkle – twinkle in the light through her faux bay window.

I could be cruel, tell her we're off because the only time Dan and me row is when she's mentioned, that their whole dick-splash family's poison. That moving's the only thing left that might heal us.

'We're not running away. It's an exciting opportunity.'

'*It's for you*. Every breath he blimmin' takes is for you.'

'It was his idea! Look, I don't want to fall out.'

'Neither do I!' She tears a sheet of kitchen roll and begins dabbing her eyes. 'But you're so clever, twisting things, twisting everything to get your own way, breaking my brother's heart at Mum's—'

'Open your eyes, woman. Your brother broke his own heart – all by his bloody self. And you knew it wouldn't last, you said yourself at their wedding! Gracie had a lucky escape. You know that, too.' I stop for breath. 'But anyway, what about you?'

'What about me?' she asks, surprised.

'Are you sorry? Half-chat, half-breed. How I was confused and didn't know how to be a mum to the boys because I was torn between two races? Where's my apology, hey?' I'm trembling too now, two jelly people in her pristine kitchen. I could stop, but her silly mouth is gaping open, as though she can't quite believe I'm daring to say it, to unearth all that's grotty in her top-end (but still only B&Q) kitchen. 'All your worshipping of Nigel Farage, and dickishness over Facebook. The racism—'

Stunned, eyes wide, she's baffled I could think her capable of such a thing. 'You've overstepped the line. I don't wish anybody any harm—'

'The racism. Yvonne, who wouldn't meet my eye. Budgie making fun of Mum's heritage. Never a thought for the kids, that it's their background, too. But they're watching you, Penny, watching how you parrot everything from this.' I pick up her paper and toss it, Frisbee-like, across her dining table. 'This shit you call a paper. Don't you dare start telling me I'm a twisted person, because I've never met anyone so small-minded and ridiculous as you.'

'Just get out!' she screams. 'You monstrous bitch. Of all the ungrateful—'

'Look in the mirror, Penny, if you're really wondering why we're going.'

Shit's sake. I could have left it perfect, my point made more cohesively than I ever thought I could. But I've let myself down. I don't want to see her sobbing.

'I loved you, Monica. Like a daughter.'

'You tolerated me.' I pick up my handbag, heading for the door. 'And I tolerated you.'

24

Old Tricks

Mum's pleased to see me, but the concern's obvious. And as much as I know this could shatter our progress, there's really no one else.

Who'll understand exactly how I feel.

I sputter to begin with in her little front room, finding it hard to put the past twelve years in order – so she can see, comprehend, how it's happened. I tell her about meeting Penny, and those early, strange days that followed, where she'd pretend to be ill, always some last-minute emergency invented to keep Dan and me apart. I describe the rest of the family, the old bastard Nana Yvonne, who'd once regaled at some shindig how she'd directed her new Bangladeshi neighbour, a young woman with a handful of English and two wailing toddlers in a pram, to the wrong bus. How I'd been huge and ready to drop, and Penny had joked that the family were referring to my baby bump as the ball of confusion.

Wearily, I spill, as Mum huffs, tired herself, picking down at the raw sides of her thumbs in the same habit that I remember. She'd pick at her feet too, the insides of her heels where no one would notice, catching at the drier parts, picking it loose in flecks, until she caught good skin, healthy live skin, that she'd peel like a mushroom till it bled. With words and tales, I do the same, offloading, exposing every tiny injustice I can remember, certain there's more that I can't, as she sits very straight, her eyes hell-black serious as she wordlessly absorbs it all, still pick, pick, picking.

'Dan's said, a million times, that I'm oversensitive. Some things have been so small, it doesn't enter his head that it matters. But it's hurt, Mum. It's made me less . . .' It's so difficult to word, and I can't think of the right ones.

It's made me less.

'And what's Dan saying now?'

Dan doesn't know about the argument – not from me, anyway. His attention comes in waves. One moment he's Norwich this and Norwich that, and the next he's silent, staring into corners, like he's ten tons of shit on his shoulders. And I keep hearing Penny in my head – *makes us wonder what you're running away from*. It's the *'us'*, the still nagging sense that they all know something I don't, that's got me sleeplessly grinding my teeth at night.

'I haven't told him. It'll probably lead to another row.'

Another row? I feel her searching square into the soul of me, and I stiffen.

But whatever she finds, she leaves alone. Pacing to the window, she shakes her head, hands balled and parked on her hips. 'Who's Peggy to judge – you, or anybody else? Her only platform's the one in her head. Stupid family. First-class embarrassments.'

There it is – beneath the surface, a rumbling of her dominance and fury. Still the same old, as though she's developed a terrific cramp in her limbs, her nose tense, as if it's about to expunge smoke and fire.

Only today, I like it.

Understand it.

'Do you think it'd be a mistake, uprooting the kids for Norwich? We could be jumping ahead of ourselves – nothing's certain yet.'

But it doesn't matter. Even if Norwich falls through, we need to get away. It's the only way. One clean shot to put things right; we owe it to our offspring.

'Live,' she says, without hesitation. 'Moving, and *who takes back control* then? Your family *are yours.*' She punches her fist into the palm of the other. 'Don't live beneath the nonsenses those idiots have fed on since time began.'

'But they never see it.'

'*They don't want to see it.* Better being top dog over someone than sitting on the bottom. Ask yourself what, besides their puffy Britishness, they've got to show for themselves? It's power, Moni. Scary, too, that whiteness might not be so special after all. Power and fear make a curious concoction – one that's—' She stops, swallowing. 'Haunted me since I got here.'

Puffy Britishness. As we drink from Avril's best china, in her gleaming little shoebox of a house, having apologized earlier for it being a mess. Her intentional British quirks now entrenched. She's got all the chat, yet none of it sits.

'You should've gone home.' I look to the sole reminder of her old life, a boot sale find that she said she didn't like, but Dad bought and hung anyway. A landscape print, by the Trinidadian artist Cazabon, of a world identical to that in the faded little picture of her as a girl. A world that must surely be dreamlike to her now. To arrive here at seventeen, a stranger, her black skin proving it, unable to hide it, landing in this grey cold world, chocked to brimming with grey cold arseholes who didn't want her, who hated her on sight. 'Given the first chance, I would've.'

'You didn't come home. Not when he did.'

'Who?'

'You know who,' she says, changing tack. Clever. So clever it works, and I lose my footing, swapping the warmth between us for retrospect; the shame she can't help but remind me of.

I left home under J-Man's instruction, thus preventing any more scandal. Alone in a bedsit he paid for, my school, friends, parents – everything familiar – disappeared.

Leaving nothing else to think about, other than how to please him.

Every day began with glamming up in front of a film. The rest revolved around fitness videos and living off Ryvitas. I'd change knickers three times a day, going to bed in full make-up in the obscenest of garments, in case J-Man popped by after work. With a tiny allowance, twice a week, as a treat to myself, I'd have an all-day breakfast and two frothy coffees, my only meal for the whole day, in the café opposite the library. Before the morning fry-up, I'd pop in for a browse, only ever borrowing one book at a time. I'd begin reading once I'd ordered, keeping a running list, along with a little summary and a rating. In five months, I'd read almost forty books.

It's funny, in a sad way, that in all those words and stories, not one moment of clarity ever jumped from the pages to bite some sense into me. Instead, I became ever more passive – J-Man picking up the bossy reins from my mother. And when it was over, we finished on J-Man's terms, too. Fluffy, forgiving wifey was ready to try again; J-Man was returning to his family.

I remember the night. J-Man lingering over only one beer, watching the telly, looking me over, now and again, with sadness and hunger. Him in the only armchair, me by his feet, in a sheer red dressing gown, feather fluff slippers to match, looking like I lived in a Wild West brothel. A high ponytail that wasn't mine, sleek and ridiculously long over my shoulder. I'd felt the goodbye all evening, but he took me to bed without saying it.

In the morning, I found it instead – written on the back of an envelope stuffed with enough rent for another month.

Memory fucking lane.

Yet all this shit pricks at something else, too. The small flirtations that I witnessed growing up, those expert, rare moments of Mum – just for once – holding all the cards. To this day, I mirror how she carries herself, know the reaction it'll guarantee. Because that smitten neighbour in our kitchen wasn't the only man.

But it was the absolute instant that I wanted to grow up just like her.

'You're twisting it, Mum. It's avoidance – I play the same games myself. Did something terrible happen to you in Trinidad, is that it?' I sound like Fran; high and wavery and full of pent-up questions. 'Why can't you ever talk to me?'

'There's never been anything to say.' I watch her go into shutdown, like she's walking around inside of herself, yanking out her own plug sockets. Pushed. Too far. 'My life started here. With your father.'

'So, why can't I forget, too – why keep pulling me apart for the same old shit – why's it all right for you, but not me?'

I don't know how we got here, trapped again in the vacuum stillness of unchanged thought; the same stuck record. I remember her bustling about, chucking my *More!* magazines, 2 Live Crew and Foxy Brown albums into bin bags, desperate to obliterate any negative influences conspiring and corrupting me – none of which had much to do with J-Man. And no real difference from her precious Marvin Gaye and his luscious sexual healing.

Dad was no better. He'd sit there in the background, hidden in his piles of marking, quietly drowning in his disappointment of me. 'Those poor children, Monica. A broken home. This wasn't how we raised you.' And when he'd shake his head, I'd want to vomit.

J-Man. The sole black professional on his street, the first in his family to own a house outright. Clever in business, he had all the chat – but wasn't brainy or worldly. I knew that, even then. It was Katrina, his fluffy blonde wife and their light-skinned adult children, who helped him fit into our community's narrow ideals of ethnic tolerability. That, and his disturbing aspersions and denial of his African heritage. Less Original Gangsta. More Original Blackgammon.

But it always is easier to fit than to challenge.

My mother's a fucking hypocrite.

Still, I cut her some slack, stopping with the questions; give her truth, instead – after all, everyone's always so keen to highlight my shittier characteristics. And I'm on a roll anyway, like I'm in one of the boys' computer games, tackling the bosses, round by final round; Budgie. Penny, too.

Now this.

'I didn't come back, because this never felt like home. And I know, all that with J-Man . . . Jason, was wrong. But at least he saw me.' I never had a best friend, where all the tiniest of things got shared, but for a bit, I did with him. Not quite a monster. More a chancing, old dirty bastard. 'I was lonely, Mum. I've been lonely my whole life. If I'd had a sibling, someone that looked like me—'

For a small moment, she's desolate. 'I looked like you, Monica.'

'And it did my head in. Being black didn't have to be what you made it.'

'What on earth do you mean by that?'

'Like it was a burden. A shame. You made me carry it, too.'

She claps her hands. 'Then you fall between the teeth of the only black man in town.' She kisses her teeth. 'A predator.'

'Perhaps. But he was also just like you. Doing all the white shite. Desperate to fit.' I'd wanted his love, almost as much as I wanted him to teach me all that Mum wouldn't. And she knew it. Still can't admit it.

'How dare you. My own child, my own flesh and—'

'Yes, the same flesh and blood – inside and out. It's not my fault you're guilty of the same things, too.'

She sits straight, a hand across her tummy, her posturing parallel to Penny's, only here there's no blubbering or glittering jewellery. Avril would never give me any of that. She's a fucking statue. 'Oh, yes?' she says, brows up, eyes cast down, but still, absolutely, fixed on me – doing the very face Penny was talking about; our shared haughtiness.

'Yes; the chameleon tricks, losing your accent. I had to look up in a *Children's Britannica* what you ate in Trinidad. Bet you haven't had a scotch shitting bonnet since you left. Since you turned your back and spoiled it for all of us.' Her eyes glitter with fury, but I don't cower beneath them; I'm not finished. 'My entire bloody life, you've hidden your secrets behind my mistakes. And your worst one, the worst trick – that I've turned myself inside out over, for as long as I can remember.' I think I'm going to cry. 'Did *you* have an affair – with that man, Mum?'

'What man?' For one beautiful second, she looks wary.

'Across the road. Who'd come for dinner.'

'Matthew?' She sniffs. 'Don't be ridiculous.' But the way her face drops tells me different. Tells me what I remember of her that night was true.

'I saw you and him once.' Mum's red dress and smile; all the red I replicate, consciously. 'In the kitchen. *Being intimate.*'

Any warmth vanishes from her eyes, frosting till they're hard and unacknowledging. 'I gave birth to a witch.' With perfect composure, she walks to the front door, opening it wide.

'And it's me you call deceit.'

She doesn't even have to ask me to go.

2 5

Time's Up

'You know, this really is a form of abuse,' Joe starts, somewhere behind me. Me and Fran are exiting the Co-op, after
bumping into Joel and Toby by the Pick 'n' Mix.

My crew. Family witnesses.

'It's raining. Take her home.' I look from Joe to Molly,
clinging to his hand as he drags her along the street after us
– while Joel gives them the skunk-eye.

'She's fine.' But Joe doesn't check. Molly breaks from him,
the girls chucking their arms around one another.

'Keep walking, kids, I'll catch up,' I instruct, all quick and
firm. 'Watch Fran at the road, give me two minutes.'

Distrust crumples and colours Joel's face. He doesn't like,
has never liked, this man superglued for the past six months
to his mother. More than ever I need to reach out, erase those
creases of doubt, make him smooth and untroubled again,

but I've the sudden horrible sense we're beyond that. I watch as he stops Fran at the road, the less busy one, with the island and the speed bumps I let them practise on. Joel guides her to the middle, putting his hand up to thank the driver slowing, and my heart aches.

'Don't you care any more?' Joe no longer even sounds like Joe. 'I'm, I'm dying without you. Can't you see?' I don't know what to say. He's drawn, slack in the cheeks, as if all his clever vibrancy's dried up. 'I'll sort it out – sharpen up, like you said. Be the person you—'

'For your family.'

His laughter makes Molly jump. I rub her shoulder, delicate and fine-boned beneath my fingers. The rain's getting heavier, and though I try to warm a little comfort into her, she tenses under my touch.

'It has to stop.' I take a deep breath in. Please let him be accepting. I breathe out. 'We stop. Now.' It's hard to penetrate the drink, to strike something that might resonate. 'Look at your daughter,' I say crossly, though his tears are devastating.

'I love you,' he mouths, inaudible to Molly's precious ears, clear to mine.

'Yes.' I can't help reaching to wipe his cheeks, scuffing through prickly bristle. 'But it's no good. It's not enough.'

'Nothing ever is. What's the point?'

I misstep, out into the road before I should, colliding with a man in a grey hoody. With a mumbled sorry, I move out of his way, then thank the slowing traffic as Joel had done. My son's shadow, moments late.

'*Oi!*' rages out behind me, a Rottweiler bark that puts me on ice, as a sixth-sense tremor-like foreboding moves through me, followed by two real hands, slapped flat against my back, shoving me. I've no reflex to save myself, all natural protections emptied from shock, as I stumble, crashing to my knees, which graze and tear on the road's broken concrete. 'Watch where you're going!' He moves away from me, jumping out of the road towards the bus stop, and a fresh target – a girl in a pink hijab, a few years above the boys at school, now sat staring at the floor.

She winces down into herself, like a tiny bird that's found itself unprotected. She's yet to learn that no matter how small she makes herself, his type will always spot hers.

His type like it more when you shrink.

'An' here's another one. A bomber one.' He jumps again, swinging from the bus shelter like a primate, as she hides behind her books, screwing her eyes shut. 'What's in your bag – gonna blow up the bus?' The rain's saturating, monsoon-like, the sky rumbling, as he screeches into the sky, kicking the books from her hands as she covers her face, her shoulders leaping in fear as he yells, 'Boom!'

Joe tries for a handful of my jumper, but I slip from his grip, ignoring the pain of my knees, unable to stop or control my body as I chuck myself around the boy's neck, pulling his slippery grip loose, and him to the floor. But my punches are lightweight, girly flailing he's quick to wriggle away from. 'Who are you? Who are—'

He shoves me again, only this time my head smacks

against the metal smoothness of the lamp post. Bright white spots burst from nothing. My vision twisted. Sick-making.

'Monica?' Joe. Strange and warped, my ears as blurred as my sight. I'm going to be sick. 'Try that again, try it fucking again!' Joe's demented, his face almost lilac as he puffs his chest out, clicking back his elbows, squaring up to, Jesus, treble the size of this boy, who can't be much more than seventeen. For the first time I see him properly, like a camera coming back into focus. Skinny and pockmarked, head to foot grey marl – someone's scroaty little son. 'Do that to someone who'll give it back, you cowardly little bastard.'

'That your bitch?' I sense the adrenaline in the boy, unnatural, as he bounces from foot to foot. 'You wanna fight me, don't you?' He sticks his tongue out, making it pointed, flicking it quickly in and out of his mouth, across his teeth, coked off his tits. 'Fight for your bitch?' he says, with rapper hands and Jafaican accent. A terrible hocking noise grows in his throat, as he shoots quite skilfully a foaming lump of saliva that spatters my neck, mingling quickly with the rain.

Molly buries her head in the nook of my hip as I shield her in my mac. Trembling yet transfixed, I watch Joe grab the boy by the hood of his tracksuit. He snarls, fearless, spitting in Joe's face too, more of a shower this time.

'Should be going home, not getting in my way – My Way! My England!' He shoves Joe with enough force to send him stumbling backwards into the road as a red Fiesta slows and stops, unable to pass.

It's a slow-mo macho tussle, until Joe whacks the boy full pelt in the mouth; his knuckle cracking as it passes through the soft flesh of his pocked cheek, then into teeth and jaw. There's instant blood, a claret directionless spray that hits across their trainers, as the boy's knees give at once. He crumples to the ground, just as Joel's face peeks back around the corner to witness Joe straddle the boy, landing blow after blow on the gobby shit who just won't stop with the gibes. It's me who wrenches Joe off by his shoulders, but not through compassion.

If I don't, Joe will kill that boy.

It's a car horn that warns of the retaliation, heading toward Joe's abdomen in the form of a silver pocket-knife, slick and dazzling in the rain. Joe moves, just enough, for it to sink into his thigh instead. The boy stumbles away, leaving Joe and his labour pain screams, writhing on the tarmac.

There's no blood. I try to remember if that's a good sign as my vision spins out, and I'm sick into the kerb.

Then Joel's here, with a hand on my back, his phone alive in the other, ringing 999.

'Call ahead.' Joe's secured to a stretcher, tucked in tightly with a red blanket. 'They know me.'

'And who shall I say's coming in?' The ambulance man humours him, making me utterly sad.

'Can I go, too?' Molly's tear-streaked face looks up at me, a small scrap of worry.

I'm relieved, selfishly, that my daughter's safe. With Toby, Sir Duke and *The Wizard of Oz* – no place like home.

'Can she?' I ask the man, now shunting Joe into the back of the ambulance.

He screws up his face, thinking hard. 'Course.' He smiles, kind brown eyes, kind gentleness, just what's needed. 'You the wife? We can make room.'

26

Shitstorm Apocalypse

'Ask Mum,' he kept saying. Dan's voice inches to life, break-ing the silence we're all but set fast in. 'Shitting himself that he'd dropped you in it.'

Time's up. Proper.

'So, I'm not asking Joel. I'm asking you. Where he lives, what he does, what . . . what he looks like. I hate that I want to know!' His palm crashes onto the table. It makes a flat smacking sound that echoes around our kitchen, emptied now of the usual noise and lightness and family-pack tightness.

'Has he been here – in our bed, met the kids?'

Oh, God. 'Never here. I'd never let him in our home.'

'Let him in you, though.' Dan is so removed from normal, I can no longer read nor fully recognize his face. Only his eyes are the same as they've always been – hurt, yes, but still mesmerizing. There's comfort in spotting the familiar. He's still Daniel Petersen somewhere: husband, breadwinner, family man extraordinaire. Still Danny-boy, the blinkered, self-righteous, path-walking perfectionist. Mine – by a thread.

Mine, all the same.

Because didn't we wake up together, in our IKEA king-size this morning, happy enough, making plans for the weekend ahead of us? Swimming with the kids early Saturday, tiring them into an easy day that'd end with a takeaway in front of shitty ITV evening telly. An early night. House viewing in Norwich on Sunday. All of us safe, healthy, together.

Together. The most important thing.

'I'd take it all back if I could. On my heart.' My face aches so much, even my teeth hurt. My eye's bloodied and swollen; pure agony. 'I'm a terrible person.'

'I've never thought that.' He stops, as if searching for the words to devastate. 'But they were right. Mum. Nan – bless her. She knew. She knew exactly what you were. What you are.'

I could defend myself, tell him that lust and secrets are all I've known, but there'd be no fight in it. I slag off Penny's materialism, but, Christ, my hungry vanity . . .

Before Dan, I pigeon-holed all white men between either my dad or the poisonous warnings from J-Man against dating them – 'I swear, Monica, they'll never marry you. Best remember that. In a white man's brain, you'll only ever be good enough for practising on.'

It's sad that the drip-fed message of my limited value still comes so easy to hand in my thoughts. How twenty-odd years can pass, and I still question my worth to the white man, because Jason Robinson, the whitest black man I ever met, sowed the seed and said so.

Dan's eyes stay on mine until the hurt gives, leaving him emotionless, slicing us into strangers.

We sit in silence at the dining table, chosen years back to accommodate our growing brood, their smeary fingerprints still decorating the cupboard handles and drawer fronts around us. On my spice-stained wooden worktops, the same old cutlery pots sit next to the same old pen pots that probably don't work but act as paperweights to the stacks of school notes, Tax Credit renewals and party invites. Our sun-kissed faces still smile out from holiday photographs, still stuck to the fridge with the same old watermelon-shaped magnets.

The happy chaos – of a past life.

Even Sir Duke's eyeballing me from Dan's feet, with as much venom as his precious master. Everything's shit and out in the world.

But I knew the shit would come. This is always how it ends.

'So. This man. This other man.' Dan stands, scraping his chair on the tiles as he always does, heading for the cupboard with the booze. Two tumblers get set on the table, side by side and almost touching, the Jack Daniel's poured. Nudging one towards me, Dan raises his brows as an order to drink.

He knows I can't bloody stand Jack Daniel's.

'Wipe your eyes.' He flings the tea towel that's dangling from the back of Fran's chair at me. Fran. She couldn't even get to six with us intact. 'Talk. Describe him.'

Describe Joe. I close my eyes, and like when your time's up and it all expires, everything between Joe and me flashes through my mind. The fun. So much fun. And the awesome sense of wellbeing, in all the best of ways, that came from him, in every greedy orifice.

'Well, he's local. He works, up – up at the hospital.' I clear my throat, avoiding Dan's face. 'We haven't been seeing each other long—'

His hand slaps down, catching the edge of the overfilled fruit bowl, sending a lone satsuma tumbling across the tablecloth. 'It's fucking, Mon. You've been letting him have you. My wife.' Dan's eyes glisten as he balls his fists, crushing them into his chest. 'Mine!' Reaching for him, he jumps away as if I'm rabid.

'It just happened, Dan. I'm sorry.' *'It just happened'* – used in billions of moments just like this one, all over the world since the first flushes of time, in books and soaps and messy Wickes kitchens. An excuse; the weakest of them all. As it falls from my lips, it tastes cliché, lazy. 'He's like an older version of you, really – only ... damaged, coming up for fifty—'

'It's that bloke, isn't it? Posho from up the school.' Dan's eyes roam the ceiling as if it's all making sense. 'All the walks, the disappearing bullshit. The spa ... of course, the spa.'

Catching my eye, he smiles to himself, sadly. Sadly. 'You watched me shake his hand.'

We're lost. Done. Love hasn't been mentioned for a long time. I try remembering when I last told him that I loved him.

I can't remember. I can't fucking remember.

'You've even felt odd, you know? To hold. To be with. You've felt ... unfamiliar.' Dan's hands rake through his hair, turning it fluffy and bedhead, like our children's.

Our children. Flesh evidence of a good love.

Like my romantic past, only reversed, Dan had never dated anyone brown, either. When we met, Nancy named us 'the magnets' to wind Penny up.

She also said it because it was true.

'How long?'

I waver, but there's no reason to twist and lie. 'Five months. Off and on.'

'Off and on? Like when things didn't go your way here?'

What can I say? It was exactly like that.

'How many times have you and him—'

'Please, Dan.'

'Too many fireworks to count, as well.' His face turns unkind. Nasty. 'So, what is he, then, some sort of rampant, ageing pony? Because from what I remember, he looked like a tubby old scruff who liked a drink.'

'Which is why I backed off—' I catch myself. 'What with us and wanting to move—'

'He's an alchie?' Dan nods along with me. 'I'd laugh, if this wasn't me. *If this wasn't us.* A rich old soak humping my wife. Humping poor miserable little Monica, so bored at home. And to top it all off, a hero now as well.'

He's cheapening it. Like Joe's nothing but some posh white saviour. It irks, despite the guilt.

'You sign up for a degree on a whim.' Here we go. Dan counts off my sins on his fingers. 'Volunteering in that bloody library – or was that a cover, too? Digging up your parents; tearing the family apart—'

'He was just so present, Dan. Right when I needed it. Everything appealed.'

'What the hell does that even mean?'

'He heard me.'

'And I didn't?' Dan meets my eye. Holds it. Knows full well that's only half of it.

'No,' I tell him, not flinching away. 'You didn't.'

There was truth, in Joe's Garden of Eden damnation of me. It goes without saying that I could've, could *always* have been a better wife, perhaps a contented one, if I tried harder. Mirroring Eve's first temptation, that thirst for more, to sate some subversive stirring, just out of my reach, has always been my battle, too. I'm not the only one, though – it's human bloody nature; we're wired to forever crave more, to have it all – only some desires are safer than others. Dan's wants stayed material, acceptable, an eager subscriber to the pre-prescribed life of the aspirational and trendy. Society's crude veneer. Don't, for fuck's sakes, peek behind it. Climbing the slippery social ladder, selling out, little by trickle. Throwing himself at the golf, which he's never really liked, would much rather have a West Ham season ticket but thinks he should be on the greens instead of the terraces. To please whom? And why?

Parental showboating, wife muting, shapeshifting, masking himself into what he thought impressed other people.

Other people.

Who I've learnt, at last, don't fucking matter.

'It makes me feel shit. What happened to you.'

'If it hadn't been for Joe, it might've been worse.'

'I've got to swallow that,' Dan spits. 'Another man, defending my wife.'

His arrogance is astonishing. I think twice before I say it, know there'll be no coming back.

'You had years to do the same.'

'So, this is my punishment?' He laughs, oblivious still to his own racist family and to his own faults, no matter how obviously spelled out. 'Cuckolded for being the peacekeeper.'

The tattered state of our marriage is defeated by Dan's basic bullshit.

Pride. Property. The 'My Wife!' posturing, comparing not only the size of his privates, but the size of his bravery – and didn't Dan even mention Joe's riches too, not three minutes ago?

I feel less apologetic by the second. 'You're only bothered because Joe did what you've never once been able to.'

Our little world, blown open for the bigger world to inspect. I think of Nancy and Hunter, ushering in the children earlier, their soothing low voices, avoiding my eyes. My sole good fortune is that Penny and Clive are in Spain. But she'll be back in a flash, I know it, as soon as Dan fills her in properly, armed to the back teeth with vials of fresh poison and I told you so's. Dan the victim. Me the merciless slag of a wife, driven by cock and currency.

And it was about the cock.

But it was Joe's kindness, too. That I never once had to prompt, explain or ask for. And I'll say thank you when I visit him in hospital. Hurt. Seriously hurt. Because of me.

'You know, the second you step foot on that ward, my bags are packed.'

Amazing how well attuned we can be.

Fresh tears plop on the oilcloth, white polka dots on the red background, same as when my eyes shut. I screw them tight as my left eye shrieks into fresh agony.

But the physical is mere inconvenience, compared to the ruins we're in.

I never once had the bridal fantasy, of the big dress, those gushing crowds of admiration. Stress, and the attention of a day like that, held little interest. The sunshine freedom of just me and Dan on our wedding day was all that I'd ever hoped for.

But it was never just the two of us. Dan never wanted a life that way.

His parting words refuse to be forgotten – 'I always tried to make you happy. Be everything you didn't have. A husband when it suited you, a parent a lot of the fucking time. A best friend.'

I never claimed to be infallible. But I do know, understand myself better now than I ever have before. Not the heritable history, all the familial baggage Dan takes for granted, but my character; my flaws and my values – because I do have both.

In five Mondays, I'm forty. Reaching the identical age J-Man was when he introduced me to my weak spot. My lifetime's downfall. I placed desire over my marriage. Over my family. Again.

And I can't undo it.

Dan communicates by text if it's about the children, and to inform me that he's now (predictably) at Penny and Clive's, who've returned ASAP to support him. I bet it's like DANAID round there; she's probably getting t-shirts printed, having a charity gig street party for singletons, in the hope of finding a decent Aryan replacement for me. Perhaps she's even dug up Becky, the Goldilocks who got away. Anything to scrub clear the dirt memory of the half-black Jezebel with the full-black heart who destroyed her son.

I'm exactly what Penny's prejudice conjured. Black-hearted. Black-spirited. Black. Forever stuck by the wickedness of the negative. Even the dictionary says so.

Then my rage returns. Know I'm not fully to blame.

And if I could, really could, click my fingers, make it like the fallout never was, roll it back to when I was quiet and good, I'd hesitate.

27

Scorned by Proxy

Collecting Fran from school is the second worst part of the day.
The first is dropping her off. All my old avoidance tactics are
thoroughly redundant – I'm a lonely lemon anyway these
days. I wait for Fran at a distance; off to the side near the trees.

I'm hopeful that, again, I'll fly just enough beneath the
radar to swipe Fran quick then leg it. Surging forward with
all the other parents, I end up behind Lynda's entourage; a
group of five, including Kathryn.

'We're supposed to stick together,' Lynda's saying to her
audience. 'I swear, if she'd ever gone near my Roger.'

It doesn't take Stephen Hawking to work out who she's
talking about.

As bloody if, anyway – Roger looks like he hasn't evolved
from the foetal stages. I keep my head down. This is part of
the punishment process.

They can do what they want. But if they do it in front of the kids, in front of Fran—

'Apparently, the father's in one of those big bungalows near the allotments. Thank goodness there's family nearby to pick up the pieces, that's all I can say.' It isn't, for she carries on. 'Then there's the other family. Poor Bella,' Lynda says, as if they're now best friends. 'You just can't imagine.'

Despite being an official playground ghost, Poor Bella's become an official playground martyr.

'It was obvious she wasn't a girl's girl. Showy. So obvious.' Lynda cups a hand to her mouth. 'And those awful hoop earrings. I'd have sent him for a tetanus.'

I wonder if she'll organize a witch-hunt; have me, Mrs Ghetto-slagulous, run out of town by her angry gaggle, scorned by proxy over the crime of the century. Crime – they don't even know us. We're just fodder; village gossip. And the gossip will move on, soon enough, to some other unfortunate. It always does.

My worry is, will I? I haven't slept since Dan left. And I could just about handle that, but with Joel's distance, too, my days tunnel, endless, something I push myself through, if only for Fran and Toby's sakes, unsettled themselves – Fran now wetting the bed. Last week, I caught her in front of the telly, her hand on her chest at the bit where the Tin Man knows he's got a heart because it's hurting. I'd take the mess back and suffer a lifetime of shit, for them.

Not for Dan. But for them.

Joel ignores all my attempts to communicate and apologize for what he knew to be true. When he's home – which is rare, preferring Dan's company – there's frostbite silence, and when he's not, all I have are his movements, from the school app on my phone, telling me that he arrived safely. What lesson he's in.

I'm neither whole nor human without him.

'Why,' asks Kathryn, 'couldn't it be Joe's fault, too?'

'Men are like cats, Kath,' Lynda says condescendingly. 'A bit of comfort, and they'll go with anyone – or anything.' I catch the edge of her eye as she watches me over her shoulder.

She wants me broken, and sorry. But I'm not – not in the way she hopes. Yes, things are undoubtedly shit, but I have never felt more me, more sure of myself. And I'm certain, too, with witch intuition, that Lynda's biggest problem with me is that Joe didn't fancy her.

'But he's not a cat.' Kathryn puts her hands on her hips. 'He's a grown man.'

'Oh – I'm sorry. Has the talk of your new friend upset you?'

Kathryn's neck grows pink, crawling upwards to cover her ears. 'Have you never cocked up, Lynda, in all your fifty-two years?'

Lynda grows corpse stiff.

'You can't make us all read the bloody *Handmaid's Tale* for book club, then make excuses for the old goat who couldn't keep it in his pants.'

Lynda's posturing like she's ready to claw Kathryn's eyes out. *'I'm defending Bella.'*

'While woman-shaming in the very next breath. We don't know what went on between them. And you know what else?' Trembling, Kathryn stands her ground, catching my eye with a tiny smile. 'It's none of our bloody business.'

Lynda snatches her son by the wrist and storms off. As her crowd of Karens begin to disperse, I head straight for Kathryn and hug her.

'Fifty-two?' I smile, slapping a hand to my forehead, but Kathryn's all nervous energy. I wonder if, through all their years of Lynda's dominance, it'd been festering anyway, just beneath the surface. Relationship inequality is nothing new; Penny and her pushover, Budgie and Gracie. Gracie. The last I heard, Michael had chucked his girlfriend. I could join the dots, but like Kathryn just said, it's really none of my business.

Fran bounds out, pigtails flying, her face stained orange from a pasta lunch. 'Is Dad back?'

Later, after clearing the dishes from another easy freezer meal, I flop for a flick through the channels. But nothing I'd usually watch holds much interest any more. The books aren't cutting it, either.

It's now, when the kids are in bed and I've time to fill before trying to sleep myself, that I start replaying Dan leaving. I do it from the most aching moment, when he held my face, held his lips against my bruised eye. Something, in the pits of his stomach, made a noise; a low, barely audible whining – the same as when our first dog died. I recall it lucidly; Dan, resting his hand on Joel's head, fingers turning through his curls, as we wept our goodbyes.

More fucking tears. Still laced with the same ache. Of emptiness.

Then the doorbell. Sir Duke starts up his deep and protective bark, sending my dinner back up my throat.

Fear is a terrible thing.

Any sudden volume, and I'm back on my knees in the rain, watching that terrified girl. Sana Begum from Danes Lane – gymnast and guitar hero. Her mum and dad bought me a bouquet so enormous it could hardly get through the door.

I don't know what they got Joe.

I slide silently to the door in my slippers, pull the curtain a slither, try and fathom—

It's Mum. All straight and starchy, with a small wheeled suitcase on the doorstep.

Falling on her uptight little shoulder, I sob my guts out as she pats me gently.

'Your house, Moni. Your rules.'

'It won't stay broken.' Mum places my wedding picture back in its place on the bookcase. Me, in a floaty lemon sundress, my beachball stomach, like I'd swallowed the world. 'There's too much love.' She sits across from me, in the flower-power

Ercol, cleansed and glowing in an apricot fluff dressing gown. We've a glass of Chenin Blanc apiece.

Weeknight wine. Even in life's current shitstorm, the moment is perfect.

'How did you know?' I swallow, still a little nervous of this warm, maternal Avril. 'About the split.'

'Facebook. You're as popular as brown royalty.'

'At least she's a husband who understands.'

'Just wait. Smart people can only be stupid for so long.'

'But Dan's not the only stupid one, is he? Taking up with an alcoholic doctor – you couldn't make it up.'

'Has he contacted you?'

'He's not allowed.' I roll my eyes. 'Posh rehab, innit?' And posh wife, too.

'And what about when he can?' Mum asks, in that shrewd way she's got. Like she knows, despite our decades of distance, that I'll see Joe again. Holding her tummy suddenly, she seems pained, but shakes her head at me crossly. 'Don't fuss.' She finds a pack of Rennies from the bag tucked by her side. 'I'll tell you when I'm dying. And you are not stupid.'

'I never learn, though; I see what's coming, then just dance after it, anyway.'

'It's called living, Moni.' Mum exits, leaving me baffled, worried I've somehow triggered her again. I'm so fearful she could take off any moment, I stay quiet. Then I hear the freezer drawer; the cracking sound of ice twisted out.

A minute later she's back, and I'm touched when she carries in two glasses of water. Perching herself, she drinks deep before speaking again. 'In Trinidad, I wasn't from anything. You could say, dirt poor. Electricity and water, but no bathroom. No privacy – I shared a back room with five other kids, none of whom were my siblings. I was looked after by an aunt, some friend of the woman that was . . . I never knew my mother. No one told me anything about her. And I never asked. Kids didn't back then. Really, there's never been much to tell you. I was quiet. Worked hard and saved harder. It was always my plan to leave, knew that if I didn't get out, I'd be stuck. Stretching out too young, by some boy next door. Then I come here, and it happens anyway.' She drinks the rest in a single stream down her neck. 'Tiny little place. I don't miss it.'

'But Essex, though?'

She laughs. It's a beautiful sound. It's a beautiful sound because it's real. 'Yes, and like I said to your best friend Peggy, England wasn't what I expected. Then, living got me trouble. Got me crazy in love with your dad. But somewhere, and I don't know when, reality got the better of me.'

'Not completely.' I think of her making eyes at Mr Tom Selleck security, but don't want her to clam up again. I hesitate, but only for a second – because where's she running to, at ten past eleven at night, in her dressing gown, with bald eyebrows and no bra? 'What about our neighbour?'

'Matthew? A boost. Nothing more.'

'You sure?'

'I worry what you take me for.' She tuts.

'That's the problem. I love you, Mum. But I don't know you.' It's true. Outside of the hints, the smutty novels and penchant for red that she's tried smothering for God, I've never really known her.

'Which is why I'm going to stay. Support. And, girl, I know there's plenty between us that'll take longer than Brexit to iron out, but here I'll be.' She reaches across the coffee table, giving my toes a squeeze. 'Until you tell me to go.'

She beds down in Dan's spot, on her side, facing the wardrobe.

And I sleep.

2 8

The Already Shifted

I get ready, dabbing my trusted old scent behind my ears and the backs of my knees. It's a perfume I've been groomed by advertising to believe is my signature, worn for my best moments – yet it's not my intention to go to bed with Joe. I tell myself this, as I select the bra with the most lift, the tights without holes. Shutting up the ghost house. Double-locking the front door. Knowing it's only my key that'll open it.

My key. To my house. Most things have rotted into the singular. Our bed is now my bed. I talk about this to my new counsellor, see the links of my life joining nicely, the pattern of it all. It's my brain that's the ultimate torturer, so she says, my weighty thoughts enough for two people. I'm a jigsaw, too, apparently – slowly coming together, only I'm a thousand pieces and nothing but red scribble on a blank background, like those pictures in Tate Modern that me and Joe thought we could mimic.

But though I'm still mostly scribble, restoration's possible.

Joe stands in the entrance of his small front door, straight off a side street, smack in the middle of town. It's a tiny terrace, with a Nepalese restaurant on one side and a barber on the other. A place where you'd start, a first flushes couple's nest, or, in Joe's case, a weekend parent's home. Not the family houses we're used to. It looks inviting, shadowy, its butter yellow lamplit softness spilling into the outdoor dusk.

He pushes the wooden door shut behind me, sticky from ancient lashings of white paint. I fight the urge to sink my fingernails into the woodwork, know they'd mark in the gloss, leaving behind fat pithy dents. This house reminds me of Horn Road.

'Drink?' he asks, leading me into the kitchen.

'What are you having?'

'Tonic water. It's the only thing I can almost convince myself as being fun.'

'I'll have the same.'

Grateful the moment's dealt with, Joe starts circling his tiny kitchen, pulling plates out and checking the oven. There's a calm efficiency about him. A sense of peace. 'Stroganoff,' he explains, as a hot waft of meaty deliciousness fills the room. 'With brown rice – you do like brown rice?'

'I do.' I can't help but think of the old days, his bacon baguettes and crisps.

'It'd be fine, you know,' he says, twisting free some ice. 'Just because I can't drink doesn't mean you have to suffer.'

'It's hardly suffering. You're cooking, looking after me.' I sip, the bitter fizz pleasant on my lips.

'Let me show you around, then,' he suggests, pinching my elbow. 'It'll take less than a minute, but still.' Joe grins, gesturing me into the hall. 'Living room.' With an elaborate sweep of his arm through the doorway, I stick in my head.

There's a small bay window, naked from nets and fuss, just the liquid night blackness of glass, offering a strange science fiction sort of privacy. A woodburner stands within the recess of the old chimney breast, sandwiched between shelves and shelves of books. Other than a new-looking grey sofa, and an artsy standing lamp, bent like a Conran Shop crone, the room's barely furnished at all. It should feel empty, but it's the books, polychrome and multi-sized, haphazard and beautiful, that make the room home. On one sofa cushion rest his glasses, atop a pile of reading material; incoherent scribblings in a notebook.

'How's work?' I point at the pile of papers.

'Brilliant,' he says. And I believe him.

It's difficult comprehending that this is the same person from a month ago.

'How's Bella,' I start, ready to use the word I've never said to him aloud, 'now she knows about your alcoholism?'

Without a glimmer of insult, Joe assures me that both Bella and Molly are fine. His parental duties have now relinquished into twice-weekly supervised visits. Like Joel, Molly had a child therapy assessment, with a follow-up appointment in three months' time. Unlike Joel, she's since been to Disneyland Paris with Bella and Bella's parents.

Rather than crumbling – and my conscience is glad, so very glad that she hasn't – Bella's simply disassociated from Joe. Work's been considerably more supportive to him, and after insisting on rehabilitation, he's back, with continued support from a specifically assigned work mentor. I don't suppose Joe could be in a more apt or understanding environment.

'Bella's concerns are to take me to the cleaners. Adultery and alcoholism will make it very easy. She wants to move.'

So do I – and not just for the privilege of anonymous fresh beginnings, either. I still don't feel safe, can't help but check the faces of every person I pass on the street, travelling as close to my destination as possible, so I don't have to walk far alone.

Because alone equals vulnerable.

It's an enormous daily effort to conquer the fear of it happening again. The worry is that the day I stop worrying will be the day it happens, which is what's keeping me rabbit keen and almost skinny. And older-looking. I've at last squashed the notion of passing as early to mid-thirties, and it seems to have happened instantaneously – that about twenty per cent of my hair is now white; not old lady grey, but brilliant white – as wild and curly as the black.

I don't really mind any of it.

'We were over the minute Bella pieced it together,' he tells me. 'With all the doctors around my sick bed, and her demanding to know everything. Then there it was – like projectile sick. I did feel rather cleansed,' he jokes, despite the sad eyes, chucking me under the chin. 'So. Dan knows.'

'Yes. Dan knows everything.'

'But he doesn't know you're here.' The corners of his mouth fight to remain still. 'It was good. When it was good, Mon – wasn't it?' The lure of him returns as he watches me, those strange grey eyes dusted free from the crimson cobwebs. From a month and no whisky.

'I've missed you. Like this.'

'I ballsed it. Once I got you, I ballsed it.'

'I couldn't leave. I'd never really have left.'

'Why d'you think the odd whisky was needed?'

'Odd? Bottles more like – and all the pot.'

He smiles, naughtily, as if perhaps I don't know the half of it.

I wander to his shelves, studying the titles and the spines, keen to read between the lines. Among his big books, the typicals of a clever hungry reader, and the rows of reference books, are the skinny spines, the plays and poetry pamphlets – his truth. This is Joe. Not a pompous manly hardback in sight. On the lowest shelf are his notebooks, a horizontal stack, sheaths of paper oozing like cream filling from a layered cake.

'The books are pretty much all I took,' he explains, standing next to me. 'It's not been pleasant, has it?' He kisses my cheek. 'Come, let me show you the rest.'

*　　*　　*

We eat, sparklingly sober in his hot-box kitchen, with more gusto than I have for weeks, then retire to the living room – my favourite room – though I love everything about this house. Love its peaceful energy. I stack his paperwork neatly by my feet, making room for us on the sofa, as Joe lights a joss stick and candles on the floor around the fireplace.

'There.' Pleased with himself, he stands, dusting off his hands on the fronts of his trousers as I pass him his coffee. 'Clever blighters. They disguise a multitude of aromas. Alcohol's one thing, but herbal sobriety's out of the fucking question. Surely I'm entitled to *some* fun.' He squeezes me. 'But no herbs tonight.'

'What's it like,' I ask, 'being alone here?'

'It's the best I've felt. Probably ever.'

I understand that. Pure independence. It's in me, too. Days followed on my own terms and decisions, which make me more tolerant. A better mother. A non-wife.

'And I'm writing,' Joe says committedly, without the usual awkwardness whenever his writing's mentioned. 'It's mostly scraps, but I think I've got a book coming.'

I clink his mug with mine, impressed. 'What's it about?'

'Not us, don't worry. I reckon the world's had more than its fill of reading about men like me and their urges.' He smiles. 'It's about addiction. You know, I might brave it, submit a few chapters.'

'Be brave. I'm sure it's marvellous.'

'You know, there's tons of A4 down there, dedicated to

you.' Joe pats my knee, his directness as strong as ever. 'Dan still dangling his inevitable return like a carrot?'

'I'm getting used to his absence.' It hurts to buggery, same as the day he left me. All I've done is learn to manage. Thanks to Mum's visit. Thanks to Dr Luximon, my counsellor.

Perhaps we could be fixed if I begged for absolution. Perhaps it'd be okay, a relief, at first – until the tiny things grow, like when my phone rings and I tell him it's a sales call from Kettering. Or when we're out and a handsome heft of man walks by that I'd be dead not to notice, and Dan subtly lets me know he's not forgotten. Life could turn full circle for the sake of fake normality – me full-on grateful again. Back to the life of pretending. I didn't want that life.

I still don't. I miss him terribly. But I don't need Dan.

'I give the kids my everything all week, and the weekends, well, they're not quite so never-ending any more. I'm seeing a counsellor.' Why that feels confessional, I don't know. 'Mum suggested it. Although the attack's all we first talked about, we've gone right back to the blueprint – my parents, my teens. All those missing-part feelings. Why I am as I am. But you know what I think?'

'What?' He watches me, proper mesmerized. Still.

'I think I'm just me. Life's cause and effect, but they're only patterns that I've used to either excuse or justify myself.'

'So, you didn't cheat because you were born wicked?'

'I cheated because I wasn't happy.'

I secured myself to Dan to make myself good; fused our genes to make us unbreakable. I didn't foresee that by nailing myself in I'd be left with no escape. But, then, I never thought I'd ever want to. There were other ways to make Dan see, better ways to free who I was. I didn't need to spear my heart onto the groin of another to break the chains of my Garden of Eden.

For the first time tonight, I wish for a proper drink in my hand. But, then, we wouldn't be like this, cogent and honest. I couldn't be dry forever, but between me and Joe, this is one of the freshest moments we've ever had.

'I wasn't happy, either.' Joe: twinning, in all our myriad ways.

It's not hard, dreaming us up as second-time-arounders; overly tactile and glued at the hip. Me barefoot, in one of his shirts, as he gropes me from behind, night on night on night. Perhaps in that doorway, right there. The fantasy lives on.

The kids are adjusting, slowly, to the simple routine of just us. They're ecstatic to see Dan on Fridays when they all disappear to Penny's. She got her wish, to tell the world she was right all along, but there's been no showdown between us; Dan's not allowed it.

Dan – who still can't acknowledge, nor find it in himself, to understand.

'What you did. That disgusting boy. Thank you will never be enough.' Tears fall on my grasped hands. 'It compounded everything. That gut feeling that I've never belonged, that I'm never truly equal, or good enough.'

I don't belong. The current political disorder's exposed a societal split, but worse than that, it's made a concrete platform for hatred. I'm nothing more than a crime number – far from the only one. My own privilege of being born here, my Essex accent and white educated father means fuck all, so it's up to me, to value and accept myself, my whole self – make my children proud to do the same. All externals have ceased to matter.

'I've got to stop viewing myself through the prism of other people's ignorance. I can't pass all that shit on to the kids.'

I choose to align with my own self-worth.

'Which'd hurt far more than that hideous eye you got.' Joe strokes my hair. 'I'm glad. You've spent too long bending. How is the delightful mother-in-law, anyway?'

'We aren't allowed to talk.'

Joe raises his eyebrows, mirthful at this. 'You're a brilliant person. Come here.'

I don't need asking twice. Thinking I was past this, past the tears, I dissolve into his chest, nuzzling into his lovely solidity. 'I've missed this,' I admit. 'Lost without a man in my life, shame on me.'

'D'you think you're the only one? People crave familiarity. We stick with what's comfortable, fulfilling or not.'

'*We* didn't.'

'No, love.' He gazes down tenderly. 'We didn't.'

'Do you think we'd work – properly?' Wanton indecision. I irritate myself.

'Who knows?'

'But you always think you know everything.'

'Yes, but I'm sober now.' Joe's face breaks into its familiar lines, then he sighs. It's the most cavernous sound I've ever heard. 'You'll reunite. I'd put money on it.'

'But you'd normally be asking by now what does this mean? Do you want Dan or want me? Why aren't you doing those things?'

'Because you're here,' he says, very simply.

'And?'

'Thanks to my nightly gratitudes, I'm at ease with that fact.'

Cripes alive – who is this mindful, twelve-step-following-fellow-of-calmness? But it's better. Tons better than the sloshed, pompous, fedora-wearing, jealous Joseph from the big house.

'I start my degree in October. Even if Dan doesn't come home, I won't have time for another husband.'

'I'll still settle for the fact that you came tonight.'

'I come first, now – after the kids, naturally.' I'll never let any man become all my life, ever again. I think this, as I fasten myself back around his body. 'Could you rekindle with Bella?'

'The job suspension, even my little rehab visit, perhaps we could've got over it. But you. Once she knew about you.' Eyes wide, he whistles. 'Beyond salvation. Unlike yours.'

'Dan can't even look at me.'

'Which is beneficial. And very exciting. We've never had a legitimate bunk-up,' he says, and I give him a playful shove. 'I'm in good working order, but I'll have a slight limp, they reckon. It'll give me something distinguishing, don't you think? Everyone'll wonder if I walk like that because I got stabbed through a nerve, or because of my cumbersome cock. I'll never be more popular.'

His laughter almost overpowers my phone, ringing somewhere in the blackout depths of my handbag – the kids my first thought, as I pull it free.

Nancy.

'Reception's better in the bedroom,' Joe says as I stare at the screen, unsure.

I disappear to answer. Nancy starts speaking first, her lovely face filling the screen as her laughter fills my ears. 'Have you heard about Dan whacking Budgie – knocking him sparko?'

But my head can't work out if Facetime means we're friends again. Me and Nancy haven't spoken since life exploded.

'I said she wouldn't know,' Nancy says over her shoulder, a three-way convo we've done so often before. 'Last week – Dad saw the lot.' She laughs again. 'Said he only wished he'd had a camera.'

'Better late, hey, Mon?' says Hunter. 'I miss you.'

I smile. 'I miss you both, very much.'

'Thought it might help – give you a full picture.' Her tone's changed, the warmth fading to nothing, resurrecting my bone-deep guilt, putting me back on the outside looking in. 'I wish you'd talked to me—' She stops, suddenly emotional.

'He's your brother.'

'Exactly. We can't fraternize with the enemy. Even if you are the closest thing to a best mate I ever had.' She sighs. 'So, you can't stay the enemy.'

'Why did he hit him?' Regardless of all that's unsettled, I still want the deets – of Dan's machismo retribution, of Budgie flying feebly into a pyramid of beer kegs.

'Budgie kept starting on this kid, down the pub. Dad said he had to drag Dan off – but not straight away.' Nancy's back smiling again. 'That's between you and me, though.'

'Good old Clive.'

'No one hates you, Mon. Not really.'

'Have you talked to Dan?'

'That first week you split, pretty constantly actually. Two, three in the morning, sometimes. Broken more than he'd ever let you know – again, that's between you and me.'

Our call ends before I get to tell her that I love her.

It's getting late. Through Joe's front window, I see the slim doorway for Yes Minicabs! I noticed earlier. 'Cabs on your doorstep. Very handy.'

'Would've been when I couldn't drive.' He chuckles. 'I can take you home.'

'The kids don't need any more gossip.'

'I'll come across with you, then.' Coming back with our coats, he reaches past, opening the door enough for me to slip my fingers around the edge.

'This has been lovely.' I kiss his cheek. 'Thank you.'

'I'm on earlies, could drop you in the morning – away from prying eyes, of course. Because. Seeing as we're,' Joe peels my hand from the door, finger by finger, 'temporarily free.' He places his palms on the hem of my dress, gathering it in little pinches, past my knickers, peeking through the patterned gusset of my tights. 'We could play some tune-skis; I've rediscovered Gil Scott-Heron.' Joe kneads my thighs harder. 'Share the rest of your cheesecake for break-fast. What do you say?' He smooches across my throat, his thumbs orbing my breasts. Pulling at my collar, so I'm stuck on his terms, Joe's lips rediscover mine.

But as his persuasion grows, it's odd to find that I don't begin slipping as quickly into the desire as I thought I would – as I should, perhaps; after all, there's been six weeks with-out any physical contact. The longest sexual abstinence of my adult life. I could, very easily, let him bend me over that sofa, and take what I know up to now I've freely given. And much as I'm sure I'd enjoy it, I just don't very much feel like being taken. There's still no doubting our attraction, but I know, as sure as I know that he's trying to impress me with Gil Scott-Heron, that Joe as a permanent could never, ever work.

And there's also the kids. Who do come first, though I know my priorities have been unforgivably off-key.

Then there's Dan.

'You're different,' Joe recognizes, releasing me. 'It's different.'

And he's right.

29

Giving Peas a Chance

We've been put in a tiny side room, suspended in the strange vacuum of time that exists only within hospitals and airports. Paint peels around the skirting, freckled with the shedded skin of worried relatives. Chairs line a windowless wall, upholstered in a beige leatherette that's retained the heat from years of anxious bottoms, waiting for news.

Like us.

Dad sits opposite me, tapping his leg, and when he catches himself doing it, he squeezes himself to stop. But the leg just keeps on tapping. He's asked me twice since I got here, to confirm I'm not angry, but it's all right. I understand.

Stomach ulcers raised concerns in a biopsy many months ago, long before I connected. Now Mum's in hospital. Death's door ill—

'What good are we both here?' Dad says, breaking my thoughts. 'I'll call if there's any change.'

'Absolutely not.'

Because Dad wouldn't just ring in the middle of the night. Neither is he one for dramatics. Mum's in Intensive Care, at the mercy of strangers, who – God be willing – know how to save her. I think of the pained look of her at times that I'd dismissed as age or bloody indigestion.

All those boxes and boxes of tablets in their bathroom. Too lost in myself to put two and two together, why she was no longer working. And me keeping her up till all hours, sifting my troubles together.

I really am the most self-absorbed creation on earth.

And now I'm wishing her better for the most selfish reason of all – I don't want to be left with hurt like this.

We've come so very far.

Three ulcers, one perforated is now infected. She's been vomiting blood with a sky-high temperature while I've been offloading my problems.

'This transfusion business. You know, we've been here before. She's strong,' he says, 'like you.'

'Crikey, you really don't know me at all.' I'd laugh if I had more energy. One moment buoyed, returning home from Joe all self-congratulatory because I'd managed to keep my legs together. Bed with an Earl Grey, a clean smug Little Miss Puritan; not even the usual tears, while stroking the Dan-shaped dip in the bed.

But then came the call around three. And the first horrible thought, whenever the phone rings at that time of night.

'Perhaps,' he says sadly, 'but I talk to your mother.'

'I'm sure.' I smile, feel the falseness of it. 'No doubt about the absolute mess I've made of everything. Again.' I stand, but it's more for something to do than an urge to leave. I sit back down.

'Do you know how hard it is, to raise, to shield a child from prejudice?' Dad's voice is far louder than usual. He leans forward, legs parted, hands clasping their respective knees. 'I do. I know. A family unaccepting. Ignorance to the point of rancid aggression.'

'The Giant.' He could never be Grandad to me, a Pops – or even a Mr Parker. Always the Giant, your dad, and later, that old cunt, which was, of course, expressed privately.

'Yes.' He sweeps his fingers through his hair with a swish, left to right, which falls into its perfect place. 'We're stronger than we think, Monica. How do you suppose humans have survived all this time? We're adaptable, resilient.' Dad's words could be Joe's words. 'How else could I spend all those years without you?' His legs back tapping again. 'My brother, who I abhorred with an absolute passion, didn't even tell me my own father was dead.' He stares into the wall opposite, eyes wet; the lower half of his face trembling independently, agedly – making me long to hold him.

But I'm glued to my seat.

'For too long I ignored the terrible time they gave Avril.' Dad's breathing falters as his words crack apart. 'They never could see her. Not just her beauty, but how she meant, *means*, absolutely everything to me. You've done a wonderful job, shielding your wonderful children from the things I couldn't.

362

My lovely girl.' I rush to him, our hands squeezing together just as his tears hit the floor. 'I am so very proud of you, Monica.'

I can't get close enough, would shrink myself if I could, rewind every second, every life-defining moment, bittersweet or agonizing or happy as they came to be, live my whole life backwards, just to become the kid again.

Then he'd be young, and so would she – and we'd never have to be parted.

'I can't bear the loss of another daughter any longer,' Dad cries into my hair, 'can't bear how much we've missed—' He pulls away, wiping his eyes, saddened more, it seems, by my utter bewilderment. Then I think of that picture, tucked within ours in Mum's bible. Baby Ashley. 'Thirty-nine years ago, for eight perfect minutes.' Eyes streaming, Dad cups my face. 'I had two girls.'

Eight minutes. A pain so unimaginable, I'm terrified to empathize. 'Oh, Dad.'

'We thought it'd be kinder. *Easier*. Quickly, it was obvious we should've told you—'

'Obvious?'

'Such a short time in the world, but Ashley left a terrible hole. You'd even talk to Avril's tummy when you were very tiny. The books, imaginary friends, the badgering for a sibling.'

And every time I asked, it reminded them. Of the loss, the hole in myself that I've felt forever. I feel a sudden comfort.

My loneliness, our loneliness, was real.

'Was I . . . fraternal or—'

'Like Toby and Joel. Identical. Passed on from you.'

It explains the breaking of the Petersen pattern. It wasn't their pattern at all.

'I'm so sorry, Dad.'

'You've nothing to be sorry for.' He rocks me slowly, but I can't stop saying it. Because I am. For Ashley. For everybody and for everything.

I'm devastated.

'Mon?'

I daren't, but even now, my eyes are on the tips of his shoes, his best pair – for high days and nights out. Dan perches on the chair next to mine, and when I lunge for him, find none of the reticence I expect. And I feel it, feel it, that he needs to hold me, too.

Dad slips out, leaving us alone.

Once we're parted, I notice Dan properly. He scoots into the next chair along, as he enquires politely about my mother. I fill him in, leaving my hand on the seat between us, upturned and asking, but he ignores it. Outdoor cigarettes and remnants of cologne linger on his new shirt, dove grey, crumpled now in a Joe kind of way.

'I came straight here. Seems I can't shut off as easily as some.' He stands to stride around the room, but I already know it's too small for anything as dramatic – plus, he's slightly wobbly on his feet.

'A work do,' he reveals, with a tired shake of the head. 'I was asked after you, funnily enough. Said we were all fine.

As usual. Just fine. I had the old, "cling on to it, son, they're not little for long, cherish these moments", bollocks, bollocks.' He laughs. 'You know I haven't even told them? Forty hours a week and they know fuck all.' Dan sits, and for the first time in weeks meets my eyes. 'Isn't this where your alchie boyfriend works?' He raises his brows, waiting for my response. 'I half expected he'd beat me to it.' Dan's spittle hits my arm. He's weathered, by shades of sad and jaded. By life. 'Not even five minutes, and I'm back measuring myself against that fucking cesspit of a man.' More spittle flies from his mouth.

'You won't believe me, but I had finished things.'

'Do me a favour.'

'The second you mentioned Norwich, we . . . I—'

'Sticks, does it?' Dan does a mean little grimace. 'But I can't believe that, can I, because I can't ever believe a word you say.'

'You're right. I've always hidden what's important, never speaking when things were wrong. Your family—' I put out my hand, talk over him. 'They swallowed us. Made me deny myself. And I feel more ashamed of that than anything else. My parents, Joe too actually, helped me be me again.'

'Doctor Joe. Bless. Sharing the ins and outs of all our private moments.'

'Not ours. Mine. My life.' I slap my hands on my legs and stand up. It's hard, tolerating the drinkers when you're lucid. 'I was a person before we met.'

'Yeah, the big mystery past.' He rakes his fingers through his hair. 'That you'd never bloody—'

But I'm distracted by the three doctors rushing past the window in the door.

Dan looks too, as another doctor bolts past. We both rise in sync, rushing for the handle, as I hurl myself into the corridor, firing frantic questions at the backs of the rushing doctors. The far double doors sweep open by the metal foot of a hospital bed. Two porters push through, quick and determined, yanking the bed into a sharp right. My mother, small and sunken, lies between the sheets, her eyes closed.

Dad stumbles through the doors, his face in his hands.

'Please.' I'm begging, caught in my coat that almost pulls me over. 'It's only just all right.'

'Okay, love.' Dan's tone is soft as he hauls me up straight, putting our devastation aside to comfort me in this new unbearable sadness.

Our past few weeks of togetherness, her happiness and ease. I can't not know the warmth of her again. My awkward, stubborn, beautiful mum.

My shattered, shattered heart.

Dad takes my hands, trembling himself. 'Sepsis. That's as much as I know. The sooner they operate the better.' He sniffs, standing tall. 'And that's what we must cling to.'

Dan's adopted the strange look, too, sobering instantly, our fragile reality palpable. Dad takes me gently by the arm, like I'm made from glass, but I'm reluctant to let go of my husband.

'I won't leave you.' Dan drops his head, kissing my shoulder. 'I promise.'

'I was thinking about when the twins were born,' Dan says. After doling out coffees, he allows his knee to rest against mine.

It's galling, utterly galling, that I considered these tiny contacts insignificant. I want to recall them all, bubble-wrap and treasure them.

'How ill you were. The pre-eclampsia. I don't think I'd known terror, proper terror, in all my days till then.' He tries for a cautious sip, then thinks better of it. 'Then Fran. That same fear again. Now look at us.' His voice drops to a whisper. 'Twelve years, three bloody kids. Fran pissing the bed.'

'That's stopped.'

'Joel, who can't stand the sight . . .' Dan chews his lip. 'I want to love you, but I can't stop going over why you weren't thinking about them, when you were letting that old soak climb all over you. Don't think I never had offers, that I've never been tempted. Recently.'

'I'm not surprised you've had offers. Or recent ones.'

'Me and Gracie.' He lets it hang, blows his drink. 'Had some . . . private words. Said she'd seen you in Stratford, that she thought it was me you were with. At first.'

A piece of work. What a fucking piece of work.

'All over me, she was. I still didn't. I couldn't.'

'You're so perfect – the only thing Penny got right.' I point at his knuckles. 'Bet she's not thrilled you smacked her brother, though.'

'Don't think it was about you,' he says, exposed. 'Or him. Mr Lover-Lover to the rescue.' But I do think that. Dan's muscular point to prove, all too late. 'Budgie had it in for this lad behind the bar. Provoking, all bloody night. Boy, Son. Sambo before you know it. Then I was hitting him.' Dan looks at me. 'And you know what? He was smiling. Smiling as I fucking thumped him.' He covers his face, huffs through his shield of shaky fingers. 'How I let him hurt you – I'm not proud of myself, Mon. But you didn't make it easy. It's hard, trusting a mystery.' I only need think of my mother to know he's right about that. Cross with himself, he wipes beneath his eyes, quick. 'I got it wrong.'

He'll fight me off, but I do it anyway, wrapping my arms around his neck, testing our old skills to communicate, mutely, that nowhere's ever felt better. Because I know my words are useless to him.

So, please feel it. I love you, Dan. I love you.

I love you.

'I'm not here to fight, is what I'm saying.' He extricates himself, all faux concerned about spilling his drink. 'This is for your mum.'

I can't expect more.

We're jolting, frazzled coffee nuts by seven, when a doctor in operating scrubs puts us in the picture. But I know by his

368

face as he comes in the room that the news won't be terrible. They've stemmed Mum's bleed, removed the infected tissue and are finishing up. She's still here, but for the intravenous and potent antibiotics.

Despite the caffeine, sleeplessness and worry, Dad's hit some new serene level, like someone's slipped him an E; he's all smiles and loving hugs – everything beautiful again. 'Go. Get some rest, Monica.'

'I'm not leaving her. Or you.'

'Good job you came, then.' Penny's stood by the water fountain, Joel next to her. She kisses him goodbye, with a nudge in my direction. 'Insisted on coming, didn't you?'

Joel's kitted out in head-to-foot Superdry – sympathy treats, I imagine – his arms dangling awkwardly at his sides, as he does all he can not to look at me, keeping the distance that I've just let be. But I can't do it anymore. I rush for him, so very pleased to see him, smell him, and smother his worried little face with kisses, shrivelling into more tears when he holds me back, his grip slowly growing tighter. 'How is she?' he asks, muffled by my hair.

'Stable,' I tell him truthfully. Stroking Joel's head, I sniff him again, overwhelmed and thankful.

'Fighting,' adds Dad.

'I'm glad to hear it,' Penny says. 'And . . . we were sorry, Monica. When we heard what happened to you.' She draws an imaginary circle around her eye. 'No lasting damage though, by the looks.'

Looks. The external. What more do I expect?

From Penny, it's acknowledgement.

'Where's Joel?' I sit up, disoriented. There's a wet patch just above Dan's knee. I rub at it with my sleeve, warmed that he's let me rest my head.

'Gone to Marks and Sparks with a fiver for supplies.' Dan pushes my hand away. 'Leave it. It doesn't matter.'

'And Mum?'

'No word yet. Your dad was asking questions not long ago. Reckons you can both see her soon.'

I throw my head back and exhale as a little more ease creeps into my bones. 'I need the loo. Then I'll hunt Joel down before he spends the lot on Percy Pigs.' There's a tiny smile. A real one, to cherish and remember. 'I am sorry, Dan.'

'Yeah.' Dan looks at me. 'I'm sorry, too.'

'When that man got you on the ground, I wanted you to die.' Joel's voice travels round the bend of the hospital corridor. There's a crashing sound, like a packet, like a packet of Percy Pigs hitting the floor. A scooping scuffle to perhaps retrieve them.

'Sounds understandable,' Joe replies, with obvious remorse. I take a quick peek around the corner, clocking them both; Joe in his glasses, with a bundle of notes. Working. Of course. 'Your mum's a very easy person to fall in love with. I know it won't mean much, mate, but I'm truly sorry. We never meant to hurt any of you.'

'I'm not your mate. I never was,' Joel says boldly. 'You were like bacteria, growing all over her. You knew she was sad. Now everything's broken and it's all your fault. Dad hates her. I hate her.' He clucks his lips. 'Not as much today, maybe,' he admits.

I'm caught. How long have they been talking? Do I step out and protect, or is this growing; a moment Joel will learn from? A moment I don't need to be part of.

'I'm not crying because of you.' Joel sniffs, quick to set things straight. 'You don't mean anything to me.' My need to smooth things over is all at once quashed. Joel has this in hand. All my worries, for a few brief seconds, are replaced with overwhelming pride.

My lovely, lovely son.

'Your mum and dad. They'll be all right in the end, I promise.'

'Grown-up promises are full of shit.'

Joe laughs. 'You'd usually be right. Do you know what a cliché is?' he asks, and Joel must, because Joe continues. 'There's a poem, a predictable one, but I've always liked it. It's about becoming a man. How you know you are one by your actions and—'

'Yeah. Kipling's "If".'

I imagine Joel's face, the expression on it, and I must picture it right, because Joe chuckles again.

'That's your mum, and her books and cleverness, that's made you so smart,' Joe praises him, impressed. 'When I feel terrible, and trust me, Joel, I have, especially lately – I think

371

of that poem, how to be a good man. Seeing as you're an expert – who gets it – perhaps you'll know what I mean about those words.'

'Have they helped you?' Joel's interested, despite himself.

'Not yet. I haven't learnt to be a good man yet. But I'm trying.' He sighs, and the atmosphere changes, such is the finality of it. 'I've a good feeling about your nan,' Joe says gently. 'You won't be seeing me again.'

I head back, still needing the toilet, only numbed to the desperation. Joe's decision, the right one. From absolute goodness.

Without me.

But no time to think; Dan's waiting, grinning, taking my hand to lead me into a side room, where it still feels like night and the air is electric. Mum's eyes, twinkling in grateful recognition, as she gives us a smile that's sure to deplete the very little vim she has left.

'Dan slipped through the net. Presumptuous bunch; presumed he was mine.' Dad sees my eyes on the Next of Kin Only sign. He smiles up from his seat, pushed as close to my mother as physically possible. Her hands rest sandwiched between his as he stirs his thumb across the top of them, concertinaing her skin.

Dan squeezes my hand, releases it. Says, 'I'll find Joel.'

And I go to my mum.

'Do you want to share a cab?' Dan asks, now we're in the stark brightness of white cloud.

'I'll walk for the bus, thanks. Fresh air at last.' I've the feeling we'd like to say more, but though we don't, we still don't move. Because we're out now, gone from Planet Hospital where the rules of real life are adjourned, and we can all love and care again.

'Perhaps,' Dan says, 'when I drop the kids home later, I could pick up fish and chips – stay for dinner?'

It must be my way, to cherry-pick the words that mean the most. Home. Stay. Faultless monosyllables. Epic levels of comfort. 'I'd love—' I bite it down, curb my enthusiasm. 'Yes, please.'

I kiss Joel goodbye – happier still, because he lets me.

'Something your mum said – poor woman, she could barely say anything.' Dan gives me another slightly less guarded smile, fuelling another small flicker of hopefulness. 'Smart people can only be stupid for so long.' He tilts his head as he studies me. Draping an arm on our son, they head for the cab rank.

'That's an Avril phrase.' I'm awed by her knowing. 'If ever there was one.'

They don't turn around. Dan acknowledges, instead, with a thumbs-up.

Smart, maybe. What I know for sure is that there's no place like the home we made together. Our own back garden is the blessing to be thankful for.

And with my heart, full of courage, that's enough.

Acknowledgements

Love and thanks:
For their lifetime contribution: Mum, for those early library visits and Dad for paying for The Writers Bureau course when I passed my GCSEs – incomplete to this day – I hope the book makes up for it.

To Sarah Armstrong, and all your encouragement and talent, thank you for being my earliest support and champion of Monica. Sarah Bower, thanks for your critique and kind guidance, and to all the lovely folk at the National Centre for Writing, without whom I may still be clueless.

To Kit de Waal, your continued support is a thing to treasure. You are inspiration and proof indeed that representation matters. Love also to my tribe – The Common People. Who knew a book could create a family? I am so proud to be part of our awesome collective. We Are Coming.

To Yvvette Edwards, wise woman extraordinaire – it's both a privilege to be your grasshopper and to call you my friend. Thank you for everything.

Hugest of thanks to The Good Literary Agency, and to my most incredible agent, Abi Fellows. Our serendipitous meeting sparked such joyous things – being born within the same moon phase surely having *everything* to do with it. My words cannot thank you enough for believing in me and Monica.

To Clare Hey, enormous thanks and gratitude to you for falling for *Lives Like Mine* and being a brilliant editor and guide throughout this process, and to all the marvellous people at Simon & Schuster UK and Australia that I've had the pleasure of working with and learning from: SJ, Anabel, Judith, Rachael, Amy, Polly, Jess and Sabah – you are fantastic.

Big thanks to the amazingly gifted Yasmine @findingevesroots, for both your gorgeous cover art and support of the novel.

To my most amazing creations, Zoe, Joanie and Eliza, who've weathered every writerly heartbreak and jubilation. I hope I've shown you perseverance and ambition, but most of all I hope this has taught you how beautiful life is when you dare to be yourself. I love you with all that I am. Thanks also to my lovely family, sisters, and dearest of friends, Jen, Rose, Fi, Martin, Reg, Blousey, Sooz, Lorraine, Emily, Anna and Viv. To Chloe, the biggest of thanks for being brave enough to question my fragile first draft by asking, 'Who are you writing this for?' which improved the book in an instant.

And to Mon, for lending me her namesake.

I wrote it for all of us ♥

Shedloads of love to my canine homeboys, Marlon and Steve, and especial thanks to my husband, Matt, for never questioning or doubting my dreams, just letting me try to fly with unfaltering support. It helps that you are hot, but you are my heart and we are everything good love should be.

Love to my mother-in-law and astral traveller, Glennie. I'm sure the publicity campaign you're fronting for me up in heaven is nothing short of stellar. We miss you. Every day.

And to Gordon Brown – without working family tax credits I'd have neither my first-class degree nor a book deal. I truly appreciate your invention.